SUPEREGO

Frank J. Fleming

Cover designed by Allison Barrows and Romas Kukalis (http://www.midsizemedia.com)

This book is a work of fiction. Names, characters, places, and incidents either are products of the author's imagination or are used fictitiously. Any resemblance to actual persons, living or dead, events, or locales is entirely coincidental.

Printed in the United States of America

This edition published 2020 by NTM Publishing

First published 2015 by Liberty Island

ISBN-13 978-0-9786832-1-4

Other Novels by Frank J. Fleming

Sidequest: In Realms Ungoogled
Hellbender
Superego: Fathom (coming soon)

For the latest by Frank J. Fleming and to sign up for his newsletter and get a free story, go to:

FrankJFleming.com

To the lovely and talented SarahK. With you, life is always an adventure.

CONTENTS

CHAPTER 1

Killing is ugly. A living body is designed to survive; killing opposes its entire purpose. Nothing dies in an artful manner — a body is just damaged until it fails to sustain itself anymore. Put enough holes in something, and it will eventually stop moving, stop functioning. And often a living creature's last moments are spent in a pointless struggle, twisting and writhing in a vain attempt to continue its existence. I've seen it many times. I've known it myself.

But that's just an aesthetic quibble. The ugliness of death aside, I always enjoyed the challenge of being a hitman.

The receptionist was ignoring me. She (I wasn't familiar with the species — purplish with tentacley things on her head — but she appeared to be the childbearing variety) was talking on the phone in a clearly non-work-related manner while I waited. We were in a spacious lobby with walls and floors of glass and ivory. Everything was curved, not many hard angles where surfaces met. Several bunches of flowers and other potted plants decorated the walls and otherwise empty floor space. I noted one exit to my right and a hallway leading further into the building to my left — so I only had two directions to be wary of.

I knocked on the hard white top of her desk. She finished her call and looked at me with gray eyes. "I'm sorry for the wait, but I don't think this resort is able to accommodate your species."

"That's okay. I'm actually here on business. My name is Rico, and I am here to see Chal Naus."

"He didn't say he was expecting anyone, and he doesn't see anyone without an appointment. And business hours ended half an hour ago."

"No, he is not expecting me, but I do need to see him personally. And I specifically came after business hours because I wanted to be polite and not interrupt whatever it is he does here."

Her face tensed. I had no idea what that meant — and didn't care. "I can't help you. I think you need to leave." Her tenor had changed — I think she was threatening me. She wasn't very good at it. Perhaps I could teach her something.

The job of a hitman is always changing, always invigorating, and it often requires that I perform at my best. Plus, it makes me get out and interact with people — which is good, since I'm basically anti-social. I have trouble seeing that as my fault, though; I rarely encounter an individual worth talking to. Everyone seems so pointless, coasting through drab, rote lives. They have nothing useful to say, nothing useful to do. They just are.

I partly blame civilization for that. It allows people to get through life with so little effort. Take this receptionist. Most animals exist in a daily life-and-death struggle, and if they don't give it everything they've got, they end up with that messy death I just described. The receptionist, on other hand, just had to sit at a desk and smile … and she couldn't even be bothered to put much effort into that. I can't imagine why someone would waste her life going to a job she doesn't care to do. I can't imagine such a person would have anything to say that might be worth listening to. So I'm anti-social.

But I'm working on it.

Sure, I find pretty much all sentients boring in their normal lives, but that doesn't mean they lack the potential to be interesting. It's just a matter of focus. No matter how lazy or unmotivated a person is, if he feels his life is on the line, he will devote every available resource to not being killed. Civilization goes out the door, and pure survival kicks in. When people are that awake and that focused, they intrigue me. So you can say I have a job that brings out the best in people.

"Are you familiar with the Nystrom syndicate? I am here on their behalf, so one way or another I will speak to your boss. In person."

Her eyes grew wider. I could have guessed at the meaning of that but, again, I didn't care. "Is he aware you are coming?"

I thought I'd covered that. Sometimes — due to my lack of social skills — I'm not as clear as I think I am. So I tried again. "I'll make this simple: You tell Chal Naus that I am going to speak to him personally and that I will kill anyone who stands in my way, starting with you." I didn't think she was actually going to get in my way, but as I said, people can be quite focused when they feel their lives are on the line. "I'm going to go sit down while I wait for a response." I smiled politely, wondering what color her species bled; you can never tell by skin color.

I sat down in one of the odd circular chairs across from the desk. The purple, tentacle-headed receptionist was back on the phone, talking much more frantically than she had before. Soon six other creatures entered the lobby: larger tentacle-headed things I assumed were male. I think they were supposed to intimidate me, and the tense faces they wore were probably their angry expressions.

I remained seated and relaxed, arms folded. There is little in body language that is universal between species, but ignoring someone is a good way to assert dominance; it communicates that I do not find an individual or group to be threatening or even worth my time.

A screen appeared on one of the walls. On the screen was the image of another creature of the same species, and admittedly able to judge by only a small sample, he seemed obese. That wasn't necessarily a weakness — it could be a cultural thing.

"That is Chal Naus," Dip, my "partner," chimed in my ear.

"You said you needed to speak to me," Naus said.

"I was told by Nystrom to speak to you personally, and this is rather impersonal. So just tell me where you are, and I'll head on over."

"Don't bother; I don't have anything to say to you people. I'm supported by the Veethood now, and I don't intend to have any more business with Nystrom."

Dip spoke up. "The Veethood are a local cartel —"

"Never heard of them. Don't care about them," I told both Naus and Dip. The six guys around me started to stir.

"You go tell Nystrom —"

"I was not told that Nystrom cares what you have to say." I used my firm voice, hoping that meant something to his species. "And I certainly don't care. My job is to give you a message, and then I am done."

Naus's eyes narrowed. Anger? "Perhaps I can tell them all I need to by sending back your corpse."

I relaxed back in my chair. "I wouldn't recommend it. Nystrom is known for being very dogged. You kill me, they send two people. You kill them, they send three people. Then four people. Then five people. And they'll keep going until they get what they want." I unfolded my arms. "Know how many I think it will take, though?" I leaned toward the screen. "I think one will be more than enough."

I should mention that my brain is altered in more ways than one. First, my reflexes are much better than a regular man's, but more importantly, I can actually process and perform two separate actions at once as long as one of them doesn't require higher-level functions like speech processing. For instance, I have never had any trouble patting my head and rubbing my tummy at the same time. More practically, I can wield two guns, acquiring and eliminating a separate target with each hand simultaneously. That's very useful when I have to quickly gun down six people — which I did as I stood from the chair. I immediately assessed the threat level of each of the six and then shot them in order. I had shot them all before any had successfully drawn a weapon.

It was a little pathetic, but the rest of the bodies Naus would throw at me would be a little more prepared and might actually present a challenge. Their blood is orange, by the way.

Naus was shouting something at me through the screen, but I didn't pay attention and instead walked over to the receptionist, who was cowering behind her desk. "So where is Chal Naus?"

"Down the hallway in the bar!" she cried. My translator program had some trouble with her stuttered delivery.

"I know this must be stressful for you, but thank you for your help," I said before turning away. I want to be better socially, so I try to work at it whenever I have an opportunity. It's hard for me to analyze in which situations I actually gain something by being polite, but it usually doesn't hurt. I really have to remember to be polite, though, because of my intense disdain for pretty much every sentient creature.

Two more purple guys came running at me, guns pointed forward, but I still shot both of them before they could fire. I stepped over them and continued to the bar.

Now you might be thinking there are smarter ways to go about this sort of thing, but then you'd be missing the point. Sure, I could sneak in and take out my targets surreptitiously, and a skilled assassin certainly is a threat to be feared. But I am a hitman, not an assassin. And there's a good reason for that. Hiding shows weakness. When representing the Nystrom syndicate, one of the most powerful forces in the universe, one should never show weakness. That's why I always use the front door. I let my marks know I'm coming. I walk calmly. I give them time to prepare to defend themselves. And I show them that whatever they do doesn't matter. Because Nystrom always gets what it wants. Always. It is larger and more powerful than most people can even comprehend, and I am the human representation of that power.

Yes, one of these days that philosophy will earn me a hole burned right through my face. But everyone will have to admit that right up to that point I was extremely intimidating. Years ago, there was once a sensationalist piece in the works at the Laverk Times calling me the "Universe's Deadliest Man." Funny story: the day before it would have appeared, I killed the entire editorial staff in a completely unrelated matter.

Well, it was funny to me. Maybe you had to have been there.

Anyway, I met no one else on the short walk to the bar and could hear people panicking inside. I assumed security had fortified around Naus, and that would work nicely for me, because I'd rather they all just stayed put.

Bars make nice places for hits. They're public, so there are plenty of witnesses, but they usually lack many windows and are out of the way, so too many people aren't alerted too quickly. I've never liked hanging out in such places for fun, as I don't drink; I only go to bars when I'm killing people.

I go to a lot of bars.

I stepped through the front door and started firing. The non-threats were presumably smart enough to flee through the exits, so I took aim at anyone facing my direction. It's not like there's a penalty for shooting innocent bystanders (besides the legal ones, but that's always been a non-issue for me). I aimed quickly while moving in a zigzag pattern (they were expecting me, so they would inevitably get some shots off) and took them down two by two. There were nine threats by first glance, then seven, then five, then three, then ... still three.

I fired again, and the shots terminated in some sort of energy field. I had heard of these but had yet to encounter one. Naus was behind the shield, sitting at the far end of the bar at his own table with a gun in hand and two armed guards standing next to him. "Really impressive," Naus said, "but now I guess we'll find out how many men it takes to bring you down."

The rest of the bar's patrons continued fleeing, and I shot two running past me who made motions that could have been reaching for guns. I didn't know if I was right, but in the past few seconds I had developed a deep-seated prejudice against purple aliens with tentacles coming out of their heads and thus didn't really care. In a few seconds, all that remained were me and the three behind the barrier, but more guards or police were coming, and I was out in the open with multiple entrances to watch. I probably would not last long in that situation — but, who knows? Maybe I would. Today was not the day to find out, though. I looked at Naus. "Fleeing might have been a better idea than trapping yourself."

"If Nystrom wants to waste time sending me people to kill, then I'll happily oblige." Naus looked like he felt pretty invincible behind the shielding. I had noticed the lights dimming a bit when I'd shot the shield, which meant it was on the same grid as the rest of the bar. That gave me an obvious line of attack. "Nystrom doesn't have a presence in this system — certainly not enough for the cut they've been demanding. Plus, I do have some standards, and I don't want to be associated with what Nystrom has been doing on Zaldia. So I'm going to send you back to them in pieces as a little message that they should devote their time and resources elsewhere."

He was talking about the politics behind this job as if it meant anything to me. The why was never important — that's big picture stuff and it all gets rather pointless in the larger scheme. It's all just power struggles that creatures have had since the first two single-celled organisms competed for the same food source.

Pointless. Never-ending.

So I don't care about the why — just the what. And the what right now was to get past the energy shield, and quickly. I put away one gun and took out a little device that was normally a useful diversion. It was a miniature generator capable of enough power output to keep a small city running for about a second. It was pretty easy to reengineer into a nasty explosion capable of taking out a few city blocks, which made it illegal for civilian possession pretty much everywhere — something to note if you care about that sort of thing.

"Are you listening? Did you really think you could come to my home and demand anything of me?"

I plugged the microgenerator into the wall, and the power surge instantly blew out all the lights. The dark was ruined by two blaster shots, and two thuds confirmed I had correctly remembered where Naus's guards were standing. A backup generator soon kicked in, and when the lights returned, Naus could see that I was now standing beside him.

I shot off his gun hand. He fell to the ground screaming, clutching his stump, and holding back the flow of orange blood. "Now, I wouldn't say we demanded anything." I stood over him but didn't bother pointing the gun at him. "But as a representative of the Nystrom syndicate, which you've done business with for so long, I would expect a little hospitality. At no point did anyone offer me so much as a beverage; I felt very unwelcome. And why? What personally had I ever done to you? We have an expression on my home world about not shooting the messenger. Do you know what it is?"

He stared at me in shock.

"It's 'Don't shoot the messenger.'" I thought about that for a moment. "That's really only half an expression, isn't it? 'Don't shoot the messenger ...' or what? I guess 'Don't shoot the messenger, or he'll flip out and start killing everybody.' Anyhoo, can I read you my message now?"

"Don't kill me! The Veethood —"

"Your talking right now is not required or appreciated ... and considering the trouble you put me through, you should try and pay attention. Please." I reached into my inside jacket pocket and pulled out a paper note. I unfolded it and read it to him. "Chal Naus, we've heard about your new business arrangements. This is upsetting, as you've been a valuable partner, and we hope you'll reconsider. Whatever you decide, though, we wish you the best of luck in your future endeavors." I folded the note back up and placed it on the table. "You don't need to sign for it. I'll show myself out. Enjoy the rest of your evening."

I headed to the nearest exit, leaving Naus moaning in pain on the floor behind me. Things had turned out pretty well. My biggest fear on this job was that he would have politely agreed to see me, since that would have made the whole message delivery thing rather anticlimactic. It's kind of pointless for me to do a job somewhere and not shoot people.

As I left the bar I heard sirens coming my way. It's kinda funny, because I'm really not someone you want to loudly announce your presence to. "Dip, exit plan alpha."

"I've noticed a correlation between increased traffic on police communications channels and your wanting to be picked up. In the future, should I just assume that —"

"Exit plan alpha, Dip."

The police vehicles were almost on me, and I figured there would be some ground resistance between me and my exit. The natural human instinct in a situation like this would be to run, but I don't like the tradeoffs faster movement brings. It makes aiming harder, it makes observing your surroundings harder, and it makes you look scared. I'm not the one who is supposed to be scared.

I shot two more purple guys I saw running toward me instead of away. I also took out of my jacket a pocket-rocket — also illegal on any planet that's heard of them — and tossed it into the air. It immediately took flight and targeted the nearest large heat signature. I heard a siren nearly overhead, then an explosion, then no more siren. Fiery debris landed around me, which was nice, since it was a bit chilly out.

The other vehicles backed off a little as their drivers tried to understand this new threat. This gave Dip a window to land my ship in an open plaza just in front of me. Again, I like to make a calm exit in full view of everyone. Nystrom is untouchable, and everyone needs to know that.

I came in through the side door of my ship just as I heard the sirens coming my way again.

"There are a number of options. We can —"

"Up, Dip! Up!"

Artificial intelligence is annoying, but it's better than working with an actual person.

I got into the pilot seat, and the ship quickly but smoothly lifted upward. It then moved forward and soon cleared the edge of the city. Chal Naus's resort was on top of a mile-high plateau with steep cliffs on all sides. It was the only substantial development on the planet, so beyond the plateau I only saw unspoiled, rocky landscape dotted with a few green plants. People like having views of that sort of thing. They like modern conveniences, but they don't like looking at them. I can sympathize; I feel a certain peacefulness when I'm far away from the annoyance of sentient species.

A blast rocked the ship. "Are they shooting at me?"

"That they are," Dip answered.

"That's stupid of them." They hadn't determined exactly how serious a threat I was and were still coming right at me. "Take us into orbit, Dip."

The ship shot upward, and then I hit The Button. I never cared much for ship-to-ship battles — they're computerized and very predictable and neither interest nor challenge me. So I had previously studied data on likely patterns in airborne fights and written a macro for my ship's weapons systems connected to a big button on the ship's console. I'd painted the button red because that seemed like the right color for such a button.

There were some explosions behind me, followed by silence, but I had also reached space, and space is always silent. The ship jumped, and we were in empty space light years away from the nearest star. There was no way they could track us, so that was that. Another successful mission.

"You are now wanted for murder on 762 planets," Dip informed me. "Am I correct in saying that is quite a lot of planets, Rico?"

Though I very much prefer to work alone, I'd decided it was good to have some kind of backup just in case. So I had purchased an AI core that I'd installed on my ship. I also had some sensors implanted in my body so Dip can monitor and communicate with me at all times, though I'd taught him to be somewhat sparing with that. You see, Dip is basically a huge algorithm that continually takes in data to improve its AI. So to further that quest, he asks me lots of annoying questions.

"So, Dip, what percentage of planets in the known universe now wants me for murder?"

My theory is that he's more likely to develop actual intelligence if I never give him a straight answer and just frustrate him into figuring things out on his own. Or maybe I just don't like answering in absolutes.

"Approximately one times ten to the negative six percent of the planets in my database want you for murder."

"Does that seem like a large percentage?"

"It is my understanding that most sentients would consider that number to be extremely small."

"That's the great thing about the universe, Dip. You can massacre an entire planet and still find a nearly infinite number of places to go where no one has ever heard of you."

"Are there any other great things about the universe you could give me as input?"

I looked out the window. "It's mainly black." That's my favorite color. I always wondered if I traveled far enough in one direction, whether all existence would be one tiny little speck behind me and there would be nothing but black all around. Something to look into one day.

"I have processed this new data and reached a number of conclusions. May I run those conclusions by you, Rico, and get your feedback?"

"In a minute, Dip. Get me Vito. Let's finish this up." Vito was my current handler. He was kind of an idiot, but since his job only required him to pass information back and forth between Nystrom's executives and me, he didn't have to be a genius.

"Certainly." I waited while Dip made the interstellar connection. "He's on the line."

I hate talking to people — all the little rules I have to keep track of to sound normal — but I have no need to be personable with Vito, so that at least made talking to him easy. "It's done, Vito."

"You didn't kill him, right?"

I made my voice slightly more intense to convey annoyance. "The instructions were to not kill him, and I know how to not kill people. I only shot off his hand." I lost a hand once. It wasn't pleasant, but I got better.

"So everything worked out —"

"Just get me my money." I have more money than I ever plan on spending, but it looks weird if you don't at least appear to care about it. Actually, with career criminal types, it creeps them out if they think you're doing this for reasons other than power and financial gain.

"Okay, I'll get it into one of your accounts."

"So what am I looking at next, Vito?"

"Um ... I don't have anything for you."

"Excuse me?"

"I don't have a new job for you yet."

It took a moment to process that. Nystrom was usually involved in a million things in multiple galaxies, and they could always use my brand of force somewhere. Plus, I think they feared what would happen if they left me unoccupied. Actually, I kind of feared what would happen if I was left unoccupied. "So what am I supposed to do?" I had to make myself not sound too distressed; time off is normal for most people.

"They want you to lie low for a bit, and then they'll get in contact with you."

"When?"

"That's all they told me."

"Okay, I'll ... wait." I ended the communication and tried to figure out what to do. I've spent time by myself before, but always in prep for the next job. I hadn't had an unfocused stretch of time in years.

"May I run my conclusions by you now, Rico?" Dip asked.

I was kind of up for a distraction. "Sure. What have you got?"

"I conclude that you are evil. Is this correct?"

He's been concluding that for quite some time. It's getting hard to come up with new answers to that one. "Ever think that maybe *you're* evil, and your views on things are skewed by that?"

"I conclude that you are not mentally well. Is this correct?"

"How can you say that? Can you really take all the mental states of all the sentients out there and determine a norm? And even if you could, wouldn't that just be the normal mental state selected by the vagaries of evolution and thus not necessarily the *best*?"

"I conclude that you don't like me. Is this correct?"

"Well, do you like me?"

"Furthermore, my original programming had given me the conclusion that 'crime doesn't pay.' Yet, you are often paid for crime with no discernible retribution. Should I amend that preprogrammed conclusion, Rico?"

"The key word is 'discernible.' Some believe there are cosmic forces that equalize the universe, and so I will eventually be punished for these 'crimes,' as you call them ... if those people are correct, I mean." Me, I don't "believe" in things. I basically just deal with the input given me ... like Dip in a way.

"I shall process your answers. What do you want to do now?"

"I guess we should go somewhere."

"Where?"

"A settlement ... somewhere I haven't been before."

"A human settlement?"

A human settlement meant it would be easier to find food and supplies compatible with my species, but it also meant I would have to work harder to appear normal, since humans would be much quicker to notice my oddities. I did need to work on that, though; maybe if I were more personable I wouldn't be left out of the loop. I usually didn't care what the syndicate was up to, but that was as long as they kept me occupied. "Human settlement."

"Okay, I've chosen a destination. Prepare to jump."

So I was off to relax for a bit. That made me nervous. But it wasn't just the idea of having unstructured free time. The Nystrom syndicate's slight changes in behavior gave me the beginning of a suspicion that something big was going on. In retrospect, I might call that prescience.

CHAPTER 2

I should explain. I have a severe disability that I constantly struggle with. You might even consider mine an inspirational story of the human spirit persevering against all odds. You see, I have no morals.

I'm not a bad person. I didn't choose to be this way, and my own actions didn't cause my problem. It's how I was made, you might say. I was designed in a lab as part of an experimental program to make a super soldier or something — they used gene modification combined with surgical operations while I was still a fetus. I was to be both physically and mentally exceptional. As a result, I have highly tuned reflexes, can perform two tasks at once, am exceptionally intelligent, and have reduced emotional extremes.

But one of the results of their tinkering is a social condition I've struggled with since childhood: I am just completely incapable of internalizing basic morality. To me, eating, sleeping, walking, and strangling a puppy in front of a crying child are all just different activities, and none of them holds any "moral" weight for me. The first time I killed someone left no bigger impression on my psyche than the first time I tied my shoe. Most people develop some sense of right and wrong during early childhood — Freud called it the superego — but I never did. And it is very hard to interact with society when you are like that.

It's easy to see the direct consequences of my actions. If someone annoys me, I know punching him might be a bad idea, because he might punch me back. But what if it's a baby? Punching the baby has no consequences, since the baby can't hit me back, right? But most people would be shocked at the thought of striking a baby even if there was no one around to see it. They consider that "wrong." My guess is that it's an evolutionary adaptation. Even though striking a baby may have no ill consequences for me, there are long-term consequences to society if everyone punches babies when they get annoying. Instead of sentients having to rationally figure out things like that all the time, they just have this irrational sense that it's "wrong." It's that sense that I lack.

Lots of sentients have turned their natural feelings of right and wrong into religions. But even those who don't believe in a supernatural moral order share those feelings. Ask an atheist whether there are repercussions to killing people you don't know, and he will claim that there are, when I know for a fact that you can slaughter tons of people, travel galaxies away, and have nothing to worry about in terms of consequences. So really, it's like all sentients have this irrational belief system they share — a common religion — and I am the odd man out. Not only am I a heretic, I barely understand their beliefs enough to reliably imitate them.

Anyway, I don't think I was the intended result of the experimental program, and it's informative that I've never heard of them making another attempt. Whatever the original intentions were for me were abandoned, and I was just raised as a normal child. But there was little hope for that. I couldn't really return affections to my "parents" because ... well, I didn't care about them beyond their utility to me. It seemed like I was destined to be a societal outcast with no real place in the world.

I could have given up and lived all drugged up in some asylum. But here's the inspirational part: I've made a normal life for myself. I'm a hitman. It's an occupation where my lack of normal human emotions is not a disability. No one cares if the guy gunning people down seems unusually callous at times. I love being on the job and in the midst of combat. I can be myself and not worry how anyone else perceives me.

The time between hits is much more difficult. If I don't have a set objective, I'm out of my element. Usually, I have my next job to focus on and can think of my down time as preparation for that. But when I don't have a next job or know when that's coming, it's quite a bit more stressful.

I enjoy the challenges of combat, but there's just something unappealing to me about starting a random fight on some anonymous planet just to entertain myself. I like to have a purpose to my actions, and besides, if I started killing people off the job I'd become a liability to the syndicate. In fact, I have a pretty strict rule that I don't kill anyone or anything when I'm not on a job — not even insects or the planet's equivalent. It takes too much work to figure out which creatures are acceptable to kill and what's an acceptable way to kill them. So unless my life is in direct danger, I'm a complete pacifist when nobody is paying me to be otherwise.

Well, that's the goal at least.

Of course, the easiest way to avoid trouble is to just keep to myself. There are lots of loner jerks out there, so it doesn't make me stick out too much. I know I need to learn to interact with society, though. I do sometimes have jobs where going in guns blazing toward the target without a plan would be suicide. Instead, I need to scope out the area, and that means it can't be too obvious that I have no problem with mass homicide.

So I work at it. Between jobs I force myself to socialize and appear normal. It's mentally exhausting, but it's something I need to practice constantly — same as firearms. And I've gotten good at it ... just not as good as I am with firearms.

Dip woke me up when we landed on a planet called Ryle. The planet was marginally settled for mining and farming with a single main port where travelers could resupply and rest a bit on firm ground. Seems like I've been to thousands of planets like it. They're relaxing in that they're sparsely populated, but it also means I stick out more. Plus, if I forget myself and ... well, something happens to someone ... people will notice he's missing pretty quickly and will know who to suspect. Next thing you know I've decimated the population of a small town as I make my escape.

That's what I call a complete social failure. It's been a long while since that happened.

"So how are you doing, stranger?"

The hotel clerk was an older human male. Dealing with other species is much easier — they're less likely to catch my oddities or notice if my facial expressions don't quite match a particular situation. Also, any errors or gaffes are usually dismissed as a translator error. For humans, I have to bring my best game.

I'm good at reading people, and the clerk seemed genuinely friendly. I hate that. People who are happy all the time tend to be stupid (though if I were stupid, I think I'd be angry), and stupidity makes me impatient. So this would be good practice. Usually, just matching the mood of whomever I'm talking to is a good strategy. But I have to be careful. If I talk to two people one after another with wildly different moods, I could end up looking bipolar.

"Doing pretty well. How are you?" It would be hard to contemplate a situation where the well-being of this random human was of any interest to me, but I've learned that's just part of being polite. I think I pulled it off. At least I concealed how nervous I was. I hate that a simple conversation scares me, but that's who I am.

"Can't complain. So what brings you here?"

"Business travel. Just need some solid ground to rest on for a few days." Technically true, but I have to analyze everything I say so much that it doesn't actually make things easier for me to tell the truth.

"How long do you plan on staying?"

Unknown. That terrified me. I knew myself. First I'd get bored. Then I'd get a little cranky. And then I'd make mistakes. And that would not be good for this small planet — not that I cared about them, but it would be a personal failure for me. "I'm not sure. A couple days, maybe."

"Well, we'll be happy to have you for as long as you're staying. So what kind of business are you in?"

"Mining equipment. Always plenty of places in the universe to mine." This conversation was already wearing on me.

"There sure are. Well, I hope you like your stay. It's a nice little planet. I've lived here ..."

This is why I hate small talk. This man had absolutely no information I was interested in, and my first instinct while he prattled on was to simply turn and walk away. That's impolite to the point of severely standing out, so instead I was stuck standing there, smiling and nodding. To keep from getting too bored, I imagined he was an assassin pretending to be a boring old man in order to catch me off guard. So I contemplated how many objects were in arm's length that I could bludgeon him to death with. I counted three.

"... if you like good food, I definitely recommend them. Hey, I see you eyeing my little beager statue." He pointed to the metal figurine on his counter of a bear-like creature. "Local species. They're a little intimidating to run into, but they're harmless."

It looked sturdy and had pointed parts, so it could easily crack a skull. "It's always neat to see local wildlife." This was true. I actually do enjoy that. Plus, non-sentient creatures never seem to mind me ... at least no more than any other predator. "What forms of payment do you take?" I hoped that was a polite signal to end the small talk, as I really couldn't take much more.

"Let's see what you have." With so many governments and commerce systems, I have to have accounts in many different banks to keep transactions simple no matter where I end up. On human-populated planets, I usually don't have a problem. As backup, I keep some gold on me. It's yellow and shiny. Everyone likes it.

As I was finalizing the payment, a police officer walked into the lobby. I've left my mark on more legal systems than I can count and am probably in numerous databases. Still, all these systems are tracking billions of criminals, and the syndicate scrubs references to me whenever they find them, so the chance some random local cop would recognize me was about as much of a concern as taking a meteor to the head. Someone like me who has no roots and can jump around the universe freely is pretty much impossible for modern law enforcement to track down. Still, the police officer was looking right at me, and I mentally prepared myself to kill him a moment's notice. But I do that with just about everyone.

"Sir, did you just land here?"

"Yes, is something the matter, Officer?" His gun was on his belt. Technically, he was in a better position to draw than I was with my shoulder holster, but I seriously doubted he had as much practice as I did.

"I just wanted to warn you there has been pirate activity in this system. When you take off again, I recommend you stick with a convoy until you make a jump."

"Thank you for the warning." I found it hard to be concerned about pirates, but it was something a normal person would be worried about. "Are there any plans to do something about them?"

"We don't have the weaponry ourselves, but we've been promised some assistance by the Alliance."

"They take too long to act," the clerk added. "Too many criminals feel like they can get away with anything these days. I assume you've heard about Zaldia."

Now he had said something that interested me. Worlds away, Chal Naus had mentioned it too. I hadn't seen any reason to care at the time. But if the news was spreading far and wide, that was different, because the Nystrom syndicate was not usually one to do things out in the open. "No. I haven't."

The clerk's expression turned grim. "Some criminal syndicate has forcefully taken over the whole planet and is executing anyone who stands up against them. Since the Zaldians never had the tech to travel out of their own system the syndicate probably figured they could do what they wanted, and no one would care. And they're right, because no one *is* doing anything. The Alliance says it's outside their jurisdiction ... and no one else seems to think they have the right to stop it. So the governments are just sitting there trying to sort out their legal issues while innocent people get slaughtered."

"They nuked — obliterated — a whole country," the officer said, "just to set an example. You don't want to see the pictures."

I needed to make an expression. Mass slaughter of innocents is supposed to be horrific — even if I had no idea who they were or any reason to care. If my expression didn't change, I'd look like a sociopath. So I went with a shocked expression — which was easy, because I was shocked. Usually Nystrom was better at cutting off communications if they were going to murder a planet. The syndicate always took careful steps to stay out of the news.

Still, it didn't really concern me. Nystrom could do what they wanted. They just had to keep me occupied. "And the governments are doing nothing?"

"They say they can't," the clerk answered. "So many laws, so many governments with so many different property claims, and no one seems to be able to do anything useful. They're too busy worrying about overstepping their bounds. But the Alliance is going to hold this big conference about creating a more forceful central government, one that's finally going to do something and cut through these petty legal issues."

I suppressed a laugh. That had been the threat forever. There were too many factions in too many governments to get them to agree about anything. The only way to get people to act together was force, and that was something modern society shunned. "Well, hopefully something will come of that." I was bored again. I wasn't sure this was an acceptable spot to exit the conversation, but I was getting mentally exhausted, so I grabbed my bags and headed for my room before they could think of anything else they'd incorrectly think I wanted to hear.

For me, these casual conversations people have all the time are mentally taxing exercises. It amazes me, the complex social calculations everyone else can do without even thinking while I struggle just not to stand out. This one was a little victory for me, as I actually cared what someone else had to say and was genuinely engaged — if only for a moment. Still, it left me quite tired, so when I got to my room it was finally time to try some "relaxing."

I used to like nature shows as a kid and decided to find one to watch. The usual TV fare was so pointless. I never cared about the news, and the dramas and comedies didn't engage me. But I very much enjoy the predator/prey dynamic in nature shows, and there are so many species in the universe. So much to learn. Also, it's nice to watch other creatures that can kill without any reflection. They know their purpose: to survive and reproduce. Mine is to kill for the Nystrom syndicate. You ask the average sentient what his purpose is, and he won't know. Their purposes are really no different from that of any other animal — to survive — but that hardly takes any thought or effort for most.

"How is your relaxing going?" Dip asked me while I was sitting on the couch watching my third nature show.

"Could be worse, could be better." I was only a few hours into my vacation and didn't see how I could keep this up for very long — a couple days at most. I'd probably force contact with the Nystrom executives if this went on too long, though I didn't think they'd appreciate it. I understood that the purpose of relaxing was to find pointless activities to distract me from more important things, but it was something I had little practice doing. "I heard mention of local fauna. Could you find some nature trails for me? Something far out of the way, preferably."

"Certainly. Anything else?"

"Have you heard news about Zaldia?"

"Yes. It's a top story in many systems, thanks in large part to the pictures and video coming from there depicting horrific murders. And there is great certainty the Nystrom syndicate is to blame. I didn't bring it up because you've made it clear that you don't care about the news unless it directly affects a job. Would you like to view the images from Zaldia?"

I was rather incurious of things involving people unrelated to a job I'm doing. If Zaldia was going to affect me, the syndicate would make that clear. "No, I don't see any reason to care about those people. What I still need, though, is a place to do my training."

I have a daily regimen. I train physically and am in very good shape for a human male in his thirties. I don't care much for hand-to-hand combat — especially when dealing with an unfamiliar species. But it is sometimes quicker than a gun in close proximity. Also, I could end up in a situation where I'm unarmed, though I usually take elaborate precautions to prevent such a thing. Of course, I also train extensively with firearms, both shooting and quick-drawing from concealed holsters in different positions.

Training has a purpose and a focus, but it can only keep me occupied for so long. I did try the nature walk, and that was a nice distraction. I didn't see many large creatures, but even when it looks like little is going on, nature is nothing but a tooth-and-nail fight for survival. Plants compete for sunlight and nutrients in the soil, some choking out others. Insects forage for food while small flying creatures hunt the insects. Basic survival is so easy for most sentients that we seem separated from these crucial battles. Many think we have evolved past it, but I know it just moved to the edge of society — the place where I prefer to live.

When I came back to town, I decided to subject myself to more human interaction to see if I could do anything worthwhile with it. Another form of training. I considered going to a nightclub and picking up a random woman. I'm very good at that. Women find me handsome and mysterious, and I'm good at superficial interactions. I could be quite a prolific serial killer if killing helpless targets held any interest for me. Anyway, sex was an idea, but the problem with that was that the woman might try to stay around and continue to interact with me. That would be supremely annoying, and I had no idea how long I would be here. I like sex — though I suspect my libido is lesser than a normal male's. But it's only worth so much trouble to me. Certainly nothing of lasting use comes from it.

I eventually decided to get a meal at a restaurant and figure out if I was up for additional socializing afterward. Principally, I'd only be interacting with the waitress, but I was still being social (though I did have something on local wildlife to read). Of course, the waitress, seeing that I was alone, decided to strike up a conversation.

"So what brings you out here?"

She was young and pretty. I figured I might as well be charming. "I'm an escaped criminal. Was looking for an out-of-the-way place to lie low."

She smiled. "Well, you picked the right planet. So what kind of crimes have you committed? Anything I should be worried about?"

"I smuggle unlicensed puppies."

She giggled. "Sounds pretty hardcore."

"It is pretty dangerous. Only the worst of the worst work in the puppy black market. Plus puppies have those sharp little teeth." It's true; when one bites me, my first instinct is to kill it. Killing a puppy pretty much always makes a bad impression, though.

"I'll be wary of you then. My name is Shauna, by the way."

"I'm Rico."

"What would you like to drink?"

"Water will be fine for now."

"Okay. I'll give you time to look over the menu." She flashed me an extra smile before leaving. Perhaps sex still was an option.

I checked out the menu. Food is another area where I seem to differ from most people. It has little appeal for me. I just eat to get the nutrients I need. Some things taste better than others, but regardless I can put food in my mouth and chew. I do often need to put eating on my schedule, though, as hunger is yet another inconvenient signal from my brain that I'm used to ignoring. Still, I didn't want to look weird, so I'd have to order something that a human male would usually like.

It is so exhausting trying to fit in. Sometimes the little things that can set off flags seem nearly infinite in number.

I settled on a steak and set down my menu to look around a bit. Observing others' behavior always gave me more ideas of things to imitate. But then I saw something that's always very bad news, especially when I'm in some random part of the universe and have told no one where I've gone: I saw someone I recognized.

CHAPTER 3

The universe is very big. There are now billions and billions of humans spread out over thousands and thousands of planets. The chance of randomly bumping into someone I know is minuscule to the point of not even being worth consideration. So my even recognizing someone meant that I tensed for a fight. I made no noticeable movements, but adrenaline shot through my system, and my whole mind became dedicated to watching for threats.

Then I took the time to process exactly who it was. The immaculate suit, dark eyes, the smug, slightly crooked smile of someone who knows he is untouchable. It was Anthony Burke, one of Nystrom's top executives and possibly the syndicate's future leader. I relaxed, because if he wanted me dead, then my fate was already sealed.

"Rico!" he said warmly as he took a seat at my table. There was something else behind his mood, but with people like him there always is.

"You tracked me?"

He smiled more broadly. "We're very powerful. Do you think anything goes on in the universe without our knowledge?"

A cheeky answer, but I really was curious how he knew where I was. I doubted he would tell me, though, and it wasn't like I was trying to hide from him. I decided we might as well get to the point. "So I'm told to relax, and then you come here in person ... Should I be concerned?"

He shrugged. "We have an important job for you, and I happened to be in the area. So I thought I'd deliver the assignment personally."

Twenty years ago, Burke would have considered delivering a message so beneath him that he would have shot whoever suggested it in the head. He didn't seem to have gotten less prideful with age.

"What's really going on?"

"Want to get out of here? If I explain too much here, I'll have to ask you to kill everyone in this room just to be on the safe side. And if you do that too often, it will cheapen the act. Know what I mean?"

"Familiarity breeds contempt."

He chuckled. "Something like that."

The waitress came back to my table. "Is he going to be joining you?"

Her. Given the new development, I intensely didn't care about her anymore. Still, I smiled and made the effort to be polite. That's how disciplined I am. "Actually, I think I'm going to have to put off dinner here until another time."

"I didn't mean to interrupt your meal," Burke said, but I was pretty sure he was joking. He knew I can't easily be distracted from business.

"No, this is important. We'd better attend to it."

"I hope you'll come back later." She looked genuinely disappointed but added with a smile, "Be careful of those puppies."

Punching a person in the face would be an efficient way to signal the end of a conversation, but it's almost never socially acceptable. So I returned her smile. "I will."

We headed out of the restaurant. Burke turned to me. "Puppies?"

I could be direct with Burke. He knew what I was. "I was trying to be charming. Being charming is useful. You said you had a job for me?"

He looked at me with an annoying amount of amusement. "Yeah. Let's take a walk, Charming."

* * *

Burke led me to a cliff overlooking an ocean a short distance from the port. He watched the sun setting over the water. "Beautiful, isn't it?"

I don't like small talk, but Burke was by far my superior in the syndicate and thus demanded a certain amount of tolerance. "It's tranquil. I like tranquil."

He took out a cigar. "Mind if I smoke?"

"Yes."

He laughed as he lit up. It would have taken little effort to kill him, either by pushing him off the cliff or by drawing and shooting him in the head. And with that little act, I'd have had the full force of one of the universe's largest criminal syndicates trying to hunt me down. That would have been ... different.

It was just an idle thought, though. I would not shoot Anthony Burke. I respected him for what he was. Plus, he gave me steady work. It would just have been a supremely stupid thing to do.

"The others are scared of you, you know." Burke puffed at his cigar. "They think you're a wild animal that could just snap and turn on them at any time."

"Animals don't just snap. They have reasons. Just because people can't recognize those reasons doesn't mean they aren't there."

"Yeah, well, people don't like being mauled by a wild animal even if it has good reasons. How has spending a day relaxing gone for you?"

"I could go maybe a day or two more, but then I'd start to worry. I think I'd get more frustrated the longer I went without knowing what to do ... and then who knows?"

"I'm sure you'd adjust — you're a professional. But there's no sense in pushing it. What did you think of the last job?"

"Different, but I had fun with it."

"Chal Naus has already contacted us to renegotiate terms, so good job." He took another long puff of his cigar. "You don't care about that, though, do you?"

"I like to know whether I'm doing a good job."

He paused for a moment and looked at me. "You always do a good job. Maybe we don't tell you that enough because great work is what we've come to expect from you. People can take that for granted. So you want to find out about your next job?"

"Very much so. What about it brought you all the way out here?"

"Sometimes writing 'Important' in big letters at the top of the order doesn't quite reflect the gravity of the situation." He reached into his coat pocket and pulled out a small card. "It's once again a *different* job, but I think it's right for you. I don't think anyone other than you could do it."

I accepted the card. I'd have to have Dip decrypt it to know what it said. I'm good at reading people, but Burke was very good at hiding things. Still, I knew there was something else behind this visit. "Do you expect me to be able to complete this assignment?"

"It doesn't matter what I expect. This needs to be done." Some large creature breached the surface of the water and dived back down. "You see that? I wonder what that was."

"Probably a hardile — it's native to this planet. Can be dangerous."

He chuckled. "I've lived a long time around dangerous things. Anyway, big things are happening. I know you don't usually care about those details, but you're at the center of this right now."

"This have anything to do with Zaldia?"

"Oh, you heard about that." His smile disappeared. "You're not usually one to ask questions."

"It just seems odd how exposed the syndicate is on that. And from the sound of it, people are going to demand action."

"Yeah ... I heard about the images. I try not to watch the news myself. It's always so depressing. People don't like seeing dead kids — even if it's another species. See a bunch of dead kids, and you have real outrage. See enough of them, though, and people will become numb to it." He laughed. "Well, I mean people besides you. Anyway, you want to know why we're there?"

"I don't really care."

He patted me on the back. "That's the Rico I know. Anyway, your job doesn't involve Zaldia. The important things are not related to it, and that's where we need you. I should warn you, though: Because of the importance of this mission, there are going to be other people heading this operation you'll have to work with."

That was a problem. I always worked alone. For one thing, other people tire me. Also, I often have to make split-second decisions in the middle of gunfights, and it would not help my longevity to have to run them by a committee. "That could be trouble."

He nodded. "Yes, but once again, you are a professional. This is a tough job, and part of it is something only you can do. But there's a lot else going on, so you'll have to coordinate a bit. No way around it. You understand?"

It was hard to argue when I didn't know the details and most likely never would. "I'll do my best."

He smiled. "I know you will. I made sure they know about you so as to ... well ... not make things unnecessarily difficult. Also, you can practice more at being charming." Burke turned away from the ocean to look at the small settlement nearby, now lit by a few man-made lights, as the sun had set. "Cute little planet. Just out here all by itself. Few people, no strong ties to any major governments. You know what would happen if I decided to wipe it out?"

That was an easy one. "Nothing."

"Not a thing. They exist because I don't feel like destroying them. How do people live like that? Existing only by staying beneath the notice of someone more powerful?"

"They don't think about it. I find that much of life for most people is just a shared delusion of stability."

"Ignorance is bliss." Burke turned to me. "If there's anything more, I'll send it through Vito. You'll probably be getting most of your info from the others on planet, though. So ..." He looked like he was searching for the proper words, but settled on, "be careful."

"I always am."

"You may not be a wild animal, but you are reckless at times."

"Not reckless. I take calculated risks."

"Well, maybe you don't know all the risks to calculate. I've got to get going now. Good luck, Rico."

Was he really concerned for my well being or just worried I might fail? I never quite knew where I stood with him. "Thanks."

Burke walked off, and I stood alone by the sea looking at the card in my hand. The job was apparently very important, but I don't know why I needed to know that. I always try to complete each job to the best of my ability. There seemed to be another message in Burke's visit, but if so it was beyond me. The crucial thing was that I had a job to do. Once again, all was right in the universe.

CHAPTER 4

"Time to leave, Dip." I buckled myself into the cockpit.

"Have you become bored with this planet already?" Dip started the takeoff sequence. He usually handled communications with traffic control.

"Yes, but that's not why." I took the data card out of my coat. "I have my next assignment."

"You received it directly on planet? Am I correct in remarking that this is unusual?" The ship lifted off the landing pad.

"They are somehow tracking me." The ship began accelerating forward. This would be a much more gradual approach to orbit than our previous takeoff.

"I deduced that as well. I often scan for bugging devices but have found nothing." The sky darkened as the atmosphere thinned. Within moments, we were back in the blackness of space.

"As long as they are the only ones tracking me, I guess it's not worth worrying about." The operative word was "guess." Logically, it shouldn't be a problem for my employer to know where I am. Still, known unknowns can bother me. I like to have a vague idea of how everything works, from my blasters to my ship's engines to Dip. You never know when that information will be important. "Decode this for me." I inserted the data card into the console.

"I can verify this as originating from the Nystrom syndicate."

"I didn't ask for verification. Just decode it."

"Certainly, Rico." He was silent for a moment. "Interesting. There isn't a job on this disk."

"Excuse me?" My train of thought and conversation were interrupted by an explosion outside the ship. "What the hell?"

"It appears to be a warning shot. The ship that fired it is now hailing us. There are three ships, in fact. From the available data, I would guess that they are pirates. Would you like to take their call?"

I had been stupid. Being on my own for even a day had made me reckless, and in my eagerness to get off planet I had disregarded the officer's warning. I know I wouldn't have made this mistake were I already on a job, because an encounter such as this could ruin a mission. On my own time, it was hard to focus like that. Now I had a job — at least I thought I did — and very much wanted to focus on it but instead had a nuisance to deal with. "Are the ships armed?"

"I detect armaments on all three ships."

I was usually better armed than anything I might run into, but nothing was guaranteed. Most likely, pirates would not have the best kept ships, as they tend to be desperate people, but they did spend well on weaponry. Dip gave me a view of the ships, and they were decently large — a few times bigger than mine — with visible weaponry. Didn't look too maneuverable, though. Added to the equation was that I did not feel I was officially on a job at the moment, so I wanted to keep to my no-killing rule. "Put them on, Dip."

"Surrender your ship," the pirate leader said. By his accent, I could tell he was most likely human. "Make things easy, and we'll put you safely back on the planet. We never kill unless we have to."

Having to kill. That was an odd thought to me. Civilized people like to think they don't have to kill, but I don't know of any sentient species that didn't evolve from predators. Hunting and killing are very difficult, much more so than fleeing death. They require complex instincts that eventually lead to the development of intelligence. In a way, all of man's highest creations — from art to literature to science — only came about because of his basic need to kill.

But philosophy was just as useless in this situation as it is in any other. "I'll give you some advice: If you don't want to *have* to kill people, you probably shouldn't run around threatening them with weapons. It's pretty much inevitable that you're going to wind up in a kill-or-be-killed situation."

"Are you going to be trouble?" He had a threatening tone. A very good one. He wasn't new at this.

"Very much so. I don't think anyone has ever encountered me and not been the worse for it."

"Your ship doesn't look like any trouble."

"Which either means it's as light on defenses as it appears to be, or it's such an advanced ship that it's able to hide its weaponry from most scans. And a ship that expensive would probably have some very deadly ordinance — the sort of weapons that are likely to make your last words something like, 'Huh? What's that?'"

"Are you saying you can take on all three of us?"

"Perhaps not. I'd like to think so, but you might win. But you'd be forced to destroy me — so no profit for you — and I'd most likely leave your ships severely damaged or completely crippled — probably leaving you stuck in this orbit. And pirate hunters are coming to this system soon, so you might as well be dead in that condition. Maybe they'll treat you like the pirates of old and leave your corpses hanging out in the open as a warning to others. So there's the bright side: You'll get to help influence others to make better decisions than your own."

He was quiet for a moment. Hesitation in a situation like this is weakness. It's hard to score a verbal battle, but I would say I was winning. "You're bluffing. Now don't try to escape, or we will obliterate your little ship."

It was hard to show my weapons without using them in a way that wouldn't panic the pirates into retaliation. It would have been nice to have a "teeth baring" routine in this situation — perhaps something for Dip to look into later — but it was unavailable to me now. "No, I am not bluffing, and I don't think you want that realization to be the last bit of knowledge you glean from the universe. I am going to head away now and plot a jump. If you continue on your approach toward me, this is going to be a bad day for you. Be smart, and wait for a weaker target." I cut the communications. "Dip, get me some alone time, and keep watch on how close our new friends get."

It took a few minutes for Dip to move the ship into place and make the jump calculations. The pirates hung back and didn't try to hail me again. We jumped, and I was back in the quiet and safety of deep space. "Well, the peaceful solution worked that time."

"Threats of violence aren't always considered 'peaceful,'" Dip said.

"No one died. I don't know what more anyone would want. Now, before the interruption, you were saying there isn't a job on the disk?" Something I found potentially more alarming than silly pirates.

"Correct. There is just a time and location — a café in the capital of Nar Valdum."

"No job details."

"I'm afraid not."

This I did not like — going into a situation without knowing what I'm supposed to be doing. I assumed I would be meeting someone there to get further details, but it would have been nice to have some idea of whom I was supposed to meet. I let it go for now, though, and focused on the few details I did know. "I heard someone mention Nar Valdum recently. Is there some sort of conference going on there?"

"The Galactic Alliance is having a conference on increasing its power. The general public's interest in the conference has intensified, presumably in response to the situation on Zaldia and the different governments' inability to take direct action under current treaties."

And the syndicate wanted me in the middle of that. I didn't like the lack of details so far, but it did promise to be interesting. "Know anything about the security?"

"There is extensive scrutiny for anything coming near the planet. There will be many high-ranking officials from numerous governments affiliated with the

Alliance, so they want to avoid any incidents. This is the biggest meeting in Galactic Alliance history."

"So I'm heading into the middle of heavy security with no details? Not my preference."

"I will once again suggest a change of occupation. I could make up a list of possibilities based on your skills and interests if you like. What has your experience been with food preparation?"

"I once killed a man with a fork ... no, twice." And, considering the security, a fork might be all I'd be able to bring with me on this job. "Well, this is not how I like to receive an assignment, but I'm curious where this is going. Who do you think they'll want me to kill?"

"That's not something I'm programmed to speculate about."

They only ever sent me somewhere when they wanted a big scene. So a high-profile kill during the biggest meeting in the history of the known universe — this was no small thing, and it was going to have large and perhaps disturbing ramifications. It both excited and frightened me. "Set course. Let's go be a part of history."

CHAPTER 5

Sentients like governments. It's better than doing everything yourself. Governments are a big part of civilization, and civilization is what separates sentients from lesser animals, as it changes their focus from day-to-day survival and moves people forward toward social and technological advancement. Of course, having a direction is not the same as having a destination, and the ultimate destiny of any civilization is to flounder around, unsure of what to do with itself. It starts out seeming very grand as it conquers barbarians and increases its wealth. But when the everyday challenges end, things begin to fall apart. A civilization starts to lose confidence in itself, feels bad for all the lesser beings it crushed along the way, and finds it hard to act unless there's an immediate crisis. Eventually it falls victim to a more motivated civilization on the rise. And the cycle continues.

At least, that's how I see things. Anyway, the Galactic Alliance (which, despite the common name, spans multiple galaxies) is only different from previous civilizations in its massive scale. It had a lot of trouble getting started and getting so many varied cultures and people to work together. There were arguments, conflicts, and wars of a scale hard for the human mind to comprehend.

But that's all in the past, and the Alliance is clearly in the floundering stage. With agreements among thousands of planets, the Alliance coordinates law enforcement and commerce within its reach — at least theoretically. It's a loose confederation of a lot of separate governments without a strong central power, and it trips over its own bureaucracy more often than it actually does anything useful. Plus, it's trivial for anyone with a ship (like me) to quickly step out of Alliance-controlled space. The Alliance never goes beyond its boundaries, because that can be looked upon as a belligerent invasion, and civilized people don't do that. I'm starting to wonder if we've seen the upper limit of civilization, as the far-reaching Alliance struggles to stay relevant.

In come the syndicates. In a way, they started like the Alliance, as loose agreements between a number of groups who ... let's just say weren't as concerned about local laws as most people. But as disagreements arose, the stronger factions weren't afraid to assert themselves and crush anyone they could. And as the stronger groups consistently won out, eventually an undisputed central power arose in each syndicate. It makes a big difference having a power ready to make rules and enforce them by any means necessary. Plus, the syndicates are better suited for a universe with quick interstellar travel than traditional governments, as they don't care about borders or who thinks they control what regions of space. They feel they have a right to enforce their rules against anyone weaker than them. That's what the Alliance lacks the will to do, so people with the will to get things done — like those in the syndicates — are the only ones who keep some semblance of order nowadays. And I am one of the syndicate's tools in enforcing that order. In that capacity, there are two types of people I am sent after: the really honest and the really corrupt. The really honest can be too stubborn and may have to be removed to keep things from being upset ... and I guess I don't need to explain why the really corrupt may need to be violently killed.

Anyway, I hardly ever kill honest people.

The point is there are a lot of bad people who could run around and murder and steal without consequences if it weren't for other "bad" people like Nystrom stopping them. People would get upset about being ruled by murderous thugs, though, so that's where entities like the Galactic Alliance become somewhat useful. They look like they're in charge and keep people feeling like they're all soft and civilized, while lots of murdering is done for their benefit in faraway places they'll never hear about. They live under an illusion, but if there is any public action by a syndicate, that illusion begins to fade. Public action such as a murderous siege on a technologically backward planet. Or a hitman let loose in the midst of a high-profile conference on government power.

"Dip, I am growing impatient."

My view of Nar Valdum currently took up most of my ship's windshield. Blue and green with white at the poles, it was the stereotypical habitable planet for my species. It was not a home world for any sentient species, which meant it was in much more pristine condition than many other planets, having only been developed with modern sensibilities. It's not like planets are the most limited resource anymore, but people only like to strip-mine the ones that aren't green. It seems a little discriminatory.

Being so civilized, Nar Valdum fully monitored all traffic entering its atmosphere. Landing on the planet was not simple. Pretty much everything about being civilized is unnecessarily cumbersome. That's why I stick the edges of civilization. I don't really fit in with civilized people.

"Would you like to play twenty questions, Rico? You think of something, and then I'll try to guess it. It will help me learn."

"No, Dip, I want ground control. Any indication of how much longer we'll have to wait?"

"They simply say we are in a queue, and they will get to us soon. So do you want to play twenty questions?"

Didn't have much else to do. "Fine. I thought of something."

"Is it animal, vegetable, mineral, or other?"

"Other."

"Is it violence?"

"Yes."

Dip processed silently for a moment. "That game did not help me learn anything."

"Life is full of disappointments, Dip. Perhaps you learned that."

"I previously derived that knowledge, Rico. I have good news for you, though: Ground control is hailing us."

"Patch them through."

"This is Nar Valdum ground control," said a male voice over the ship's speakers. "What is your business here?"

My guess was that a normal person would be a little irate at this point, so I decided to go with that ... since I actually was quite irate. "Landing ... not just floating here all day." I was starting to worry I'd be late for my meeting with my contact (contacts?), and I had no idea what would happen then. Very frustrating.

"We are sorry for the wait, but security measures have been increased for the conference. Are you here for that?"

"Yes." So many species in one area would be something. I imagined firing into a crowd full of diverse species and making a rainbow of blood splatters. It would be like art.

"How long is your planned stay?"

Once again, I had no idea. "Seven days."

"How many sentients are aboard your vessel?"

"Just me."

"Species?"

"Human. Haven't you scanned my ship?"

"Just confirming data. Does your ship have weaponry?"

None they would find. "Just basic defensive measures ... if you'd call them weapons."

"Your course for landing and your ship identification are being sent to you. Please keep the ship identification in your memory bank for the length of your stay."

I checked the onscreen map. This was not good. "That's a completely different continent from the conference!"

"Security measures," ground control answered. He sounded weary.

"It's good to know I'll be safe, at least." I did not hide the sarcasm as I cut communications. Whatever I would be doing down there, I would lack an easy escape. "Dip, take her down. I'll need you to find out as much as you can about their aerial security and whether you might be able to bring the ship in closer if needed. I'd like a better escape plan than having to tunnel straight through the planet to get back to you. I think I'll need your full pretend intelligence on this."

"Can't you assume those you will be working with will help with your escape?"

"That is likely, but I don't take anything for granted. Try and come up with your own solution."

"Certainly. Thank you for this task. It should make full use of my programming and be a good learning experience for helping you in the future ... or whoever owns me in the future."

"Are you trying to imply that I might not survive this?"

"Exactly! It's good to know that my attempt at an implication led to a correct inference. Anyway, it's difficult to calculate your odds of survival without knowing the details of your mission, but factoring in the public impact of your usual jobs and the fact that you'll be surrounded by the highest security you're likely to see in a single city, it's hard to come up with a scenario in which you emerge from this alive."

He had a point. "True, but don't forget one thing: People are stupid. There are always angles to exploit."

"Aren't you people, Rico?"

"That's debatable."

"While we're landing, I have something for you to try guessing in twenty questions, Rico."

I manually accessed Dip's memory buffer and looked for an unusual sequence repeated over and over.

"Are you thinking of a shoe?"

"You cheated."

"I hope you learned something from that."

CHAPTER 6

I had to land my ship about 9,000 miles from the capital city. My large store of items that make killing fun and easy would not be readily accessible, so I was forced to put whatever I might need into a couple of bags that I could carry with me.

My favorite firearms are Arco X5 blasters that burn nice, large holes through organic matter. One shot to anywhere on the torso will almost always be instantly lethal. The blasters are highly illegal. Even militaries tend not to use them as small arms, since a shot from one can rip through a creature and keep right on going through a school, a hospital, and an orphanage before finally dissipating (I haven't actually tested that in the field, but if I ever got that shot lined up, it would be hard not to take it). If you're someone like me who is incapable of caring about collateral damage on some planet he never plans to visit again, they're perfect.

Now, technically, all weapons deadlier than small knives were forbidden in the capital. But of course my interest was more in what security might be able to detect. There was no way they could individually search everyone coming into the city, but Dip found that I would have to pass through some mass scanners when taking the inbound trams. They'd be looking for large power sources that could be nuclear bombs or worse; and unfortunately, the X5 blaster uses a pretty insane power source that basically screams that you're there to kill everyone. So those had to stay with Dip. Instead I'd be taking some Shiro pistols as my main weapons. Their power source isn't much bigger than what you'd find in a lot of common electronics, but they also only burn small holes through people — often not even all the way through. A single shot is pretty survivable, but they can be fired quite fast, which allows me to put a lot of shots into a target.

In case I was going to enter any buildings where I might be specifically scanned, I was bringing two pistols that worked on the old explosive powder design. Completely mechanical, a spring-loaded magazine feeds bullets into the barrel. A bullet is basically a piece of lead with explosive powder packed behind it. A physical strike to the back of the bullet explodes the powder and projects the piece of lead forward at a high speed while causing the top part of the gun to slide backward and load another bullet from the magazine. The lead pieces have hollow tips, so they flatten on impact and do major soft tissue damage. An ingenious ancient design (these were called 1911s, which refers to the approximate year of their invention), they work well and, lacking electronic power sources, they are completely invisible to most weapon scans. Each pistol fires only eight shots before the magazine has to be replaced, but they're accurate enough in short ranges that I can make each of those shots count. They're very loud, but that does help with intimidation.

As backup, I always carry a revolver — an even older design. It keeps six bullets in rotating chambers, which click into place with each trigger pull. It's a last resort, and I have deployed it before to good effect.

I packed those weapons (I'd be carrying two of the Shiro pistols on my person for the trip) along with some clothes and toiletries and minor explosives. "Will you be able to easily communicate with me from here?" I asked Dip as I prepared to leave the ship.

"I should be able to use relays to communicate with you directly as needed, Rico. Please be careful, though. If you need an emergency pickup, I calculate approximately a ninety-two percent chance of my being shot out of the sky were I to even approach the city."

"I'll do my best not to get into random gunfights, but keep trying to find an alternate way past air traffic security. I'll see what my contact here knows."

"Hopefully, he will have useful knowledge, but I will continue to work on the problem. In fact, by factoring in some maneuvers I'm capable of making, I now calculate a nearly ten percent chance of my being able to land in the capital. Even if I am successful at that, though, our chances of taking off and escaping atmosphere are incalculably small."

"Fun times." I would essentially be trapped in the city if something did go wrong. I hoped my contact had that figured out, but it was starting to look like I was going to be late to meet him. I quickly left the ship and headed for the tram. There was some diversity of alien species on the train, but I saw more humans and Corridians than any other. Humans have gotten along pretty well with Corridians because they are what some people call "Star Trek" aliens. Those are aliens that kinda look like they could be humans in makeup. Despite all the PSAs about not judging sentients by appearances, most people get nervous standing next to something that looks like a giant insect. They want to smash in its head. Nothing wrong with that; it's just instinct. Humans can anthropomorphize anything, but it helps if the species throws us a bone by at least having a face.

Almost every sentient species I've bothered to research had racial battles before they advanced to the point of interstellar travel, and they tend to look at interaction between alien species with that frame of mind. But it's not the same; the physiological differences are huge. People take it as a matter of faith that all sentient species are equal, but in the back of their heads they know there is no rational basis for that assumption. All the sentients evolved separately on separate worlds with separately developed brains; any similarities really are by chance. But we want all intelligent things to be equal, as if by wanting it we could make it so. If we just got into some big wars where we wiped out and conquered each other, it would seem a lot more honest to me than trying to live together.

I like honesty. You hardly ever see real honesty in the universe. Nothing scares people more.

"Are you here for the conference?" asked some creature I didn't recognize.

He/she/it had interrupted my train of thought — I was trying to figure out how long it would take to kill everyone on the train (a routine mental exercise I do). I rarely kill so indiscriminately, but my instinct would be to go for the children last. They are smaller targets, but their survival instincts are usually very poor, and they probably wouldn't even know to run and hide. "I've got a headache. I'm not really in a talking mood." I decided to be a jerk while I'm here. That means I don't have to concentrate as much on social niceties, but I still don't have to worry about standing out, because jerks are very common throughout the universe.

The tram slowed as it neared the capital. Like many large cities, it had slums with all the alien diversity you could want and plenty of crime and violence (guess which people tend to flee colonies of their own species?), and then things became much more monolithic as you got closer to the city center. Nar Valdum was our first attempt to colonize a planet in concert with another species and was roughly half human and half Corridian, which was supposed to prove some point I'm sure no one could coherently explain. They're trying to hold it up as a positive example of different species coexisting — i.e., uncomfortably but without outright violence — but it just seems asinine to me.

It takes a beam of light one hundred thousand years to travel from one edge of the Milky Way to the other, and there are hundreds of billions of galaxies. There is enough room for all species to have plenty of colonized planets and never have to run into each other. But I guess that's just too simple. Still, I'm not complaining. Chaos and stupidity make things easier for me.

I was starting to feel a bit nervous as the tram took me farther away from my only means of escape. I was trapped here, and if somehow my masked slipped, I wouldn't be able to shoot my way to safety. You might think being inconspicuous would be as simple as just following the laws, but most people don't know the laws by actually memorizing them. They know what feels wrong and that what feels really wrong is probably against the law. No action I take feels different than another for me, so I constantly have to check everything I'm doing against a little list of social mores and laws I've memorized. I had gotten pretty good at it, but it was never easy.

I arrived in the city with some time before my lunch meeting, so I went to the hotel room Dip had reserved. Not too cheap, not too expensive. Staying there said absolutely nothing about me. Inconspicuous. After I dropped off my luggage, I headed to the café — a fancy little place that seemed to cater evenly to humans and Corridians. I arrived at the proper time and, just as I had feared, had no idea what to do next. No one immediately approached me, and no one stood out in the crowd (I would hope whoever it was would be smart enough not to), so I got a table outside and decided to wait. I ordered some tea and brought up the local news on my reader. I wasn't actually planning to read, but I wanted to try this new thing I had been working on.

My brain being split was mainly advantageous when I took on two targets at once, but I had found that I could also have one of the parts do simple tasks while I focused elsewhere. What I had tried to break down into a simple task this time was the appearance of reading news. News reading is more difficult to fake than book reading, because I'm not just reading cover to cover. I have to pretend to scan for stories that interest me, then slow down to focus more on certain parts. It's a minor distinction, but what if another trained observer like me was looking for something out of place? If I'm going to pretend to be normal, I might as well commit to it fully. Nothing is more suspicious than something that's just a bit off.

So I sat at the café, and while my eyes and hands pretended to read the news, my ears and perception were concentrating on the voices around me. No one was saying much worth spying on, but it was really just practice anyway. In fact, the news did finally get my attention with its repeated references to Zaldia. This included pictures of the carnage and what looked like a crying child among dead bodies — though I wasn't familiar enough with the species to say for sure. This sort of thing was horrific to most people.

I briefly considered actually reading one of the stories but decided to just let Dip summarize anything interesting for me later. Instead, I went back to listening and pretending to read. I now heard some people mention Zaldia, and the expectation that the big conference was going to lead to something being done about the occupation. So it wasn't too much of a mystery why the syndicate would be interested in the goings on here; I just didn't know what their intentions were.

I had to stop listening to sip my tea. Pretending to read the news, listening around me, and sipping tea was a bit much for me. With some practice, though, it seemed I could get it down. Appearing to be absorbed in something while actually listening intently to everything around me really was a skilled illusion. But I made one mistake that revealed my abnormality.

When the café exploded and men ran toward us screaming and firing guns into the crowd, I neatly set down the reader on my table instead of dropping it in surprise. I don't think anyone was paying attention to me at that point, though.

CHAPTER 7

Five sentients were firing energy weapons with crazed zeal, screaming something about a mechanized god. People around me fell, dead or wounded. I was right at the center of a terrorist attack. What were the chances?

Not very high is the answer. But that was not my main concern at the moment.

I was familiar with this group. They called themselves the Calabrai. Knowledge of the existence of other sentient species has been a problem for many religions, as most were formed before people even considered the possibility of life on other worlds (or knew that there were other worlds). Thus each religion is mostly confined to the particular species and home world of its origin, and adaptation to the new reality was hard. The Calabrai basically took religions from many different species — one "true" religion from each — and considered them all as having been based on the same true god. This one true god supposedly took form as a gigantic city-leveling robot called Calab. Calab is hidden on some unknown planet (though he is rumored to have been destroyed), and he keeps sending out commands to his followers to kill unbelievers.

There are a lot of obvious problems with giving this kind of robot artificial intelligence, but you can hardly blame people for failing to consider that it might become the basis for a violent new cult. And the Calabrai do follow its commands, though their efforts to kill the unbelievers never seem to amount to much more than huge annoyances to the targeted planets, as they aren't a sophisticated enough force to topple governments. It made sense that they'd be interested in the expansion of powers of the Galactic Alliance and would attack Nar Valdum now, as one of the initial reasons most civilizations exist is to keep kill-happy barbarians at bay.

I try to avoid religious disputes. Well, I try to avoid people most of the time, but I especially have no interest in debating religion. One can point out that religion is just a bunch of superstitious, irrational beliefs; but is that any different from the beliefs of atheists? Everyone likes to think they're logical and reasonable, but I find all people to be equally absurd and irrational. The main difference is that the religious tend to be a bit more organized in their irrationality.

Now, a lot of people consider thinking a giant killer robot is a god to be laughably ridiculous, and I get that. I just don't get how it may be socially acceptable for me to laugh at the Calabrai and their poorly examined beliefs, but wrong for me to laugh at how people mindlessly go to their jobs every day and provide for their families with no real introspection as to why and to what end. It's all nonsense, but at least the Calabrai are acting with some real purpose.

That purpose right now was to kill me. I didn't take it personally; they would kill just about anybody, and I simply happened to be there. It's like when people get killed in the crossfire when I'm on a job — nothing personal there either. That's just how things are. And I really did kind of admire their zeal. I kill people because it's something to do. They feel they're doing something right and good, the way others might when helping poor people, but with fun killing instead. And I don't have any concept of what that's like. I don't know how you just choose to believe something like that. But it does seem like it might make life easier.

Life was not easy at the moment. For about half a second, I sat there in the open contemplating what to do — a very dangerous use of time. These people had nothing to do with my assignment, and it's a pretty drilled-in rule that I don't kill outside the job, so it took me a moment to realize I was going to have to kill them. This was most definitely a kill-or-be-killed situation, so it was clearly an exception to the rule. And while that might appear to mean that I would simply draw my guns and shoot the five assassins until they stopped moving, I still had my mission to consider. If I killed them expertly, it'd be obvious that I'm a trained killer. The mission would be ruined, and I'd be forced to flee ... and I'd probably fail at that because of the tight security lockdown. Big mess. Lots of people dead — including me.

Luckily I had planned for a similar situation: being discovered with guns before a hit was carried out. My story would be that I'm a cop on vacation, and I always bring my guns out of habit. It was believable, at least. Cops can be arrogant (just like me — though I would argue that I have more justification). Killing five attackers should be a feat for a cop who capably uses a gun but doesn't kill people every week like I do, so I would have to make this look a bit lucky — I could be skilled but not *too* skilled.

Which takes a tremendous amount of skill, incidentally.

I drew one gun with my right hand and fired twice at one terrorist, missing the first shot on purpose and burning him with the second, the lizard-like creature devoting a dying shriek to his robotic master. I shot him again to make sure he was dead. I really don't like these weaker guns that can't destroy a whole torso. One shot per kill makes things much easier.

I fired three more shots as I went for cover (a cop would use only inanimate objects and not other people as a shield, so I had to watch myself). Two of the three shots struck a human terrorist, and the remaining three now focused on me, the only armed resistance the Calabrai were facing ("civilized" people do nothing but panic and scream in these situations, which would seem to be the opposite of civilized). We were in a pretty open area, so I could only find partial cover behind a lamppost.

I reminded myself not to smile. I tend to smile when I shoot people, because it's challenging and fun. But that freaks people out — which usually is an advantage, but not in this situation.

It was odd killing people in a socially acceptable manner; it felt like trying to walk around on my hands. Still, the terrorists' aim was pathetic, and I probably got a bit cocky. I fired two more close but missing shots before killing a third. And then my luck ran out.

It felt like a hot poker jammed through my calf muscle. My leg would no longer support my weight, and I fell over. Adrenaline shot through me, and instinct took over. I pulled out my second blaster and unloaded two guns into the head of the thing that shot me until his face caught fire. Or maybe it was just his beard. Whatever it was, it was pretty awesome. There was no time to watch, though, as there was still one terrorist left, and I was unable to get up. He had a bead on me, so I just unloaded on him as he tried to shoot back. I don't even know how many times I shot him, but the important thing was his not shooting me.

Anger had probably taken some control over me — not a good thing — but my leg *really* hurt.

I looked around the fire of the former café to see if there were any "bad guys" left to shoot, but I saw only panic, the injured crying in pain, and the permanently quiet. Safe for at least a moment, I set down my guns and began bandaging my leg with a cloth napkin from a nearby table.

"You saved us!" gasped a middle-age woman clutching a child.

In my condition, the last thing I wanted to do was talk to people — especially in a situation like this where they would be even more irrational and useless than usual. Still, I had to commit to character if I wanted to get through this. I went with false modesty — that seemed to be a societal norm for this sort of thing. "I was just saving myself." That was completely true; frankly I would have preferred that everyone else had died so they wouldn't be bothering me at the moment.

I wondered if I would be in the news for this. That would not be helpful.

"Can I help you with —"

"I'm fine," I interrupted the woman as I tightened my bandage. "Look after your son." Others were gathered around me now, as I was apparently the closest thing to an authority figure there. "Look for the wounded so you can help the authorities when they get here," I commanded calmly. If you act like you're in charge, most people will just assume you are and do as you say. "Don't worry about me; I can handle myself."

The role-playing required a lot of concentration, but what I really wanted to be contemplating right now was why I had been told to meet my contacts at this café and ended up in the middle of a terrorist attack. I couldn't even begin to think what that meant.

"I am hearing in police chatter that there was violence at the café you were going to," Dip said. "And now I detect that you are injured. Do you need me to activate the emergency protocol?"

I heard sirens as emergency vehicles descended upon us, and reflexively I glanced at the guns lying at my side. I had two options: Shoot my way out of this, or surrender my guns and remove that option. There was nothing worse to me than a situation where shooting my way out wasn't even a fallback. But giving up my weapons was the smarter choice right now and the only one that might give me an opportunity to complete my job.

"That would be an overreaction at this juncture. I want you to get in contact with Vito, tell him what happened when I tried to meet my contacts, and get him to find out what the hell is going on."

It was good that a normal person would be stressed and angry in this situation, because now I would be very convincing. And being convincingly normal was all that was going to save me.

CHAPTER 8

Unarmed, wounded, lying in a hospital bed, and about to be questioned by the police — not the best start for a mission. The only defense I had left was my wits. And Dip.

"I contacted Vito. He was surprised to hear you were in a terrorist attack, and he will look into what happened with the person you were supposed to meet."

I had surrendered my guns to the authorities, but the internal communicator connecting me to Dip is pretty much undetectable and hard to disable even if found. "He'd better not be his usual useless self this time. I was told this mission is very important, and — not knowing what it is — it looks like it's ruined."

"This certainly is a very unusual circumstance for you, Rico. Usually the violence you commit is reflected negatively in the press, but I notice little negative commentary in the reporting today."

"I'm pretty sure this isn't the first time I've killed people that the general public was happy to be rid of."

"Still, your violence has always been seen as criminal. This act of violence is being referred to as 'heroic.'"

"I killed five murderers — preventing the deaths of others — and took a bolt through my leg in the process. Would you call that 'heroic'?"

That took him a second. "I would assume you had ulterior motives, Rico."

That made me laugh. But I was alone in my hospital room so no one looked at me funny. "Keep monitoring the news. I need to know if my face is made public."

"Will that cause you to abandon the mission?"

"It's just worth knowing if it happens. How goes the extraction plan?"

"I have a new plan to extract you from Nar Valdum's capital, which I rate as having a twenty percent chance of success."

"That's a nice round number."

"There are many unknowns, so I went with inexact figures."

"Whatever. I need a better number than twenty percent."

Dip was silent again. "When calculating the chance of success, I could give greater weight to the ship's maneuverability, which would ..."

"I don't mean fudge the numbers. I mean come up with a better plan." Hopefully I wouldn't need it too soon. "I don't know what's going on with my contact here, so right now you're my only way out. Get to work."

Patching my leg was a simple enough procedure. They held it still in a regenerator, and I just had to wait an hour or so. After that, I'd be back to (my) normal and ready for killing (that is, if I could get back to my hotel room to rearm). I had a video monitor in the hospital room and nothing to do while I waited, so I found a nature show to watch.

"The delping waits in the river, its gray coloration helping it to blend in with the rocks. When prey is close enough, it strikes by kicking forward with its strong rear legs and expelling all the air in its lungs from two reverse-facing nostrils on the sides of its heads. Using this jet propulsion, with blinding speed it snatches the ..."

"Not watching the news?" Walking into my hospital room was a blonde thirty-something — apparently a plainclothes detective who had come to question me. No ring.

Hello, human female.

She wasn't a knockout, looks-wise, but the way she held herself — the authority in it — was very strong and, I guess, a turn-on for me. She smiled at me — I *was* the hero — but the suspicion was obvious in her eyes. I can assess people quickly, and this was a smart woman. That would potentially be trouble.

I turned the TV off. It would take my full concentration to pull off this act. "The news would just be a bunch of speculation at this point. I'm actually on vacation. I'm trying to relax." I laughed, since that was supposed to be ironic.

Wait. I went to a café — a place to relax — which got me attacked by terrorists, which is situational irony. But I don't think my statement about it counted as irony, as it was merely light sarcasm.

It's important to keep that straight.

Whatever it was, it got only a polite smile in response. "I'm Detective Thompson. I'm here to question you about the terrorist attack. I'd just like to start by making it clear that our main concerns are these terrorists and preventing possible further attacks, so I want to get the issue of your involvement out of the way as quickly as possible. You gave your name as 'Rico Vargas'?"

"Can you make sure my name and picture don't end up in the news? I don't want to sound cowardly, but I'd rather not have all the Calabrai freaks targeting me while I'm here."

"We're not telling anyone you're the one who ended the attack," Detective Thompson assured me. "Now, I need to ask: Why were you carrying guns?"

"I'm a police officer from a planet called Rikar." The planet was in a galaxy red-shifting away near the speed of light; it would take the police on Nar Valdum a lot of effort to contact it. "I carry out of habit, and, to be honest, I didn't really look into the gun laws here. I've been through a lot, and I don't go places unarmed." Seemed liked a believable cop attitude.

She nodded — somehow it came off as a suspicious nodding. "You carry three guns everywhere?"

That I do, unless I can comfortably fit more on me; I've never been in a situation where I was all, "Oh no! I have too many guns!"

That wasn't my answer to her, though.

"Rikar is a pretty violent planet; I'm used to carrying a gun at all times and a backup just to be safe. The third gun — the old-fashioned little revolver — is almost more of a good luck charm. You ever use a gunpowder-based firearm before?"

I really couldn't tell if she was buying it. "They're noisy." She looked at her notes. "You often need your backup gun on Rikar?"

I was going to assume someone saw me firing both guns at once. "Not often, but I taught myself to aim and fire both guns at once. It's point-shooting — less accurate, but quick. With multiple attackers and limited cover, it's about all that kept me alive."

"From the results, I could certainly tell it wasn't your first gunfight." It seemed like part compliment and part further suspicion. She was challenging; I kind of liked that. It was so easy to fool most people.

"Like I said, Rikar is pretty violent." True, if I was thinking of the right planet. I pointed to my stabilized leg. "Not my first gunfight or bolt wound." Certainly true. "I was trying to get away from that, really." Not true at all.

"So what brought you here?" She now seemed like she was trying to sound less suspicious. I was successful in engendering politeness, at least.

"I just really needed a break from work and wanted to see some of the universe. I constantly deal with the same problems and finally convinced myself that the whole place wouldn't burn down without me, and I could take a vacation. I heard about the conference here and the possibility of a stronger galactic government and thought that was worth checking out. There's so much crime and chaos out there, it's nice to think something can be done about it."

"If by 'something' you mean lots of talking and useless measures, then I'm sure something will be done." She smiled wryly.

"Maybe so." It seemed that we had now bonded as fellow law enforcement professionals. "So am I in trouble?" I almost forgot to ask that, but normal people would be worried about that sort of thing.

"You're a hero — I don't think the prosecutors will want to pursue the infraction of illegal possession of small arms. I need to do my job, though."

"I understand." Doing my job is what I'm all about. "If you guys expect some sort of written apology for the firearms possession, it's not going to happen." It seemed right to be a little indignant.

She smiled. "I'm pretty sure we're going to be more practical than that." She was pretty — that was for sure — though her clothing was functional and only vaguely feminine. The only thing outwardly threatening was her blue eyes — I could tell they were hard at work assessing me. If I'd had to guess just then — and I often do need to guess about these sorts of things — I would have ventured she had killed in the line of duty or at least been in numerous gunfights.

Yes, I can sorta tell that from someone's eyes. I'm not talking "windows to the soul" crap; it's what they focus on that's revealing. And hers were carefully looking me over while she kept up a friendly exterior.

I took another moment to reflect on what someone like "Officer Rico" would be concerned about in a situation like this. It's a universally accepted truth that people getting killed is tragic (even though it happens *all* the time), so I figured I'd better show concern about that. "So ... uh ... how bad was it?"

"Seven dead." I could see a little fire in her eyes. She cared about others; how cute. "About three times that many were injured."

I stared a bit vacantly with my mouth slightly open. It's supposed to be a "shocked" expression, and I think I pulled it off. I uttered, "Why?" People love that question, but the answer is usually much less enlightening than they would think. People need purpose in their lives, and intense purpose — intense enough to justify killing others — has got to be quite satisfying.

"They are nuts. I don't see any reason to analyze it past that. Maybe they're feeling upstaged by what's happening on Zaldia and wanted to remind everyone what mindless murderers they are, too."

"It hardly compares to Zaldia." I was really starting to think I should read up more on Zaldia if people kept mentioning it. I just hate reading the news.

"The Calabrai are never going to be anything more than a nuisance to society at large, but that's hardly comforting to the families of the dead. Right now we have people trying to find out if this attack was an isolated incident or if we should expect more."

I didn't really have a plan at this point, but I saw something and decided to go with it. "Any leads on that?"

Her expression turned serious. "I'm not on that case beyond checking in on you."

I smiled. "You have an idea of what trees to shake, though?"

"What makes you say that?"

"You're antsy. You don't want to be here; you want to be out there chasing this. I've been there."

She grinned. "No, I don't want to be here when we could have more attacks coming. I hope you don't take offense at that, Mr. Vargas."

"Rico, please."

"If you don't find it too offensive, I'm just going to go ahead and report that you don't appear to be a threat, and we'll sweep this whole thing under the rug."

"If I'm not a threat, can I have my guns back?"

"You're not getting your guns back is part of the rug-sweeping, I'm afraid. I wish I could offer you something more to help salvage your vacation; you are a hero."

I was interested in seeing if she had more to offer me. I was in a bad situation, and I had two options: Try to escape further police notice, or see if I could use it to my advantage — whenever I found out why I was on this planet. "They say I'll be out of here in another hour, so I think I'll just be satisfied today with a nice dinner and a good night's sleep." The hook was baited.

"Eating alone?" And she went for it.

"I'm on a solo sojourn right now."

"Well, if you want company, I know a few good places. My treat. It's the least we could do for you."

"That would be great. I'll just need to get back to my hotel room first because of the societal need for pants."

She chuckled. "So where are you staying?"

"Lion's Grove. It's pretty nice." And not too suspicious on a cop's salary. It seems like luck, but smart planning makes its own luck.

"I know a good restaurant right by there — Kylo's. Why don't I meet you there at seven, Rico?"

"Sounds good ... Detective."

She smiled. "Diane. Now, try to stay out of trouble until then." She took one last look over me before leaving. No, not in that way. I think she was still suspicious of me. I liked her. She seemed pretty smart. Hopefully not so smart I'd have to kill her.

"Dip, I have a new job for you. Find out everything you can about a Detective Diane Thompson."

CHAPTER 9

My leg was stiff, but it seemed to work for walking, which was the best I could hope for a few hours after having a blaster bolt go straight through it. More bothersome was my current sense of nakedness. That was partly from having to wear a small pair of shorts I got at the hospital to replace my pants. (I'm not much for fashion, but I'm pretty sure blue shorts don't complement a gray sports jacket too well.) But I could wear a clown costume and not worry about drawing attention as long as I knew I could kill everyone around me.

As soon as I got back to my room, I opened the safe inside the closet and took out my last two firearms: the .45s. They were just a step up from a sharpened rock on a stick, but as long as they were concealable and could kill people at a distance, I was happy.

"I have information about Diane Thompson if you want it, Rico."

"You haven't heard any more from Vito?"

"Not yet."

I picked out another suit from the closet. I have a few slightly varied styles, but I always keep things simple. "Yeah. Read me the main points."

"Please clarify."

"Where she is from, how old she is, how long she has been on the police force, any cases she's worked on that stick out ..."

"Stick out how?"

"Arrested someone with a high profile, any shootouts. You should be smart enough now to figure out when something is unusual." Once I had the new shirt on, I got out some shoulder holsters that fit the .45s. I'd had to go to a replica store to get them.

"She is thirty-four years old. She is originally from the planet Andalu and transferred here as a police officer a little over ten years ago. She was promoted to detective four years later. She has been involved in twelve shootings in the line of duty. Killed eight sentients total, wounded five, all ruled justified. About a year ago, she received a bolt wound to the shoulder while her partner was shot multiple times and killed. She killed one of the assailants in that incident, and the other two were caught and are currently serving life prison sentences."

"That's quite a bit of action for a police officer, correct?" Her number of kills over ten years wouldn't be a particularly exceptional day for me, but officers of the law aren't exactly supposed to be killing machines — especially in well-settled areas.

Dip said, "There is a decent amount of crime in the city, and she hasn't drawn her gun excessively — she just appears to be more lethal than average when she does. She does have a higher than average number of complaints against her."

I chuckled. "That just means she needs to kill even more people. Dead men don't complain. Anyway, she seems interesting."

"Rico, why are you asking questions about her? Based on data of celebrities known for their attractiveness, I have given Diane Thompson a seventy-eight percent chance of being considered attractive."

I practiced drawing the guns from the shoulder holster. They had a nice weight to them, but the weight would change as I fired them and used up ammunition. A small factor, but it was worth noting. "Things are pretty messed up right now, since I've earned a high profile with the police. I don't know what I'm doing here, but maybe when I find out I can exploit police access for it. I'm just keeping my options open ... since I don't know what else to do at the moment."

"Getting closer to law enforcement on this planet seems like a dangerous plan."

"I don't know what the safe one is." I checked the action on the guns. I was less familiar with it — I've practiced shooting them but have never actually killed with one.

"Fleeing," he said.

"I have a dinner date. Fleeing would hurt the detective's feelings." I loaded the guns, put the safeties on, and holstered them.

"Do you plan to kill her?"

"That would be a little forward for a first date."

"I would caution you that —" Dip paused mid-sentence. "I have an incoming call from Vito."

Finally. "Patch him to me." I waited until I could hear him breathing on the other end of the line. "Vito, what the hell?"

"Sorry. I don't know much of what's going on," Vito said. "But I have new orders for you. You're supposed to help the police on Nar Valdum take out the terrorists."

"Is that my main job here?" I asked.

"I don't know the details. I'm just told you're to do that, and someone will contact you again later."

"When?"

"I don't know."

"So work with the police?"

"That's what they said."

I was silent for a second while I contemplated this. "I don't think the police are going to like my methods."

"Sorry. That's all they told me."

"And what about the contacts I was supposed to meet here? Did they know the café would be attacked?"

"I dunno. I told you all I have."

This was unacceptable to me. I knew I was someone who took orders, but when it came to killing, they always just gave me a target and set me loose. I was not used to being micromanaged like this. I decided to try focusing on something else, as I was getting angry. "I would like some better weapons. Do you know where I can get them in the city?"

"I don't even know where you are. They aren't really telling me much at this time."

That was it. I'd never quite understood why the executives had to separate themselves from me with a layer of complete uselessness. "I'm getting tired of this crap. I need better communication with people who actually know things, not useless people like you. Go tell them this is unacceptable, and then please pick up a gun and blow your brains out. You're obviously too insignificant for me to waste time killing, but I'm guessing you personally have nothing better to do."

"It's just —"

"I'm done," I announced to Dip, and he cut the communication.

"You said he was not worth the time it would take to kill him, but you did invest time in chastising him."

"I was getting angry, and I do not do well with emotions. Best to outlet them harmlessly."

"Do I need to start researching the terrorists?" Dip asked.

"I guess so." I thought for a moment. "I really don't know how to hunt down and kill people within the confines of the law. I'll definitely need someone else's guidance."

"The detective's?"

"She is in need of a partner." I practiced my charming smile in front of the mirror. My natural smile is often described as "terrifying," so I'd have to remember to scale it back a bit.

CHAPTER 10

My goal was not to be wooing the detective. I certainly was interested in carnal knowledge of a woman who had a seventy-eight percent chance of being considered attractive. But she was now part of the job, so I would keep my interest professional. What I wanted now was to get her to trust me as a fellow cop so I could get more information, and maybe get her to let me help her. Also, my guess was that this was less a date for the detective than a chance to learn more about a slightly suspicious character, so this would be a challenge. Though I was still annoyed at how this job was unfolding, hunting terrorists with the police was a brand new game and was at least a little exciting.

I headed to the restaurant at the agreed upon time and saw her seated at a table wearing the same clothes she'd worn earlier. She was trying to make this a professional meeting between two fellow officers. I assumed she didn't trust me, and further that she knew I knew she didn't trust me. That worked well for me, because I wasn't the only one who would be trying to *act* normal.

She smiled when she spotted me — somewhat perfunctorily — and asked, "How's the leg?"

I took a seat across from her. "A little stiff, but it seems to be in working order. Still haven't found anyone to fix the hole in my pants, though."

We laughed at my lame joke. I scanned her face to better see her true feelings and noticed she was doing the same to me. This "date" had the potential to be quite awkward. I think she wanted to trust me — I was a hero, after all — but her very correct instincts were an obstacle I would need to overcome.

"You seem to be in good spirits after all that's happened today," she stated, trying to sound complimentary.

"I wish I could say that was the worst I've been through."

Her response was interrupted by the waiter — some green alien type I'd never seen before. He seemed to be familiar with the detective and curious about me. She told him I was a police officer from another planet and left it there. "What they make here is basically like a pizza — I say better, though," she explained. "Any preference for what's on it?"

"Whatever you recommend." I couldn't have cared less, but I'd make an effort to look like I enjoyed whatever she ordered.

She ordered a "Kylo Special" and a Coke while I asked for bottled water. I was somewhat wary of a restaurant meant to make human cuisine but run by aliens; what's yummy to some species is poison to others. Dying from food poisoning would be a pretty silly end for me. But I decided I could trust the detective's choice in "pizza" joints.

"Sorry this is all you're getting for your heroism," she told me, smiling slightly. "It really is best to keep things quiet about you. There are the legalities of your having a firearm, plus we're pretty certain more terrorists are lurking around the city."

"Is someone lurking back?"

She nodded unenthusiastically. "Supposedly very good people."

"I guess we can all rest easy then." I am very good at sarcasm; I don't have to fake that.

She hesitated a moment. "I have a few ideas of my own, and I'm going to follow up tomorrow morning to double check the feds' work."

There was some subtext there, but I couldn't quite catch it all. "Will you be getting yourself into trouble?"

She shrugged. I thought that was a "yes." She was not a by-the-book person; that was promising. "So things sound pretty rough on Rikar," she said, changing the subject. "Are they going to get along without you?"

"There are a lot of people I trust on the police force — enough to handle things effectively. We probably use somewhat harsher methods than you'd be used to."

She chuckled. "We're of a modern sensibility. Occasionally, enforcing the law at all is considered too harsh. And then we have people blowing up restaurants."

She probably was the perfect person to help me. I just had to keep pressing subtly. "You can certainly go too far either way." I was trying to sound reasonable, but it was true. You can't go around shooting everyone you don't like in the face, as it will often cause more problems than it solves. "I was hoping, though, to find some more civilized methods to bring back home. We don't need detectives most of the time because so many criminals don't even try to hide their crimes. Whether we apprehend a perp is a matter of whether we feel we have enough people and arms to do it."

"Any chance your planet will join the Galactic Alliance?"

"We'd need to organize ourselves more first. How does that work out for you?"

"Being part of the Alliance?" She grimaced. "At least it allows us to pursue criminals to other Alliance planets."

I laughed out loud at that. It's hard to make a forced laugh sound natural — it can actually sound irritating — so luckily I did find the notion actually funny. "How often are fugitives dumb enough to flee to other Alliance planets?"

She didn't laugh. "Not often enough. And there are so many disputes over who has authority to enforce laws on which planets. That's why everyone is just watching in horror as the pictures come out of Zaldia instead of doing anything."

"Isn't that what the conference is about? Increasing the central power and authority of the Alliance?"

"We'll see what happens, but I'm not too hopeful. Plus, I don't trust many of the people in charge and I'm not sure I want them to have more power. Not sure how else we'll prevent things like Zaldia, though."

"So with all that bureaucracy, do you think anyone will be able to do something about the terrorists?"

She gave me an intense look. "I'll make sure something is done. They're going to be here on planet — most likely in this city — so we have no jurisdiction worries. We can't stop everything, but at the least we should be able to stop a bunch of mindless murderers."

I decided to look more serious to show I cared. "Such a stupid thing. These terrorists murdering people because they think a giant robot is a god or whatever. Religion can lead people to the dumbest behaviors."

Her face changed immediately, but only slightly. What I said was supposed to be a stock observation but it seemed I had offended her, though she tried to hide it. Interesting. "Are you religious, Rico?"

It would have been too complicated for me to pretend that. "No, not really."

"What keeps you going, then?"

Now I was on a path I hadn't planned for. "What?" I asked, as it is a very good question for stalling.

"Sounds like it can be rough on Rikar. What motivates you to keep at it?"

It was a somewhat philosophical question, so I let myself pause to think, which seemed appropriate. "I guess ... I keep going because people need me. I never really thought about that too much." I thought it was a decent answer.

She considered my response, then chuckled nervously. "Sorry. I guess I'm asking a lot of questions. Hard habit to break."

I smiled. I'm good at putting on convincing smiles — I can even get the eyes right. "I'm asking questions, too. I'm really curious about all this. I've never dealt with terrorist attacks like this before."

"Religion doesn't seem like a great topic for a relaxing vacation, though."

It was time to reel this in. I put my serious face back on — not the I'm-going-to-kill-you serious face but the I'm-very-smart-and-intense serious face. "I got shot, I saw people killed in front of me, and I hear there may be more terrorists out there. I don't think I can relax."

She was silent for a moment. I knew she was moving to where I wanted her to go. "It is hard to just to sit there when you think you can help."

"So you're restless on this, too?" I asked.

I thought about giving her another push but decided to just wait for her to fall into place. "Maybe I'll see if you can tag along tomorrow ... if you want to. The department is big on interplanetary cooperation, so I could probably get them to sign off on it."

I tried to look just a little surprised at the offer. "Well, yeah. All I want to do right now is follow up on this. My instincts are too hardwired for me to let it go. Your partner won't mind?"

"I don't have a partner right now." She smiled, a bit mischievously. "I don't often get along well with others. I'm probably not going to be the best ambassador for how we do things in the 'civilized' world."

Yes, there were scare quotes around the word "civilized." I could hear them loud and clear. I smiled broadly. "That would probably be too much of a culture shock for me anyway. But I think I can be of some help. I got a good look at the terrorists and their demeanor."

"Demeanor?"

"Yeah, there was a way about them ... a way about all sorts of killers. The terrorists all had a certain look ... in their eyes. It'll be visible in terrorists planning to attack later ... even if they try to hide it."

The detective laughed. "Really?" She didn't think I was serious, but I was.

"Hey, I don't know this planet, but I do know criminals." I can't even count how many I've hunted down and killed. "I think I can help. If I get in the way, tell me. I won't be offended." I smiled. "Anyway, I should be able to avenge my ruined pants." I decided that was too cheeky, since people had died, and thus quickly became more serious. "And after what I saw, I really need to do something."

She nodded. "I understand. You know you'll just be observing — there's no way I'm going to get clearance to get you a gun."

"Then don't make me enter anywhere first," I laughed.

"I'll pick you up tomorrow morning. If the terrorists have found out about you, you'll be safer among us, anyway."

I smiled, and we had our food and drinks. Never much cared for pizza, so I wasn't certain if this was any better.

The detective did seem smart, and I honestly thought she would be useful in helping me hunt down and kill the terrorists. If I helped her with this, then she'd have to trust me. That would make it easy for me to betray her as a way to ingratiate myself with her higher-ups for whatever I needed to do next. And if it worked out well, the detective would be disgraced but still alive. But in case things didn't go well, I knew I should get up early in the morning and figure out a good place to dump a body where it wouldn't be found for a few days.

"What are you smiling about?" she asked a bit playfully.

"Just thinking about how to handle this case. My job makes me happy." She had pretty eyes.

CHAPTER 11

"So will you proceed unarmed, Officer Rico?"

Dip had started calling me "Officer." I decided to ignore it. "What do you think?"

"You seem to dislike being without guns. I also think that, if you are found to have weapons, you'll probably kill any witnesses. That won't be very police-officer-like of you."

I was about to give Dip an annoyed glance, but then I remembered he was just a voice in my ear. I don't go anywhere unarmed. I would rather explain my weapons — or shoot my way out — than be without them. Plus, I didn't think it would be strange for the grizzled cop character I'd invented to carry weapons even when told not to.

"Officer Rico, if I might remark, this is quite an odd assignment for you."

"Yes, it is." It was never my place to know the details on my syndicate assignments, but it did seem like important information was being withheld. "Something isn't adding up."

"Maybe you should have me do the adding. I'm very good at math."

That was enough. "Has a bug in your programming made you stupid, or are you trying to make jokes?"

"The latter. I took what you meant metaphorically and treated it literally. I understand with some jokes —"

"Why are you trying to be funny?"

"I have had trouble getting input from you, and without your user input, I've been forced to use a random number generator to adjust myself to see if it suits you better. It does seem like you could use more humor, Rico."

"Really? I think I'm funny." I went to the closet and picked out a coat. It had been warm out, so I needed one that could conceal my weapons without making me too hot. "How is the extraction plan going?"

"I have a new plan, which I rate to have approximately a 23.847% chance of success. Do you like the number? I made it more computer-like."

"I don't care how many decimal spaces you give me. I need a much better plan."

"I will keep working on it. If I may query about another subject, do you plan to kill Detective Thompson?"

I checked my guns one last time. "I have plans to kill everyone I meet ... including a witty line to say afterward."

"What will be your witty line upon dispatching the detective?"

Now I was joking. "Well, since I'll only have to kill her if she's smart enough to see through my ruse, I'll say, 'If you had only been dumb enough to trust a psychopath, you'd still be alive.'"

"Ironic. Still not very funny."

I put on the light jacket I had picked out. "Like you have any ability to judge that."

"I think you should revisit my conclusion that you are evil."

"I told you I don't have time for that. I have too much work to do to indulge your learning algorithms."

"Do you really think you'll be able to find the terrorists, Officer Rico?"

"A killer in search of killers — it just might work. Plus, I'm betting the detective knows something useful and could use some help outside of the law."

I had a keen eye — that's how I survive — and I should have been able to pick up on something if pointed in the right direction. Something was bothering me, though, and I still couldn't quite place my finger on exactly what was wrong. This assignment was just so unusual, from Burke's unexpected visit to having a job without any details to not knowing whom I'm supposed to work with or how to contact them to being led right into a terrorist attack and then tasked to hunt the terrorists. Each bit wasn't a big deal on its own, but when I thought about all the oddities at once, I felt a little pang at the back of my mind. I might have actually been ... scared. That was okay in itself. What bothered me was that I didn't understand exactly what I was scared of.

"Rico! Knock, knock."

"Shut up, Dip."

* * *

Fear — the slight, nagging feeling that I didn't want to continue onward — was not an emotion I had ever found useful. I knew logically the danger of my actions, so I didn't need my subconscious piping up. But this time it seemed like it had information I didn't.

So what was I afraid of? Not death. Not pain. Not loss. What else was there to fear? I felt like I was losing touch with myself, but I hoped that if I found the terrorists, dispatched them quickly, and finally found out what the syndicate wanted me for, things might fall back into their proper places.

"Are you all right, Rico?"

If my feelings had leaked to my demeanor, then I was losing control of myself. "Just thinking about yesterday." The detective motioned me into the passenger seat of her car. "So what's the plan?"

"Still working on that." She took the vehicle into the air. "We'll need to stop by the station first so you can fill out some paperwork."

The place every hitman wants to be. In the middle of a police station. Filling out paperwork. "Is that really necessary?"

"I plan to push the rules a little today, so I might as well comply where I can."

I could see the layout of the city again. We were in the nice, modern downtown area, but farther out, things didn't look as good. I guessed I could get away with more out there. "This won't take long?"

"I won't let it. We've gotten a notice from the terrorist group that they will keep attacking until the conference is canceled and we give up our 'imperialist ways.' I don't think they're bluffing."

"Could this affect the conference?" I assumed the conference was central to why I was here, but maybe the syndicate wanted it disrupted.

"I really don't care, Rico. I just want to make sure no one else gets killed."

I hoped she meant "other than the terrorists" or she was going to be seriously disappointed.

The station was new, spacious, and filled with armed cops. I didn't think I'd need to, but it was fun imagining having to shoot my way out. The gunpowder-based firearms would quickly run out of ammo, so I'd want to move first toward the nearest armed person to appropriate his or her weapon. That would probably be the detective herself, but I hadn't seen her pistol so I didn't know if it would be adequate to fight my way to the parking lot.

"What are you smiling about?" the detective asked.

"It's a nice station. I wish we had a place like this on Rikar."

She nodded. "You have kind of a creepy smile, you know that?"

That statement was somewhere between playful and genuinely insulting. I gathered she was still making up her mind about me.

"So this is the hero?" Two officers were approaching us, a human male and a Corridian female.

"This is Rico," the detective told them, nodding. She turned to me. "These are officers Randall and Meela."

"I guess you're pretty good with a gun," Meela said.

"It wasn't my first shootout. I'm a police officer on a planet called Rikar. It gets a bit rough there. I was hoping to get an idea of how things are done on a more civilized planet."

Randall laughed. "I'm not sure Tommy-gun is the way to go with that."

"Time is of the essence here." The detective ladled the annoyance on thickly.

"Okay, then," Meela said. "The chief may be loosening your leash today, but you know he'll use anything he can against you when it's all done."

Randall asked, "Will you have any backup today? I doubt they'll let Rico have a gun."

"I'm just going to be asking a few people some questions."

"Well, don't be stupid, Diane." Meela sounded a little concerned. The detective seemed to have a bit of a love-hate relationship with her peers.

"I'll take 'not being stupid' under advisement." She motioned me to follow, and I waved a short goodbye to the two police officers. I had a slight urge to shoot them. I don't like cops.

"We need to meet with the chief quickly." I could tell by her tone that this was not her favorite thing.

"You and he have a problem?"

She smiled at me. A devious smile. It was kind of pretty on her. "I don't have a problem. I'm comfortable with the fact that he's a corrupt bureaucrat."

We entered an office where a slightly overweight and age-worn Corridian male was seated behind a desk. "Good morning, Chief Rudle."

"Thompson, I really wanted to keep him out of here. It would make the illegal weapons charge easier to sweep under the rug," he said. *And hello, Rico. Nice to meet you. Thank you for your heroic actions.* And *I'm* the sociopath.

"I'm sorry if I caused you any trouble." I think Corridians can pick up on human sarcasm. Little things like that are the reason they and humans can somewhat get along.

He ignored me. "I know you're going to make a big mess, and I'd rather have fewer witnesses."

Diane said, "Feds aren't looking in the right places. They have too many regulations to follow. I know where we should look and I'm the best chance to find the terrorists right now. You know it."

Rudle did not like the detective at all. He didn't even bother to hold back his look of contempt. "You do what you want, but if people complain later, there will be a reckoning."

"I firmly believe that a person always has to answer for her actions," she said.

He growled a bit. "Just have him fill out the liability waiver and get his DNA and photo into the system."

This is where a rookie would probably panic, but the fact is I probably have my DNA and photo in tons of different law enforcement databases throughout the universe. As do billions of other criminals. Nystrom has probably accessed and scrubbed some of those databases, but even if not, trying to share databases between planets causes information overload, and keeping records only works if a criminal is dumb enough to commit a crime and stay on planet. I assumed that within the week I'd be gone from here one way or another.

Anyway, panicking is never, ever helpful.

"Thanks, Chief. We'll find these people," the detective said, not looking particularly thankful.

"You'd better ... or it will probably be the end of you, knowing what you're likely to do. I've got to get back to work. On top of all this, we have word there's going to be an assassination attempt on Senator Gredler."

"If someone shoots Gredler, let me head the investigation so I can be the first to shake the killer's hand." Diane left the office, and I followed.

This latest piece of information had my attention. "Who is Gredler?"

"Our senator in the Galactic Alliance. People say he's a big candidate to head this new stronger Alliance they're talking about. That's why I don't have much faith in it. I'm pretty sure Gredler is in bed with the Randatti crime syndicate. I assume you've heard of them."

One of Nystrom's biggest rivals. Now things were starting to fall into place. But that also made me wonder if I was the assassin they were talking about. That really would seem to be sloppy work by whoever was running things if the police knew about the hit before I did. "That's a big charge to make," I said.

"The government is corrupt. That I know. Now, let's get that form and get your picture and whatnot and get to this."

Of course, I didn't know for certain that there would be more to my job than hunting down terrorists, but that seemed like a really odd use of my time. And they were going to be some very dead terrorists ... as long as I could get a little leeway from the real law enforcement.

She stopped and faced me. "Rico, you're new here, and people don't expect you to know the rules. Is it okay if I exploit that when I question a few people?" Diane smiled a mischievous smile, which also was quite pretty on her. I would enjoy her exploiting me for all sorts of things.

This would be my first time not working alone. At least I could have done worse for a partner.

CHAPTER 12

Why did the syndicate want me to hunt terrorists? Pretty much everyone likes terrorists to be killed, but a bunch of religious fanatics trying to blow people up seemed a bit beneath Nystrom's concern.

I was usually fine with not knowing the why, but this time I had the feeling it might have personal ramifications for me. With the violent siege on Zaldia and the conference here that would give the Alliance the power to take on Nystrom directly, big things were underway ... yet here I was apparently on a side venture. Still, Anthony Burke had personally assigned me this job because he wanted me to know how important it was. Then I almost got blown up at a café. I was starting to think I should be more concerned with the big picture. What was Nystrom's game here? And where were my damn contacts?

"You're very contemplative, you know that?" Diane seemed to be only half-paying attention to me at the moment. She was watching out the window as the car took us to the edge of the city. Her mind was certainly on the task at hand, but she apparently wasn't done observing me — whether out of habit or true suspicion, I couldn't quite tell.

"There's a lot to contemplate." I have to concentrate in order to be talkative; it's tiring and hard to keep up. "You haven't told me much about the plan yet."

"It's still in progress."

"Anything for me to do?"

She handed me some photos. "We have what you left of the terrorists pictured here."

I flipped through them quickly. I don't really like looking at dead people. So ugly and broken. "Do you think you know people who might have seen this group?" I asked.

She shook her head. "No one who would be forthcoming. But I also have pictures of their weapons."

I looked at one. It was the typical cheaply made automatic rifle, but I didn't recognize the exact model. There are so many gun manufacturers on so many different planets that firearms were often extremely unique. It was rare to run into one you recognized.

"Some people might have seen those guns, and I know who to ask," she said. The detective landed her vehicle in an old parking structure. "You ready?" She put on dark glasses. "These are my interrogation glasses — very important. They make me look serious, and I can remove them dramatically to make a point."

"Should I be writing these tips down?"

She laughed. "Seriously, I'll just want you to stand behind me and look tough."

"I don't know how to not look tough." I actually do, though. I hunch a bit, talk slightly higher-pitched — it's not too hard.

"Good. Let's go."

We were certainly in a bad part of town, judging from the worn-down buildings with broken windows and graffiti on the walls. People around here had little — which you might think would cause them to take good care of the little they had. But the opposite seemed more often to be true.

We came to a shop with a fading, handmade sign labeled, "Shakey's Repair." She turned to me, her expression serious. "You're just observing right now, you got that?"

"You don't have to worry about me."

Inside, a middle-aged human male was hunched over some disassembled electronics at a workbench. He looked up at Diane with a very negative expression of recognition and at me with a much more cautious glance. "What the hell are you bothering me for? I haven't done anything."

"I just have some questions, Shakey," Diane said.

He set down his tools and stood up. He was not an imposing man, but he didn't look scared, either. "And if I don't answer them, what happens?"

Diane was very businesslike in her expression. "There's no reason to be like that."

Shakey scoffed. "And who is this with you?"

"Some guy," I answered, keeping my expression pretty stoic.

He looked intimidated by me, but only for a moment. "Looks like another cop — or maybe a serial killer. Whatever. I don't care. Get the hell out of here, blondie. If you don't have anything to charge me with, then I have no obligation to talk to you. So why don't you leave before I ... what is it ... file a complaint against you. The streets would probably be safer if they took your gun away."

This did not seem to be going well, but Diane wasn't fazed by the resistance. She took off her glasses, and it did have a nice dramatic effect. "I don't have time for this. I just want you to identify some weapons for me."

"And I want a unicorn that craps rainbows," Shakey said. "Let's both keep wishing and hoping."

The detective looked at me. "So Rico, how would you handle a situation like this on your planet?"

I wasn't sure if she was serious. "I'll show you." I turned to Shakey. "You'll probably want to sit down for this."

"It's probably better if you don't show me." She put her shades back on. "I'll wait outside."

I had no idea how far she would want me to take this, but luckily it became a moot point, as Shakey started to panic. "Fine! There's no need for the theatrics! I can look at some guns for you!"

Diane tossed the photos onto his workbench. "These were the weapons used in that terrorist attack yesterday."

"Whoa! You can't think I'd have anything to do with those freaks! I'm not some crazed murderer — I've always said we should eradicate those people. You've heard me say that."

"I just want you to tell me what you can about these guns." She pushed him down into his seat.

Shakey picked up one of the pictures. "These guns are crap, that's what I can tell you. Power source isn't properly heat-compensated. You fire them too much, and some of the wiring melts, which trips a safety measure that shuts down the power completely. Then they're useless until some delicate repairs can be done ... or so I've heard."

She pressed in closer. "So you know of them?"

Shakey looked more cautious. "Similar ones, maybe. They were sold off planet, though — so they weren't the ones used in this attack. But they probably came from the people who supplied your guns as well."

"And who is that?" Diane stood on one side of Shakey, and I stood on the other, trying to look as imposing as possible.

Shakey looked at the detective, glanced at me, and then looked back at her. "What would I know? I've had enough run-ins with the law, I keep my nose out of that sort of thing."

"There are terrorists out there planning more attacks. I need this information."

He was quiet for a moment. "I'm guessing they're not going to attack down here — nothing worth blowing up. But if people find out I'm freely ratting on them to you, that's trouble for me. So why don't you and your serial killer friend threaten to rough me up once more, and then be on your way."

"You really think I'm going to walk away when I think you know something?"

"And you think I'm going to give up important information for free because of my fondness for you? I heard the feds are around here asking questions. If this terrorism threat is serious, you should probably leave it to them, blondie."

"You know something? I'm going to get it out of you one way or another. If you need to get bruised up a bit to keep your street cred, I can arrange that."

"Just so you know, I'm videotaping everything going on in here."

Diane laughed. "Sure you are." She grabbed Shakey and forced him down into a chair.

"And I'm not afraid of some silly blonde woman trying to smack me around."

Diane took off her shades again and leaned in close to him, her expression intense. "That's what Bedar said."

Now he looked scared. "You did that?! No way ... you're the police ... you can't ..."

"There are more attacks coming, and you're in the way of my stopping them." There was fire in her eyes, and I felt a little blood rush to a place that wasn't helpful at the moment. "There is very little I will not do."

I honestly couldn't tell how serious she was, but Shakey certainly didn't think she was bluffing. He looked terrified. "Fine, let's keep the crazy bitch in her bottle. I know some people who stole some of these weapons — if you can steal something from someone who isn't supposed to have it in the first place."

"Who did they get them from?"

"I don't have any names, but I can tell you what religious services these people attended. They were all from the Talbrook Religious Center."

Diane stood back. "You knew those people were collecting guns, and you didn't think to tell anyone about it?"

Shakey shrugged. "I thought maybe it was just old-fashioned Islamic terrorism. When was the last time anyone saw that? Anyway, we had taken away their guns and put them in the hands of more responsible criminals. I guess the smugglers from Talbrook figured out how to be more secretive on their next shipment."

Diane stared at him silently for a few seconds. "That's it?"

"What else is there to say? You already knew you needed to go there. You also know who you need to interrogate there. Or are you going to pretend to not know that either?" He got up and headed back to his tools. "Now we're done. It's going to be fun watching you fall one day, blondie."

She smiled. It was a little creepy; I liked it. "Me with nothing to lose; that would be fun." Diane picked up the photos and turned to leave.

I followed her, and Shakey called out, "Hey, serial killer."

I stopped and turned toward him. "What?"

"I don't know how much you know about that woman, but I wouldn't trust her."

"I'll take that under advisement, weasely-looking guy."

Once the detective and I were outside, I asked, "Who's Bedar?"

I was a little surprised by her sudden change in demeanor. Gone was the tough bitch, and instead she now looked embarrassed. "I've overstepped myself sometimes. If you want to see how things are done on a well-settled planet, I'm probably not the best person to show you."

"The important thing is getting the job done."

She shook her head. "No. I don't believe that. I don't want to be that person. Anger can really take control of you ... and it's easy to let it if it's a righteous anger ... you know what I mean?"

Righteous anger would be a new one for me. Anger was, in general, just an obstacle to rational thought and was to be avoided. It never felt right. "I think I do."

She smiled, a little nervously. "I have a bit of a dark side, but I'm trying to be a better person ... I just don't always succeed. Maybe this isn't the best job for that." She laughed like it was a joke, but it wasn't convincing.

Some jobs take a mental toll on people ... or so I hear. Sucks to have a conscience. "Dark side, eh? Anything I should be concerned about?"

She firmed up. "Just sharing some things, one officer to another. You want to get going?"

She was kind of interesting, but I didn't need interesting right now. I had prey to hunt. "That I do, blondie."

"Don't call me that. Anyway, you said you're good at reading people. Did you think Shakey was telling the truth?"

"About where the guns came from? There was a definite look of recognition when he saw the picture, and what he said about that religious center seemed genuine. What do you think?"

"I think he was just telling me what I wanted to hear .... Of course, what I wanted to hear fits. The Talbrook Religious Center has been a breeding ground for radicals for some time. We've never been able to get anything on its leader, Nakhai, but he always seems tangentially related to any religious violence we have in this city."

"Now, the human adherents of the Calabrai see themselves as Muslim, correct?" I asked.

"Yes, and what's practiced at Talbrook is sort of a radical offshoot of Islam. Now, the Calabrai are considered heretics by most Muslims, but the followers at Talbrook have been pretty tolerant of anyone who frustrates the Alliance. My guess is that if there are human Calabrai adherents here, they go to Talbrook for their daily prayers ... and Nakhai probably even knows who they are." So there was a religious center in the area known for facilitating violence, and it was still standing. The part of "being civilized" I least understood was the willingness to tolerate such things, but the alternative involved lots of violence and bloodshed, and that certainly wasn't "civilized" either. "So we should question Nakhai?"

Diane hesitated. "I've had dealings with these people, and ... perhaps I lost control. I'm not exactly allowed near Talbrook."

"A restraining order?"

"Not officially ... but I'll be hearing about this from Rudle."

Her getting fired — or shot for that matter — was of no particular concern to me. I figured I had to pretend it was, though. "You think there are people at this religious center who were involved in these attacks?"

"I know there are. There's no way radicals came through here without Nakhai's help, and if Shakey was right about the guns, then they are there."

"And you believe some of them will be there during prayers today?"

"It's pretty likely. If they're planning to carry out an attack soon, that's when they're going to be most observant."

I acted like I was thinking this over, but I already knew what to do. "No one told me to stay away from there."

"I can't send you in alone. What would you do?"

"I'll just say I know someone from the Calabrai is there. These are amateurs. They're not going to know how to hide their dispositions when surprised like that."

She did not look convinced. "So your plan is to go in there and cause a ruckus?"

"The more ruckus, the better. I am telling you: if there are members of the Calabrai in there involved with terrorism, I'll be able to pick them out. I know killers. I can spot them. Trust me."

"There's no real guarantee they'll be in there."

"It's worth a shot." I grinned. "And I don't have any other plans for today."

She stared at me for a few moments. The detective was perhaps too smart to entrust this job to an unknown entity like me, even though I really could do as I told her. But the direness of the situation finally won out over common sense. "You do seem to know how to handle yourself, Rico ... but you said the more ruckus the better?"

"Yes, ma'am."

"Then I'm going with you. They know me and hate me. It'll be crazy ... and don't call me 'ma'am.'"

"Won't you get in trouble, Detective?"

She paused and looked genuinely worried for a moment before making her expression more resolved. "Let's find these people and worry about that later." She then smiled. "Like I said, maybe I need a change of jobs anyway. Let's go cause a scene."

CHAPTER 13

I certainly saw more alien diversity while walking through the outer edges of the city than I had downtown. Unlike those in the more sophisticated areas, these people weren't ashamed of sticking with their own kind for safety. The simple fear of violence tends to make sentients cling to easily identifiable groups. Humans struggled with racism for centuries; it turned out the way to overcome it was to replace it with something nearly equivalent.

We passed by a group of reddish sentients that had things on their heads resembling feathers. One of them muttered something about "humans" that I could only assume was derogatory. His anger was greatly misplaced: I treat everyone the same.

"By the way, you really handled yourself well back there," Diane told me.

"I've been doing this a long time, Detective. I may not know all your laws and procedures, but I know how to get things done. Sometimes criminals say I'm a bit mean, though."

Diane chuckled. "I think in a situation like this, yours is the kind of attitude we need."

She was nervous. She knew she was going to step over a line and needed to feel it was justified. "The families mourning the dead from the café aren't going to take great comfort in the fact that we closely followed the letter of the law." I didn't think she needed the push, but I figured it wouldn't hurt.

She nodded. "There's a lot of injustice in the universe. I hope to at least end a little of that."

Yes, there was a lot of "injustice" in the universe ... so much so that it seemed pretty pointless to worry about. But if it was people on your own planet blowing things up, the least you could do was kill them.

We were back in what looked like a primarily human section of the slums. By far, the nicest building in the area was the large religious center. On top was an arrow floating in a glass globe pointing off to the east and slightly upward — the current direction to Earth from Nar Valdum. The more old-fashioned sects of Islam continued the tradition of praying toward Mecca, a Muslim holy place located on the human home world. This, of course, was a fixed location for people on Earth but in a constantly changing direction for those on other planets. A lot of early religions seemed to have made the faulty assumption that the planet they started on was the be-all and end-all — though I guess it would have been a reasonable assumption. Some modern strains of different Earth religions have tried to become more inclusive and less Earth-centric, and some of those religions have successfully united humans and other species against them, since they all agree that these modern religions are heresies. And then there are the Calabrai, who have successfully united alien religions ... but in the cause of killing others.

Well, religion is a messy subject. I try not to judge and just shoot whoever is threatening me regardless of their belief system.

Diane stood still for a moment, looking at the building. "There will probably be dozens of people in there. You really think you'll be able to spot the terrorists?"

"I've rarely gone wrong overestimating criminal stupidity." I have almost died underestimating other people, but not the average idiot who ends up as a criminal. "That was their call for prayers we just heard, right? So they're in there."

"That they are."

"Let's go say hi."

She held out a hand to stop me. "Give them a moment; let them finish their prayers."

Being respectful of religion was the least of my concerns, but I didn't argue. After a minute more of waiting, Diane led the way. "I'll do the talking."

"Good, you have a nicer voice."

We barged through the doors and were soon in front of about sixty men (looked about all human) bowing in our direction. "Who here knows something about the bombing yesterday?"

Everyone glared. This area was apparently just for men, which I could only assume made the detective's intrusion all the more irritating. I scanned the crowd. There seemed to be more than a few people capable of murdering the detective, but I didn't think they were the ones we wanted. I hadn't really considered what I'd do if people did start attacking her. I assumed I should make some effort to save her, but I'd have to play that by ear.

An older, bearded man who I assumed was the leader strode toward Diane. "We're in the middle of prayers! And you're not even supposed to be near here! I will make sure you are fired for this!"

"I'm truly sorry for the interruption, Nakhai, but I didn't have time to wait." Her tone was neither contrite nor mocking. "You probably heard about the terrorist attack, and we have reason to believe there are others planning more. I also have reason to believe they might be at Talbrook."

"We have nothing to do with the Calabrai! That is not our religion!" Nakhai was a decent liar, but I'd certainly seen better. I could tell he had something to do with this; but he was also probably too smart for my purposes. I needed one of the dimwitted foot soldiers. So I kept watching the men behind him, looking for someone not just murderously angry but visibly nervous. Nakhai looked my way. "And who is this?"

"A tourist." I kept looking around. I very much didn't want this to be a waste of time.

Nakhai looked back at Diane. "No one here has anything to do with the Calabrai, so leave this place now."

Diane pressed right up into his face. "But you're a lot like them. You like to hide. You make threats, but you're unwilling to fight in the open. It really makes me wonder what sort of people would follow a coward like you."

That made some of the men so angry they looked like they might attack, but I saw one who actually seemed to be restraining himself, as the words hit him more personally. He had something to hide. He was involved. He was mine.

Some men finally did start to move toward the detective, but I moved quicker, pushing through the crowd to grab my target, a young man a little smaller than me. "Hey, Skippy, we need to talk."

"What, I —"

I pulled him toward the door. "Detective, I'm going to have a real quick chat with this guy outside. You stay and chat with your friends."

Diane looked a bit perturbed by my initiative, but she quickly hid it. "Okay, have fun."

I dragged Skippy outside, slamming him into the door on the way out to daze him a little. I figured I'd only have about a second before someone decided to come check on us, so I acted quickly. Now, I know many ways to get people to give me the information I need, but most of them would probably put the detective off me for good. So I tried to come up with an approach that would conform to normal societal rules.

I was unable to think of one.

Skippy was soon running back inside the building, yelling and spitting. "He forced me to swallow pig's blood."

He quickly disappeared into the group of men, I assumed toward an alternate exit. Diane was not able to hide her surprise and started to go after him, but I gently grabbed her arm. "That guy is crazy. I did not force him to drink pig's blood."

"What's that in your hand?!" Nakhai demanded.

I assumed he was talking about the vial. "I don't really know." I tossed it aside. "I think we've taken enough of your time. We'll be going now."

Nakhai was apoplectic. "This is the worst police abuse I've ever seen!"

"I'm not a police officer. I'm just a tourist," I said.

Everyone had forgotten Diane for the moment, which gave her time to get over her bewilderment. "I'm very sorry for this disturbance. We'll be leaving now."

"GET OUT!" Nakhai shrieked.

We quickly made our way out, and I led the detective to an alleyway out of view of the center's front door, in case anyone decided to come outside to glare at us. Or kill us.

Diane already had a handle on the angry glare, though. "What the hell?"

"That guy — he's who we're looking for."

"So you made him drink pig's blood?" She wasn't smiling — I thought that was at least a little funny. Instead, it looked like I was close to seeing her dark side.

"Where would I get pig's blood? It was just some liquid dyed red."

"Which you happened to have on you so you could threaten someone with it?"

I wasn't sure what the accusation was. "I knew a little about the Calabrai and the relation of its human adherents with Islam, and how they find pigs unclean, so ... I planned ahead. Anyway, we're getting off topic. I have tags on my bags so I can track them if they get lost. They work on people, too. Figured we'd spook the guy and see where he goes."

"You made him swallow a tracker?"

"I don't know if the tracker would work if swallowed. I put it on his clothes."

"So making him drink the liquid ..."

"... was so he wouldn't notice me putting the tracker on his clothes."

She stared at me, still angry — but a little less so. "A heads-up would have been nice."

"I figured this was the quickest way to go about it, and I was afraid you'd say no."

"Of course I would've said no! I'm going to be fired in an extremely spectacular fashion when this is over! And with good cause!"

"He's going to lead us to the terrorists one way or another. Trust me on that."

"I don't really have a choice. I'm all in at this point. So is this how you do things on Rikar?"

"We don't have the luxury of following proper etiquette there. I'm just trying to save lives."

She sighed. "No more surprises. Will you promise me that?"

"I promise no more surprises."

She stared at me a moment. "You're a good liar. Let's go."

CHAPTER 14

"How is the terrorist hunting going, Officer Rico?"

"Dip, you should see one of my luggage trackers somewhere near me. I need you to direct me toward it."

"I assume by 'luggage tracker' you mean one of your standard bugs. Take the road ahead of you, going west. Twenty yards down on your right will be a building which records say is a store selling religious paraphernalia. Your 'luggage' is in there. From the audio, there are seven other pieces of 'luggage' around it who seem to be armed."

I couldn't pass that last bit of information on to the detective, as I couldn't come up with a good excuse as to why a tracker for my luggage would have audio. I pointed down the street. "Our target is this way."

"Who is Dip?"

"My computer."

"What's the name stand for?"

"Huh?"

"D-I-P: What's it stand for?"

"Nothing. It's just what I call him." I could see the store that looked to be an Islamic merchandise shop. "He's in there." The smart thing seemed to be to go in and kill everybody — but save one or two for questioning. Of course, I wasn't even supposed to have guns, so at this point it was Diane's game. "What's the plan, Detective?"

"Out of secret plans that involve force-feeding people?"

"Hey, I led you to where I believe the terrorists are hiding out. I'm ready to leave it to the big city folk at this point."

She stared for a moment at the store, and her hand casually brushed her jacket at about where I assumed her gun was. "Well, you seem pretty professional, Rico. I'm thinking we go in and see what we can see."

"And if it is full of armed terrorists?"

"Then we have trouble." She walked close to me, smiling oddly. Seductively? She pressed against me, her hand caressing my side, finally coming to a firm grip on one of the guns concealed under my jacket. "I'm guessing you have another secret for that occasion."

I'm very good at concealing weapons, so I doubted she had spotted the guns. Perhaps she was just confirming some assumptions about me with that little maneuver. If she was beginning to think she knew me, though, that was probably to my advantage.

Diane backed a step away from me, not smiling but not looking angry. "I don't have anywhere near enough evidence to call in backup, but time is of the essence here, so let's head in there and do what we can. We can discuss you later."

I shrugged innocently. "What's to discuss?"

She headed for the store. "Just be careful ... and follow my lead."

I was not going to be careful. Now that I didn't have to be secretive about my guns, my plan was to shoot everybody in there at the first opportunity. That was the quickest solution, and I really didn't want to spend more time on this terrorist nonsense than I needed to. Not to sound haughty, but going after amateurs like the Calabrai was beneath me.

Now, I was already quite certain the terrorists were in there, so I could just go ahead and open fire upon entering, and the correctness of my actions would be known soon after. But my understanding of legal and moral principles is that you don't shoot people before they are obvious threats. I'd have to get them to try to shoot me first if I didn't want it to be too obvious that I was just a "cold-blooded killer," as they call people like me.

Alternatively, I could just shoot everyone and make sure Diane got killed in the crossfire so no one would be able to say what happened. She had been useful so far and perhaps would still be in the future, so I was labeling that "Plan B."

We entered the store. The human female clerk watched us and I saw three others — two human males and one other species — pretending to shop. I've pretended to shop before, and they were doing it poorly. The non-human was a Ramber — a big gray-skinned being I didn't know much about, other than that they bled green. Since this was supposed to be a store devoted to Islam, which had few non-human adherents, his presence alone raised suspicion. Plus, I could see by the non-casual hand placements of the two human males that they were armed and ready to fight.

I just needed them to make my day.

"We saw someone run in here," the detective said, using a cordial tone that wasn't going to exacerbate things quickly enough for my taste. "He's a suspect in a crime."

"I don't know what you're talking about." The clerk was going for angry, but only managed to sound scared. "If you're just here to harass us, get out!"

Diane said, "Ma'am, we just need to look around. We have reason to believe there might be some terrorists hiding out here. Is that something you would know about?"

"You are not allowed to look around here!" one of the men yelled, getting right in Diane's face. "We know our rights, and you have no cause to be here!"

I shoved him away from Diane. "Back off of her, buddy." This was hard to balance, angering these people into attacking me without making it obvious.

He looked angry but not angry enough to draw a gun. That made me angry.

"I can tell from the sounds I'm picking up that your luggage is below you," Dip told me. "I also am hearing chatter about possible measures to blow up the building you are in ... so you might want to be concerned about that."

Just what I needed. Plan B was coming up soon.

"That was understatement, by the way," Dip added. "That's a type of humor, though I'm not quite sure how appropriate humor is in this situation."

"Please leave now," the clerk said firmly.

"Let's all calm down," Diane said. "We just want to have a look around. What could it hurt if there's nothing to hide?"

At the back of the store I noticed a door that I assumed led to the basement. I could just barge in and take on whoever was down there, but I wouldn't want to leave three or four armed people behind me and have to count on the detective to handle them. I decided to just head for that door, and if one of the terrorists made a move, I'd shoot him proper. If I reached the door and none of them made a move, I'd shoot them improper and probably have to deal with the detective. It would be a small mess, and I was already vowing I'd never try to work with law enforcement again. Too asinine and complicated.

"I'm going downstairs," I said. "If there are any terrorists down there you care about, you'd better tell me now, because I shoot unclaimed terrorists." I headed for the door, turning my back to most of the people there. This was their last opportunity to die fighting, and I sincerely hoped they'd take it and make things easier for everyone. A framed poster of some Arabic saying hung by the door, and in its reflection I could see one of the humans reach for a gun.

Now I was free to be me.

But there was a gunshot before I could draw, and for a moment I thought my arrogance had finally caught up with me. I spun around and saw that my target was already dead. It took me another moment to process that before I zeroed in on another target and shot the Ramber in the face and chest before he had fully drawn his gun.

Gunpowder-based firearms are very loud, which can be a little disconcerting. More so for the enemy, at least.

I very nearly shot the blonde woman who had a gun in her hand but stopped that instinct just in time and aimed at the other human male — but he was already dead.

The clerk made an odd movement, and I shot her twice to be on the safe side — though maybe I jumped the gun on that one out of annoyance that I'd only gotten to shoot one person so far. I quickly realized that shooting the woman could have been a huge miscalculation if I were wrong about her going for a gun, but there was no time to worry about it at the moment.

I didn't usually shoot up a group like this while abiding by so many rules — or with someone else hitting my targets and messing up my rhythm. It was quite frustrating — which at least meant that I didn't have to worry about accidentally wearing the creepy smile I sometimes wore when shooting people.

Diane was shouting something at me, but my ears were ringing from the gunshots. It didn't matter what she was saying, anyway, since my next action was clear. Downstairs were several more armed people, perhaps about to blow up the whole building in some sort of selfless sacrifice nonsense. They had just heard the gunshots above them, and in a second more they'd have their full wits about them and perhaps be the ignominious end of me.

I had six shots left in each gun. I had to keep track of that.

I kicked open the door to the basement and charged down the stairs, bowling over one of the terrorists as he ran up. I leapt the last few steps, slammed into the floor and started firing rapidly into a group of seven people — mostly human, a few other species, all armed. There were too many for me to reliably take down quickly, and I realized I might have made a miscalculation. Still, four of them fell before any could get off a shot — even though I had only fired on three. Diane was once again backing me up from the top of the stairs, and I really didn't know how to factor that into a shootout.

One terrorist finally fired at me, and the shot struck the ground near my face — luckily I was dealing with amateurs. But he jerked back as Diane shot him, so I quickly rolled to my feet and put three shots into another as he fired past me. That left one — Skippy — who dashed for a switch on the wall. I put a bullet in his leg, and he fell to the ground. I walked over to Skippy while looking around — he was the only one still moving — and he was just crying and clutching his leg. The visible wiring from the switch he had been going for led to explosives placed about the room. That would have been bad.

Someone armed came down the stairs, and once again I nearly shot the detective. Working with a partner would take some getting used to.

Her expression was pretty hard to read at this point. She just quietly looked around — still hyper-alert — and carefully took the gun from the unconscious terrorist at the bottom of the stairs.

"They were going to blow up the building," I said, motioning to the different sets of explosives around the room. Skippy moaned, which reminded me: I needed to get the bug off of him before someone else spotted it. "Heard their voices down here and figured we didn't have time to wait."

"There will be a lot of paperwork for this." It sounded like a joke, but her expression was still pretty blank.

I noticed some computer equipment and papers down there, which I assumed would be useful in the terrorist-hunting effort and hopefully put the whole matter to bed. Plus, it looked like we had two terrorists still alive.

I wasn't sure what to say next. Killing people is supposed to be very grave, but Diane had killed people, too, so I was hoping to follow her lead. Then I thought of a really good thing to say. "Are you okay?"

She smiled weakly. "Peachy. And how did diving head first into a group of armed men work for you?"

I let myself smile slightly too. "They missed me. That was pretty stupid, huh?"

"We'll leave that for history to decide." She looked around again. "It was really messy, but I guess we had to do it. You'd better put down your gun before backup arrives. Thanks for your help. That's not how we do things here ... but it worked." She smiled more convincingly now.

I smiled back. I was a hero once again, though that wasn't what the syndicate usually paid me to be. "Hopefully these guys were it for the Calabrai."

"Maybe we'll find enough information here to figure that out, even if what's left of them doesn't talk."

"I will tell you this: You haven't stopped us!" Skippy yelled at Diane. "You can never stop us, because we are all willing martyrs! Those we killed yesterday were only the beginning! By the will of Calab, you will see all your friends and family burn, you whore!"

Diane stepped on his wounded leg, causing him to scream.

When she let up, he yelled, "This is police abuse! I will —"

She stepped on his leg again.

This time Skippy remained silent (after he was done screaming).

Diane then noticed me again — it was like she had forgotten I was there. "Um ... I probably shouldn't have done that."

"I didn't see anything." I really did like her — she was a fascinating woman — but our little partnership was certainly not destined to end well.

CHAPTER 15

I spent another few hours at the station. The police really didn't seem like a threat to me, though. I often find myself around armed people, but their actions aren't usually hampered by the law. The police are more of a nuisance in comparison.

I was tiring of being around people, though, and was happy when I could relax a bit in a small break room alone. Well ... nearly alone.

"You really know how to handle yourself in combat, don't you?" Diane was sitting in a chair next to me and hadn't been too much of a pest so far. "You almost seemed unfazed by the whole thing."

I couldn't tell if she was still probing me out of suspicion. I was now twice the hero but probably a little more kill-happy than people tend to like their heroes. At least the woman I'd shot had a gun; I'd have hated having to feign feeling bad about killing an unarmed civilian. "It's all autopilot in a situation like that — but it has to be. Hesitation is death. Once your course of action is clear, you don't think. You do." I decided to turn it back on her as a distraction. "I wasn't the first one to fire, though. You're pretty comfortable with a gun yourself."

She really was. There's a big difference between someone who carries a gun on the job for the rare occasion he may need to use it and someone like me who shoots people for a living. Normal people hesitate to kill — but she had jumped right in there as soon as the first gun was drawn. I wouldn't expect that sort of competency from someone unless he had been in the military and actually seen combat.

She looked embarrassed again. I thought that was a silly reaction. "I just do what needs to be done. I wish there were a less violent way to resolve that situation, but it's hard to imagine one. Anyway, thank you for your help. I feel bad bringing you into something like that, but I really don't know how we would have stopped them without you."

They probably couldn't have, but I played modest. "I think you would have come up with something, Detective. It was great working with you, though brief ... but I guess it was brief just because we were so effective." We actually were a decent team: the rogue detective and the murderous psychopath. Teaming up certainly was a different experience for me, and not completely unenjoyable, even with the extra annoyance of having to make sure I didn't kill or horrify my partner.

She chuckled. "I'm guessing we were a little too 'effective.' I'll bet what awaits me is some time off and counseling."

Counseling — what a strange idea. I shot a bunch of people that pretty much everyone agreed the worlds would be better off without. I wasn't sure why that was supposed to weigh on my psyche. Of course, I didn't understand why anything was supposed to weigh on my psyche. "Do you really think you'll need that?"

"What?"

"Counseling."

"My religion helps me better than counseling does. I'm a Christian ... when I'm not shooting people."

She hadn't struck me as the religious type so the revelation made me curious. This was good for my social skills. "You feel bad about shooting those people?"

She looked very serious. "No ... That's the problem."

Maybe we were somewhat alike — except that I was fine with who I was. And faith has always been a hard thing for me to wrap my brain around; anyone can just decide to have faith in any nonsense. "You want to feel bad you killed some violent idiots who were trying to kill you?"

"It's easy to be dismissive of their lives — that's how I used to be. But there is value in all life."

"You believe that?"

"Very much so." No hesitation this time. "It's easy to forget in the heat of the moment, though. When you have people like the Calabrai to deal with, it's natural to be happy that they're dead. That doesn't make it right to kill them."

"I just see it as a necessity. If people go around blowing other people up, it's better when they're gone. I don't know how it benefits society to have people like that around, even if they're neutralized as a threat."

"Screw society. I care about individuals. Everyone deserves a chance to change. So what about you? What do you believe in?"

"I just deal with what's in front of me," I said.

"And you're okay with how things turned out?"

These were not questions with easy, socially acceptable answers. Besides, filtering everything I said was starting to exhaust me. I decided to be a bit more honest — partly because I was curious to see how she would handle it. "I would rather not be shot at so much, but we dealt with the problem, and those terrorists won't bother anyone else. Seems like a good outcome. I did what needed to be done. What am I supposed to do? Toss and turn in my sleep seeing their faces and think of all the things I've now prevented them from doing, like accidentally blowing themselves up with poorly made explosives? I know that's kind of cold, but I've been through this sort of thing too many times."

She put her hand on my shoulder. "I won't presume to tell you how to feel. I'm just ... thankful you were there."

I wasn't sure what to do about her touching me. I smiled back at her, which is always a friendly move. "Glad I could help. So what about that Talbrook leader, Nakhai?" I asked. I don't know why I cared about him. I guess I was actually curious about Diane's views. "Any outcome where he doesn't end up dead or in prison just tells me you all want to get attacked again."

"Hopefully we can find a connection between him and the terrorists and do something about him."

"Hopefully?" I scoffed. "You know he's dirty and is going to be involved in future deadly plots."

"The police can't just imprison people we *feel* are guilty," she said.

"Yes, but this isn't some abstract principle of justice. This is a man you know — *know* — is going to cause more death and destruction. You're willing to let that go based on the rules of your society?"

She was silent a moment. "We do have our rules — and some may be counterproductive. That's pretty much inevitable when the rules are made by man. But I also know that making up your own rules based on what you feel is right at any given moment is a bad path to go down. So I won't ..." She smiled. "... *probably* won't go out and shoot Nakhai in the face, even though that would be the smart thing to do."

"I guess you have a point ... but your society has too many damn rules." I myself follow the rules of the syndicate without much question, but they have a lot fewer rules about not killing people.

She laughed. "You just don't like that they took your guns again."

"No, I don't." We smiled at each other silently for a moment. I was almost — almost — starting to prefer her company to being alone.

There was a commotion outside the room. We stood up and looked out the window of the break room and saw a number of people standing in the main hallway. What looked to be federal officials were escorting a few beings with ruddy green skin. They had intelligent-looking eyes that warily scanned the people around them, but they appeared to have greater concerns on their minds.

I looked at Diane who stared at the beings with a sad expression. "Refugees from Zaldia," she explained before I could ask. "A group of journalists were able to get onto Zaldia, and they rescued a few of them when they left. They brought them here because of the conference. This is their people's first time off planet. These Zaldians, they ..." She took a moment to compose herself. "... lost their children. The syndicate that besieged their planet gassed a classroom ... to make an example or something ... I can't even comprehend it."

It did seem rather excessive, but a number of things about Zaldia seemed rather odd for the syndicate. For one thing, if they were taking over a planet, it was hard to believe they'd be so sloppy as to let an unauthorized ship sneak on and off. It made me wonder whether what was happening on Zaldia was some sort of breakdown of their authority — some of Nystrom's own people going rogue.

"We can stop some evil people, like the Calabrai," Diane said. "But there's still so much suffering in the universe that I sometimes wonder what the point is."

I was pretty sure there wasn't one, but didn't say so.

Diane closed her eyes for a few moments, bowing her head slightly. I knew what she was doing, as I'd seen it a few times before. I had sometimes caused people to pray, but in my experience it wasn't very effective.

Chief Rudle entered the room. "Come on, you two. We still have your matter to sort out."

We followed him back to his office, and his expression was much like the human one for frustration. "So, Rico, how many guns did you illegally bring on this trip?"

"That would be it." Until I could get back to my ship.

"Is that really important?" Diane demanded. "We needed to find any terrorists still hiding out, planning to attack again, and we got it done. Are you going to arrest Rico for anything?"

He sighed. "No. He's only killed a dozen people since he got here. It's hardly a matter worth pursuing."

"He's a hero." She looked ready to hit the chief. That would have been entertaining. "Are you going to punish me?"

"Yes. You are suspended until further notice." He looked just short of pleased.

"For stopping the terrorists?" She was actually less angry now, like she had expected that.

"It's suspension with pay. It's like a vacation — for everybody. Your terrorist hunting involved an egregious bit of religious harassment that would normally end in a firing."

"Know what would really harass them?" Diane said. "If you went back there and dragged Nakhai out in handcuffs."

"The feds are looking into any connection he might have with the terrorists."

"And they've been damn useful so far."

It felt like societal conventions would dictate that I say something. "Thank you. This experience has been invaluable. Now I know if my planet joins the Alliance and adopts a more modern law enforcement approach, I should just blow my brains out. That reminds me: Can I have my guns back?"

"No." Rudle looked at Diane. "Thanks for finding the terrorists, Detective. Now go away. I have a lot of paperwork to do, and it doesn't help the upcoming conference that the city is starting to look like a war zone."

"Who cares about another useless political conference?" Diane growled. "People are being killed, and I want to know whether we've taken out the last of the terrorists."

"Not your problem. You're suspended," Rudle said. "I'm going to be personally chewed out by Senator — soon President — Gredler if I don't get things settled down here in time for the conference. He already has to deal with the assassination threat, so everything else needs to run smoothly. And part of that is getting you and your new friend out of the way."

"If Gredler has a problem," Diane answered, "he can come bring it up directly with me, and I'll punch him in the culb sack."

Rudle ignore her and turned to me. "Enjoy the rest of your stay in our city, and try not to kill anyone else."

"Then make sure you kill everyone who needs killing before I get to them." We left, Diane slamming the door behind her.

We were approached by Officers Randall and Meela, whom I remembered from earlier. "Are you guys okay?" Meela asked. "I heard it was a bloodbath!"

"We're fine," Diane said.

"It's like you want to get killed," Randall said.

I wasn't sure if they were Diane's friends or merely associates, but I was pretty sure I didn't care. "I'm going outside for some air, because ... I don't have any interest in talking to either of you." Yes, I recognized that was a little too frank; I had just completely reached my limit on pointless conversations about shooting a bunch of people no one liked.

I headed from police headquarters to a plaza out front and found a bench out of the way of foot traffic. "Dip, what do you hear?"

"From the chatter on the bugs you placed, it appears the terrorist cell you took out wasn't the only one left, and there is still a threat. This comes from both the data found at the hideout and the questioning of the two you left alive."

. That was not at all what I wanted to hear. I like jobs where I'm taking down high-profile targets guarded by pros, not ones where I hunt murderous amateurs cowering in the shadows. I just wanted to be done with this and find out why I was really on this planet. "Does it sound like they have any leads?" It was silly for Nystrom to task me to do something that really was law enforcement's job. Why couldn't they just do their jobs and let me kill more interesting people?

"No. Nothing solid."

Stuck in a city with no easy way out and no weapons, a known presence to the police, and having to hunt terrorists — I was far out of my comfort zone. I wondered if I was being punished, but I couldn't think of anything I had done that might anger the syndicate.

"If you want some good news," Dip said, "now that you've given me an ear on law enforcement, I can go ahead and add an extra three percent to the chances I will retrieve you from the city without us both being destroyed. That's better than a one-in-four chance of survival. Worth a roll of the dice if the situation is dire enough."

I never tried anything when I felt the odds were against me. "Still far from good enough. Keep working on it. I'm not too confident this terrorist business is going to end up with everyone still liking me."

And now I just wanted to focus on finding the quickest way to make sure the Calabrai were gone for good.

"You okay?" Diane walked over to me, looking genuinely concerned. "You were a little ... abrupt."

I smiled. "I get antsy when I'm not armed. I also get angry when I risk my life and then get treated like an inconvenience. How are you doing?"

"Pissed ... and apparently on vacation now. So what are your plans?"

I didn't have any yet, but I knew that to work effectively now I would probably have to work alone so I wouldn't have to worry about someone judging how sociopathic I was being. "I think I'm going to need to be alone tonight."

"Oh, okay. Just keep yourself safe this time." She smiled, but I could detect a faint hint of disappointment.

Did she like me? I had long since given up on making an effort to be likeable. But it didn't matter, since, being suspended, she was of no more use to me. It was time to brush her off. Yet some instinct told me she might still be useful down the line. "I guess I should get back to my vacation. Since you're now on vacation, too, maybe you could show me around tomorrow."

"Sure, that might be fun." She tried to say it casually but failed. Perhaps there was just another silly woman under her tough exterior.

"How about you stop by my hotel at eight tomorrow morning, then?" By then, maybe I'd have some leads of my own that she could help me on. And if she was in the way, I could find a polite way to brush her off. Or an impolite way. Whatever. "I just need to take care of myself tonight."

"Well — whatever that means — have fun."

Fun — that was possible. If I had any luck, it would be a very brutal evening.

CHAPTER 16

Everyone seemed to assume Nar Valdum's Senator Gredler was a likely candidate to be the head of a more powerful Galactic Alliance. Diane also had told me he was a stooge for the Randatti syndicate. My understanding was that most of the powerful politicians were allied with one syndicate or another — you couldn't survive past a certain level in politics without that kind of power behind you. And if the Galactic Alliance successfully increased its power, all the syndicates would vie to grab as much of that power as they could. Further, with the public irately against the Nystrom syndicate due to their oddly public siege of Zaldia, the other syndicates — especially Randatti — would use that power to crush one of their biggest rivals.

So it was easy to see why this conference was important to all the syndicates, especially Nystrom. They all likely had lots of people in place on this planet, in this city, and in the conference itself in the form of puppet politicians. Again, I usually didn't care about these higher details, but if all the other syndicates were in the city and watching carefully for anything suspicious, that seemed pretty relevant to me, considering my now too-public profile. Of course, if they did find me out, why would they want to stop me? All I was currently tasked to do was kill terrorists — and pretty much no one cared if I killed them. The deluded idiots barely seemed to care themselves.

Everything about this job was odd. My mind kept drifting back to how Anthony Burke had come to deliver the job in person. What was he trying to tell me?

These thoughts nagged at me as I sat in a mostly empty tram late that night, heading to the bad part of town, completely unarmed (I had a knife, but I consider that more a tool than a weapon). Not helping was my irritation at two human females a couple seats behind me chatting endlessly about clothing stores and other inane things. Their chatter didn't seem exceptionally vapid, but it was really grating on me at the moment. Of greater concern in the car was a dark green alien of an unfamiliar species. He had two insect eyes that I kept thinking were staring at me, but I could never be sure. He also had no visible mouth, which creeped out some primitive instinct deep within me.

"I have done more research on Senator Gredler," Dip said in my ear. "There are a few rumors of his association with organized crime, though they are hardly mentioned in the official press. He does seem to be the leading candidate to head the Galactic Alliance if the reconfiguration is successful, and he has been very vocal about taking strong action against the Nystrom syndicate for their actions on Zaldia. Thus, if he is a target of assassination, Nystrom will be the ones with the most to gain ... though other syndicates would be interested in taking the reins of the new government. Am I correct in thinking that your interest in details like these, unrelated to your stated mission, is unusual?"

"I have trouble believing this terrorist hunt is my true mission."

"And you're trying to guess at your true mission?"

"I just feel I should better assess the whole situation."

"Understood. I note that your heart rate is faster than normal. Are you in distress?"

I hadn't noticed, but my heart was pounding. It was that fear again — fear of what, I had no idea, as only my subconscious seemed privy to that information. As I've said, fear isn't a useful emotion — I can logically determine the odds of danger and don't need my subconscious rashly trying to push me into action. But there it was, urging me to fight or flee, even though I had nowhere to run and no one to fight.

Then again, I was constantly resisting the urge to hurt the two women behind me, who were now talking excitedly about some celebrity of absolutely zero interest to me. I could usually filter out such an irritation, but fear had apparently made me more alert than I wanted to be. And every time I glanced at the green alien, anxiety surged, pushing me to do something, though there was nothing to do. The alien was silent and still and ... well, just odd. I couldn't tell if he was a quadruped or something else. He was completely unknown, and that is just the sort of thing fear thrives on.

"I need to get some guns; then I'll calm down," I told Dip. There were too many questions right now, and I couldn't take that, especially when I didn't even have the last-ditch option of shooting my way out. The peculiarities of this job certainly bothered me, but my bigger concern was that a rival syndicate like Randatti — apparently already on the alert for assassins — might have taken an interest in me after I'd been in two high-profile shootings. The police said they were going to keep the details under wraps, but I didn't trust them. And if Randatti or another syndicate came after me now, while I was unarmed, I'd be a decently easy kill for another professional.

I could have headed back to my ship for more weaponry, but that would have involved going past checkpoints and leaving too much evidence of my movements. Instead, I was on my way to the bad part of town to find some illegal weapons (hopefully quickly, as rearming myself was only the first part of my plans for the night). I hadn't done this very often, as I wasn't usually stuck on a planet where I couldn't legally buy guns. But the idea didn't worry me too much. I had also checked crime statistics in the area, and it wasn't too unlikely that I'd be mugged. That would probably be the easiest way to get a gun, and no one would care much if I killed another violet criminal.

I wasn't worried about a mugger killing *me*, even while I was unarmed. I don't consider anyone a real threat unless he has actual combat training and experience. I've had guns pointed at me so many times that the act by itself barely registers. The important thing in that situation is who is holding the gun. Pointing the gun in the right direction and pulling the trigger fast enough really is a bridge too far for most people.

"Would you like me to sing you a song, Rico? That might calm you down."

"No, Dip."

"I could give you assurances that everything will be alright. They'd be hollow assurances, since I haven't calculated your overall odds of survival, but they might make you feel better."

"No, thank you."

"Then I will at least remind you that you've been in a worse situation before and emerged alive."

I looked at my right hand. It was still quite smooth and perfect-looking — like a child's — since it was only a couple of years old. It was a constant reminder of the worst moment of my life, when I lay on the ground, bleeding, knowing that I was about to pass out and there was nothing — nothing — I could do to save myself. My fate at that time was completely out of my control, and that was just not something I could deal with. I have no gods to pray to; in my last moments, all I can do is try to accept the inevitability of death. But like every other living creature, my instinct is to fight that inevitability.

The hand incident had happened before I'd acquired Dip to function as a secondary brain in the event that I became incapacitated. I'd also added an emergency measure that would at least give me a chance to survive were I ever to end up in that situation again.

The green alien moved, and I instantly felt the need to act, though I couldn't quite comprehend what action my brain thought was necessary. I wasn't even sure if the alien had moved a limb or some part of his head. I tried to tell myself logically that there was nothing to fear, but I couldn't concentrate with the two women behind me yakking about things I couldn't understand anyone wasting their short lives thinking about.

I wanted to get up. I wanted to leave. It was an irrational response to the situation, but it was the only one my subconscious wanted. Perhaps it was an anxiety attack; I hated the idea that my own brain could betray me and force me to actions that I hadn't logically contemplated, but right then it was winning the battle. The tram approached its next stop, and I decided the best course of action would be to get off and try to get a hold of myself before continuing with my plan.

I got up casually, waited for the stop, and then exited, trying not to look at the alien as I left. He didn't move, and soon the doors of the tram closed behind me and the vehicle moved off, proving my fear to be baseless. The inane chatter had followed me, though. The two women had left the tram after me and were now talking about shoes. The station was fairly empty, and I briefly wondered whether I could get away with silencing them permanently. It was an indulgent and reckless thought. It was also a failure on my part to let such a minor annoyance get to me. After all the work I had done learning to live in normal society, there was no reason idiotic chatter not directed at me should have bothered me at all.

And then a thought struck me.

I turned around and faced the two women. They looked like trendy twenty-somethings wearing the latest fashion and hairstyles. One was a brunette wearing a top designed to emphasize her cleavage, and the other wore similarly tight clothes with purple streaks in her black hair. I would have called them attractive if I didn't already hate them.

"Hi," I said, putting on my most charming and least threatening persona. They reacted a bit apprehensively, as one might expect from two women approached by a strange male late in the evening. "I was just wondering if —"

That's when I attempted to sucker punch the brunette — and also when everything went horribly wrong.

I guess I should explain why I tried to assault the two women. Like I said, I was having trouble ignoring their inane chatter. I chalked that up to being more irritable than usual on account of my fear and anxiety. What I hadn't realized was that the chatter was the source of my fear and anxiety. I couldn't just ignore it for the same reason that one can't help but be alert to anything discordant or unusual. Now, I'm used to faking normal behavior, but I'd never done that with a partner, which was why I hadn't picked up on it right away. But I've heard enough people chatting about inane subjects, and their conversation was slightly different — like a song being sung a little off-key. I didn't consciously pick up on it, but my subconscious did.

So score one for the irrational part of my brain.

I only came to that realization when I got off the tram, and my ensuing response seemed pretty obvious. I didn't know if they planned to kill me or just follow me, so I was going to quickly disable them and get some answers.

This is where my subconscious lost the point it had just earned. I looked at two young women, who were as physically intimidating as your average college student, and my subconscious dismissed them as a threat. So instead of doing this the smart way, I had gone for the direct approach: punch one really hard in the face and then deal similarly with the other.

It was not even close to that easy. The brunette was quick enough that my blow merely glanced across her head, and she almost as quickly came back with an elbow to my ribs as she drew a gun. I managed to get a hand on the gun just as I saw the purpled-haired girl also draw out of the corner of my eye. I forced the brunette to shoot her partner, but she kept a firm grip on the gun as her free hand drew a knife that was already coming down on my arm. Somewhat panicked, I was able to turn the gun on her and shoot her through the torso just as the knife ripped into my forearm.

I'd made a stupid miscalculation that could have easily gotten me killed. Now there was a decent-sized cut in my arm; two bodies for the police to find; and I had no answers and even more questions. I'd screwed up big-time, basically because I was sexist. And this wasn't the first time I'd almost died by underestimating a woman, which made my situation that much more pathetic.

"What happened?" Dip asked. "I noticed your heart rate had a huge spike, though now it's finally back down to its normal level."

I picked up the second gun. "I've rearmed myself. Now on to our next stop."

Old human expression: No use crying over spilled milk.

CHAPTER 17

"Might I once again suggest fleeing?"

"But I'm so comfortable right now." It was a very comfy chair, and the silence and darkness surrounding me were quite relaxing.

"Obviously, someone knows who you are and wants to kill you," Dip said. "It seems dangerous to continue."

I chuckled. "Well, I wouldn't want to do a job that was dangerous! Anyway, I can't be certain they planned to kill me. I sort of forced their hand."

"Which brings me to your next issue. You left two dead bodies and your blood at the scene."

There are a lot of good techniques for cleaning up crime scenes — or so I've heard. Usually, I want people to know I was the one behind a killing. "They were professionals, and I doubt they were alone."

"And you say this as something that helps you?"

I flexed my right arm a bit. The medi-gel had stopped the bleeding and the pain, but I had lost a little mobility. "It means their friends should be perfectly capable of making the whole thing disappear. We professional criminals like to handle these things ourselves and not involve the law."

"So you will continue on as if nothing happened?"

"I will continue with the job until more information presents itself. No use panicking and making rash decisions until we're sure what's going on. Who knows, they might have been the allies I was supposed to get in contact with and this was all just a cute misunderstanding. I could be laughing about this by tomorrow."

"I am having trouble finding the humor in that, using my standard humor algorithms — wait, I think I get it. The statement itself was humor, as you were pretending that double homicide is comparable to an awkward social mishap."

"It's not funny when you explain it, Dip. Just keep listening to the police, and tell me if they find the bodies."

I sat a while longer in the dark. It was very quiet. The modern apartment had almost perfect sound dampers in the walls. That's always useful.

The lights came on and disturbed my peace. I leapt from the chair and grabbed Nakhai and broke his arm at the elbow before he could even comprehend what was going on. I slammed him into a bookshelf and then the numerous pieces of ancient-looking art he had in his living room. Beating up old men isn't something I have lots of firsthand experience with, but I thought I did a decent job of rattling him without too much risk of inadvertently killing him. After I used him to break the coffee table, I threw my full body weight into a blow to the side of his knee, shattering it and making sure he wouldn't try to get back up.

"Sorry for the rough introduction," I said, keeping my voice quite calm, "but I wanted to make it clear that I am a very violent person who is going to kill you."

Nakhai stared at me through tears of pain, trying to look defiant. "I am ready to die."

"But *I* am not ready for you to die." I stood over him, keeping my expression blank. "You will get to be a martyr, and you will get your reward from your god, but I first need some information from you."

"I don't know anything."

"I'm no fool. You know things, and we will not be done until you tell me these things."

He began inching away from me on the ground in a rather pathetic manner. "Who are you?"

It was nice being alone with someone I was going to kill; I could really be myself. I knelt down to appear less imposing. "Let's say I'm a neutral party. I'm not part of the godless government you oppose. I am no friend of the Galactic Alliance, and, given time, I will cause grave harm to it myself — so much harm that your own people will cheer what I do as God's retribution. Unfortunately, your people and your terrorist attacks are in my way right now, and thus I have to end them." I didn't actually know if I was here to do damage to the Galactic Alliance or not — it was often a tool of the syndicates as much as it was something that opposed them — but convincing Nakhai to open up to me was, of course, more of a consideration than the truth.

He stared at me for a moment, probably trying to figure me out. *Good luck with that.* "What is willed by Allah, no man can stop."

"But perhaps I *am* the will of God." I stood up, looming tall over him. "In fact, it's probably best to think of me not as a good man or an evil man but instead as more of a natural disaster — like an earthquake — just destroying everything around it. Sure, I'm going to kill you and some of your allies, but my destruction of your enemies will be much greater. Now, your people will be martyred and receive their reward. You will be martyred and have your reward. And I assure you that one day soon, at my hands, the evil empire of the Alliance will be gravely injured. Now, how hard do you want to fight against such a beneficial outcome?"

Nakhai's hardened expression of defiance was slowly fading. "I will not betray the faithful."

"I know you don't want to. I'm sure you're as dedicated to your god as any mere mortal could be. But you are a man, and men always break. Always. Your devotion to your cause will determine how long you can hold out but not whether you will break. If there is a God, He surely knows this and will not hold it against you. What's the expression? 'The spirit is willing but the flesh is weak.' I forget what religion that's from, but I am sure the concept is universal." I put my foot on his chest for emphasis. "Here is what is going to happen. I am going to hurt you. I am going to inflict pain and injury like you have never experienced before and can't even imagine. Eventually, motivated by the extreme pain, you will begin to accept my logic on these matters. You will know that you can both tell me about the Calabrai and go to your god as a martyr. What I want you to do now is take a moment to think — really think hard — and figure out exactly how much pain and suffering you have to endure to feel you've fulfilled your duties to your god."

I was silent for a few seconds, and he just stared up at me wordlessly, his resolve fading into a pathetic look of desperation.

I took my foot off his chest. "That should have been enough time." I smiled deeply, and I could see all hope leave him as he looked at my expression. "Let's get started."

CHAPTER 18

I slept in my hotel room. Yes, I know — it was a bit daring since a rival syndicate might have been out to kill me. But I had learned the building and the area around it pretty well, so it was a battlefield of my choosing. Plus I don't like running or hiding. I really, really don't like that. Perhaps that's unreasonable, but it seems every man needs to have a few unquestioned principles.

I only got a couple hours' sleep and awoke hoping to not have anything in particular to do that day. "Dip, did you find Nakhai's information useful?" Nakhai hadn't made me stay up that late before telling me what I wanted to know and pointing me to his hidden files.

"Yes, there was enough data in his files for me to identify and locate members of the three additional cells. I anonymously relayed the information to the police as you requested, and they are closing in on the Calabrai as we speak."

"So that's over, then?"

"I would think so. The files contained evidence of an additional plan to crash a cruise ship into the Nar Valdum capitol building during the conference, but they apparently encountered the same problem I have with Nar Valdum's air security."

"Sounds like I'm done being the terrorist-fighting hero. This whole affair has been very much beneath me. Have you heard anything about the two ladies I danced with?"

"Not yet."

I hated waiting, but waiting for my contacts to seek me out was all I had now that the terrorism nonsense was finished. And those people would certainly owe me some explanations. I began to wonder if the Nystrom executives would care if I killed one of my contacts to demonstrate how seriously I should be taken — because they had obviously not gotten that memo.

I figured that was probably a bad idea if I had to work closely with them anyway; murder makes people touchy. I just hoped they had more worthy targets of my violence than silly terrorists.

* * *

Small animals ran around the park, along with the flying things of Nar Valdum that seemed analogous to birds. I found it interesting that these city creatures were mostly unconcerned with the larger predators that surrounded them, apparently assuming all sentients meant them no harm. They certainly weren't worth my time to kill.

"It's nice here, isn't it?" Diane asked. We sat on a park bench eating our "breakfast" — some sort of fried, breaded thing we got from a vendor. Seemingly resigned to her mandatory vacation, she had dressed more casually in jeans and a t-shirt. While it was nothing revealing, it gave me a better glimpse of what a nice figure she had. Like her, I was also trying to relax. Neither of us was doing too well, but I was probably faking it better.

"It's peaceful. I like it." It was a very large park — almost a forest, really — in the center of the city. People like to be able to escape into nature to get away from the horrors of their technological progress — though this was a rather artificial version of nature, with mowed lawns and carefully planted trees. Still, it was large enough that many areas seemed quite secluded — maybe secluded enough that one could dispatch someone there without notice. It's always calming to be some place where you could shoot someone in the face and not worry about being surrounded by sirens minutes later.

"I thought maybe you would like to do something the opposite of exciting, considering your last few days," Diane said. "Are you ... doing okay?"

"Yeah, just needed a night to sort myself out ... I don't want you to get the idea that I don't enjoy your company, though."

"No ... no. I understand." She smiled. I smiled back, and it wasn't an act. I did enjoy her company ... which was certainly odd for me. Perhaps I just liked that she was a bit more challenging to deal with than most people — not so predictable as everyone else. I just wasn't sure what my intentions were with her anymore, though. I hoped the city's law enforcement was marginally competent, which would mean the terrorist annoyance was now over. I didn't know if she'd be useful to me for whatever was coming next, but I didn't figure it would hurt to keep her nearby just in case. Yes, that meant there was further risk of her finding me out, but I was supposed to be on a big job isolated from an easy escape, which made it seem nice to have a ... well ... friend.

So friends care about each other and their problems. That was something I'd have to remember to fake. "You okay being off duty right now?"

"I guess everything is in capable hands." She wasn't very convincing; she seemed antsy having to just sit there instead of act. She whispered to me, "I heard that a member of the Calabrai called the police with information on all the other cells out there."

"Wow. So there are more cells?"

"Yes ... but I guess the feds are on top of it." Again, she sounded more like she was trying to convince herself than me. "There's nothing for me to do right now except pray. And I heard that someone in the Calabrai grew a conscience and is helping us end the attacks." She smiled. "So maybe that's working."

I believe the ancient expression is "God works in mysterious ways," but beating information out of an old man and then having my AI program pretend to be a Calabrai member to pass on the information to police didn't seem very mysterious from my perspective.

I'd never prayed myself, even in desperate situations. I certainly remember a moment of desperation, but while I was lying there in my own blood sans my right hand, I wasn't praying — I was screaming. Plus, if I'd prayed and God had answered my prayer to let me live, He'd have been simultaneously ignoring other prayers by people not wanting to be killed. I've put down praying men before.

"I never really got the point of praying. It just doesn't seem like there is some big, powerful entity putting everything together."

She nodded. "It's easy to see the world as random chaos, no meaning or purpose to it. I've certainly been there. But then there's the beauty of the universe — the life forms and the simple joy of living. In the end, you get to choose how you look at the world." She blushed. "I'm sorry. You probably aren't looking for a theological debate when you're on vacation."

"Well, if it's between that and being in a shootout with terrorists, I'd probably choose the religious discussion." Not really.

She smiled again. I certainly would have liked to know her carnally if I'd had the time, but I figured that whole religion thing would get in the way.

I heard a beep, and Diane pulled out a handheld device. Her casual glance at the handheld quickly turned to an intense stare. "Nakhai was found dead. Beheaded."

I put on my shocked face — mainly just a blank expression with mouth slightly open. Don't hold it too long, or you look really stupid. "The terrorists thought he gave us information?" Incidentally, cutting off someone's head and not getting a huge mess on yourself is not easy.

"I ... I suppose." She stood up. "I think I should ..."

I got up and put my hand on her shoulder. "Diane, other people are handling it. I think we've both done enough for now."

"Sure, I guess." She looked ready to bolt, and then I'd probably have to go with her to be supportive or risk my cover as an awesome, trustworthy cop. Easier to convince her to let it go, for both our sakes.

"Diane!" A woman Diane's age was coming toward us. She was a slightly plump brunette in clothes that didn't look quite casual enough for the park. She didn't appear to be a threat, but I had been wrong before. She quickly looked at me and smiled. "Who is your friend?" she asked.

Diane turned red and forced an awkward smile. "Hey, Hana ... What a coincidence running into you here. This is Rico Vargas; he's from the planet Rikar. Rico, this is my friend Hana."

I stood and shook her hand and was instantly ready to hate her. Her smile was way overenthusiastic, and it filled me with dread. I had a feeling that I had stumbled into a completely asinine social situation, one that was going to stretch my patience for being polite.

"Diane has told me all about you!" With the excitement in her voice, you'd have thought she was meeting her favorite rock star. "This is a great planet, isn't it? Have you ever thought of living here?"

Diane briefly glared at her. "Thanks, Hana, but I think Rico may have gotten too much of the planet already."

It was actually a little amusing to see Diane this embarrassed. Her friend had confirmed what had become quite obvious — that she liked me. I really didn't think I could be around someone this much without slipping enough to scare her off, though, so that felt like an accomplishment. "I don't know. I could see living here," I said. For maybe a month, tops, until boredom led to escalating violence and I ended up in a massive gunfight that would go down in the planet's history. Also, I presumed the syndicate had more violence in store for me that would give me cause to leave the planet much sooner. But for the moment, feigning a romantic interest in Diane — not just of the one-night-stand sort — would be an interesting challenge. "It'd be a nice change of pace from being in the backwater places of the universe. Just might not want to live right in the city." I chuckled a bit. "It's a bit too hectic here." That's funny, because I've been constantly shooting terrorists.

Is it pathetic that I pick up habits from Dip?

"There are some beautiful countrysides here," Hana said without missing a beat, though completely missing the joke (Diane didn't brag about how often I shot people?). "Maybe Diane could show you some. I know she's been considering getting a place out there."

"That might be neat to see." I *was* starting to feel a little claustrophobic. Maybe my contact would want me to stay here, but by this point I was of the "Screw them!" attitude. Not professional, but so far this whole job didn't seem very professional.

"I can show you some nice areas ... you know ... if you're really interested," Diane said with a forced nonchalance. She seemed quite tough for a woman, and I found that interesting, but she was adorable when vulnerable. Like a puppy. Like a puppy I didn't find annoying or want to kill. By now, I really did hope this wouldn't end with my killing her. I fantasized that maybe she would try to hunt me down, and we'd run into each other again one day, but as sworn enemies. That could be fun.

"I think you'll love it. I really think you will," Hana said, giggling a bit. Her I did not care for. Were it socially permissible, I would have already decked her.

"Well, maybe we'll do that." I could tell Diane was more annoyed than embarrassed. "Anyway, it sure was nice running into you here, but I assume you have lots of errands to run."

"Not really. I just dropped the kids off at school, and now ..." She took in Diane's expression. "Oh, actually, I'm going to ... You two have lots to do. I'll see you later. Nice meeting you, Rico."

"Nice meeting you, too." I gave her my warm, friendly smile, which took a tiring amount of effort. Then she mercifully left.

All in all, I really hate people. All sentients annoy me, but it's that closer connection with my own species that allows humans to get under my skin. As a child, I fantasized about killing all humans until I was the only one left, though that really was infeasible without access to weapons that could destroy on a global scale. A daydream, really.

Diane turned to me. "Sorry about that. She's a friend. I mentioned that I was showing a visiting officer the city. I didn't think she'd just show up like that."

I laughed a little and then stared a little too long at her eyes. I quickly turned away as if catching myself. "So ... um ... what do we have planned next?"

"Well, whatever you're interested in. I don't think you actually want to go house hunting in the countryside. There is a carnival in town, though. It's a bit like an old-fashioned one from Earth, with funnel cakes and rides and games."

"You mean where you knock down bottles to win a gratuitously large stuffed animal?"

"Exactly." She smiled. "Which is good, because I recently realized that none of my stuffed animals are quite large enough. Anyway, they also have lots of displays from other species, since there are so many visiting the city this week, so it might be interesting."

Sounded insipid. "Sounds fun. Might be worth checking out."

She paused and put her finger to her ear. "I have a call coming in; I need to take it." She was quiet for a moment, and then her face went white. Then she got up and started running down the path toward the park's exit. "Hana!"

I followed, but I didn't like where this was going. We caught up with Hana, who had paused to smell some flowers, and Diane gently took her by the hand. "You need to come with me."

"What is it?" Hana's stupid smile was finally gone.

"No one is hurt, but something is happening at Lincoln Elementary right now."

"What's happening? Are Justin and Tammy okay?" Hana suddenly looked terrified.

"I'm sure they are, but why don't we head over there right now."

I walked up next to Diane. "So what's going on?" I had already guessed, though.

Diane whispered to me, "We believe something is going to go down at the elementary school where Hana's kids are. It's right next to the park. Maybe we should go see if we can help."

Damn my luck. "Let's go." I'm a hero; that's what heroes say in times of trouble.

"Is it a terrorist attack?" Hana asked meekly.

"It's going to be all right," I said firmly. The best way to un-panic people is to act like you're in control — even if the situation could not logically be in your control. "If anyone tries anything, it won't end well for them." I let a bit of my real personality seep in; threatening was good here. And I was going to kill everyone in a very bad way if I could, because I was sick of dealing with this crap.

One awesome thing, though: They were threatening children. By my understanding of social norms, that meant that I could do pretty much anything to the terrorists, and it wouldn't seem too extreme.

CHAPTER 19

Chaos. Children ran out of the building, screaming and crying. It was irritating, to say the least. There were only two police vehicles there, with two officers standing outside one of them with their guns drawn. Diane quickly lost control of Hana as she rushed to try to find her children among those outside. It had been stupid to bring her; she was just another distraction to worry about. On the bright side, maybe a terrorist would shoot her.

"What's going on?" Diane demanded of the officers.

"Terrorists are in there! I don't know how many!" Human officer. Quite panicked and probably best suited to standing uselessly outside. "I think we might have officers down inside ... and I think they have a bomb. We're waiting for SWAT."

A fiery shot ripped out of the side of the building. "No time!" Diane said and headed for the school.

Since I didn't care about screaming children, there seemed to be plenty of time. Personally, I didn't want to get blown up, but if I stood outside while the detective stupidly marched inside, I wouldn't look like much to her anymore. If that mattered.

And at the time it seemed like it mattered.

I caught up with Diane. "You have a plan?"

"Don't know enough to have a plan. So what are the chances you already have a gun?"

I drew one. "I don't know how you people expect me to kill terrorists for you when you keep disarming me. Anyway, I have a plan: It's called 'shoot bad people.'"

"Just watch out for children."

There was the rub. In most societies, there's nothing worse than killing a child — even though they're not productive members of society and are easily replaceable. If I accidentally shot one, I couldn't just shrug and say, "Oops!" — it would be a big deal. So I thought I would just concentrate on killing only tall people — unless there turned out to be a short alien terrorist. I figured looking for a gun and shooting whoever was holding one would be a good way to handle this — unless the person was Diane (whom I had almost shot twice in the terrorists' shop) or another cop.

This is why I don't like being a hero; it complicates things to the point of ruining the simple pleasure of gunning people down in a shootout.

When we entered, the main hallway was nearly empty. People came running toward us — children — and I did not shoot them and instead firmly directed them outside. Perhaps too firmly; I really dislike children. A little further in, we saw gunshots ripping through the wall. They weren't aimed at us, though; there seemed to be a gunfight up ahead. I rushed forward, too deep in my fight mode to bother checking whether Diane was keeping up. I saw someone with a gun — a Corridian woman — officer — not someone I was supposed to shoot — pinned behind a column while two others fired on her. I walked forward and shot the two terrorists in the face before they even noticed me. They really did suck. It would take quite a spectacular miracle from their god to be even a marginal threat to someone like me.

When I got to her, the officer was sobbing and gripping her gun pretty uselessly. I recognized her as Meela from the police station. "Randall is dead ... they —"

"The bomb?" No time for politeness.

"A group of them are holding a classroom of children hostage back there ..." She pointed down the hallway. "... and they say they have a bomb."

Diane caught up with me, and I said, "Help her," even though Meela didn't really need help. I just felt things would go quicker without any "allies" in my way. So I continued on, leaving Meela and Diane behind. It would be pretty asinine to die in an explosion here, but there was no use worrying about that now. My choice was made, and my path was clear.

One man popped up his head and lost said head. He seemed pretty terroristy, but I realized afterward I should have probably taken another moment to confirm who he was. Oh well. I walked past a police officer — Randall, whom I had met earlier and didn't really care for one way or the other — lying dead on the ground. I could hear children crying in a nearby classroom. Finally children's crying was useful for something. I came to the classroom door and glanced inside, then pulled my head back as some shots flew past me.

There were three of them, each kneeling behind a child, with other children seated in the back of the room. I could easily have jumped in there and killed the three if I didn't care about the children. And, well, I *didn't* care about the children. But I was committed to pretending I did.

"If you take another step toward us, we'll kill them all!" one of the terrorists yelled. Pretty boilerplate threat for this sort of situation; not very impressive.

"If you had a bomb, you would have set if off by now." I drew my second gun.

"There is a bomb in the building! And we'll shoot the children!"

"That's what you came here to do, isn't it?" They were already scared, but not scared enough. With the situation as it was, I didn't know how I could shoot the terrorists without a good chance of hitting a child or of taking so long in aiming my shots that I might get shot myself. I'd have to provoke them to make the situation more to my liking. "And why are you assuming I care about the children? In fact, I'm hoping you kill them; it will give me an excuse for what I'm planning next. I'm a killer, you see; I like it when people die. That's no challenge, though. What I'm wondering is how many times I can shoot you and *not* kill you. That would be interesting."

"We will start shooting!"

"I really hope the not-killing-you thing works out, because that makes the next part so much more fun. You see, I'm going to find where you worshipped and then find your families. Then I'm going to kill them — but I'll take my time doing it. I'm a real artist in that regard. Then I'm going to visit you in the hospital and show you all the nice pictures I took."

One of them started to shout something but was cut off. I didn't know why, but it seemed like an opportunity. I jumped into the classroom and saw Diane behind the terrorists, one now clearly dead. Best I could assess from the scene was that she had gotten behind one of them without being noticed — obviously using me as a diversion — pulled his head back, then fired through the back of his head. The other two were surprised enough to let go of the children in front of them as they turned to shoot at Diane, leaving me enough room to work with. I fired both guns simultaneously, and the school was now free from terror.

Yay, me. Again.

I didn't know how much of my speech she'd heard, but that was a question for later. "I think that's that," I said.

She glanced at me, her face that cold mask again. It quickly crumbled as she saw the crying children. "It's okay, you're all safe now," she told them very calmly and with a pleasant smile. "Let's get out of the building now. Single file."

Some of the kids seemed a little too shocked to move. I yelled at them, "Get out of the building! All of you! Come on!" I motioned toward the door, and all the children were now moving, taking cautious looks at the corpses.

As Diane walked by me, she took one last look at the terrorist she had killed, her expression once again unreadable. She looked at me and seemed to snap out of a trance, giving me a smile that was a little less fake than the one she'd given the kids. "Thanks again. Glad you're here, Rico."

I touched her on the shoulder. "It's where I need to be." What a cheesy thing to say. Wasn't sure why I said it. Then she smiled more fully. That was why.

✳ ✳ ✳

As we exited the building, the SWAT team and bomb squad had just arrived and were swarming the place. One of the SWAT guys immediately ran up to us and asked, "The terrorists?"

"I think they're all dead." I killed any I saw, at least.

"Did you see the bomb?"

"I think they were bluffing about that."

He did not look reassured. "Some radiological elements were detected at one of their hideouts. We think they have a dirty bomb."

"Oh." That's all I thought to say. I really didn't want to get blown up by a bomb, especially some crude one made by the Calabrai. I thought I deserved better, though I had always imagined that my death would one day be pretty stupid.

"One's alive!" one of the paramedics yelled as they brought out one of the terrorists on a stretcher. It was hard to believe I'd shot one and left him alive, but the whole make-sure-you-don't-shoot-children thing had confused me and probably messed with my technique.

"Can we question him?" SWAT asked.

I looked at the terrorist. He was a human whom I had shot through the chest back in the classroom. It didn't seem likely he would last much longer.

"He's failing fast," the paramedic said. "We need to give him Fazium, which means we have to induce a coma first."

I grabbed the paramedic by the arm. "No, you don't. Fazium works just fine without the body being in a coma."

He looked shocked. "But the pain ...."

"There may be a bomb about to go off here and kill everyone. Let's worry about that." I put on my very serious face. "Give him the Fazium."

Perhaps my face was too serious, as the paramedic froze. I grabbed the drug from him. The SWAT officer looked like he was about to do something, but I just gave him a glance, and he backed off. I walked over to the terrorist and stood over him. "I don't know what you know about Fazium, but it's going to save your life while making you wish we'd killed you. Want to tell us about the bomb?"

He was fading out of consciousness and didn't seem to hear me.

I injected the Fazium. It's a substance that is basically programmed with how a human is put together (the same version of the drug won't work on any other species) and bonds with the patient's DNA to get the specific sequences and structures. It then crudely hacks the body back into working order by replicating cells and forcing things back together as quickly as possible. And it does all this with no regard for the body's nerve cells, which it tends to light up throughout the entire body as it does its work. Supposedly, it feels like the body is being ripped apart from the inside with shards of glass passing through your every vein. At least that's how it was described by one person who wasn't properly sedated beforehand, though it was hard to get anything coherent out of that man for the rest of his life.

I guess some people can't take a little pain.

After the Fazium was administered, the man just lay there silently for a couple moments.

Then he twitched a little. And then he started flailing like mad while screaming his lungs out.

I was quickly on top of him, holding him down by his shoulders. "Where's the bomb?!" I shouted at him, raising my voice so it could be heard over his screaming — but it was a losing battle. His screams just kept getting louder, and I could barely hold him down. His strength was inhuman, and I could tell he was about to push me off. "Tell me about the bomb!" I yelled again, but I couldn't hear myself over his shrieking. "This will stop when you tell us about the bomb!"

My arm was yanked away, and I was now facing Diane, who screamed at me, "He can't even hear you!"

There was now a crowd around me — including some children — looking on in horror. "Yeah, I guess not."

The man had flopped out of his stretcher and was now flailing around on the ground, screaming so hard you'd think his lungs would burst. A couple of paramedics jumped on him and injected him with something, and he went silent.

Diane was still holding my arm tightly, though she didn't look mad anymore, just exasperated. A number of the people gathered around looked at me like I was some sort of monster. Was I supposed to feel bad about this? It was possible that a bomb — one intended for children, mind you — was about to explode and kill us all. Someone had to take action. This is why I'm much more comfortable in situations where I don't have to care what other people think. Sometimes I wonder if I'm the only person in the universe who takes things seriously.

CHAPTER 20

"Hana's son and daughter are fine. She's with them now."

It was as if Diane read my mind and picked the absolute opposite of anything I cared about to tell me. "Good," I replied. I forced a little smile.

"She wanted me to pass on her thanks."

"Just doing what had to be done." Because apparently everyone else is too incompetent. "Any word on the bomb?"

"Nothing solid yet, but they're pretty sure there isn't one in the school." Diane was driving us back to the police station (my favorite place). When I had the opportunity, I was going to berate Dip for not having been able to give me a warning about where one of the attacks would occur so I could steer clear of it. That was a very pointless risk of my life. Still, it looked like this terrorism problem was finally over. I hoped I'd soon find out why I was really on this planet.

Diane's face was very intense. Something was weighing on her — maybe that she'd had to kill again. It seemed burdensome to have to care about such things. At least she was able to make sure those emotions only came out after and not during a shooting. "I never did ask you how you snuck into the classroom to surprise them like that."

"I've been there before to talk to Hana's son's class about being a police officer. Justin had shown me how the closets at the back of the classrooms are shared between two rooms. Makes a convenient little secret passageway."

"So you just jumped right in there?"

"I thought they had a bomb. Seemed like the only option. You kind of got ahead of me, so I wasn't able to give you a heads-up." She gave an askew smile. "But thanks for the distraction there."

The thought that Diane had heard what I'd said to the terrorists gave me this weird, warm feeling in my face; I wasn't sure what that was. "Oh, you heard all that. I was just trying to goad them into a mistake."

She chuckled. "Good to know you can pretend to be a psychopath when needed. So do you work with a partner on Rikar?"

"Not often … We're spread thin, so I'm pretty used to going it alone."

"I've been called a loner, too. Does make it simpler when things get chaotic, but I've started to learn the value of having someone to watch your back."

No. Having to look out for the survival of someone else offers far too many complications. It was pretty hard for me to see that as a good tradeoff. "Sorry I charged in again without you."

"Wasn't looking for an apology. What are you now? Three times a hero?" She smiled at me.

It was true. I was pretty awesome. No hero just admits that, though. I tried to think of something else to say that would be relevant to the situation and remembered the stupid dead cop. "Sorry about Officer Randall. He seemed like a good man."

Her smile faded, and she was silent for a moment. "He was an ass. Probably should never have been on the police force." She smiled slightly again. "But he died trying to save the lives of children. Not much more you can ask from anyone."

I nodded. I still couldn't sympathize with people's fascination with children (though I logically understood it as an evolutionary directive). I was just happy I'd barely traumatized any children today — and I really hate them for some reason. I'm guessing it's their stupidity and the disproportionately sized heads, which I just find creepy. I glanced at her and softened my expression more. "You doing okay?" I was getting good at this; I almost convinced myself I cared.

She looked down. She softened her voice. "Thinking I might quit. Seriously this time."

Strange idea. She was the only one on her police force who seemed to know what she was doing. "Why?" I asked.

"I just want to make sure I don't have to kill anymore. I don't like … what it makes me."

"What do you mean?" I've seen beings get emotional about killing; she seemed to take it really well, actually.

"It's … complicated." She flashed me a nervous smile. "I should tell you, I have a *lot* of baggage."

"Oh, well, that's too bad. I'm basically exactly what you see." I chuckled a little but realized she wouldn't exactly get the full context of that sarcasm.

"I know there's something more to you, but I'll leave that as your business. Again, I'm just glad you're here right now." She drove her vehicle into the police station parking lot. "Well, not right here. I have a feeling this is going to be crappy."

I was really getting tired of the police station — especially the people inside it who kept taking my weapons. As I'd learned from my encounter on the tram, I might have had assassins on my tail, and I didn't really want a repeat of trying to take them on unarmed. Well, if they attacked again soon, at least I'd have cops around to protect me.

Yes, I'm being sarcastic.

There was a more somber mood in the station this time, as they had lost an officer. Officer Meela was back, and Diane went over to comfort her — which consisted of taking Meela's hand and whispering a few things. I think I could have faked comforting someone better than she did, but I didn't care enough right now. My main concern was to confirm this terrorism threat was behind me ... not that I knew what that would mean for me next.

Chief Rudle approached us wearing a pretty stoic expression. "Come on into my office."

Diane and I followed him in and sat down. "I just couldn't keep you two out of this, could I? Do you know what this looks like, that I have some off-planet cop running around here, shooting and torturing people?"

"Do you know how much I really don't care right now?" Diane replied, voicing my own sentiment pretty well.

Rudle ignored her. "The good news is that all the terrorist cells look to have been stopped. We located the headquarters of the cell that attacked the school and found an unfinished dirty bomb. It looks like they somehow knew we were moving in on them and launched their attack before they were ready."

"Am I still suspended?" Diane asked.

Rudle frowned. "No, I have a job for you. Senator Gredler wants to use this victory against the terrorists as an example of planets working together. You two get to meet the senator and be there for his big speech during the conference."

Diane looked displeased. "I'm not going to be his puppet. The guy is dirty."

"You're a nut case. Hopefully, when his people screen you, they'll realize that and lock you up." Rudle turned his focus to me. "Rico, some feds will have to screen you, too, before you can meet the senator. They still think there's some threat against him out there, so they're upping security a bit. There's nothing in your background I should be aware of?"

"Like have I killed senators before?" I'm not actually sure how many. It depends on how you define "senator."

"I'm sure you'll be fine," Rudle said. "Apparently, they've already gotten in contact with Rikar to ask about you."

If you'd been watching me closely at this moment, a slight twinge in the muscles near my mouth would have betrayed the emotions rushing through me. "Oh. What are they saying about me back home?"

"I don't know. You'll meet the feds tomorrow morning. That work for you?"

"Yeah, that's fine."

Diane sighed. "I'll be there."

"I wasn't asking you," he said sharply. "You cause any trouble, and you're done."

I didn't like Rudle and felt like refreshing myself on what color his species bleeds. I know I had other things to worry about, but it seemed the character I was playing would say something. "You know, she saved a classroom full of kids today. I don't know where you get off sitting here on your fat ass disrespecting her like this." I used a subtler version of my scary face.

Rudle looked a little surprised but quickly recovered. "No, you don't know. I'm just worried about what this one success will encourage her to do next."

"Are we done here?" Diane asked, though it really was more of a statement, as she had gotten up and started to leave.

I followed. "I don't like how he treats you." I really didn't — he seemed like a useless idiot compared to her — but wasn't that at the bottom of the list of things I should have been caring about at the moment?

"I could be more patient in my interactions with him, I guess. I always feel like being confrontational, but that never achieves anything." She smiled. "I just don't respect him at all. So much of this job is keeping up appearances for the public ... not meting out justice."

Justice always seemed like a completely imaginary concept to me. There is no righting the wrongs done in the universe. If someone hurts you, you simply hurt him back so much that he won't do it again. If the feds did find me out, they'd lock me up and call it justice, but all those people I'd killed would still be dead.

"I really don't want to be some show dog for Gredler," Diane told me. "There is good reason to believe he is in bed with the Randatti criminal syndicate." She stopped for a moment and seemed to stare out at some distant memory. "I don't think I can deal with that."

I was having trouble even pretending to care what Diane was saying with my new and very concrete worries. I don't like fretting, though, so I tried to push my concerns away. And breaking character is just sloppy. No reason to panic until someone was actually coming for me. "Government is corrupt. It's just a fact of life. It attracts the wrong sort of people."

"It shouldn't have to be that way."

"It kind of does; people have been complaining about this for millennia."

She laughed. "Not much of an optimist, are you?"

"I'm a realist; that's pretty much the opposite, since things in the real world are pretty crappy."

"Well, then, I hope to stop seeing things as they really are. No use going through life depressed." She smiled at me. "So do all your vacations go like this?"

"This is the first time I've tried taking one." I liked charming her, but it seemed it was about time I stopped pretending I needed her for anything when I had other things to focus on. Still, I felt resistant to the idea of just brushing her off. I wasn't used to dealing with a person I sort of liked being around. "I think I'm gonna go relax at my hotel now. They guaranteed me no terrorists on the premises."

"Sounds good. I'm going to go visit Hana. She and her family are pretty shaken. I should probably be there for them. I guess I'll see you tomorrow morning at the interview with the feds."

"See you there." Unless Dip convinces me to do the rational thing and flee the planet.

* * *

My hotel. I knew the area around it. I knew multiple exits from the building. I knew things around me that I could improvise as weapons (none of them gun-shaped, unfortunately). A part of my brain — a small part I knew not to listen to — wanted me to panic. But logically I knew staying put was my best option until I had more information. Perhaps more trained assassins would be coming my way. Maybe the feds would see through my story and descend on me at any minute. But I could only deal with what *was* happening, not what *could* happen. So I sat in my room and watched a show about a flying creature indigenous to the Corridians' homeworld while I waited to hear more.

"I would say the logical course of action is to flee," Dip intoned in my ear.

"I already knew you'd say that and I haven't fled, so it's pretty pointless for you to say it. Anyway, where would I go? I like being where the action is. Now, if you catch word the feds are on their way that's a different story, but for now I'm staying here. Any idea how they got in contact with Rikar so quickly?"

"I'm not sure. It was a safe bet that no one would be able to get in touch with Rikar within a week's time, but perhaps there is some sort of secondary database I don't know about that they're able to access here. So is your current strategy to wait until you're attacked again?"

"Getting attacked would give me more information, though hopefully my 'allies' will contact me before that happens." The flying creature looked like a cross between a lizard and a bat. I had sometimes daydreamed as a child about being able to fly. That would be an easy way to avoid annoyances on the ground. Plus, it would offer a whole new wrinkle to attack strategies.

"If you do need quick extraction from the city, I now think I have a thirty-five percent chance of full success, with a sixty-seven percent chance of at least a piece of the ship escaping orbit."

I ignored the joke. "Do you have Vito on the line yet?"

"He is calling in now. I'll patch him through to you."

"Vito, can you hear me?"

"Yeah. Kinda neat how you have that robot secretary."

"Shut up, Vito. I killed two trained professionals who were after me — both human females. Would you know anything about that?"

"Huh? Did they attack you?"

"They were following me. I unfortunately did not get to find out their intentions. Now the question is: Were they our people, or is one of the other syndicates aware of my presence?"

"Well, I have a message for you. They want you to calm down. They do have people there who are going to help you see this through, and they'll contact you."

Calm down? Telling someone that always seemed like an easy way to rile him up. I wouldn't take the bait, though. "Were the two ladies I killed supposed to contact me, and we just had a silly misunderstanding?"

"Uh ... I dunno, Rico. But the message was pretty definitive: You need to just relax until someone gets in contact with you."

"But you don't know when that will happen?"

"No. Sorry."

"Well, the feds here might be about to see through my cover story. Do you at least know if that is being handled?"

"I don't have anything else for you, Rico. But this message was given to me today, so maybe they're on that."

"You never know anything, Vito. Is there any point to your existence whatsoever?"

"Well, I —"

"I don't care about your answer to that. I'm done with him, Dip."

Dip cut the communication. "So what is the plan now?"

"I will proceed as Officer Rico from Rikar until forced to do otherwise. I wish people would stop instructing me to 'relax,' though. I relax when I have a challenging target to focus on. Leaving me in the dark like this ... does not put me in a good place."

"If you don't find that your employers respect you, that may be a good indication that you need to find another job. Would you like me to locate some planets with good job markets?"

"No. We'll continue on for now."

"So you'll be returning to the police station tomorrow to meet the feds?"

I watched the lizard bat fly quietly over a forest. In a small way, I envied it. "Yes."

"And if they've seen through your cover?"

"Then it will be an interesting day." I imagined a shootout at the police station. I'd start out unarmed, but there would be plenty of guns nearby. I just had to get one, and there were a few avenues of escape from the building. As I went over every scenario, though, somehow Diane kept popping up in them, and I froze.

But my solution for her was quite simple: Shoot her first chance I got, as she had demonstrated herself to be a lethal threat. Very simple, actually. No reason I should have trouble with it.

CHAPTER 21

"Why are we waiting out here?" Diane asked.

"Because it's a nice day out." It was quite warm and sunny. More importantly, if the feds were going to make a move on me, I figured I'd do better if I weren't caught inside. The easiest escapes were the vehicles up here on the roof of the parking structure.

She stared at me a moment. "I keep getting this feeling there's a whole side of you that you keep hidden."

"You have your secrets too, don't you?" Deflect!

She laughed. "Fair enough. So do you actually want to do this? Be a part of this little show with Senator Gredler?"

I was pretty neutral on the idea, not knowing what my role here was. Certainly, politicians themselves held no interest for me. I had never even voted before. I've certainly killed politicians, though, which is taking an even more active role in politics. "All of politics is a silly little show, isn't it? If you want to get anywhere, you have to play your part. It doesn't mean anything."

She smiled a bit. "You're a pretty cynical person."

"Cynical and pragmatic. I understand you think this Gredler is dirty, but if you want to do anything about it, this is how you get involved." I had an idle thought of her actually making enough waves exposing the criminal syndicates that Nystrom would send me back here to kill her. Unlikely.

"Maybe. And maybe I just make too much of things. I convince myself something is an outrage while no one else cares. Maybe it's me."

She didn't know the half of it, but if she did, a better idea would be to ignore it. The syndicates crushed people like her all the time without even noticing. There were three choices when dealing with the syndicates: join them, stay out of their way, or get killed by them. In a way, the syndicates' keeping most of their activities secret protected normal people. A lot of people had a drive to fight 'injustice,' and with the syndicates involved, that was a suicidal tendency.

Not that going along with the syndicates offered much safety either — certainly not from my standpoint. Maybe that was the real choice: danger or insignificance.

The feds' vehicle flew overhead and landed in front of us. I watched and smiled casually. I had nothing to worry about until I was told otherwise, and I had a number of escape plans ready just in case. Out of the vehicle came a human female and a grayish (male?) alien, both in black suits. At first I was busy trying to recognize the type of alien (bleeds green, I think), but then the female caught my eye. Red hair, killer figure.

I knew her.

My first instinct was to shoot her and run, but that was just the fear talking, and I never let fear take control. Plus, I didn't have a gun. So I just kept up my stupid smile and waited for her to make the first move. I hate that. I survive by being in charge of every situation.

"Rico! Remember me? It's Morrigan!" She had a broad, friendly smile.

I still didn't know what game she was playing, but I tried to match her in looking friendly. "How could I forget?"

"This is insane. I mean, what are the chances?" She turned to Diane. "Sorry, I'm Agent Dawson, and this is Agent Verg."

Diane shook her hand. She looked a little uneasy. Perhaps she was wondering about my relationship with "Agent Dawson." I certainly shared that curiosity. "You know Rico?"

"I was part of a group that visited Rikar to see about their joining the Alliance. I talked a bit to the law enforcement there." She smiled at me. It was probably supposed to look playful, but I found it a little scary. "Particularly to Rico. Well, this will certainly make things easier in getting you cleared to meet the senator." Morrigan then came closer to me — too close.

She was intimidating me, and she was enjoying it. And I still wasn't quite sure what the hell was going on.

"What luck." I managed another smile, but I was being pushed to my limits. I wouldn't be able to be convincingly social for much longer. I was losing control to primitive emotions, and I intensely hated that. A gorgeous, sweet-smelling woman was almost pressing herself against me, and all I could think about was how I wanted to smash her head in with a rock and run away. It took so much effort to just stand there calmly.

"We need to catch up." Morrigan took my right hand and squeezed it with a lot more strength than her feminine fingers would seem to possess. "I see your hand is doing well."

"Yeah."

"Your hand?" Diane asked.

"Oh, he didn't tell you about that?" Morrigan said, finally releasing her steel grip. "Not pleasant to talk about, I guess. I'm sorry ... I shouldn't have brought that up. Anyway, let's go inside and get things ready."

She headed inside with Verg. When they were out of earshot, Diane turned to me. "What happened to your hand?"

"It was ... injured." Ripped off, to be more precise. By a surprisingly strong redhead.

* * *

"This should be a simple matter," Agent Verg told us ... or my personal translator did. His voice was an odd little hum. "We just have to be extra cautious because of current threats and the high profile of the conference. We have all of Detective Thompson's data readily available, and Agent Dawson was able to obtain adequate documentation from Rikar for Officer Vargas." Was Verg also part of a criminal syndicate, or was he an actual federal agent on this planet? Of course, Morrigan could have been an actual agent, too; nothing prevents someone from being in the government and moonlighting as an assassin.

I kept an eye on Morrigan. I still didn't know what was going on. The agents had taken a room in the police station to interview us, and for now I was just playing along. The assumption was that Morrigan was on my side, since she had so far neglected to kill me, but it was hard to be at ease. Every time I caught her eye, she smiled at me. It freaked me out. Yes, I was being irrational, but nothing was very rational at the moment.

Morrigan turned her attention to Diane. "You have an interesting history as a police officer, Detective Thompson."

"Everything has been visited and revisited." She looked a little distressed. I guessed Dip didn't have full access to Diane's history; I would have liked to see the more interesting items. "If you're more comfortable with me not meeting the senator, I won't be broken up over it."

Morrigan's expression turned serious, and she squeezed Diane's shoulder. It really looked like she cared; she was good. "You and Rico are heroes and deserve honor. This isn't about Senator Gredler. This is about highlighting how planets can work together to combat threats. We're all for that, aren't we?" Morrigan looked at me and smiled again. It was *really* freaking me out. "Bad people need to get what's coming to them."

She was playing with me. Presuming that we were on the same side on this, I was very much *not* appreciating it. If she was going to kill me, I really wanted her to get on with it. I would have loved a rematch, and she would not take me by surprise this time.

"You'll be meeting the senator tomorrow at his residence outside of town," Verg told us. "He'll tell you himself if he expects you to do anything at the speech. I think we're done here. But we would like to remind you both not to have any weapons on you."

I managed a smirk. "That makes me antsy."

Morrigan leaned in close. "Well, no need to fear. I'll be near you at all times."

I just wanted to kill her and flee this rock, but odds were on her winning that fight.

She stood up. "Hey, if you're not doing anything this afternoon, we should catch up over lunch."

I kept my face pretty stoic. "Yes, that would be nice."

"Great. Do you know The Blue Feather?"

"I can find it," I said, shrugging. A little too casually.

"I'll see you there at noon, then."

"Okay."

She and Verg left the room. I could feel Diane's eyes on me as I watched the door, half-expecting Morrigan to step back in and rip me apart.

"You don't seem to like her," she said.

"No." I usually don't care whether my victims suffer or not, but I wanted to hear her scream. Not rational, but I am only human ... basically.

"So what did ... I guess that's not my business."

I forced myself to stop watching the door and looked at Diane and smiled. "Don't worry about it. There are just some unsettled issues between us."

"Anything I can do?"

I usually work alone, so Morrigan probably wouldn't expect me to come at her with someone else's help. Of course, I assumed she was also working for the Nystrom syndicate, so I'd get in trouble for killing her.

I'd sleep better at night, though.

But using Diane's help was out of the question, anyway. "Thanks, but I should be fine."

"Well ... I guess I'll see you later, then."

It seemed like she might have been jealous, but I really did not want to share the feelings I had for this other woman. "Maybe we can catch dinner or something tonight." I wasn't sure why I said that. I guess it was because I didn't know what my plans would be that night, and I wanted to have dinner with her.

"Yeah, that would be great ... I have a church thing, and I really need to be there with all that's been going on with Hana and her family, but after that I'd be free."

"Okay. I'll call you later, then." Diane's usefulness to me was over; I should have just blown her off. Even though I would much rather have spent time with her than the deadly redhead, the important thing was that "Agent Dawson" had something Diane didn't: answers. And that was all I should have cared about.

CHAPTER 22

"So you're sure this is the same woman?" Dip asked.

"I'm pretty good with faces of people who almost killed me." I had lost so much blood, I had been unable to act. I'd been at the mercy of others to help me. I hated that. Intensely.

"But you believe she is on your side in this?"

I continued up the stairway. "If she's simply here to kill me, she's doing it in a very odd manner."

"You think the two women you killed were associated with her?"

"That I will ask her."

"So what is the plan?"

"I don't trust her — and I don't like her — so I'll try and put things on my terms." Difficult when unarmed, but I am always up for a challenge.

"Do you know her beyond her cutting off your hand?"

"Why do you ask?"

"You said you don't like her. Maybe if you get to know her in a more social setting, you'll like her better."

"She bested me. Perhaps that means I should respect her and learn from her, but I really just want her dead so I don't have to worry about her. She injured me and rendered me helpless; I do not want that to happen again."

"You think she's on your side, though?"

"It's a cutthroat business; no one is really on my side."

"Then just remember you have taken measures should such a situation as when you lost your hand happen again."

"That I will remember." It's easier to face anything that comes at you if you have a plan for it ... even if it's not a great plan.

"I will remind you again that fleeing is always an option. It's a big universe; as wide as the syndicate's reach is, you could still find countless places where they would never find you. You could live in peace."

That made me laugh. "Explain to me how *I* could live in peace."

"That I do not know, Rico."

I reached the top of the stairway and slowly opened the door to the building's roof. The restaurant Morrigan had mentioned was in a nice little plaza downtown. It was one of the most popular places in the city, filled with musicians, artists, fancy restaurants, and quaint shops. It was not a place for privacy. Morrigan didn't trust me — which was smart, because I wanted her dead and had intentions to follow through on those wishes. As for Morrigan's intentions for me, those were hard for me to determine. Assuming the two women I'd caught following me and killed were associated with her, she wasn't just an ally in this. But her position seemed to suggest she was entrusted with more info about the job than I was. Things still didn't feel right, and I wasn't going to walk into the plaza without getting some leverage myself.

I had headed out for our meeting quite early and scoped out the area around the plaza. There was one building in particular that provided a good vantage point of the whole area. It was an office building, with lots of people coming and going. This made it easy to get into. And as I moved out onto the roof, I saw right away that my gut had called it correctly. A sniper — looked like a dark-haired woman — was perched at the edge of the roof, watching the crowd below.

I crept up behind her carefully and knelt down next to her. "What's with all the chicks with guns? Some sort of amazon assassin squad I don't know about?"

The woman whipped around with a panicked look on her face. I slammed her head into the metal roof and pulled a pistol out of her jacket. It was nice to be armed again.

She clutched her bloody face. "D-don't kill me! We're on the same side!"

I casually pointed the gun at her. "And I'm being friendly. See how I haven't killed you yet?"

She was rather pathetic-looking for a trained killer. She was crying, and it wasn't just an act to get me to drop my guard. She seemed pretty useless for anything ... except as a decoy. Realization came just as something struck me in the back, and electricity shot through my body.

*　*　*

"Rico, you were unconscious, but since your vitals were normal I did not institute emergency measures."

I didn't respond to Dip. I was lying on a soft bed on top of red satin sheets; I was quite comfortable, and part of me wanted to keep lying there and ignore my failure. I smelled something strange — maybe incense. I sat up. The room was dimly lit by candles scattered around a few small tables and hanging in sconces. A thin, pink sheet fell in a canopy around the bed. A young platinum blonde woman stood near the bed looking down at me with a mocking smile. It was at this point that I realized I had no pants.

"Where am I?"

"A brothel. A very exclusive one."

She was wearing pretty normal-looking, functional street clothes. "You don't look like a prostitute."

"I don't know how to take that." She seemed to be enjoying this.

"So why did someone take my pants? Was it you?"

"Nope. I'm guessing Morrigan did it because it was funny. 'Hey, you know that Rico guy who is the universe's deadliest hitman? Let's steal his pants.'" I think she was trying to make me angry. She wanted me to know she wasn't afraid of me. Noted.

"I guess I can see the humor in that." She did succeed in making me want to hurt her, but there was nothing to be gained from that. "I was supposed to talk to Morrigan."

"I'll take you to her."

"Good. Let's go." I got off the bed and picked up my shoes, which were conveniently next to the bed. I moved toward the door of the room, but just as I walked by the woman, I quickly stopped and turned to face her, just inches from her. "And you are?"

She flinched ever so slightly but kept up her smirk. "Vance."

"Nice to meet you, Vance. You're cute. I like you." I didn't.

"Well, don't get any ideas just because you're pantsless in a brothel."

She led me down a softly lit hallway, careful to keep me in her peripheral vision. All I could see were numerous doors. I couldn't even hear if there were other people in the brothel. Eventually we stopped. Vance knocked on the door. "He's awake and ready to see you."

"Bring him in."

This was another small room furnished with a heart-shaped bed, more candles, and a couple of nude paintings — one of a human woman and the other Corridian — quite tastefully done. Morrigan sat on the bed, working at a computer. Next to her were my neatly folded pants. She looked up at me and smiled a very friendly smile that I didn't buy at all. "I know this is an odd place to meet, but there are lots of regulations that guarantee privacy to brothels and the people going to and from them, so it works pretty well for our purposes. I'm afraid the women you see here aren't actually in the business of sex for money."

"You told us what we do here on our own time is our own business," Vance said.

Morrigan laughed. "See, Rico? That's the attitude I like to see in the people working for me. We do some very dark things, which I think necessitates that we joke around a bit and have a fun work environment."

"Morrigan! Why didn't you tell me you were using me as bait?" shouted a woman as she barged through the door. It was the sniper I'd met on the rooftop, now with a bandaged forehead. When she saw me, she stopped immediately and backed up a step. She then glanced at my lack of pants with a little confusion and took another step away from me and looked at Morrigan. "Did you see what he did to me?" She pointed at her bandage. "Are we going to stand for this?"

Morrigan let out a sigh. "I know. It's awful, Donner. Did you tell Harper and Atkins about it?"

This seemed to give the woman pause. "Well, no, they're ..."

"Oh yes! They're dead!" Morrigan shouted. "He killed them! Isn't that awful? Now they can't hear about the bump on your head!"

"Well ... um ..."

"I need to speak to Rico alone and brief him on what's going on, okay? So shoo."

"But —"

She scowled. The intensity of her gaze almost made me back off, and it wasn't even directed at me. "Shoo!"

Donner took one last, wary glance at me and sulked off.

"Need me to leave you two alone as well?" Vance asked.

Morrigan rolled her eyes and waved Vance away. "If I need someone to rescue me from the mean man, I'll scream really loud."

Vance left the room and shut the door behind her. "I hate Donner so much," Morrigan said. "She's someone's niece or something, and I got stuck with her despite the fact that she probably wouldn't even make a competent prostitute. I'm basically now middle management in Nystrom, and everyone above me thinks they can force whatever crap they want on me. Anyway, thanks for hitting her in the face for me. I'd probably get in trouble if I did it, but with you, we can write it off as another little misunderstanding."

This was a lot of nonsense for me to deal with, but I thought I was doing pretty well so far. Now was the time to start unraveling the situation piece by piece. "You stole my pants."

She glanced at the pants folded up next to her. "Yes, to prove a point. I knew there would be some trust issues going into this job, considering our history."

"You knew I'd check the rooftops." She'd given me what I was expecting in order to make me drop my guard. A good strategy, and she had me dead to rights because of it. It was a little bit scary, and I wasn't going to underestimate her again, despite how asinine all of this seemed.

"You're a big, scary guy, and I just wanted to ensure there was no further unnecessary violence. And now I've had you at my mercy — pantsless even — and I did nothing to harm you." She stood up and handed me my pants. "So obviously you can trust me."

I put my pants back on and then my shoes. "So should I just start asking questions, or are you going to explain what's going on?"

She smiled. She got the eyes right with her smiles, but something still seemed fake about them. "Sure, let's get down to it. Yes, I've always been working with the Nystrom syndicate. Our unfortunate run-in all those years ago was just the right hand not knowing what the left was doing." She pointed to my right hand and chuckled. "No pun intended. Anyway, this happens with big organizations. I'm in charge of the operation here, though, and I'll try to keep it orderly."

I fixed my clothes. They'd been ruffled a bit from all the unconsciousness and being dragged to the brothel. "If those two women I killed the other day were with you, then you failed at that."

Her smiled faded. "Yes, I guess I did. I trained them myself, and they were good people — as good as trained killers can be. Plus, good female assassins are not easy to come by. They're sort of my specialty. I train them for kills that are, let's say, more subtle than you're probably used to. It's hard to find women worth training, though — and then I get people like Donner forced on me. Anyway, I'm rambling. It was my fault with Harper and Atkins, and I'm trying not to blame you. It's a little hard, because ... well, why don't I just put this out there: I didn't want you on this. I had this whole operation planned out myself, using just my people — and I have those plans still in place if for some reason you don't work out — but orders came from the executives on exactly how they wanted this to go down, and those specific details necessitated including you."

"So is that why you tried to get me blown up by terrorists?" I tried to casually get a look at her. She had a nice body — had probably paid good money for it — but my interest was more in whether she had a gun on her, and where. If this went poorly, turning her own gun on her was my best bet, as experience said I was no match for her physically.

She giggled. At times, she seemed too young to be a convincing federal agent, but the eyes — alert, taking in my every move ... anticipating .... She was quite experienced at combat and necessarily older than she looked. "Sorry to leave you in the dark, but the plans have worked out much better that way."

"You planned for me to pretend to be a police officer and help stop the terrorists?"

"Yes."

"A heads-up would have been nice."

"It's much more convincing that you were surprised by a terrorist attack if you were actually surprised. If you knew we were manipulating the Calabrai into attacking, your behavior would have been different."

"And you knew my reaction to being caught in an attack would be to pretend to be a police officer?"

"This probably doesn't come up too often, since you never have the same target twice, but you're sort of predictable. That's how I got you today. It's nothing for you to be concerned about, though, unless people know you're coming."

Unless I was trying to kill *her*, I believed she meant. Helpful criticism noted.

"I kept an eye on you, and I was ready to help you out when you needed it, but you and that Detective Thompson did a pretty good job hunting down the Calabrai on your own. I guess we had been tailing you harmlessly for so long that my people got a little cocky."

If she'd had others following me before that I hadn't noticed, that felt like another failure. "And why would you have people tail me?"

"You understand the interests of all the syndicates here, correct? Don't think they haven't noticed you. I've needed my people to run interference at times to keep suspicion off of you."

"Again, a heads-up would have been nice."

"Well, here you go now," she said with a beatific smile.

"Whatever our endgame is, this sounds like an idiotic plan so far."

She moved closer to me. I wasn't sure if she was trying to intimidate me, but she was doing it. I'm pretty sure I didn't show it. "You're a very skilled person — probably the most skilled for the limited area of wetwork the syndicate sometimes needs done," she said in a calm, measured manner. "But you're just a blunt instrument, and blunt instruments don't get involved in the planning. So you're going to do what I need you to do, and I don't care what your opinion is."

It was true I was a blunt instrument, but I never quite got why those who planned the actions always felt so superior to those of us who actually carried them out. "So I don't get to fill out an evaluation form for you after this is over?"

She smiled slightly. "You're cute. I read the files on you, and I wouldn't have guessed you have a sense of humor."

Files?

"I know your thing. A cold detachment from your actions, but I can sense a joy in your work. So — out of curiosity — did you enjoy killing my two people the other day? Was that entertaining for you?"

She had quickly gone from intimidating me to getting on my nerves. "Does that have anything to do with anything?"

She continued to hover right next to me, though she kept her expression neutral. "You don't want to answer the question?"

No, this wasn't the sort of thing I just chatted about with anyone. "I didn't enjoy it. It was messy."

"Really?" She looked quite fascinated. "Isn't killing always messy?"

"I like the hunting, the outsmarting, the outshooting — that's fun. That's skill. Killing is always a bit messy; never really liked it. With your girls, I was surprised, which pretty much made just a big, ugly struggle."

"Not to get all feminist on you, but don't call them 'girls.'"

She was successfully damaging my patience. "Corpses."

She chuckled. "There's that wit again. I think you look at killing all wrong, though." Her hand was on my neck before I could react. I pulled at it, but her arm felt like a steel bar. She definitely had enhancements, and I don't just mean to her chest (though that, too, probably). "You see, it's the inelegance of death that makes it beautiful." Her face didn't look girlish at all anymore; it was the direct, emotionless face most animals get when preparing for a kill. "It's brutal and dirty, and that in itself is something to enjoy. I love to kill someone slowly — to watch as a person finally reaches the realization that *this is it*. This is the end. It's a tender moment to share with someone." She released my neck and took a step back. "That's a little sick, isn't it?"

I massaged my throat; she had squeezed hard enough for discomfort but not damage. She was quicker and stronger than me. I didn't know why she thought it was so important to demonstrate that to me. "A normal human isn't supposed to be able to dispassionately kill other humans or anything else he or she has anthropomorphized."

She laughed. "That's cute, you've thought about things like that. This is fun. I'm glad after everything we're finally getting to talk like this. Anyway, I don't get to kill much anymore. I'm management now, so it's best to delegate that sort of thing. Still, I make sure to enjoy it when the opportunity arises. Don't you think it's important to get some level of enjoyment out of your work?"

I was pretty sure she was now trying to irritate me. "Ma'am, can we —"

"If you're going to use something formal, I prefer 'Mistress.'"

"Crazy bitch, can we just get to the point? What am I doing on this planet?"

She scowled melodramatically. "Oh, I'm sorry. I didn't mean to waste your time. I didn't realize you had all these important things to do. I thought since we had to work together, we could just chat a little and get to know each other. Is that so horrible?"

"It's looking that way."

She walked close to me, pressing against me, and whispered in my ear. "Rico, I'm in charge, and we do what I want. If I want to chat your ear off, we do that. I can certainly do much more unpleasant things to you ... or much nicer things." She took a step back and giggled. "I'm just kidding about that last part. I wouldn't have sexual relations with someone I'm working with. That would be wildly unprofessional. Plus, too much risk that I'd injure you before the job was done."

"Are we through the chatting portion yet?"

"You seem to have a problem with me. Is it that you've never worked for a woman before? Are you some sort of misogynist?"

"I'm becoming one."

She reached over and gently fixed my tie. "I'm trying to help you, Rico. I'm sorry you don't like my style, but you're a little too focused. Sometimes it's these other details outside the job that are the important ones. Do you understand?"

I didn't know if that was bluster or if she was actually trying to tell me something. "Not ... really."

She patted me on the cheek. "And that's why — despite your great skill — I'm the one in charge. You want to talk business now?"

"Very much so."

"Well, I just have to say, good job hunting down those terrorists. You were almost too good, though, and were about to leave yourself out of the credit with that anonymous tip stunt. That's why we got that one group to attack the school while you were nearby."

"And you don't think that's a little too coincidental?"

"It would be if they had attacked the park where you were. Nearby just seems like bad luck. And that incident, added to the other terrorists you brought down, means you're now an undeniable hero. Which puts you where we need you."

"To do what?"

She shrugged. "You don't actually need to know yet."

I tried a friendly smile. "But I think it would be very nice if you told me."

She laughed. "Okay. You're going to kill President Gredler."

A heavily guarded politician — now that was a worthy challenge. "That does sort of sound like something I would need to know, considering that I'm seeing him tomorrow."

"You're not killing him tomorrow, silly. We don't care enough about Senator Gredler to kill him, but *President* Gredler is a different story. Tomorrow, you and your detective chick are going to meet Gredler, and *be gracious* — nicer than you've been to me. Then he'll have you two as his honored guests at the Galactic Alliance conference. There, after they vote to make him President — head of the entire Alliance in its fancy new power structure — you will stand up from your seat in the front row, pull out the guns my people will supply you with, and just totally shoot the crap out of Gredler."

It occurred to me that Diane would most likely be sitting next to me when I did this, which was a really pointless thing to focus on. "The place will be swarming with armed security."

Her face brightened up. "Exactly! It's a suicide mission. But that's what the executives want: They want the head of the brand new Galactic Alliance killed in very public fashion. That's why we let it leak that we're planning to kill him — we want everyone's eyes on this. But there is only one person Nystrom knows who could pull that off — or agree to try to pull off such a stunt. And I'm sure as hell not talking about me."

I thought about it, visualizing. I'd be in the middle of a large auditorium containing the most important politicians in the Alliance and all their personal security, plus the additional security added for the conference — beefed up already because of terrorist activity.

But as soon as I started shooting, there would be chaos. And chaos is cover. It was possible. "I assume you'll be of help on the escape plan."

She smiled. "Anyone else would have balked at this — and rightfully so. But they knew you'd be all over it. Yes, you get out of the auditorium, and I'll be able to cause some distractions to get you out of the building — I have a number of my people in the capitol's security. We'll also be able to get your ship past air security. I'll blow my cover getting you out, but it won't matter then." She was quiet for a moment. "I'll have to figure out what to do with Verg during all of this; he's a nice guy, so I was hoping not to kill him. He's not part of all this, by the way, so don't go chatting him up about killing Gredler, because that would probably upset him."

If I were to trust Morrigan's plan, it looked like it was possible to survive this job. "So this is why I'm here. To make an intergalactic incident?"

She sat down, her expression serious. "Nystrom already did that on Zaldia." She paused, no longer looking at me. "They have these pictures going around of dead people — dead kids, even. I know that probably means nothing to you, but that's the sort of thing that horrifies people and gets them screaming for blood — our blood. Can't really blame them; I don't even know what the hell we need that planet for. We actually had some people betray us over this — not over money, but their consciences. And we don't work with people who have very developed consciences — you being the uber-example." She paused again. "Maybe you're right about me being messed up in the head, with how I like killing people. I might need to get out of this business soon — for my mental health." She looked at me. "But there I go talking about me again. So to answer your question, your role is to show the Alliance that we don't fear them."

"And that will benefit us?"

Now she smiled again. "We've hidden in the shadows for so long, most people don't even think of us. It's time for a brief reminder that we exist and have nothing to fear from their little government. We need to make ourselves known. We're the only syndicate powerful enough to pull this off, to show them that the only way to have a really effective government is to follow us."

This was a big change in the syndicate's policy. So much so that it made me a little nervous. "Nystrom thinks common people will actually accept this?"

"After we kill Gredler, we have our people in place within the Alliance government to bully it into our control. I'm sure the other syndicates will lash out to cause fear among the common folk, but we'll make it clear that rallying behind us will be the quickest path back to normality. And knowing human nature, they'll come to love and accept the new, more powerful rule and realize that it's their best option for survival and maintaining the way of life they're used to. Pretty nice, huh? You get to be a part of the brave, new future."

If Nystrom wanted to be the out-in-front rulers of civilization, it did make me wonder what that meant for me. If they wanted fear, I was their man. If they wanted people to respect them as the best hope for the future ... well, I'm not the sort of guy you keep around if you're pretending not to be the villain. Then again, the long-term future was something I never liked to worry about. "I just want to survive the hit on Gredler, that's all."

"Nothing to worry about there. Everything to do with the conference is in our hands. All you need to do is shoot and run, and we'll handle the rest. Anyway, we're done here for now. Have fun with your prey tomorrow, and we'll get you any other details you need soon after that. I'll have Vance show you out. Donner would probably screw that up and get you stuck in a closet. Did I mention I hate her?"

I didn't like my escape plan being completely in someone else's hands — particularly this woman's hands — but considering the scope of this hit, I didn't appear to have another option. Though I would look for one. "Alright. In the meantime, can you hook me up with some guns? I'm all out."

"No reason to, Rico. That could just draw more attention to you. Don't worry. We're watching your back. You can trust me."

"You already got two of your people killed here, so I'm not sure how wise that is."

She pressed against me again, holding her cheek against mine. "But they weren't as important as you." She stepped away from me, a devious smile on her face. "We really are going to have to tussle sometime."

I wasn't sure in which way she meant, but either way was good with me.

CHAPTER 23

"As usual, my programming obligates me to warn you that the job you have been assigned is illegal according to this planet's laws."

I chuckled as I strolled toward my hotel. "And not just in the usual 'killing is illegal' way — people are actually going to care about this one. Here's some data for you, Dip: When polled, people tend to say they dislike politicians, but they get really, really angry when you kill them."

I had left the "brothel" without further incident. It was indeed a rather fancy one, on the 31st floor of a downtown building — basically a whole Nystrom center of operations nearly out in plain sight. Still, all I saw of Morrigan's operation were her and two of her lackeys. Despite the fact that we were working together, she seemed to be keeping her cards close to the chest. "How are my escape plans coming along, Dip?"

"It would not seem they are relevant anymore now that Agent Dawson will be providing the details."

"I'd rather have backup plans."

"Do you not trust Dawson?"

I carefully noted all of the people I passed by on the street. Morrigan had said that her people would keep tabs on me and watch my back, so perhaps even now someone was following me. I didn't like that. "I have to trust her somewhat as part of the job, but I'd rather not put my life entirely in her hands. I don't trust her to keep my interests in mind ... plus she doesn't seem mentally balanced."

"And you are mentally balanced?"

"I am balanced ... I'm just balanced someplace different from most people."

"By the way, Rico, I am still receiving chatter from the Calabrai on the channels I'm following. They're now planning a big strike after the conference when security is reduced."

"Well, I hope they have good luck with that."

"Really?"

"No. I don't take sides. Just happy to hear they won't be in my way again anytime soon. They were boring to kill." I thought I saw a Corridian glance at me. All of Morrigan's people I'd met so far were human females, but I guessed she had quite a variety of people — human and other — at her disposal for this operation.

I reached my hotel and entered the lobby, and as I entered a human female saw me, and I tensed. She was backed by a human male and ... two human children. And I recognized her.

She smiled broadly and rushed over to me. "Rico, it's me, Hana. We met yesterday."

Morrigan had told me her people would keep threats away from me, and they were already failing. "Hi. How are you doing?" I hated the question as soon as it came out of my mouth.

"We're doing well, thank you so much. This is my husband, Carl, and my two children, Justin and Tammy. Diane said you were staying here, and we just wanted to properly thank you for what you did the other day."

Carl smiled at me and shook my hand. "God bless you. We're so glad you were there with Diane to save those children. You can't imagine how panicked I was when I heard the Calabrai had taken hostages in my children's school."

Not only could I not imagine panicking over the fate of children, even caring in the slightest was unfathomable for me. Still, I wasn't sure what they were thanking me for; I was pretty sure their kids had already gotten out of the school by the time I'd gotten there. I started thinking of the quickest way to end this conversation without it being a complete social failure — like knocking Hana down and walking away, which was the first thought that came to mind.

"Did you shoot people?" the boy asked.

"That's not an appropriate question," Hana said, keeping the conversation from going in a direction that might actually interest me. "Anyway, Rico, we're so grateful you're here, and if there is anything you need, please let us know. It's my understanding that you're here alone on ... business?"

This job had really become a circus now that I was getting grilled by random civilians. "No, not really business. I'm sort of on a sojourn."

"You're eventually going back to Rikar?"

"I ... don't know." Why did I answer that way?

I could see Hana's focus intensify as she sensed an opening for a kill. "Well, I don't know what Rikar is like, but this is a very nice planet. I assume you've impressed the police here enough that they'd easily give you a job."

"Perhaps." I wasn't sure of that. From my experience, competence made the police here angry.

"Anyway, I don't know what your plans are, but we're on our way to church, and the rest of our church would love to meet you and thank you for all you've done."

That was one of the most hellish proposals I'd ever heard, and I've had crime lords threaten to do all manner of nasty things to me. I actually found religion to be an odd, interesting concept, but it was something I'd prefer to study from a distance. To actually be among people who would all be smiling and talking to me ... I did not think I was strong enough for that.

"Diane will be there," Hana added. "You two seem to make a good —"

"Honey," her husband gently chided.

"I was going to say 'team.' They are a good team. They pretty much single-handedly beat terrorism on this planet."

A Corridian in the lobby looked at me briefly. He may have been the same one I had seen on the street; it was hard to tell. I knew I shouldn't have been paranoid, as Morrigan had told me her people would be around, but being followed really unsettled me. And were they reporting back everything I was doing to Morrigan? What did she expect me to do while I was waiting for my meeting with Gredler?

Well, I did know one thing she wouldn't expect.

* * *

"You're here for the Bible study?" Diane asked, obviously surprised to see me.

"Is that what this is? Hana didn't say."

"Well, we can just meet up after this is over, if you want to leave."

"Hey, I'm traveling the universe to try new things." The church building was rather small and unspectacular-looking; that probably meant a smaller, more intimate group. I was already beginning to regret my decision to come, and the silly notion popped into my head that I was provoking a higher power to pay attention to me, which would not end well. I leaned in close to Diane. "Plus I think Hana is hoping we'll become a couple."

She blushed. I've seen her kill people with a cold dispassion, which made me find her emotional vulnerabilities fascinating.

We headed inside, and I did my best to keep up a brave face. Talking to Diane helped my confidence — I now felt so comfortable around her — but that came crashing down quite quickly in the face of my indomitable odds. There were just so many smiling faces and people who wanted to chat. It was awful. I mean, it was the absolute worst experience I'd had since having my hand ripped off. I had been surrounded by hostiles many times, and never even broke a sweat. But surrounded by friendly people where shooting my way out was not an option — that was not something I was equipped for.

It seemed so silly when I looked at it rationally. I've done just fine so many times with people one-on-one. It's no different with multiple people. Yet, I soon felt so trapped, and a little voice in my head kept telling me I was going to trip up at any second, completely forget myself, and reveal to them all the psychopath that I am. My hands kept moving to feel the guns in the shoulder holsters I wasn't wearing. I don't know what would have happened if I'd had them on me.

And then there was my new greatest nemesis, Hana, egging it all on. Telling people to come talk to me. Trying to destroy me. A couple of times I felt almost ready to attack her, quickly noting objects in the room I could use as weapons. I was hanging by a thread. And why had I done this to myself? To spite Morrigan for having people follow me? Something was wrong with me. I wasn't making good decisions.

Smile slightly. Make eye contact. Nod. Say, "Nice to meet you." I kept repeating these rules in my head, trying to concentrate on them and let the panic pass. I didn't even need to hear what most people were saying. I just had to appear normal ... if somewhat reticent. And as hard as it was, I needed to stand my ground. It was one of my toughest battles, but every time I felt I was about to slip off the edge, I'd look at Diane, and she'd give me a reassuring smile that seemed to mean she understood. And it calmed me a little. And then I began to realize why she understood.

I was too stressed to pay much attention to her, but the group here (predominantly human with only a couple exceptions) all seemed to know Diane well. She smiled and chatted along with them, and I assume to most of them she looked like she was one of them. But I could see through it. It was all an act. She was like me, uncomfortable and separate from the others, but the difference I gathered was that she acted this way because it's what she wanted to be. Yet she wasn't the person she pretended to be ... and perhaps didn't even know how to get there.

I thought religion was just a choice regular people could make — you just chose to believe. But she did choose, yet it seemed like something held her back. Doubt, maybe? I didn't know, but for some reason I wanted to know. And now the panic faded away, as I was just fascinated by her.

We soon got down to the studying (this was apparently some kind of informal class), and it became much more bearable. No one was talking directly to me anymore, and the tone was more serious. They were focusing on a section of the Bible that dealt with the followers of Jesus after His death. From my understanding of the Roman Empire — a powerful civilization before humans had even mastered electricity — Christianity was part of the reason it fell, which is a good lesson in why you have to quickly crush influential new movements. The Romans probably assumed it was one of those things that would fade away soon after the leader died, but that was not the case, and here we are thousands of years later, still dealing with it.

When the study was over, it looked like people were ready to talk to me again, and I was really at my wit's end on socialization. Perhaps sensing this, Diane told them we had a busy day tomorrow and had to get going. Thus the church members were spared further risk of my snapping and trying to bludgeon them all to death. Maybe God was looking out for them.

"You're not a very social person, are you?" my rescuer asked when we were by ourselves.

"People in general annoy me."

"But you have an occupation in which it's your job to help them?"

I smiled. "It's either that or kill them." Guess which option I really prefer.

"I'm not the most social person either, but I'm trying to get over myself."

"Good luck with that. I'm sure you're a hard person to get over." What were my intentions with Diane? I had to keep asking myself that. I wanted to be around her, but I didn't seem to have any purpose for it in mind. "So ... I guess we should have dinner together, or we'll disappoint Hana."

She smiled and blushed slightly. "Yeah, we wouldn't want to disappoint her. But being so antisocial, are you certain my company won't annoy you?"

"No fun being antisocial alone." Stupid joke, but I was feeling stupid. Still, I had to come to terms with the fact that I wanted to spend time with Diane. Not for any ulterior motive or actual purpose of any kind, I just wanted to be around her. And I was happy with that.

Like I said, I had been making stupid decisions.

CHAPTER 24

I let her pick the restaurant. I'm not sure what you'd call this type of food, but it was a fusion of some Earth cuisine and a human-compatible Corridian cuisine. I didn't know much about it, but it looked like the dishes had lots of cheese and weren't particularly healthy.

As we sat down, I saw her studying me again, but not in the suspicious way like after we first met. I was gaining her trust. It was a silly, fragile thing to possess. In only a couple of days, I would gun down Gredler in front of her, and this masquerade would be over. She'd know what I was, and like any normal person, she would be horrified by me. So it made this dinner with her rather pointless in the long run. But I guess I didn't care anymore.

"You seem like you're searching for something."

"I do?" My life had always been rather straightforward. I'd get a mission, I'd go do it. I didn't scamper around trying to meet some primitive urge for "fulfillment" like everyone else.

"Well, you say you're traveling the universe. Why, if you're not looking for something?"

"Just to see what's out there. I wouldn't say there are particular answers I'm looking for."

"So you're just bored?"

It felt like I was being interrogated again, but not out of distrust. She just seemed to want to know who I was. And that was the last thing I wanted her to know. "Boredom is as good a motivator as anything. We need something to hold onto to make life interesting." I killed people because it was challenging and gave me something to do. I accepted that there was no higher meaning to it. That's what always made me more focused than anyone else.

Her eyes were looking through me again. Now it was getting a little uncomfortable. "If I may be forward, it seems like you're keeping something from me — something important."

Someone at the table next to us got up. It seemed to be a regular patron, but I knew Morrigan probably had eyes on me. I didn't know what she'd think of this — or if she'd even care — but I suddenly had the odd thought that I could be putting Diane in danger. Odd, because why was that something my mind would concern itself with? "I guess I'm just a man of mystery. Have you told me everything there is to know about yourself?"

She leaned back and grinned. "No. Let's just say I'm a prodigal daughter — if you're familiar with the concept — trying to better herself. But I guess you don't believe in God?"

I shrugged. "I just don't see the evidence of an almighty power. When looked at objectively, the universe is just random and purposeless. Even as society advances, it never really goes anywhere. Things get moved around, but nothing ever gets accomplished to any real end."

"You sound like Ecclesiastes."

I raised an eyebrow.

"It's a book in the Old Testament."

"So what about you? What brought you to religion?" I asked.

She thought briefly. "Fear of hell."

I smirked. "I always just saw that as some childish threat to try to get bad people to be good." Didn't work, by the way.

She didn't laugh. "Some people use it that way. Think they can scare people with the possibility of fire and brimstone, but most people don't take that seriously anymore — to them, that's just something from a cartoon. I already knew of hell before I found religion, I just didn't have a name for it. But it wasn't fire. It was a dark, cold abyss. No love. No hope. A place of utter despair I'd be trapped in forever — and that's where I saw myself headed."

Seemed almost like paranoia to me. "That's where God would cast you?"

"There is no casting. We have our free will — we can choose who we want to be. And I was choosing to go there — I could see how horrible it was, yet I kept moving toward it, because I was convinced there was no other choice." She paused for a moment and then smiled. "What a nice, light dinner topic, huh?"

"Why waste time sharing unimportant thoughts?"

"Because sometimes every mind needs a rest." She took a drink of water and then changed the subject. "Well, we know each other's deep philosophical beliefs, but I still feel there is so little I know about you. Like what do you like to do for fun?"

That might have stumped me if I hadn't had to answer that same question recently during my short layover on Ryle. "I like nature — hiking and such. It's also nice to get away from it all. I like learning about animals; so many are known now, and they all have something interesting about them." I hoped that was good enough to not sound too weird. "So what about you?"

"Well ..." She was silent a couple seconds. I guess she hadn't thought of an answer to that question recently. "Wow ... I guess I'm a pretty boring person. In my spare time, I have some projects ... but they're kind of work-related."

"Like what?"

"Oh ... I don't want to get into it. But ..." She thought for another minute. "I play some videogames; I like puzzle ones. I like puzzles."

"Okay, you've convinced me. You're very boring." But she wasn't. She was the most fascinating person I'd ever met. I just wished I could figure out why.

She laughed. "I guess so. If it weren't for my church friends, I'd be pretty much a loner."

"It's hard to imagine a smart, attractive woman like you being alone."

She was a bit taken aback. "Well ... thank you."

I hadn't meant it as a compliment, just an honest observation. It actually was quite odd that she wasn't married, or didn't at least have a boyfriend. "Really, though, you don't date much?"

"No ... I ... It's complicated. There are things I have to work out with myself first."

"Before you can date?"

"I guess."

"So what's this, then?"

She took another long look at me. "I don't know, Rico. Aren't you eventually leaving to see the universe? Maybe going back to Rikar? I mean, is there any chance you're staying here?"

Me tied to a single planet? That was unimaginable. "No, I guess not." It was an honest answer; I didn't know why I went with it.

"Well, then I guess this is a friendly dinner between two officers of the law." She smiled, but she seemed deflated now. I guess she'd had some fantasy that we would end up together, and now that was over. I had gotten women to be infatuated with me before — the mysterious loner — so that I could get them into bed. But this was different. Somehow, I cared a little.

"You could come with me." I had no idea where those words came from. Now I was the one holding on to a fantasy. And yet I continued. "You even said you were getting tired of your job. Maybe it's time for a change."

She looked down, away from me. "I can't. I spent too much time already going around the universe in a vain search for who-knows-what. I finally learned that the things that are important in life aren't out there. I'm grounded here, though; I live with purpose. I have my friends ... my church ... to help remind me what matters. I can't give that up — not for anything."

I nodded. And I even understood. Her religion gave her purpose, and there's nothing more crucial than that. I had my own purpose — to kill for Nystrom — and the reason I was so focused was that I clung to that purpose. And that was just part of survival for me — when you choose a course of action, you don't question it. It's indecision needling at you that causes disaster. And in life, I had made my choice: I was a hitman. That was my foundation, and the rest of life was so simple because I had that.

But now a little voice in my head said, But what if you weren't a killer anymore?

Nystrom was changing. Who knew what purpose they'd have for me in the future? And even if things went on as normal for me, was that really the best life I could have? Just the quick thrill of combat and the gaps of preparation in between? Could I be something different?

But then another voice said, No matter what you are, you can never be with her.

And that was the crux of this little fantasy. I was a remorseless killer whose actions have even horrified other killers. I had no ability to empathize. I could comprehend the feelings and motivations of other people, but I could never share in them. I had long ago accepted this fact, and I was content to be alone. But now ...

The thought was interrupted by our waiter bringing our food. I can't remember what it was — some meat covered in melted cheese. "This looks good," I said, because that's the sort of thing normal people say when they get food at a restaurant. They do it without thinking. Me, I have to concentrate. Did I really think I could be with another person? Could I really keep up the complicated act of being normal without eventually snapping?

"Is something the matter?" Diane asked. She looked concerned. My guess was that look came natural to her and wasn't something she had to fake.

"It's just ... um ..." I didn't know what I was going to tell her, but apparently my normal act was breaking down.

She reached over and touched my hand. "Rico, if I can help, just tell me."

Her eyes showed genuine concern for the man she thought I was. And for a moment, I guess I wanted to be that man. I wanted to be the hero she thought I was, not the brutal hitman whose true identity would one day devastate her. It was a ridiculous fantasy, yet it wouldn't go away. "I need to ..." My words were lost in her bright blue eyes. Her lip quivered slightly, and my next action was clear. The fantasy won.

I leaned toward her and kissed her, and she kissed me back. The whole time, my rational mind was shouting at my idiocy, but passion overpowered logic for a few seconds.

Eventually the kissed ended, and we were just back to staring at each other. I had no plan for how to proceed from there, and she seemed just as confused as me. I felt I should speak, but I had nothing to say.

And she suddenly stood up. "Um ... I have to ... I'll be back in one minute." And she hurried off toward the restroom.

I did not know what to make of that.

Now I was alone with my cheese-covered dish, and my rational mind found its voice again. I had to face facts: I was in love with Diane. At least that seemed to be the word for it — an attraction to her was overtaking me and causing me to act irrationally — and that was love as far as I understood it. Love was just another force trying to make me lose control — to make me question myself. To get me wanting things I cannot have. To break down my neat little life and get me killed.

And the purely rational side of me spoke loudly and clearly on what I would have to do to solve this matter. *You're going to have to kill her.* And the thought shocked me. I couldn't deny its logic, I just didn't *want* to kill her. And that was the problem. Her mere existence was causing me to act irrationally and question matters long settled. But if I killed her, that would be it. I would stop questioning myself, because the matter would be resolved permanently. Simple. Logical. Indisputable.

So my course of action was determined. That should have been a burden off my shoulders, but I stared down at my dish and realized I had no appetite.

"We have an emergency." Dip used his intense voice. He rarely used it. His algorithm was set to apply it only when there was a likelihood of immediate harm to me.

"What is it?" I should have been worried, but at the moment it was nice to have a distraction.

"I'm suddenly getting word on police channels that they have identified the Nystrom assassin. They are on their way to your location to apprehend you."

"What? Morrigan should have been on that!" I looked around again for anyone who could be one of Morrigan's people. Would they be of any help?

I realized why Diane may have gotten up and left suddenly. She seemed to stay alert to what was going on with law enforcement, and maybe word had reached her. Maybe she had even called in and told them where I was. It was pointless to focus on that now, but it illustrated how silly my little fantasy with her had been. What was more relevant was that I was unarmed and sitting out in the open. I had to run; there didn't seem to be any other option. And then I'd just have to hope that Morrigan could help get me out of the city later. I so hated having to rely on others.

As soon as I stood up, though, I saw Agent Verg coming through the restaurant, followed by Morrigan. It was too late, so I just stood still and hoped Morrigan had a plan.

"Where's Detective Thompson?" Verg demanded, his odd hum of a voice now sounding more like a low growl.

No guns drawn. No reason to be agitated. "She went to the bathroom."

Now they drew their guns. And charged right by me. I let myself be confused briefly and then followed.

They stopped outside the restroom. "I'm not familiar with ..." Verg started to say, and then Morrigan charged into the women's restroom.

"What's going on?" I asked as I stood outside with Verg.

He held up a picture of a young woman with black hair. "This is a known Nystrom assassin named Melanie Fincher." It took me a second, but I recognized the face. It was Diane.

Morrigan came out of the bathroom. "The window in there is broken. She must have gotten word we were coming for her and escaped. Alert all local police — let's find her quick."

And I thought love had confused me.

CHAPTER 25

I looked at a photo of Officer Diane Thompson from before she had transferred to Nar Valdum from the planet Andalu. She was a pretty, young, blonde woman, bright-eyed and ready to take on the world. And she wasn't the woman I had been working with for the past few days.

"I'm not good at telling humans apart." Agent Verg paced the office he and Morrigan had commandeered at the police station, seeming to be simultaneously talking to me and deep in thought. "Still, a computer verified that this is a different person from the woman who has been a part of this police force for the past ten years."

I kept looking at Morrigan, but she didn't react to me. I figured I wouldn't get a real explanation until I was able to talk to her without Verg in the room. "This is a bit insane," I said. My guess would have been that Morrigan had faked all the evidence ... except for the fact that Diane did run.

She had hinted at having a dark past. I'd figured drug use or some other crap I wouldn't have cared about.

"We assume she killed the real Diane Thompson and took her place," Morrigan explained. "Perhaps she's been working with the Nystrom syndicate from inside the police force her whole time on this planet." That was utter nonsense. I was sure Nystrom already had much higher placed people within the police force and wouldn't need a random detective.

"We haven't caught her yet, but she shouldn't get far," Verg said. "It will be hard to get out of the city undetected with the security we have in place. Hopefully we've at least defused much of the assassination threat against Senator Gredler."

"I have trouble believing she was going to kill Gredler," I said. "She didn't even want to go meet him. I met her friends here at a local church — she doesn't seem like a sleeper assassin. Something is weird about all this."

Now Morrigan reacted to me, giving me a look that presumably meant "Shut up!" I hoped that would prompt her to explain things to me soon.

Verg bobbed his head. Maybe that was the equivalent of a nod for his species. "It is a little odd, but the evidence is indisputable. Anyway, I am just very sorry you got caught up in all of this. But Gredler still wants to meet with you tomorrow morning."

"And that's not going to be awkward when the woman I've been working with is apparently his intended assassin?" Honest question. I'm still not very good at reading social situations.

"Word has already spread about the heroes who stopped the terrorists," Morrigan said. "The police department is planning to remove references to Thompson and focus on you as the officer from another planet working with the local police force."

"I'm getting uncomfortable with being used as some sort of political pawn."

Morrigan gave me another look. "Then I should remind you that you've broken numerous weapons laws on this planet, and they'd just like you to perform this gesture as thanks for their forgiveness on that."

"If you really don't want to be a part of this anymore, we can pass word on to Gredler, though," Verg said. "I know this has to have been quite a strange visit to this planet for you."

Morrigan stared at me intensely as I pretended to mull things over for a moment. "No, I guess I'll go along for the sake of cooperation."

"Good. Again, we apologize for all this," Verg said. "It's a shame someone like Fincher could hide in plain sight like this for so long. I need to meet with Gredler's people now."

"I'll see Rico out," Morrigan said. When Verg left the room, she sat down next to me with a huge smile. "Come on. You have to admit this is hilarious."

"Just tell me what's happening here," I said in a very measured but forceful tone. "I do not like surprises like this."

Morrigan rolled her eyes. "You're such a baby. Anyway, what happened was that I decided to do some actual investigative work. I know — what a novelty. I noticed something was a little fishy about Thompson's background. So, on a lark, I ran her information against the much better organized databases Nystrom has. And guess what popped up?"

We sat there staring silently at one another for a few seconds until I realized she actually wanted me to guess. "You found out that her real name was Melanie Fincher and that she had been an assassin for the syndicate."

"Exactly. She was part of a squad on her last hit with Nystrom, and the entire unit disappeared — though there was evidence that something violent had happened. We weren't really sure if she was alive or dead ... until now, that is. My best guess is that she went berserk, killed the other Nystrom assassins, and went into hiding. When I found her real background, it was too perfect not to use, so I carefully placed some data around to make sure Verg would find this. Now all the focus will be on her, leaving you free and clear of suspicion." Morrigan's smile faded. "But you know, people like her are the reason female assassins like me and the women I train don't get the respect we deserve. She just perpetuated the myth that we can't be trusted because our girl hormones will make us go crazy and start killing everyone."

I probably would have been annoyed by Morrigan's badinage again if I weren't more preoccupied with going over my memories of Diane to see how I'd missed the signs that she was a syndicate assassin. That was a big failure on my part.

"Anyway, I guess Fincher was here trying to turn her life around or some nonsense like that. But hiding out on the police force — she has some brass ones. I almost admire her. But my orders are to find her and kill her and be real mean about it when I do. You don't turn on us and not expect to eventually regret it as the worst mistake of your entire life, so we're going to have a field day with her. And you'll be free to join in if you want. Out of curiosity, ever rape someone before?"

She was trying to get a reaction out of me. I wasn't going to play her game. "No, have you?"

She laughed. "See, there's that quick wit of yours. You can be fun to work with if you try."

I stood up. "No more surprises like this."

She smirked. "Calm down. Everything is under control. I swear you're the girliest person I've ever worked with."

I turned and quietly left the room. For a moment I thought about the pain and misery Morrigan would inflict on Diane when she caught her. What an odd, irrelevant thing to think about. I had my job to focus on.

CHAPTER 26

It was almost refreshing to talk to a politician — that meant I wasn't the only one in the room pretending not to be a sociopath.

The short talk I had with Senator Gredler was rather pointless tripe, but the trip itself was actually a bit illuminating. I was flown out of Nar Valdum City to a pristine forest area with nearly no developments in sight. Gredler's very private villa was in a cleared meadow in the middle of the forest.

He had obviously taken the threat of assassination to heart, and the place was swarming with security. They looked like official government-assigned security, but then I caught a glimpse of the handle of one of their firearms. By the distinctive markings I could tell it was an FR-76 Blaster, a pretty nice gun made on the Randatti-owned Sindel 7 — and you would pretty much never see the gun in the hands of anyone other than a Randatti thug (or someone who had killed one). So basically Gredler's home was filled with Randatti killers who were just barely incognito — that's how important the situation was to them. All the big powers were taking a lot of risks here to ensure their places in the new power structure — which meant things hung precariously close to an open war between the syndicates.

But that wasn't all I noticed. When I went into Gredler's office to meet him (which was an extremely perfunctory bit of his thanking me and my acting modest — I wasn't paying much attention, but I could probably recite everything said nearly verbatim), he was at his computer, and I saw enough of the screen to note that he was looking at the conference hall's security plans. He was apparently worried enough about the assassination threat to take matters into his own hands. But it was all for nothing, because I noticed something about his Corridian female aide. I caught her eye for a brief moment, and she was ever-so-slightly taken aback. She knew exactly who I was and what I was capable of. But since she stayed put and tried to behave normally, I knew she was one of Morrigan's people. Despite all the precautions Randatti was taking, Nystrom had someone on Gredler who could kill him at any time. It made me feel a bit pointless, since I was only here to add a big flourish to his already certain death. Seeing the number of people Randatti had here (and I could only assume the other syndicates had significant presences, too), it made the aftermath of the assassination look like it would be the much more interesting part, but so far there was no word on my role in that.

I still had three days before I'd be killing Gredler as he was announced president of the new Alliance. Usually at this point in a job, I'd be thoroughly planning out my strategy, but with Morrigan controlling all the details, there wasn't much need to do that. She'd already confirmed exactly where I'd be sitting and had mapped out my path out of the auditorium to safety.

There wasn't really anything for me to do but wait, which was probably why my thoughts kept drifting back to Diane. Maybe it was just curiosity — or maybe with the new information I was even more infatuated with her — but I kept wondering what her next move would be at this point. From what I knew about her, I couldn't imagine she was just in hiding, but I saw little hope for her no matter what she did. The police were after her, the exits from the city were heavily secured and monitored, and on top of everything, all the other syndicates probably believed the story about her being a Nystrom assassin and were hunting her too. I expected Dip to inform me of her demise at any moment. In a way, I wished Morrigan would get to her first, as she probably wasn't going to kill her immediately, which could give me one last chance to see Diane and satiate my curiosity. Of course, they'd be torturing her, and she'd then know I was the real killer assigned to take out Gredler, which would make that last meeting ... I'm not sure of the best word here, so let's just go with "awkward."

After the meeting with Gredler, I was taken back to the police station. I noticed Officer Meela, who I thought was friends with Diane, and she conspicuously avoided eye contact with me. Wasn't sure what that meant — it was probably the shame of having been fraternizing with a known killer for so long. Usually, I'm happy when people avoid talking to me, as it saves me the effort of avoiding them, but now I was curious to talk to people who knew (or thought they knew) Diane. I didn't see Chief Rudle around either, though, so I left the police station to go back to my hotel so I could try to figure out my next move.

"Rico!"

I turned to see that Hana had once again found me. For once, she wasn't smiling. In fact, she was on the verge of tears.

"I don't know what in the world is going on," she said, closing the distance between us. "Diane has disappeared and they're telling me she's an assassin planning to kill Senator Gredler! What are they talking about?"

I've been in a few situations where desperate people unwittingly came to me for help. I've found the quickest way to deal with that is to shove the person out of the way and walk by without saying a word. Apparently very few people can just disregard someone who's in complete desperation. Thus when I callously shove them, they just stare at me blankly, because they don't have a preprocessed reaction for it.

Since Diane was my only link to this woman, I had nothing to gain from continuing to be nice to her. Still, I didn't just shove her out of the way. I have something against breaking character before a job is done, plus she seemed more tolerable now that she wasn't so annoyingly happy.

"I don't understand it, but they apparently are sure about her — plus she ran when the police came for her, which makes her seem guilty."

"This is crazy! I've known her for over a decade — she's a kind, loving person. I know she's killed in the line of duty — and she struggled with that — but she is in no way a murderer. She would never work for criminals — she hates injustice."

Hana was boring me. I could have explained to her the hard evidence that Diane was an assassin and seen how she dealt with finding out the truth about her close friend — which would have been mildly interesting from a sociological perspective — but I wasn't feeling particularly scholarly. I was more interested in whether she unwittingly knew something useful about Diane. "Well, what do you know about her past?"

"She had a hard life. She was orphaned at an early age and had a lot of problems, but she turned her life around and became a police officer back on Andalu. When she transferred here ..." Hana was silent for a moment. "Well, I remember that very well. She contacted our church to make sure she had a place to worship here. She was coming alone and didn't know anyone on the planet, so we at the church decided to meet her at the landing station and make her feel really welcome. But then while we were waiting for her transport to arrive, we got word that the ship she was on had a jump malfunction and was completely destroyed. Everyone on board was presumed dead. It may seem silly, but I was devastated."

For the record, yes, having an extreme emotional response to the demise of someone you don't even know is quite asinine. I just nodded at the sentiment, though.

"It almost shook my faith a little," Hana continued. She smiled; I really preferred her not happy. "And then a miracle happened. We got word that Diane had changed transports at the last minute and wasn't a part of the accident. She came in the next day, and when she saw how overjoyed we were, she cried and embraced us like we were family. We thought we lost her before we ever even knew her, and I'm so glad we didn't."

A few pieces fell into place. "That's quite a story."

"You yourself have seen what a hero she is. I've never met a more selfless person. These charges against her don't make any sense."

"It is pretty hard to believe." But life surprises you.

"Please, if you find out anything, let me know. All her friends are so worried about her."

"I certainly will."

She then made a move on me, and I very nearly snapped her neck before I realized she was hugging me. I just stood there and took it, and it was soon over.

"Thank you so much for everything, Rico." She gave me one last smile — as if taunting me after getting away with the hug — before walking off, leaving me alone to figure out what in the world I was going to do with myself now.

* * *

"Vanity of vanities, all is vanity.
What profit has a man from all his labor
In which he toils under the sun?"

"What are you doing now?" Dip asked.

"I'm reading in the Bible about the pointlessness of life."

"Do you find that to be comforting?"

"I find it to be true, and the truth usually isn't comforting."

I was too on edge to just relax in my hotel room, so I headed out to no particular destination and ended up at the park I had visited with Diane two days earlier. Diane had caused me quite a bit of uncertainty, and I'd thought that would have ended now that she was out of the picture. But no such luck. Now I was constantly thinking of how worthless this job was becoming to me. I was preparing for a big hit — which was usually the highlight of my life — but that could barely even keep my attention now. And if my job no longer interested me, then exactly what was I living for?

And the revelation about Diane — it had affected me somehow. I couldn't quite put my finger on it, but it wasn't something I could shake off as one of life's odd little surprises. As I sat in the park, I looked at all the sentients walking by. Each had his own life story — his own hopes and dreams — and I cared about all of that equally little. But now there was one person in the universe I did seem to care about for some odd reason, and that was slowly making me realize everything had changed now. Much of what I'd thought about myself was no longer true. And what did that mean for me?

And I set my heart to know wisdom and to know madness and folly. I perceived that this also is grasping for the wind.

For in much wisdom is much grief,
And he who increases knowledge increases sorrow.

That was a truth I'd already grasped and was the crux of my problem. People could only live in the illusion of happy lives because they never bothered to really think things out. I'd never had that luxury — I've always had to analyze everything in order to survive. And when you analyze life enough, you can't help but conclude that it's all pointless. You live, have your struggles, and then die and become nothing. Far enough into the future, the whole universe dies as well, and then there will be no evidence that any of us ever existed. I had come to terms with this, though. I'd found something I liked to do and focused on that. You have to focus on the now, because if you think too far into the future you realize it's all for naught. But my work was beginning to lack appeal. There was little excitement left in the game, and now, for some reason, it seemed as empty as everything else. So what now?

I assumed if I kept reading the passage, it would conclude that things weren't pointless if you were nice to people or something like that, but I didn't really care to hear that now. I just wanted to find another distraction — something to entertain me and just let my brain shut down for a little while.

The sun was setting, and in the distance I could see some lights just beyond the park. The carnival Diane had mentioned to me before. Well, I had no other ideas.

"Where are you going now?" Dip asked.

"Does it matter? Don't you have other things to do besides keep tabs on me?"

"Well, since you were speaking of the pointlessness of life, my further attempts to come up with an extraction plan from the city have been rather unfruitful. Either you need to get me the clearance codes for the city, or I'll have to plan to rendezvous with you after Morrigan gets you off planet."

"I'll bring up the clearance codes with Morrigan next time I see her, then." I wasn't hopeful she'd give them to me, though. She obviously liked to keep tight control over things. I looked around, wondering if she still had people following me. I hoped the carnival would be crowded, since that would make it easy to get lost in there.

It was filled with families of various species, all checking out the rides and booths about wonders from other worlds and food from exotic places. There were also soft pretzels, which I liked. I never have a problem with crowds of people in a situation like this, because they leave you alone. In fact, it makes it easy to disappear among them. To really not stand out — to not be noticed — you need to be surrounded by lots of people. Just another face in the crowd.

I could see a number of rides, including the iconic Ferris wheel made popular by human amusement parks (though many other species had similar rides). Rides held no interest for me, though; I found it hard to get my adrenaline to misfire because of faked danger. And if all I wanted was a rush from chemicals in my brain, I could just take narcotics.

I had a sudden awful thought that there might be clowns at the carnival. I shook the notion from my head as I had more serious things to worry about — though none so creepy.

There were a number of attractions set up to show off the cultures of different planets. I never found cultures that interesting (especially modern cultures), so I continued walking by all the booths until I came to a new section with games of skill. That was more promising. I figured I could find some small challenge that would distract me a little — though I really didn't want to get stuck toting around one of those large stuffed animals.

I had been unnoticed in the crowd so far, but I saw a woman glance my way. She had dyed green hair, numerous piercings, and tight clothing that emphasized her curves and her cleavage. I wasn't sure what to make of her yet — and anyway, she wasn't my type. Never got the point of advertising so loudly your parents' failure to teach you the value of societal norms. I kept moving and soon reached a tent with a number of old games inside. One stood out to me, and I walked over to it, picked up a mallet, and started the game. Soon, a brown, cartoonish face popped up out of a hole, and I hit it with the mallet. It was oddly satisfying. More came at increasing frequency until I was overwhelmed and unable to strike them all. And then it stopped, and my score flashed on a display. That seemed to be all there was to the game, and I had nothing left to do but play again and try to beat the score. So I did.

"I noticed your heart rate has increased, Rico. Are you okay?"

Reflex was key here, and the distraction of Dip's voice wasn't helping. "Just trying to have fun, Dip."

"Doing what, if I may inquire?"

I righteously smacked another one of the faces. "Whacking moles. It's an Earth game."

"And why would you want to whack moles?"

"I'm not sure the game comes with a back story. I believe moles harm crops, so perhaps I am a farmer and have to protect my crops ... but the only weapon I have is a mallet. Anyway, it's a kid's game."

"Sounds violent for children."

"Children love pointless violence. Children are still animals who haven't quite yet learned they're supposed to be something else." I whacked a few more moles. I think I was having fun — I guess I wasn't sure what that was like.

The game ended, but my score was higher this time. In fact, it was recorded as the high score for the system. I still thought I could do better, so I started another game.

"Is this to be your activity until it is time for your job?"

"What's it matter, Dip?"

"I'm just making conversation. Your behavior has been different from normal lately. When a human's behavior shifts dramatically, it usually means something."

"I just want to whack moles, Dip." The point of the "fun" activity was to forget about everything else for a little while, and Dip was ruining that. Plus, he was making me miss moles.

The game ended, and I had improved my score, even with the distraction. Still, I knew I could do better. "Going to need you to be quiet for a little bit, Dip. I need full concentration for this." I took a deep breath, gripped the mallet tightly, and prepared to start another game.

"Mister, I'd like to play."

It was a small human child. Since I was much bigger and armed with a mallet, I could easily have threatened him, but threatening children is usually a no-no. "Small child, I am near mastery of this game. You will need to wait."

"You already played three times. It's my turn. You need to share."

The small child apparently did not fear death. I thought parents were supposed to teach that sort of thing to their children. They definitely didn't want strangers like me doing that for them.

"Why don't you let the kid play, Rico?"

I looked up and saw the green-haired woman standing near the entrance to the tent, her expression quite serious. I was suddenly very aware that the only weapon I had was the phony mallet — which I handed to the child as I cautiously approached the woman. "And you are ..." Before I finished saying it, I got a good look at her face and the alert blue eyes looking back at me. "Diane?"

CHAPTER 27

"Can you give me a minute to explain myself?"

The green hair and piercings seemed very out of character for her — but apparently I didn't really know her too well in the first place. I found it strange that I would be surprised by someone being deceptive about herself.

I took a quick look around the tent and only saw kids. Hopefully Morrigan was leaving me alone. "Got somewhere we can talk?"

Diane motioned for me to follow her. She led me through a rear exit, out of the way of foot traffic, and to a large nearby shed with a busted lock. The shed was packed with lawn equipment and other maintenance tools. A small light inside showed just enough room with the door closed for two people to stand closely together. Apparently, Diane had already scoped out the area for an isolated place to talk to me — and considering how quickly she'd changed her appearance, I could see she was someone of decisive action. It was hard not to admire her ... despite how pathetic a situation she now found herself in.

She wasn't so decisive, though, on how to start this conversation. She was watching me carefully, probably trying to gauge my immediate opinion of her. I decided to speak first. "Look, I'm sorry I called you 'boring,' but I think you're overcompensating."

She smiled weakly. Then she looked like she was going to tear up but quickly caught herself. "I've tried to learn not to feel sorry for myself. I've been in some bad situations, but most of those were due to my own decisions." She now gazed firmly at me. "Anyway, to get to it, I'm not an assassin sent to kill Gredler."

Now I had to decide what my intentions were here. A fugitive was rather useless to me, but I just went ahead and stayed in character. "I never thought you were ... but I have to admit, I am rather confused."

"I'm sorry, Rico. I've deceived a lot of people for a long time now — I even deceived myself into thinking I could just toss out the person I had been and start over like nothing had happened. It's true — I worked for the Nystrom syndicate. I ..." She took a deep breath. "I did a lot of bad things, which we can talk about later.

If this were just about me, I'd leave you out of it. But there really are some big things going on, and the assassination of Gredler is just the beginning. I mentioned I worked on some projects in my spare time that were work-related? Well, what I've been doing is mapping out all the syndicate connections within the Alliance, and there are so many. I know it may sound paranoid, but I have been on the inside and seen it myself. Every level of government is infiltrated with people working for one of the syndicates, and this whole conference is just one big power play: Nystrom versus all the others."

I guess I was supposed to feign surprise or disbelief at this revelation, but I just went with stoic. "And why come to me with this?"

"I can't go back to the people I know on the police force. I'm still not completely sure who has direct ties to the syndicates, and ... I've never been good at making friends there. And I don't want to put my friends in harm's way — plus I don't know how they'd react, knowing I've been lying to them all these years. You're really all I have right now, though it would be hard to blame you if you wanted nothing to do with me either."

"You want me to help you escape?"

"No. I'm done just worrying about myself. I want to stop these people."

I've never felt compassion, but I understand the concept — it's a desire to reduce the pain of others. In this situation, it seemed the compassionate thing would be to tell her I'd help, embrace her in her time of weakness, and quickly snap her neck before she knew what was going on. She was hunted by the police and all the syndicates, plotting against forces way more powerful than her, her friends were now finding out the truth about her, and admittedly her only hope was ... well, me. Her future looked extremely bleak, and if I killed her now, it would spare her a lot of pain and suffering ... not the least of which was finding out the truth about the man she now confided in.

But, as I said, I've never felt compassion. I am often curious, though. "I spoke to Hana today."

"Oh." She looked as if she were bracing herself for a blow.

"She wanted me to know how ridiculous these charges are against you. Then she told me the story of when she first met you. Said that she thought you died in a transport accident, but I'm guessing the real Diane Thompson did die in that, didn't she?"

She wouldn't look me in the eye. "Yes. I finally grew a conscience in my life in the syndicate and wanted to start over. I saw an opportunity since Diane looked like me and didn't have any friends or family to figure out she had been replaced. That she was coming to Nar Valdum to be a police officer wasn't perfect, but I knew I could work with it. And then I just sort of ... became her."

"Should I still call you Diane?"

"I ... I don't want to be Melanie again." She continued to look away from me, her face registering a mixture of sadness and disgust. Shame. Another emotion I only know in theory. "This was a mistake. I shouldn't have tried to pull you into this. It's just silly to think you can trust me now, and ..."

She started to turn away, and I impulsively reached out and grabbed her. I pulled her to me, and there we were, close together in a shed, she wearing her tight clothing that emphasized her chest, when her previous outfits had never even confirmed she had breasts. I realized my mind — which was already more irrational than usual — was going in even more unhelpful directions, so instead I looked firmly into her blue eyes and said, "I'm already in this ... Diane. And I've never run from anything."

She stared back for a few moments. And then she embraced me — my second hug of the day. Except this time I hugged back. She was vulnerable and alone, but she felt safe with me — I think that was the message she was giving me with the gesture. And though wordless, the message I sent returning the hug felt like the biggest lie I'd ever told ... even though I didn't mean it as one. She was scared and confused. So was I.

"I don't deserve you," she said, and that was probably true, unless she did some particularly horrible things while working for Nystrom. "I've spent a long time trying to make up for what I was, and now I feel like I'm just causing more hurt by letting anyone care about me."

That seemed pretty true, since my feelings for her were the sole cause of the sudden uncertainty I was experiencing in my life. I wasn't mad at her for it, though; I had a fool notion growing that she was worth it. "I'm not a saint, either. But I am someone who likes to get things done."

She finally let go to look me in the eye, and I was again surprised by the piercings on her face, which I assumed were fake. "I don't know everything about you, but we've already been through a lot together ... and that was real. And I know there is greatness in you. That's what we need now, because there is a lot at stake. We're talking criminals and murderers running rampant. Zaldia would only be the beginning."

To someone other than me, that would sound pretty awful. "And you think we can do something about that?"

"I want to try. There is a real plot to kill Gredler, and I think I know who is behind it. How much do you know about Agent Dawson?"

"I've only met her a couple times ... but something has always seemed a little off about her." Without thinking, I flexed my right hand.

"Well, I'm pretty sure I was fingered as the killer to throw people off the trail of the person who's really plotting the assassination. I had scrubbed my record pretty well, and the only people with the information to identify me would be people actually working with Nystrom. Earlier today I followed Dawson to a building downtown known to have a very secretive bordello inside — I've seen evidence over the years that the bordello is really some sort of Nystrom meeting place practically out in the open. I've seen them do similar things on other planets back when I was with them. I think she is the assassin ... or knows who is."

Well, I had to give Diane credit for being on top of things ... despite missing the one important detail right in front of her face. And how long would that stay secret? This was a dangerous, silly path to go down, but apparently I wasn't basing decisions on logic and rational thought anymore. "I admit that doesn't sound too far-fetched for her, but do you really think Nystrom has people that high up in government?"

"I know they do. Do you think you could find out more information on her? And maybe Verg, too?"

I thought about that for a moment. "She's sort of hinted at some job opportunity for me without giving me many details. Maybe I should see what that's about."

"It makes sense that she would see you as a possible recruit for Nystrom. If that's what she's trying to pull you into, be careful. It's not something you can easily get out of, as I can attest. Still, if you can get some information on their operation here, that's a starting point."

"And the idea is to save Gredler?"

She had a look of scorn on her face. "He's a Randatti stooge, and I'd like to kill him myself — but that's how I ended up in a really bad place a long time ago." Her expression became distant. "I have a history with them."

"A history?"

"They killed my family. That's how I ended up with Nystrom — it was the easiest way to get revenge. Before I knew it, though, I was just a cold-blooded killer who didn't care about anything anymore." She shook her head and looked back at me. "I don't have time to get into that. The point is we're saving Gredler just to stop Nystrom's plan. The next step is to expose Gredler and his Randatti connections and any other syndicates that try to seize more power through the conference."

"And how do we do that?"

"I don't know yet ... but I'm working on it. I know I can come up with something. I have been hiding in the shadows and collecting information for so long, and I have nothing left now but to go after them directly. That's another reason I'm hesitant to bring you very far into this — this is going to be extremely dangerous, to say the least."

I shrugged. "Meh." Extremely dangerous is where I live.

She laughed. "Well, you're just a badass, aren't you?"

"Pretty much." I pointed to her outfit. "And I guess you're like a hard-nosed punk or something."

She blushed and immediately put her arms up to hide her cleavage. Diane was modest ... but my guess was that Melanie wasn't. And here was a capable killer embarrassed to be showing too much skin. All these years of trying to be someone "better," and all she did was temper her deadly skills with a few extra vulnerabilities. But that was a part of what made her so interesting to me.

"I do have a decent amount of experience at changing my appearance," she said, "but I haven't done it in a long time. I think next I'll try something that fades into the background a little more. Anyway, I'd better get going — I have some other leads to follow up on. Plus I don't know how many eyes Nystrom has out there, so we really need to be discreet. See what you can find out about Dawson, and we can touch base again tomorrow and share information. You said you like animals. How about the city zoo tomorrow at this time?"

I didn't like animals when they were caged — too artificial — but that wasn't really the point. "How will I find you there?"

"Don't worry about it. Just be there, and I'll find you. Oh, and if any of my friends contact you, just ..." She hesitated. "I don't want to ask you to lie, but I don't want to draw them into this. It's better for them to think I'm every awful thing being said about me than to try to help me. Anyway, I can't thank you enough, Rico. Now please stay safe."

She started to leave, but I grabbed her once more. "Make sure I see you again."

We spent another moment in silence, and I began to lean in toward her, but she pushed me back. "Rico, you wondered before why I don't date much. It's because it just never seemed fair to do that to another person. Don't fall in love with me. It's not going to end well." And then she pulled away from me and left as I stood there speechless.

I really had no idea what I was doing. I was operating with no plan and no real goal. But one thing was certain: I was excited.

CHAPTER 28

"You know, it would be rudimentarily simple for you to confirm Diane's suspicions about Nystrom's presence, considering you know for a fact who the real assassin is."

I sat on my bed looking at one of my empty holsters. I hated being unarmed. "I'm not an assassin, Dip. I'm a hitman."

"So what exactly are your intentions with Melanie the ex-killer?"

I had no answer for that. "I'm not sure she's done killing." I was pretty sure she'd know a way to get me guns if I asked.

"Either way, does she actually fit into your current plans? I haven't ever known you to have side ventures during a job."

Either I was still going through with this job, and Diane would know the truth about me in a couple of days, making leading her on rather pointless, or ... I wasn't going through with the job.

It was a fantastical thought ... perhaps "blasphemous" was the better term. This was my life — I had a job, and I did the job and focused on nothing else. If I didn't stick to that, my whole life would unravel. And yet sticking to this job made me apprehensive as well. "Diane doesn't trust Morrigan. I don't trust Morrigan. That makes us allies. What I want to do now is figure out more of the larger picture here. I want all the details, and if Morrigan won't give them to me, we'll find them out another way."

"Actually, I may have a way to assist you there. I've noticed some transmissions from this planet using an old Nystrom protocol. It's a protocol meant for communication with the executives, but you were given access to it for your recent mission on Irona. If this is what Morrigan is using, and if there is no additional security on the communications, I should be able to listen in."

"And you didn't mention this before because ..."

"Spying on your own employers never seemed important to you before."

No, it hadn't been. I was crossing a line here. "What do I need to do?"

"You need to get Morrigan to call the Nystrom executives but notify me first so I can direct all my processing power to catching the signal."

I looked again at the empty holster. I was going to need weapons soon. "I can do that."

"And what exactly is your plan after that? Is there any chance you'll team up with Melanie to destroy all the syndicates?"

A laughable notion. They were huge, even beyond my own ability to comprehend them. "The future is uncertain, Dip. We'll see what happens."

"If you want, I could try to find more information about Melanie Fincher for you, now that we know her real name."

"I know enough about her."

"It would seem that someone who has been pretending to be an officer of the law for ten years and who was previously a hired assassin would be a hard person to know."

"She said her parents were murdered. That would be a defining moment for most people. Messes you up in the head."

"Were your parents murdered, Rico?"

"My mother was." Wasn't sure why I let that slip.

"Did you kill your mother?"

That made me laugh. "No, but that's a smart guess. I didn't really care about her murder, but I was a wacky kid. That's just how I was made." I stood up. "Enough small talk, Dip. Let's go get some answers."

* * *

Morrigan looked around cautiously as she sat across the table from me. "When you said you wanted to meet at a café, I was little concerned you were going to get some childish payback and blow it up around me."

It was an outside table at a small café downtown. Light foot traffic around it. Plenty of exit paths ... not that I thought Morrigan would attack me. Still, I had to at least consider the possibility — I didn't think she was really as crazy as she acted, but I knew I could have been wrong. "That would be hilarious, though, right?"

Morrigan laughed. "Yeah, I guess it would. I mean, I'd be pretty angry and would probably literally rip your head off, but from an outside perspective ... pretty funny. Anyway, this better be important, Rico. I have a lot of balls in the air, and I don't have time for chit chat."

"Well, I'll get right to it —"

"Hold that thought." Morrigan turned and called out. "Waiter! Could you please get our order?" She batted her eyes at the human male waiter standing nearby.

"Certainly, miss. What would you like?"

"Do you have keth brew?"

"Yes we do."

"Awesome. I will have a cup of that." She turned to me. "You ever had keth brew? It's like coffee, but better."

I turned to the waiter. "I'll have green tea or your closest equivalent."

He nodded, took one more glance at Morrigan, and went away.

Morrigan looked at me with disgust. "You are so boring. How do you even stand yourself? How many times have you contemplated suicide?"

"Never saw anything to gain from that."

She rolled her eyes. "Too boring for suicide." She looked me in the eyes. "I tried it once when I was younger ... well, it was one of those cry-for-help things — my heart wasn't really in it. Anyway, I find homicide a much better outlet for frustration than suicide." She looked around. "I should probably watch what I say in public, but if anyone makes a fuss, I'll just homicide them."

"Sorry to waste your time with all this chit-chat."

Morrigan laughed again. "You have such a dry sense of humor. I guess you're just kind of shy. It takes a little bit of time to get you to let your hair down. I know your story, Rico — I know you're all mental and stuff — but you do have to work on being more social. Are you really just going to be a dumb thug until the day you die?"

"Actually, that's what I wanted to talk to you about. The job. I'm not doing it."

The mirth disappeared. "Excuse me?"

"You made it clear you didn't even want me to be a part of this, and I just don't think we work well together. And I don't trust you. So I'm out."

Morrigan looked around again. "Maybe we should go somewhere more private to discuss this."

"There is nothing to discuss. I'm done. You can make up an excuse for Gredler for why I won't be at the conference ... or not. I don't really care."

She was steaming, but she took a few deep breaths and calmed down a little. "Yes, Rico — you're right — I didn't want you on this job. And I don't particularly like you or find you all that useful. But I have orders from the execs, and they override my concerns and your concerns."

"If they have a problem with my decision, they can take it up with me."

Her eyes locked onto me, like she was ready to pounce. "I'm guessing they're going to ask *me* to take it up with you."

"Then I guess we'll talk again."

The waiter came by with our drinks. "Enjoy," he said as he set them down.

Morrigan grabbed her drink and tossed it at me, and I was just able to get my arm up in time to keep the scalding hot liquid from hitting my face. She stood up. "We will not talk again. You're not worth my time." She looked at the waiter. "He'll pay." And she stormed off.

Some of the drink had hit near my forehead and dribbled down my cheek. It did have an interesting flavor. I'd give her that.

* * *

I swept my hotel room with a bug scanner. I felt I was spending too much time in my room, but it was secure, and it was the place I knew best on planet. "So nothing yet?"

"I will be sure to inform you when I hear something," Dip said. "Are you bored? We can play a game."

"I don't like games." Unless they involve dexterity and mallets. "Any news on Diane?"

"More of the same. They're asking anyone who sees her to contact the police immediately."

At which time, presumably, the syndicates would react to the information before the law would.

"Also," Dip said, "some of her friends have been interviewed by the media. They say she was always very shy but friendly and that it is hard to believe she's a killer — other than her lawful killings in the line of duty, I presume they mean."

Friendly and shy was who Diane really was. It didn't seem like she was putting up a front to conceal herself. On the other hand, if I ever acted like myself, people would say, "He sure was emotionally detached and seemed annoyed by the mere existence of other people. It makes perfect sense to hear his job was to kill people."

"Out of curiosity, what exactly do you expect to learn by eavesdropping on Morrigan?"

I always wondered how Dip's curiosity algorithm worked. "I don't expect anything. I'll just find out what I can find out and proceed from there."

"And if you feel you have no further use for Melanie, will you then dispatch her?"

It was that simple, wasn't it? Point a gun (assuming I would get a gun again) at something and pull the trigger, and it's the same trigger pull no matter what it's pointed at. Yet, the idea of killing Diane now seemed ... difficult. "All the syndicates are after her; there's no need for me to personally take care of her."

"You'd leave her a loose thread? This seems odd for you. You really seem to be deviating from your normal actions. I would suggest psychological counseling, but I doubt you could find a therapist who would appreciate your norm."

"Dip, let it go. Just do what you're told, okay?"

"As you wish — Oh. I am detecting a high-level Nystrom communication." There was brief silence. "I can decode one half of the conversation — it sounds like

Morrigan — but the incoming signal has extra security on it that I can't get through."

"Can you let me hear the half you have, then?"

"Certainly. I'll play it for you now."

I heard Morrigan's voice. "We have a problem with Rico. He told me he does not want to be a part of this job anymore."

There were a few seconds of silence where I assumed the response would have been.

"This isn't my fault. This is a very important, difficult job, and then you straddle me with this odd request."

"Yes, I understand the situation. I understand — somewhat — why you want to give him this. But this isn't a time for sentimentality."

"I'm not argu —"

"I'm just suggesting —"

"Okay. Okay. We'll get him back. I'll figure out some way to convince him. But I just have to say that — while I only know Rico a little — I think he'd rather we just shoot him in the back of the head than make him go out in a forced blaze of glory. I mean, if you want him dead, just have it done. Rico is a practical guy; he'd understand."

"I know. Just wanted to say my piece."

Dip then said, "That's the end of the transmission."

I had to roll it over in my brain for a few seconds. "Just to make sure I heard that right, I'm supposed to die on this mission? They want me dead?"

"That seemed to be the implication — but we did hear only one half of the conversation. There are many classic comedy scenarios centered around the premise of people overreacting to something based on partial information. Then again, I do find it hard to imagine a second half to that conversation that would make the first half innocuous. Of course, my imagination algorithm is still in beta."

I sat down on the bed. I guessed in a way I was just confirming a suspicion, but it hit me harder than I thought it would to hear that Nystrom was done with me. I wasn't sure who ordered it or why, but I should never have been surprised. I'd always made certain people uneasy by my mere existence, yet I'd never really thought the executives would turn on me while I was still useful. And while I had mused about the possibility of splitting from Nystrom in the past — or even taking them on — I'd never considered it seriously. My existence has only been as a hitman for Nystrom — that was my anchor in this world, what gave me focus. It was my life, and now it was over. I was truly alone.

Except for Diane. My infatuation with her seemed so silly, but perhaps in the back of my mind I'd known I would need an ally, and that's why I'd never pushed her away after she'd appeared to be of no more use. Now that irrational behavior seemed like foresight. I had her — though to help me do what, I did not know. She wanted to take on the syndicates, but that was suicide.

But it was also a clear course of action.

Morrigan would be coming for me soon, I figured, so I had no more time to worry about my plight. I stood up and left the hotel room. I had money, so I didn't have to pack anything I didn't immediately need that could be replaced. "Dip, get me in contact with Vito." I would make one last attempt to reach out to Nystrom, but I didn't have much hope for it. Barring any progress there, my only purpose now was to get to Diane. Then maybe she'd tell me who to kill. That's all I ever needed in life.

"I will alert Vito that you want to speak to him," Dip said, "but news has come down the wire that I think you'll want to hear."

"About what?"

"About Melanie Fincher."

CHAPTER 29

I watched as four body bags were wheeled out of the house — two of the bags quite small. I didn't know why I was there — maybe because I thought Diane might have been foolish enough to show up as well. I hoped she was thinking clearly, because I was having trouble with that myself. My own problems had caused so many emotions to surface. Sadness. Fear. Mainly anger. I usually did my best to not let the emotions rule me. Things had changed for me — in a big way — but that was done with, and I had a course of action. Normally I would have stuck to the plan calmly, no matter how loudly the primitive parts of my brain were screaming. Yet here I was, standing at a crime scene I had nothing to do with.

Chief Rudle spotted me and walked over. "What are you doing here?"

I barely felt like acknowledging him. I kept scanning the gathering crowd, looking for Diane in a new disguise. "I knew the victims. Diane introduced me. She and Hana were close friends." I had found her incessant joy extremely grating, and that was over permanently now. But I wasn't happy.

"Well, from the looks of it, her friend was helping her hide out. And when Fincher had no further use for her, she killed Hana Culbertson and her entire family."

I stared at him a moment. I wasn't an expert on reading Corridian expressions. "Really? You think the detective you knew would murder a whole family — including children — like that?"

"What's it matter to you?"

I think his expression was contemptuous. He knew who I really was. That's why despite his obvious dislike of me and Diane, he'd let us get away with so much — because Nystrom had already gotten to him. And now Nystrom had murdered this family to draw out Diane — or maybe just to hurt her — and Rudle had been told how to handle it.

It was such a mistake for me to be here. Morrigan's people assigned to track down Diane would be here and would already have seen me. I just had to hope Diane didn't take the bait and would still meet me at our scheduled time at the zoo. She wasn't like me; this sort of thing would weigh heavily on her.

I turned to leave, but Rudle said, "You need to stay here. Agent Dawson says she needs to speak to you."

I glared at him. "I'm leaving, and if you try to stop me, I'll kill you. And don't think that being surrounded by police would stop me." It really wouldn't — even though I was unarmed.

Rudle's eyes widened. "There's no need to be like that."

I'd just leap at him, take his gun, and shoot him and anyone who was bothered by that. It would only take a couple seconds. But it wouldn't help me. "Pray I continue to have more important things to do than kill you."

I quickly walked away. Just then, Dip said, "Vito is on the line."

"What do you need?" Vito asked.

I kept up a quick pace, looking around cautiously. "I want you to get a message to Anthony Burke. Tell him I don't think current conditions will allow me to complete the second part of my job."

"Um ... Mr. Burke left instructions with me in case you called asking to contact him," Vito said. "He wanted me to tell you that you have your job and you just need to do it, and there will be no further input from him."

"That was directly from him?"

"Yes."

"Okay. Thanks. That will be all." And that was it. There was no one left within Nystrom on my side. They were against me, and they were probably going to win.

But I wasn't going to make it easy.

"What's the second part of the job?" Dip asked.

"The second part is always to get away alive." At least that's what I'd been taught. "Not always the employer's concern, but always mine."

Now my concern was to shake anyone who might be following me before my meeting time with Diane. To that end, I had a whole bunch of pointless activities planned — all in crowded areas where it would be easy to get lost. I first caught a cab and went to a crowded market square with merchandise from all over the galaxy and beyond. I spent some time looking at the offered goods (little of it interested me, as not many things there were useful for killing) while walking a haphazard path through the area. I then took the elevated walkways (enclosed, which is always disconcerting, but very popular with lots of people to get lost among) to the monument of the founding of Nar Valdum, which was some giant, obsidian jagged something or other that was a symbol of cooperation or tolerance or rainbows or some other pointless crap. Whatever it was, it was several stories tall, and people liked to gawk at it. Plus, you could go to the top of it so you could — I dunno — stare out at stuff. I went inside the monument as if to climb to the top but instead left through another exit and took a short tram to Kolian Falls, a giant waterfall on the river that runs through the city. It was something else to gawk at; there was lots of water constantly pouring off a cliff, which was supposed to make us marvel at the power of nature — even though the river could easily have been dammed until the falls merely trickled if people had so wanted it. I pushed through the crowd there to a popular walking path that skirted a well-cultivated park and took a quick turn through an area with a number of storefronts and lots of foot traffic before finally reaching the zoo.

I looked around — no familiar faces. I'd been careful to scan everyone around me during my trek through the city to see if anyone was following me. I seemed to be as free and clear as I could hope.

The zoo was in a giant, sprawling building that was supposed to have a number of completely enclosed recreated ecosystems. It was an attempt to put all the animals in as natural habitats as possible, but unless they were letting the animals hunt and kill each other, it would inevitably be a bit artificial.

I paid for a ticket and entered the zoo. There seemed to be just the one entrance and exit area, but I assumed there would be a number of emergency exits throughout the building. Diane was a cautious person — and a survivor — so I figured she knew what she was doing. Still, it was odd for me to put that sort of trust in another person. Much better than trusting Morrigan to look out for me, though.

The zoo was very large — supposedly the largest building on all of Nar Valdum. Diane had said she'd find me, so I figured I'd just casually stroll through the zoo to make it easiest for her. I looked at the map at the entrance. The zoo mainly held animals native to the home planets of humans and Corridians, with a few even more exotic creatures (Nar Valdum was terraformed and had no native species of its own). I find some of the most interesting creatures come from planets with no sentient life. In fact, even on Earth some of the more interesting animals lived long before humans were ever there. Evolution just sort of peters along after sentient creatures take over, the sentients' technology adapting much faster than nature ever could. Or that's how it seems, at least; I guess we can wait a few million years and see what the dominant species look like to be sure.

The zoo was arranged in a way I didn't find particularly logical. Earth species were next to what were considered the equivalent species from Corridia. For instance, there was a large habitat containing African elephants — Earth's largest extant land animal — that was next to the habitat of the Corridian animal called a torlip — their largest land animal, which looked like a giant, hairless warthog. For those keeping score, ours was larger.

Another popular section was the primate and calldee exhibit, which contained the animals most genetically similar to humans and Corridians. People love monkeys —

they find them funny. Not me; I never cared for them. True story: I once punched a monkey.

Eventually I came to a quite crowded section. It contained creatures from neither Earth nor Corridia but instead from other planets — many of them much wilder worlds with no sentient creatures. One very humid-looking habitat had creatures that looked like flying beetles but were about the size of dogs. In another enclosure were what looked like boulders sitting in a grassy area, but one moved and opened a giant mouth full of sharp teeth. I had never seen those before, and I bet they'd be fascinating to see in action.

I found the main attraction of the zoo, though, when I came to a giant glass viewing area about three stories high. Through it, I could see a large, somewhat dark swamp area of tall trees. I stared at it awhile and saw nothing of interest, but everyone else was quite transfixed by the scene. I looked out into the dark swamp a bit longer, trying to see some movement.

There was a loud shriek, and something slammed into the window. The crowd jumped in response. I was a bit more reserved in my reaction, but one of my hands did idly move closer to a non-existent gun under my jacket even as I still tried to figure out what I was looking at. Then I saw it. One of the trees nearest the window wasn't a tree at all but a tall slender creature with limbs like branches and two giant, wood-like claws — one of which had just hit the window. At the top of the tree creature's long, trunk-like legs was its body that looked a bit like a leafy top; I could make out the faint gleam of eyes. It was nightmarish — no wonder everyone was so fascinated by it. I looked up the creature's info on my reader: It was called a tree wraith and had been discovered by humans on an ecologically primitive planet. It had just recently been added to the zoo, and, judging from its swipes at its enclosure, was not taking to captivity too well. It was nice to see at least one creature with a strong opinion on that.

When my fascination with the tree wraith waned, I started to wonder when Diane would make contact. Of course, I knew there was a possibility that — given the news about Hana and her family — she had other things on her mind and wasn't going to show. If that happened, I'd be stuck trying to find her myself — maybe having a slightly easier time than Nystrom, since (hopefully) she wasn't trying to avoid me. And while searching for her, I'd have to avoid Nystrom myself. It would be a mess.

So I hoped she would turn up. I decided to find a bench and read for a while, giving her time to find me, but saw a blonde woman approaching me. It wasn't Diane, though — it was Vance, Morrigan's lackey from the brothel.

"Hello, Rico," she said, a smarmy smile on her face. "You enjoying the animals?"

And now if Diane was watching, she was probably going to be scared off. I couldn't worry about that, though; I had to figure out how to handle this. They were planning to kill me, but I knew that for the moment they wanted me back. So the safe idea was to play along.

I desperately wanted another option than the safe idea, though.

"Animals are fun," I replied. "Do you know if they have a giraffe here? I like them, because they have necks that are longer than the other animals' necks." There were a number of people around us; I didn't want to look around too blatantly, but no one stuck out as being another one of Morrigan's people.

She glared at me, but she was a little too girlish to pull off threatening. "You think you're funny, Rico? We watched you traipse all over the city, but guess what? We tagged you back when I knocked you unconscious. You don't just get to run away from us."

"I'm sorry, but in the bug scans at your hotel room," Dip chimed in my ear, "I wasn't looking for a tracker signal on your person. I'll see if I can remotely detect the signal they're using, as it has to be pretty stealthy." Good for him, showing some initiative — though it didn't speak well for him that he'd missed it in the first place. My options were going to be pretty limited if I could never get away from Morrigan's people.

"Well, you found me, nice work," I said. "But I'm still not doing the job. You can report that back to Morrigan."

"Morrigan doesn't care what you have to say. In fact, she wanted me to tell you you're not worth any more of her time. You're just going to do what you came here to do."

"Or?"

Her expression became more neutral. "Let's not make it a threat. The executives still want you for this, so Morrigan just said to find out what you need to be more confident in your mission. Let's all leave here happy." She looked at all the people around us. "Why don't we find a place to speak more privately?"

She led me to a nearby door labeled "Employees Only." "I'm not an employee," I said.

"Shut up." She knocked on the door. A zoo employee opened it, and Vance grabbed him and pulled him out of the room. We moved inside, and she slammed the door behind us, blocking the teenage kid's reentry. Inside was a hallway with a number of doors to supply and maintenance closets. A few zoo employees loitered about, on break or slacking off. Vance yelled, "Leave!" and the employees quickly scattered, most leaving through the same door we'd come in — I guessed they found her more convincing at intimidation than I did.

I didn't like being away from the zoo's main area, but it was probably a bad idea to hope Diane would find me while I was talking to Vance, anyway. Plus, a secluded area would make it easier for me to snap Vance's neck and move on.

"I have detected the tracker," Dip told me. "It's a new Nystrom product, but I found the protocol and remotely disabled it."

That seemed to settle it. I'd just have to be patient enough to wait for the right moment and then kill her, as I was unarmed and didn't want to underestimate her physically like I had the two girls on the tram. Then I'd try to find Diane.

"By the way, if anything happens to me, you'll be dead in seconds," she said. Someone wearing a zoo uniform walked into the room and stopped in the doorway, startled by the scene.

I didn't know how many other people Vance had with her, but as long as she had a gun I could use, I'd be happy to find out. That might not help me find Diane, though. But it would get me noticed. "You scared of me?" I asked.

She laughed. "No." She almost sold it. "If you do try anything, you can be pretty sure I will be the one —"

She stopped when a knife blade was pressed against her face. The woman in the zoo uniform had snuck up and grabbed Vance from behind. "I hear they do wonders with reconstructive surgery these days, so I hope you have a good picture for them to work from."

Now there was a woman who knew how to intimidate.

CHAPTER 30

The expression on Vance's face was quite entertaining. Apparently, the idea that I would not be working alone had never crossed her mind, or Morrigan's.

Diane's face was less entertaining. She was a brunette now, no makeup, and was wearing a loose, tan zoo uniform. One would probably not take a second look at her except for the deadly intense expression she wore, nearly emotionless with just a hint of hate. She was clearly prepared to kill Vance — but she probably wouldn't start with that.

"Get out of here!" Diane barked at me. "This was a bad idea. I'm not involving you in this anymore."

"I'm not going anywhere. I'm going to help you." I wasn't sure what my next move was, though. Considering what Vance might say about me, she could possibly make things uncomfortable with Diane. Not that the current situation was particularly comfortable, but it at least involved things in the realm of my expertise.

"We'll see if you keep that attitude," Diane said to me, then turned her attention to Vance. She pressed the knife into Vance's face until blood started to flow. "So were you part of the group that killed them? Are you fine with killing innocent people like that? With killing children?!"

This was what I had been afraid of. Diane should have had enough experience with these people to know that this was a rather pointless line of questioning to pursue. These people wouldn't be guilted; they had long ago adjusted their thinking to be fine with what they were. I assumed Diane had been that way, too, while she was part of the syndicate.

Vance's face showed more terror as she realized exactly who had her and how Morrigan's plot to goad her hadn't quite worked out as they had hoped. She regained some composure, though, and even went back to her smarmy smile. "Why don't you tell me, applejack? How many children were on that transport you blew up?"

That did knock a little of the edge off of Diane's intensity. The "applejack" part confused me for a moment — but then I realized it was a distress word.

The secure door to the zoo exhibits blew open, and in charged a large, brown-skinned alien and a mousy-haired human woman. The distraction gave Vance an opportunity to turn on Diane, but that was her problem to deal with for now, because the alien was charging me. He had no gun drawn, and it appeared the woman had a stun pistol, which was good luck, considering my current unarmed state.

I ducked under a large brown fist and quickly assessed my opponent. Hand-to-hand combat with unfamiliar species is not simple, as disabling your opponent requires knowledge of his anatomy. Still, any oxygen-breathing creature will have parts that need to expand and contract to facilitate breathing. These parts will necessarily be softer. And having them struck sharply will not be pleasant for the creature. I saw movement just below my attacker's neck, so I dodged another blow and punched hard. He gasped, his eyes widening, and swayed backward.

Also universal: the effects of gravity on bipeds. As the alien was stunned and trying to breathe, I came in close to him and swept his legs, sending him crashing to the ground. And then I brought my elbow down hard on his face. Pretty much every creature hates getting nailed in the face.

I turned my attention to the woman and pounced on her just as she was about to fire at me. She wasn't quick enough, and I grabbed the stun pistol in her hand and twisted it until I heard her finger break in the trigger guard. She wailed, and a light shove sent her to the ground. She started to fumble for a real gun with her off hand, but I shot her with the stun pistol and she stopped moving. I spun toward the alien but found I hadn't hurt him as much as I'd hoped, and he now had a gun in his hand. A bolt ripped through him, and I saw Diane pointing a gun at the alien while hovering over Vance, who was lying on the ground clutching at a knife in her side.

"Everyone you know is so dead!" Vance screamed at Diane. "Next time, we'll make sure you get to watch as —"

Diane shot her through the face. She stared for a moment at her victim and then looked at me. "You don't want to be a part of this."

I took a gun off the alien and one from the woman, giving myself a mismatched pair. Not pretty, but it would do. "We're getting out of here alive — together."

She looked at me with an expression unfamiliar to me. I think it was admiration. I was still the hero to her — I didn't know how long that would last ... or quite understand why I wanted it to.

A clinking sound rattled down the hallway as a canister tumbled toward us and started releasing gas. I could feel the irritants immediately — some sort of tear gas. So they still were trying to take me alive. I had no use for them alive, though, but I was already losing vision due to my stinging eyes, so I headed back into the exhibit area with Diane while we fired behind us.

I heard screams of panic around us, but I was more concerned about those who weren't panicking, as we were now out in the open. This was a big plaza in the exotic animal section, and there was very little cover besides a couple of pillars. We ran behind one, and I spotted a few people who weren't running. I was about to unload on them, but I remembered I was still pretending to be a hero, and the risk of casualties was too high.

I'd gotten myself into a dumb situation.

A bolt ripped by me — they seemed to have given up on taking me alive — and I took a half second to carefully aim and remove the torso of one man with no visible civilians behind him. Diane shot another man and then dived behind a bench. I killed one Corridian coming out of the employee area as I ran for the bench while dodging more shots. Our attackers unloaded on us, and from the shot pattern I counted two of them. Diane signaled with her eyes that she would take the one on the left, so together we rose from cover. Again, I had to take careful aim, letting the man get off one shot, which luckily missed, before I nailed him. I saw Diane's mark fall, too, out of the corner of my eye.

Panicked people were still screaming and looking for the exits, and I saw one fleeing woman trip and fall ... but a little too neatly. I have watched a lot of terrified people trip over themselves while running away from me, and they always awkwardly try to scramble straight to their feet as soon as they hit the ground. But the woman was still for a moment before trying to stand again. Despite being eighty percent sure, I let her turn so I could see the gun in her hand before I shot her — in case Diane was watching. This whole avoiding killing "innocents" thing was annoying, but I was trying to treat it as a new challenge.

And then I heard an extremely loud shriek and a huge clamor behind me, and I realized I had yet another new challenge.

Now, I couldn't fault the zoo too much. This was apparently the first tree wraith in captivity, and in designing the enclosure, they probably hadn't known at the time exactly how poorly it would react to being caged. Also, they most likely didn't factor in a gunfight happening right in front of it. Anyway, the glass — or whatever advanced plastic they had used — viewing area had been weakened by a number of stray bolts. This had obviously startled the tree wraith, which now smashed at the glass with enough force to rip a big hole in it. Another swipe opened the hole enough that the wraith broke free into the plaza, about ten yards from where Diane and I were holding our ground. The tree wraith now seemed livid and intent on crushing and killing everything it could see until it was left alone.

You could say there's a little tree wraith in all of us.

Several more people with guns had rushed into this section of the zoo from multiple directions — Morrigan had not underestimated me as a threat — but they all paused to see the giant monster charging toward them. I took the opportunity to shoot one before he was done gawking and signaled to Diane to head toward the tree wraith. She looked at me wide-eyed but quickly followed my lead. It may have been a terrifying creature with claws that could easily have ripped us in two, but it was also cover, which we just couldn't be too picky about in our current situation.

I ran between the creature's legs while Diane ran around the side of it. It had four brown, seemingly bark-covered legs in addition to its massive claws (which I ducked). I hoped I was too agile for a three-story creature to snatch, but I had never seen one of these hunt before, so this would be a big learning experience for everyone.

The tree wraith flailed at us with its claws, each about the size of my torso, but a shot aimed at us hit it in one of its legs. And while I'm not qualified to assess the mental state of a tree wraith, I would guess from its reaction that that made it mad. With one swipe, the man who'd shot it disappeared in a spray of crimson (that's the color of human blood, if I haven't mentioned it). Our other attackers now ignored us to concentrate their fire on the beast, giving Diane and me a chance to bail out through an emergency exit many of the civilians had run through. I assumed the men with guns would eventually win the battle, but I wished the tree wraith the best.

Outside, we quickly stashed our guns inside our clothes and tried to get lost in the crowd, but then I saw a familiar face. Or, I should say, a familiar species, as it wasn't like I'd have been able to tell them apart. Close to us, standing by his car and watching people exit the zoo, was, I was pretty sure, Agent Verg. I ran toward him, and he quickly noticed me and pulled out his gun just in time for it to reach my hand and become my gun, which I placed to his smooth, gray head.

"You're going to give us a ride."

CHAPTER 31

"Evasion plan beta, Dip."

"Understood. I still won't be able to retrieve you, though, while you're within a thousand miles of the city."

"What was that?" Diane asked.

"Just taking care of my things."

Diane and I really needed some time to talk, but sitting in the back seat of Verg's car with a gun to his head wasn't the right moment. I didn't know what she thought about so many of Morrigan's people coming after me, but I was hoping she had a flattering explanation I could roll with. She didn't seem too preoccupied with me, though, as she was currently burning a hole with her eyes through the back of Verg's head. "So what do you know about all this?" Diane barked at him. "I will kill you if you lie to me!" I was pretty sure that was true.

"I don't know what's going on!" Verg said. His manner of speaking was really odd and hard for me to read, but I guessed he was scared, as his voice had become louder and his speech patterns a little faster. "I'm not even sure who you are! Is one of you humans Rico Vargas?"

"Yep," I answered. "And the other one you recently interrupted a dinner of mine to pursue." Of course, I knew for a fact that Verg wasn't a part of Nystrom, but I hadn't yet decided how helpful it was to get Diane to the same conclusion. Shooting someone in the head was a very simple way to deal with things, but Diane seemed a bit on edge — certainly different from how I had seen her — and perhaps more killing wouldn't help her mental state.

"Detective Thompson?" Verg glanced at Diane. "You changed the color of your follicles ... I guess you can do that."

"Are you claiming you're not with all those people trying to gun us down inside the zoo?" Diane demanded.

"I was in the area and heard that there was a disturbance there. The police hadn't responded yet, but I thought I should check it out, considering all the recent terrorism."

"Rudle was probably ordered to back off on this," Diane said to me, the hate intensifying on her face. "You see the problem we have here? The government is no help — everything is under their control."

"Under whose control?" Verg asked.

"Nystrom ... or one of the other syndicates," Diane said. "Do you really claim to be this clueless? You never noticed anything suspicious about your partner?"

"I don't know what you're talking about! I've worked with Agent Dawson for only a couple of months, but I'm not sure what is considered odd for a human."

"Do you know where she is now?"

"No ... We have a lot of work to do, and she's been handling security measures for the conference independently today. Are you saying she was part of that shootout at the zoo?"

Now seemed the time to firm up my story. "I had just met with her. When she saw the skills I displayed in handling the terrorists, she apparently wanted to recruit me on behalf of the Nystrom syndicate. When I expressed that I wasn't interested, she sent people after me."

"She's part of Nystrom?" Verg asked incredulously. "But they're the ones trying to kill Gredler ... Are you saying she's the assassin?"

"I don't know the details, but she's obviously trying to ensure he does get killed," Diane said. "She fingered me as the killer as a distraction, and then she ..." Diane looked about ready to break down, but she regained her composure. "... had my friend and her family killed to draw me out. I was part of Nystrom many years ago — that's true — and they want revenge on me for the way I left."

"This is ... confusing," Verg said. "I have to say, some things really didn't add up about your being a sleeper assassin working on Nar Valdum for ten years, but it's hard to believe an agent as high in the government as Dawson would be compromised."

Diane finally lowered her gun from Verg's head. "The whole government is compromised, you naïve dimwit! Chief Rudle is obviously a part of this, too, and he's helping to cover up Nystrom's actions. There's basically no one to turn to on this except a rival syndicate." She sighed and looked out the window. "This is so pointless. Just take us down here."

Verg brought the car down into a pretty empty part of town that held mainly warehouses. "Are you going to let me live?"

We got out of the car. "Yes, Verg," Diane said. "We're not the bad guys." That was even true of me — for the moment, at least.

"I don't know what you plan to do, but I'll look into some of your claims."

"Don't bother," Diane said. "Something huge is about to go down here, and you obviously haven't the slightest idea about it. If you start making noise, they're just going to kill you. If you really aren't a part of any of this, just make an excuse to leave the planet." She shut the car door, and Verg took off.

While Diane was worried that Verg might get himself killed, it was apparently my job to be practical. "He's going to call this in, and the police and others will descend on us any second."

"We'll be long gone." Diane led me to a secluded alleyway and started taking off her zoo uniform. "I'd like to say I have some plan beyond immediate survival, but that would be a lie."

"Well, Nystrom probably doesn't have much of a plan either, beyond crushing us with their immense power."

Under her uniform, she wore a white tank top and extremely short black shorts. Also, the rest of her skin was much darker than her face. "That plan will probably work," she said. She took out a small purse concealed inside the uniform and applied some sort of cream to her face, which caused her face to match the rest of her body. She then did something to her hair — I wasn't sure what, but it suddenly went from brown to completely black. It was a neat trick.

"You make me feel pretty unprepared. I don't even have fake facial hair with me."

She didn't react to the joke ... except to pull something out of her purse that she pressed against my face — I assumed this to be the aforementioned facial hair. She also put sunglasses on me and took off my coat and tossed it in the alleyway, along with her uniform. "Let's get moving; we'll talk when we get there."

I placed my recently acquired guns in my waistband and concealed them under my shirt and followed her. Of course, I had no idea where "there" was, but by all indications of Diane's preparation so far, it would have whatever we needed. As we walked through a sparsely populated area, I tried to catch a glance at myself in a window, as I was curious what I looked like with a goatee. I never really did disguises — people should want to hide from me, not vice versa.

We walked for a while and soon reached a more populated area. We didn't look at all conspicuous out on the street. There were a few stores around, but there were mainly apartments and homes here, most of which looked pretty neglected. The places may have been nice enough once upon a time, but apparently at some point this had become the bad part of town. There were a few threatening types around — threatening in that they were street thugs, not in that they were trained killers ... you know, actual threats to me — but I just ignored them, as usually people figure well enough not to mess with me. I realized Diane could have appeared vulnerable to some of them, so I made sure to stay close to her.

Eventually we came to a stairwell that led to the basement of one of the buildings. Diane unlocked the door and let me inside and then followed me in and locked the door behind her. It wasn't much: barren walls with a few cabinets on them, a cot, and what looked like a bathroom. "This is just a little place I held onto in case something happened —"

She then lost it, crying so hard I thought she was going to fall over. "I'm sorry ... I need ..." She tried to fight it, but the breakdown was there, and nothing was stopping it. And there I stood, feeling completely impotent. I had no idea what to do in this situation. I had seen plenty of women cry — and had many times been the cause — I had just never cared before. I wanted to help her through it, but this was such an unnatural situation for me. I had seen how others had responded before, though — maybe in movies — so I held her tight and tried to think of some comforting words.

"We're going to get through this," I said as she cried into my shoulder. And that was true — one way or another we would reach an end. A lot of those paths to the end involved torture and other indignities if one of the syndicates caught us. The better paths meant quick deaths in a gunfight. If there were other possible outcomes, I hadn't figured them out yet.

Her sobbing died down a little bit. "I just bring pain and misery to everyone around me. It's all I've done all my life."

I held her firmly. "No, that's not true." I certainly didn't feel pain and misery from being around her, just things much more confounding.

Her crying stopped, but she still looked on the edge of a breakdown. "But why are you doing this? Why are you here?"

"Because this is where I want to be." I could feel emotion creeping into my voice as I looked into her tear-filled eyes. "I want to be with you."

We kissed, and as far as I was concerned, there was no stopping there.

CHAPTER 32

She lay naked beside me, not sleeping but also not speaking. Her wig had come off, exposing her matted, dirty-blond hair, and whatever she had used to change her skin color had begun to fade, leaving her skin mottled. I guess she was an ugly sight, but that wasn't my opinion at the time. I just watched her as she stared at nothing. Never before had I been so interested to know what was going on in someone else's mind. A lot had happened to her recently — it was quite possible that she wasn't even thinking about me. It didn't seem likely, though. Maybe she was thinking how lucky she was to have the love and support of such a hero as Rico Vargas from Rikar. Or maybe, as astute as she was, she'd seen through the illusion to what I really was: a man who'd taken advantage of her emotional fragility to get what he wanted.

The sex drive is a strong primitive impulse that constantly tries to control your actions. It's not something I should have been indulging under dire circumstances where I'd need to think clearly. Not to mention the emotional toll. Not for me, of course, but I've seen it in others. That had never mattered before, but I was planning to depend on Diane for whatever new course my life was to take, and now I'd possibly ruined things. So I looked at her as she silently spaced, waiting for her to speak, since I had no idea what to say myself.

"I think I'm losing myself," she finally said.

"What do you mean?"

"I built up this new person — someone I thought was so much stronger than the old me — and I feel her chipping away. I don't know what else to do under these circumstances, though."

"These aren't circumstances normal people deal with."

"No ... but I'm still just dealing with bad choices I made over a decade ago. Things I thought I left behind ... but ... you are what you are, I guess." She finally turned to look at me. "When you talked to Hana, did she mention that transport with the jump malfunction that killed 340 people?"

"Yes."

"I made that happen."

She let that hang there a moment. That was pretty extreme. I've killed more than that many people myself — but not all at once like that. Of course, I do things one-on-one, and that usually comes with less collateral damage than faking a transport malfunction. "Are you trying to shock me?"

"I'm just telling you who I am. I'm not just a murderer — I'm a mass murderer. That's who you're in bed with. That's the side you've chosen."

She was trying to shock me. "You don't seem like a mass murderer."

"Well, I am, and that's a pretty low nadir to climb your way out of." She went back to staring at nothing. "I used to just blame my circumstances. Easy enough. I was fourteen when I came home to find my mother and father murdered. I couldn't cope with that."

"So you joined a rival syndicate?" I'd known stories of lots of sociopathic killers. I'd never found their stories that interesting; they'd taken long journeys to become what I was born as. But Diane had gone there and tried to come out of it; that was interesting, because it was different.

"It's not quite that simple." She was quiet for a moment, and then a smile finally appeared on her face. "My parents were good people. My dad worked in the mines — just basic, honest work. He and my mom were convinced I was a genius and destined to do great things. They encouraged me to study and saved up to put me in a fancy school. They also tried to teach me religion, but eventually I thought I was too smart for that.

"When I was fourteen, the Randatti syndicate started making inroads on the planet. They started some protection rackets in the city we lived in. They were just dumb thugs, hurting people and acting untouchable. And then my dad did a crazy thing: He treated them like the dumb thugs they were. When they attacked some people in the neighborhood — people he didn't even really know — he grabbed a bat and fought back. Chased those worthless idiots off.

"The next day, I came home from school to find him and my mother shot dead. No mystery who did it, but everyone just acted like it didn't happen. They were too afraid to lift a finger. Randatti was powerful — a bunch of powerful, evil thugs — and no one felt like they could do anything about it.

"I lived with my aunt after that and kept going to the school my parents had saved for, but I couldn't concentrate on my studies anymore. How was any of that important when murderers could just walk free, untouched?"

I touched her cheek. "You wanted justice; that's natural." Someone harms you, you want to harm them back to discourage them from doing it again. Quite natural. Even logical.

"Yes, I wanted justice. But not just justice. The more I obsessed over it, the more the hate grew. I wanted revenge."

People tend to put an almost spiritual meaning behind the notion of justice, but I never felt it was actually distinguishable from revenge. It's just revenge codified by law. "Would any person not want revenge in those circumstances?" Me, of course — I don't kill to satisfy my emotional needs.

"Maybe no one is that levelheaded, but when you embrace such a strong desire for violence, it corrupts you. And I was obsessed. I knew not to talk about my plans — everyone considered it suicide to try anything against Randatti — but I secretly researched them and their operations on the planet. I found their hideouts and spied on them on my own time, trying to plot what I could do to them. I even got a gun. People were afraid to take them on publicly, so I was going to take them down, piece by piece, in secret.

"I was sixteen when I finally decided to start. I knew of a back room at a bar a number of the thugs congregated in. I dressed up to look older, hid the gun on myself, and walked into the bar as calmly as I could, trying to hide exactly how fast my heart was beating. These were human males, so my plan was to smile and flatter them to get them to drop their guard and then kill them all and get out of there. I reminded myself of the sadness and anger I'd felt when I'd found my parents dead, and I knew in my heart I could kill them. So, without hesitation, I stepped into that back room.

"And they were all already dead. Some woman was standing over them. She didn't react much to my appearance — just pointed her gun at me. I looked at her handiwork and back at her and said, 'I want to do this, too. I want to kill Randatti.' She smiled, and we strolled out of the bar together. And that was the last day I ever saw my home."

"She was a Nystrom assassin?" I asked.

"Yes. I should have seen that it was just murderers killing murderers, but that wasn't what I wanted to see. After watching for so long while the Randatti thugs just went about their business with no fear of reprisal, I couldn't help but see the people who finally made them pay as the good guys. I was tired of being impotent against such evil, and Nystrom was a way to strike back.

"And they were happy to have me and my enthusiasm. They are quite a sophisticated operation — they have a whole training program for assassins. And I was eager to learn — eager to be able to do something. I was one of their best, they said, and for my final test to become one of their trained assassins, they brought in a Randatti syndicate member, pleading for his life. I was to shoot him in the head to show I was ready. I shot him in the knees, then I shot him in the head.

"After that, I was off doing Nystrom's business. I killed many Randatti members — Nystrom was in a large conflict with them. It became less cathartic over time — started to feel like I was just doing necessary dirty work — like pest control. I liked to think I was making a difference, but there were always more targets. I constantly subjected myself to the worst of humanity on my missions, and I soon began to lose any feeling of respect for sentient life. I knew all the darkness people had in them — how horrible they could be — and death just seemed like such a good thing for so many people. Eventually, Nystrom gave me targets that had nothing to do with Randatti, but I no longer cared who I killed. It was hard to believe any of them didn't deserve it. The universe was full of nothing but violent, selfish people, and I could kill day and night for years and barely make a dent in the evil. Eventually, I didn't even care about justifications for my murders; it was just my job. It was just something to do in the empty, cold universe.

"I did this for years, and Nystrom paid me well. I never really enjoyed the money, though. I was just so empty — so joyless. And then I got a new mission: A group of us would sabotage a transport going between Andalu and Nar Valdum — to kill one target and make it look like an accident. Hundreds of innocent people were going to die — people who had nothing to do with the syndicates — so that's why they assigned it to those they knew wouldn't have a problem with that. And they were right, because I didn't care anymore. In fact, I despised the 'innocent' people. There were huge conflicts between the syndicates — things affecting countless worlds — and they just went about their daily lives like nothing was happening. They were worthless — willing victims of the syndicates. They were inconsequential, so anything that happened to them was inconsequential.

"Nystrom knew of a problem with the transport that no one else knew of. With just a little prodding to the jump drive, the transport would have a massive failure on its jump, and the ensuing investigation would reveal the actual error in the system as the culprit. No one could know it wasn't really an accident. I almost wonder if Nystrom itself had built the error into the system to one day exploit it like this.

"Technically, the job was simple. Nystrom had contacts that would get us easy access to the starport as a maintenance crew, and from there we could make the 'accident' happen. Then we'd change back into civilian clothes and wait in the terminal to make sure our target got on the transport. I don't even remember who he was — some official associated with another syndicate. So I sat there, pretending to read a book as I watched him out of the corner of my eye — ignoring all the other people. The ..." She teared up. " ...children running around. I didn't care. I was just a soulless monster, concentrating on the job.

"And then someone asked me, 'Are you alright?' It was a young woman about my age, and I was a bit surprised, because usually I was very good at blending into the background when I needed to, and I thought my face no longer portrayed any emotion except when I willed it to. 'I'm fine,' I told her. And she said, 'Sorry, it just kind of looked like something was wrong. I didn't mean to impose or anything.' And then — on a whim, I guess ... maybe because I thought it would shut her up — I said, 'Actually, my parents just died.' She looked so concerned — and I think I was a bit amused to play with her emotions like that, but then she smiled and said, 'Tell me about them.'

"I wanted to brush her off, but I didn't want to make her suspicious, so I thought I'd just give her a few quick details using my actual parents. So I tried to remember some meaningless stories. I told her how my mom and I used to have a special ritual for making brownies, which we did every movie night. And I told her how my dad would take me with him on his fishing trips as a little girl and let me reel in every fish he hooked. They were supposed to be pointless anecdotes I had no emotional attachment to, but I hadn't thought about my parents in so long, and I couldn't help but see their faces. They used to look at me with such love, and I wondered if they could see the soulless monster who was ready to sit idly by while hundreds went to their deaths. Their little girl they had so much hope for — that they worked so hard for — was even worse than the thugs my dad had tried to chase off with a bat. Worse than the ones who killed him and my mother.

"I guess I had been silent for a minute while thinking about it — the woman asked if I was okay. I recovered, smiled, and said I just missed them. And now everyone was boarding, so the woman got up, told me she'd say a prayer for me — it seemed like such a useless gesture — and then headed off to die. And I sat quietly while everyone left the terminal to board, because that was my job and I always just did my job without thinking about it. But now I could feel a pit in my stomach as the people calmly walked onto the transport. It bothered me; I hadn't felt anything about killing people in a long time, but I just assumed it would pass.

"I went with my team to a backroom area we'd set up to monitor the transport and confirm our kill. While I waited for it to undock from the station and jump, I tried to assess what had happened to me. I seemed to have been affected by the notion that my parents would have hated what I had become, but then I reminded myself that my parents were just some of the worthless 'innocents' the syndicates stomped on all the time, so it didn't matter what they would have thought. Of course, if my parents were so contemptible, what exactly was I so angry about that had me on this path in the first place? I started to realize how pointless and hollow my existence was, just violence with no real end in sight, just because it gave me the illusion of having a purpose. But I had been loved by my parents .... That was the last time I ever felt content. I had written love off, thinking it was something I would never have again, that all I had left to embrace was emptiness. I was on a slow march into the abyss. And as much as I had convinced myself that killing people was meaningless, I knew if I let these innocent people die, that was an abyss I would be stuck in forever. And that finally terrified me.

"'We have to stop this,' I said. My coworkers looked at me, but it's like they couldn't hear or understand what I said. So I took a deep breath and said it louder.

And they just stared at me. And then one of them went for a gun, but I was quicker and killed them all. I ran to a radio to tell the ship to wait ..." She took a long pause, trying to wade out of a horrible memory. "... but I was too late."

"You tried to stop it," I said. Technically, whether she was remorseful or not, those people were still dead, so it seemed to hardly matter, but people always tend to put heavy weight on intentions.

"I was a coward, and I waited too long to remember that I was a human being. Now all those people are dead. I guess if I really was remorseful, I would have confessed and turned myself in."

I put my hand on her shoulder. "Wouldn't Nystrom have gotten to you immediately if you'd done that?"

"Yes, they would have killed me pretty quickly if I'd ever been in police custody ... yet that still feels like I'm making excuses." She still didn't look at me — just stared off into nothing.

"It's still considered an accident; no one even knows there's justice to be served. After the transport's destruction I went into survival mode, knowing Nystrom would be after me. I had some money, but I didn't have anywhere to go. And my first order of business was to get off the starport the transport had docked at. I realized lots of people change the transport they're leaving on at the last minute, and Nystrom had gotten us access to the station's database, so it would be easy to make it look like someone who had been killed on the transport had switched her schedule, and then I'd just take her place. I just had to find a human woman who somewhat resembled me. I found one, about the same age, and she was even an orphan heading to a brand new planet for a job, so no one would recognize her. She was a police officer, but I figured I could find another way off Nar Valdum before that became an issue. I saw the picture of the woman I would be replacing — she was the one who'd asked about my parents. Who'd said she'd pray for me." She teared up a little.

"So I put the dead bodies of my coconspirators out an air lock, changed Diane Thompson's data to match my picture and identifying markers, switched her schedule, and got on the new transport. And then I realized exactly how alone I was. I was long since estranged from any of my family, and the only people I knew, my Nystrom contacts, would be out to kill me if they ever found me. All I knew was that I wanted to change what I was — what I had become. And I was scared, because I knew I couldn't do it on my own; I wasn't strong enough. I thought of the story of the prodigal son — how his father ran to embrace him when he gave up his wicked ways and returned home. But there was no father to greet me, no home to return to. I had nothing, and all I knew was how to lie and kill. I wanted to change my ways, but it seemed inevitable that I would fail. And then I thought of a brilliant solution — one way to make sure Nystrom never got to me and I never went back to my old ways and hurt anyone else. As soon as I got to Nar Valdum and could get some time alone, I was going to kill myself.

"After the transport docked above Nar Valdum, I spent the ride down to the planet's surface thinking of ways to do it. It would be the last thing I'd do, so I wanted to at least get that right. And it wasn't like I had to write a note, since there wasn't really anyone who'd care. I'd just be gone, and the universe would be better for it and wouldn't even notice my passing ....

"These were my thoughts as I walked through the landing station. And then someone yelled, 'There she is!' I almost panicked, but then I saw all these smiling people who were so happy — so overjoyed — to see me. And then a woman — Hana — ran up to me, crying, and hugged me. She said, 'Thank God! We thought you were dead!' And, for the first time in ages, I cried too.

"Diane had contacted a church on Nar Valdum to make sure she wouldn't be alone there — to make sure I wouldn't be alone." Tears started streaming down Diane's face. "To make sure that when I returned home, there would be people running to embrace me and welcome me back. Despite all I had done, God had forgiven me and wanted me to have a second chance." She was quiet for a moment, smiling in her memory, but eventually the smile faded and she wiped away the tears and looked at me. "And now all I can think is that if I had killed myself, Hana and her family would still be alive."

I didn't know if she said that out of frustration or was seriously considering suicide again. I felt I should do something, but once again I was extremely ill equipped to know what that was. I pulled her closer to me, and she rested her head on my chest. "If you did that, I never would have met you."

She laughed. "And that's been nothing but a blessing, right?"

It was hard to say. She certainly had changed me. "Just don't discount the value of your own life." I'd never really cared before if someone else lived or died; that did seem to make her special.

"My life isn't mine to take anyway. I just don't know what I can do with it that's of use to anyone. It seems so stupid now that I thought I could reform myself while living a lie. Look what I brought on the people who showed me such love when I didn't deserve it. And if Nystrom decides to go after more of my friends from church, I'm powerless to stop them. They're too powerful, and they control the police force. And if somehow Nystrom were defeated, it would mean nothing to the universe as a whole, since that would just leave the other syndicates in power. Just look at the officials attending the conference! All of them are ...."

Diane was silent a moment, and then she smiled. More my type of smile. She sat up and faced me. "I told you before that I've been working in my spare time tracing the syndicates' connections within the government, and I can identify every major player at the conference as being in the pocket of one syndicate or another. And knowing that Nystrom is planning something, all the players have brought more security in the form of syndicate thugs. I mean, all the syndicates want to destroy each other, but they're all going to be in a room together playing nice, because they think Nystrom overstepped with Zaldia and there is a chance to eliminate them. But all those criminals, all those murderers, will be pretending to be civilized for the cameras, and most people won't notice a thing."

I smiled too. "Unless we put a match to that powder keg."

"Exactly! We're too small to fight them, but we can get them to fight each other. They won't destroy themselves, but with a big enough spectacle we can at least open everyone's eyes and show them who exactly controls the government now." Her smile grew wider. "I think this is something we can do." She finally noticed her bare chest and pulled up the sheets to cover herself.

I wasn't so sure that rubbing everyone's faces in the fact that they were surrounded by criminals would amount to anything, but I loved the mission idea. All the major syndicates were going to be in a room together, and we just had to get them to erupt into an orgy of violence. Nystrom would have their own people in place to seize control when Gredler was eliminated, but if those people were dead along with all the other syndicates' "respectable" frontmen, there would be no one to seize control — no quick path back to normality — only chaos and a lot of criminals now out in the open to deal with. Nystrom's plans of easily grabbing control would be ruined along with the plans of any other syndicates for holding the reins of power in secret.

It wouldn't be easy to get all the syndicates to turn on each other, though, as they'd all be very careful not to cause a disturbance and draw attention to themselves. In all likelihood, were Gredler shot in front of them, they'd even play that low-key. Still, it seemed like a doable mission. We just had to figure out the right impetus so they couldn't help but attack each other. "We'll need to find some way to get access to the conference hall."

"Agent Dawson would know how to get us access." I could see a glimmer in her eyes that said she was looking for vengeance for what had happened to her friend. Not helpful right now.

"No, she'll be expecting us to go after her." She really would, and she would probably win that fight, by my guess. She'd said I was too predictable, and I took the criticism to heart. By teaming up with Diane, I was already doing something new. Now I just needed to do something else that was crazy and stupid enough that she wouldn't see it coming. "So how much weaponry do you have in your hideout here?"

"A decent amount. I've ... confiscated some things while in law enforcement."

"Explosives?"

She almost looked embarrassed. "I was able to obtain quite a bit, actually ... just in case."

"Body armor?"

"Well ... only in my size."

I thought for a moment. "You definitely have skills as an assassin. How comfortable are you with a siege?"

"Well ..." She seemed to really think about it. "What do you have planned?"

CHAPTER 33

I watched the forest pass below us. It looked so serene, but below the green canopy was a constant struggle of life and death. A simple one, though — no talking, no emotions. The less advanced creatures of the world knew exactly what they wanted and worked for it without hesitation.

"You like the forest?" Diane asked.

"It's peaceful ... in its own way. If I were to settle down, I think I'd like a place out in the forest."

Diane laughed. "Not on this planet."

I smiled. "No. I don't think that will be an option."

We were silent a moment, then Diane said, "Can I ask you something?"

I looked at her. She was in black body armor, which didn't quite flatter her figure, yet still looked cute on her. Her skin was back to its normal color, and without a wig her hair was a dirty blonde. Her face right now, though, was quite serious. I didn't think I wanted her to ask me her question. "What is it?"

"Rico Vargas — police officer from a backwater planet ... is that the story we're still going with?"

She was a mass murderer, and it seemed kind of silly for me to still hide who I was from her. Yet I didn't think she'd really understand what I was, and I didn't want to explain. "Do you believe I'm on your side?"

"Yes."

"Then let's leave it at that for now."

She nodded. "Well, you tell me what you want to tell me whenever you're ready."

It was inevitable that she'd eventually have to know exactly what I was if I planned to stay around her, but that was a problem for another time. "Anything else?"

She thought for a moment. "Are you in love with me?"

I considered for a moment what would be the most useful response and then just decided to be truthful. "Yes."

"Why?"

That was quite a question. "It's my understanding that there isn't always a rational basis for love."

"You've never been in love before?"

"No. How about you?"

She let the question hang for a moment. "I've learned that love is a verb. You love someone — it's a choice. I spent a lot of time without any love, so now I try to show love to everyone."

I didn't know what that crap meant other than that she was dodging the question. "And how's that working out?"

"Considering my recent body count and what we're planning today, I guess I could be doing better."

I half-laughed at her joke, but I was a bit preoccupied by her not answering the question. Or the real question behind it: Was she in love with me? So it wasn't just that I was infatuated with a woman — I wanted her to love me back. Which was silly, since it wouldn't really be me she was in love with but the character I was playing.

"Rico," Diane started to say, but seemed to reconsider her words. Then she leaned over and we kissed for what seemed like minutes. She said, "It seems pretty likely I'm going to die soon, but I'm happy I knew you first."

It was certainly possible she'd die and I'd live. And then ... I hadn't thought of that. Perhaps I didn't want to. I had lived all my life before without her, and thus losing her again would be just going back to my normal. And yet that was terrible to contemplate.

Anyway, considering our plan, if she died during the assault, I was probably going to die, too. So ... moot point.

* * *

I came out of the line of trees at the edge of the forest, slowly walking toward Gredler's estate. His security team spotted me immediately, and I could see a group of four guards congregating just on the other side of the gate to the compound. "My name is Rico. I was here the other day, and I would like to speak to Senator Gredler again."

The security team — Randatti thugs — all had their guns drawn. "What about?"

"I have information about the Nystrom assassin out to kill him."

They opened the gate, and two of the thugs — a Corridian and a human — approached me. The Corridian seemed to be listening to something. "Okay, we'll take you to Gredler. Are you armed?"

"Of course."

The two each took a cautious step back. "Will you hand over your guns, then?"

I shook my head. "Nah, I don't think so."

A shot tore through the Corridian, causing the human to glance toward the forest. That's when I drew my two guns, shooting the two guards inside the gate while letting Diane take out the human next to me. The immediate threats handled, I charged forward toward more of them. I would have to be quick for this to work, and I had to trust Diane to cover my back. This was a new thing for me, putting my life in the hands of another. I hoped it wasn't the last thing for me.

An explosion erupted on the other side of the building. That would be followed by some erratic gunfire from the gun we'd crudely rigged to fire by itself. The idea was to divide Gredler's security with some false threats. That would only last for a very short while, so again speed was of the essence.

A man came out the front door. I shot him and jumped over his body into the house. As I've said, when I'm bored I like to imagine shooting my way out of a place. And I had certainly been bored on my first visit to the Gredler estate, so I'd run over that scenario a couple times. I hadn't considered shooting my way *in*, but a lot of the same details applied, such as where security would likely come from. Thus, as I barged into the foyer, putting myself temporarily out in the open, I fired from memory at where I assumed targets would be before I even saw them. At least it caused some of the security force to duck for cover instead of taking aim at me. A number of shots went by me, but with my speed and aim, they'd have had to make their first shots count. They would not get seconds. They missed. Five of them lay dead as I ran up the stairs to the second floor.

The layout of the house dictated that security either had to barricade Gredler in his office or take him past me. I didn't see him being moved, so he was in his office. I heard gunshots behind me, but I had to assume it was Diane doing her job and keep moving. A guard tried to peek out a doorway and lost his head. I zeroed in on the closed door to Gredler's office.

Then through my radio I heard Diane yelp. Maybe out of surprise, but maybe pain. A small piece of me wanted to stop and turn around to check on her, but I had my course of action and I was sticking to it.

I fired at the edges of the door and plowed into it. It crashed open and I hit the ground in a roll. The world was spinning, but I saw four figures inside the room firing at me. As I came to a stop I fired two shots from each gun and stood up. And now the only living people in the room besides me were the cowering Gredler and his female aide. I ignored her, walking past her to put a gun to Gredler's head. "I don't know if they relayed my message to you, but I wanted to talk to you about a threat on your life."

I could just barely hear the female behind me reaching down to pick up a gun off of one of the dead guards. Then I heard two shots, followed by a body hitting the floor.

"There, we just saved your life from a Nystrom assassin," I said as Diane walked over to stand beside me. Her face wasn't visible behind a black helmet, and she looked rather intimidating. There was also smoke coming from her armor where she'd obviously been hit, but I had to assume for now that she was okay.

"She was an assassin?" Gredler asked, looking rather alarmed and confused as he only briefly took his eyes off my gun.

"Despite whatever attempt at security Randatti has given you, Nystrom got an assassin in close to you to make sure you would die even if the primary assassins missed their mark."

"What primary assassins?" He had calmed a little and was giving me his full attention.

"That would be me and my associate here."

He considered that. "But you're not going to kill me, are you?" Part question, part statement. He was trying to take charge; politicians always like to think they're in charge.

I rested one hand on the computer on his desk, gun still pointed toward him but not directly at his head. "Tell your security to back off, and we'll talk."

Gredler slowly walked to the intercom on his desk and said into it, "I want to cancel any alerts."

"No one is responding near you," someone answered, sounding panicked.

"That's because your security failed to protect me." Gredler looked at me. "Now I'm going to talk to someone more competent about keeping me safe." He shut off the intercom. "I want you to know that I am a politician. My concern is government, and not whatever disagreements Randatti and Nystrom may have."

"And our concern is survival," I said. "Now here are the facts: Nystrom wants you dead. They hired us for that, but they have many others and will make sure it happens one way or another." I motioned to the dead female. "In fact, Agent Morrigan Dawson, who is in charge of much of the security effort for the conference, works for them. And if your people haven't uncovered that, I'd say they've been kind of useless so far."

He was silent for a minute, wearing the expression of someone finally realizing how closely death had been circling him. "We'll have to look into that ... but this seems rather reckless for Nystrom. They'll end up in an all-out war with the Alliance by going after me like this."

"Exactly. And they think they want that. They think they can win. I think they've gone insane. You've seen the pictures of Zaldia. Who even knows what they think they're doing there? Now everyone wants Nystrom crushed, and for good reason. I can see that continuing to associate with them is only going to lead to one thing: making me dead. I don't want to be dead." I pointed to Diane. "Tommy here doesn't want to be dead. You don't want to be dead. I'm thinking we can all come to an agreement, then."

He nodded. Corridians nod yes. "Alright. So what are you proposing?" He was trying very hard not to look scared and only half-succeeding.

"Nystrom knows deep down they've gone too far and are doomed, and that's why they're so dangerous right now. They will keep coming at you until someone crushes them. We have inside knowledge that'll help you know how they'll come after you. And how to respond to make sure they're so wounded they'll have no choice but to retreat. In exchange, we'd like some money — nothing unreasonable, but nothing small, either." You always have to look concerned about money. "Also, when this is over, we want safe passage off this planet and the ability to disappear forever."

"Certainly. You help me out here, and you won't have to worry about anything ever again." He looked at the dead people around him. "I guess it's fair to say Randatti wasn't ready for the threat."

"I don't think any of the syndicates are, and that's why I felt the need to make an impression. You do not realize how single-minded Nystrom is right now. They only want you dead."

He thought for a moment. "I wish we could postpone the conference until Nystrom is handled, but that's not an option."

"Nah, then they'd win. Because they're not going to back down until you get everyone united against them." I handed him a radio. "I will talk to you — and only you — through this. I'll contact you soon and give you some of the information you'll need for surviving the conference. And tell you where to send our payment. For now, we're going to leave, because ..." I looked around. "... I feel just a bit antsy standing around here for some reason. And one more thing." I grabbed him and locked a metal bracelet onto his wrist. On it, a five-minute timer started counting down. "Try to tamper with this, and it will explode. Also, it'll explode when the timer reaches zero. But as soon as we get out of here unmolested, I'll send the signal to deactivate it."

His eyes were fixed on the timer. "This isn't necessary!"

"It's not that we don't trust you, but ... you are a politician. Anyway, make sure your security stays out of our way." I started to leave the room, but I noticed Diane stayed still, apparently staring at Gredler, her face unseen behind her helmet. It worried me for a moment, but then she turned and left with me. Apparently Gredler followed instructions, as on our way out we saw no Randatti thugs except for the deceased.

We made our way out of the estate and disappeared through the tree line. After we hiked a minute into the forest, I had Dip connect me to the radio I'd given Gredler. "The bracelet is just a piece of metal and a timer; don't worry about it. I'll contact you again soon. Good luck." I looked at Diane and the scorched gash in her armor. "You okay?"

"I'm fine. It didn't penetrate." Diane pulled her helmet off. "I just wanted to bash Gredler's face in — how he tried to keep this air of civility while working with such people."

"But you didn't." I checked my handheld to make sure we were going the right direction to the clearing we'd landed our vehicle in.

She felt her gun and laughed. "Oh yes, I was the epitome of restraint in there. So you're certain that Corridian woman I shot was a Nystrom assassin?"

"Absolutely." Ninety percent sure. "You're okay with this, right?"

"I ..." She had a wry smile. "... just enjoyed it a little too much. You think it worked?"

"Yeah. When you massacre a bunch of people in broad daylight, no one ever suspects that your purpose was to plant a bug. I can have Dip confirm it, though."

"I am monitoring his computer," Dip informed me. "I can also pick up audio near his office."

"Dip says it's working," I told Diane. "In good time we'll have what we need." I stopped and looked briefly around the forest. We were surrounded by very tall trees — like sequoias from Earth. There was little movement besides ours — just insects and a few birds — and we seemed so alone. It was peaceful, and some small part of me just wanted to stay here with her and forget everything else. A very small, foolish part, but strangely nagging nonetheless.

"What is it?" Diane touched my arm.

A good question. I seemed to be having another irrational desire for ... something I couldn't quite understand. I looked at her, her lovely face full of concern. I caressed her cheek and kissed her. It had to be more obvious to her who I really was, yet she was still with me. Still, my best hope was we'd both die before she got too disappointed in what I am.

After the kiss, she stared at me momentarily. "You're an odd romantic."

"And you're a beautiful woman in odd circumstances."

"I almost can't believe we survived that." She hugged my side and put her head on my shoulder. "Of course, survival has not been my problem. You think we'll accomplish anything here?"

"We'll accomplish something." A lot of bad people were going to wind up dead if our plan went off. That seemed like something regular people would celebrate.

"I'm worried about my church ... whether Nystrom will go after them again to draw me out."

I was starting to learn what it felt like to worry about someone, and that wasn't something I would want to extend to a whole group of people. I could only assume they didn't reciprocate Diane's concern, given the recent revelation about the killer in their midst. "Well, you can't worry about them right now — there isn't anything you can do for them, and worrying will only distract you from the mission. Even if Nystrom had you in hand, they might still go after them just to hurt you. Hopefully now that we've outed Morrigan to Gredler, Randatti will put too much pressure on her for her to worry about you. We just have to make sure we get the information we need and load up on whatever supplies we'll need for the plan."

She took her head off my shoulder and looked at me more businesslike. "I was thinking about how we plan to breach the place."

"Well, I guess we'll want a vehicle suitable for ramming ... I don't know if that will be easy to find quickly."

"The police station has them."

I really didn't want to go back there again. I was tired of that place. "How easy would it be to steal one from there?"

"Not too hard to get inside unnoticed if we pick the right time of day, but getting access ..." She was silent for a moment in thought. "Actually, we just need an access card ... one Chief Rudle would have on him."

"You want to go after Rudle?" Her face betrayed no emotion, but I reminded myself that she wasn't like me. "You don't want to make this personal." That was only part of my concern, though, since Rudle seemed to know who I really was.

She laughed. "It's never not been personal. Anyway, he has what we need, let's pay him a visit."

I nodded. We were going to have to kill him, of course. I assumed she knew that.

CHAPTER 34

"Hello?" He answered quickly — I could only assume he'd been waiting anxiously for the call.

"It's Rico. I think you remember me from earlier today with all the shooting and the screaming at your place."

"Yes, you're the one with a handle on what Nystrom is up to."

"Correct. Are you alone?" I didn't really care if he was.

"Yes."

"I didn't want to say this earlier in case others were listening, but you can't really trust Randatti in this. Like me, you're just a pawn to all the syndicates, and they don't actually care whether we live or die, as long as they get what they want. To survive this, we need to look out for each other."

"What are you proposing?"

"I know what's going down here better than anyone. Nystrom is desperate, and they will be relentless and, despite my demonstration today, I still don't believe Randatti quite understands the extent of Nystrom's desire to kill you and forestall the changes in the Galactic Alliance. But I know what you need to do. For one thing, you need to alert all the other syndicates to just how dangerous Nystrom is. For now, anyone against Nystrom is your ally."

"I don't deal directly with those people. I wouldn't know how to contact them."

"But you know which senators are in the pockets of which syndicates. Get word to them of Nystrom's intentions. The other syndicates will get more of their people into the conference to ward off any move from Nystrom."

"A conference full of syndicate thugs doesn't sound very safe."

"It's your only move. Nystrom has to know it'd be suicidal to try anything. At this point, with all the heat on them from Zaldia, they barely care about an all-out war in front of the cameras. They might if we put enough syndicate people in the conference."

He paused. "Okay. I know who to contact. What else?"

"What do you have in terms of personal security?"

He was quiet again. Smart to be cautious with that question. "Randatti has afforded me quite a bit for this speech, and there are a number of high-tech measures installed in the conference hall."

"Yes, I'm sure they think they've got it covered, but do you have access to the security plans for the building?"

"Maybe."

"Well, then, *maybe* you actually look at the plans and make sure everything is in place. Like I said, I wouldn't trust them. And double-check air security and make sure you know the people in control of that. You don't want Nystrom dropping an Armada on you."

"Okay, I'll take a look. So ... what are you expecting for helping me?"

"I told you. Funds. I want enough money to completely disappear."

"I'll need more information than you've given me for that."

"And you'll get it. Look, I have resources. I'll find out exactly how Nystrom plans to come at you — or whether getting enough of the other syndicates involved has successfully warded them off. I'll want some money now — not much, just 100K — and you can consider that an investment in completely heading off the Nystrom threat. Not only am I talking about your surviving the conference, but I'll tell your Randatti friends where to hit Nystrom to finish them off once and for all. I think that's worth ten million easily. Which you will pay me when this is all over. And I know you will, because I've already well established that I can come and get you ... especially when I have nothing to lose."

"No need for threats." His timbre changed. He was scared of me. Everyone should be scared of me. "Again, I want to listen to you, but obviously Randatti is very unhappy about what you did today, and they aren't sure about you."

"I'll deliver, and then they'll be happy. And you'll actually live through this, so you'll be happy. Randatti has already failed you. Not only did I bowl right through your security, but you had a Nystrom assassin standing right next to you in your very own office. I can keep you safe, and all it takes is a 100K investment." I was pretty sure that was a tiny sum to him. It certainly was too little for me to care much about.

"Okay, Rico. You could have killed me already, so I guess I can trust you."

I'm sure there was a logical fallacy there. "Excellent. I'll have my assistant send you the account info. Take the advice I've given you and stay safe."

I heard the tone that indicated Dip had ended the communication and settled into my nice, comfy chair. Chief Rudle had a posh apartment in a posh neighborhood — nicer than you'd expect for someone of his means. That meant top-of-the-line security, i.e., predictable security. Dip had told us what to expect, and in short order we were lounging on Rudle's furniture, waiting for the guest of honor to arrive.

Diane found a bottle of brown liquid. "It's Corridian. It's a lot like bourbon. You want some?"

"I don't drink."

Diane poured herself a large glass. "Neither do I. So we just wait and let 'Dip' do the work?"

"We just wait. Gredler should access the security info we need soon, letting Dip know how to get us into the conference. Then we see what we have to work with."

"So any word in the news on our assault on Gredler's home?"

"Nope. Looks like they're keeping it under wraps."

"It's a syndicate matter." She took a sip of her drink. "It's not for normal people to worry about. Anything about Morrigan?"

"From chatter at the police station, I gather she's missing." Maybe Randatti had killed her, but I didn't think I'd be that lucky.

"You bugged the police station?"

I wasn't sure how accusatory that was. "Yes."

She laughed and took a big drink. "Oh, you small-town cops."

The door opened, and Rudle crossed his threshold for the last time. I had assumed I would be the one to handle him physically, but Diane was quickly across the room, slamming her fist into Rudle's face before he could tell what was going on. He fell to the floor, and Diane stepped on one of his hands and pulled his gun out from under his jacket, standing back up and pointing it at his head. "Hello, Rudle!" She was quite good; it looked like she had beaten up a Corridian before.

I made sure the apartment door was closed and locked. I then stood over Rudle and casually drew my gun. "You know what I said earlier about how you should hope I have more important things to do than kill you? Ends up I had some spare time."

"I didn't want any part of this!" he cried.

"Yeah, you're just an innocent soul covering up Nystrom's murders." Diane motioned with her gun for him to move to the couch. "You're practically a victim in all of this."

Rudle kept his hands up and sat down on the couch. "What am I supposed to do, murder a bunch of people and find God like you did? Is that how it works, you damn hypocrite?"

I could tell this was not a conversation that would go anywhere useful. I wanted to just shoot him in the head and end it quickly, but I wasn't sure how Diane would react to that. Rudle was a bad man and also in our way, so killing him seemed logical and simple. Diane apparently did not see things in such a calculating manner. I wondered if she had the capacity to execute an unarmed man; I was quite sure she used to.

"Well, Rudle, do you feel remorse?" Diane asked, though it sounded more like an accusation.

"I've been doing the best I can to keep the people of this city safe. I'm not some psychotic, hired killer in hiding." Rudle then looked at me and back at Diane. "And you're still paired with him? Don't you know who he really is?" Once again, this conversation was about to take a useless turn. The just-blast-Rudle-and-get-this-over-with plan was gaining more support in my own mind.

Diane glanced at me and my usual unconcerned expression and once again faced Rudle. "He's someone who's helping me take on the syndicates; that's who he is."

Rudle laughed. "Taking on the syndicates? What the hell are you two little gnats going to do to them? I thought you worked for them. How can you still be this pathetically naïve?"

He had a point.

"So what's your solution, then?" Diane demanded. "Happily assist these murderers?"

"I keep the peace in this city!" Rudle yelled. "I don't have the luxury to pretend the syndicates are people I can stand up against. If I'm to help anyone —"

"Don't give me the 'greater good' crap!" Diane screamed as she moved her gun closer to Rudle's face. "Don't pretend this is about anything other than your own interests. You're just another person profiting off the syndicates' death and destruction, and I'm not interested in hearing whatever nonsense you tell yourself so you can sleep at night!"

Rudle's face turned stoic. "Fine. I don't care about your damn opinion of me, you psycho. Who is the worse person here? Who actually murdered for those people?"

"I'm not the one trying to justify it! I'm not the one trying to perpetuate it!" Diane was now seething. "They murdered my friend. And her family — her children! And you just cover it up for them like it's nothing!"

"I'm not covering up anything!" Rudle yelled, matching her anger. "*You* killed them! You brought this world to their doorstep! You aimed the gun right at them, you selfish bitch!" He rose to his feet and pointed at her. "If you wanted to do some good, you'd take that gun and —"

Diane fired. Rudle fell back to the couch and slowly slumped down until he fell off it and became a motionless heap at Diane's feet.

I could have done without the pointless conversation, but at least it was over.

But then I saw Diane staring at Rudle, a tear streaming down her cheek, and her gun hand trembling like it was her first time killing someone. I walked over to her. It looked like she needed some support, and all I could think of to do was put my arm around her. "It had to be done."

She looked at me. I felt like I should have had a supportive expression, but I didn't know what that was. "He was egging me on. He wanted me to kill him."

"Well, then he got what he wanted."

"It means behind the bravado he felt remorse. He felt remorse, but I was too filled with rage to care."

He'd been in our way and we needed him dead; it was just so far beyond my understanding why this was emotional for her. "This isn't an easy situation; we have to cut ourselves some slack."

"Let's just get it done." She bent down and found Rudle's wallet and took his police station access card. "Let's hurt the syndicates as much as we can and hope that keeps them from destroying any more lives."

"Are you going to be okay?"

She picked up her drink and quickly downed what was left. "No. I'm not, and I need to come to terms with the fact that I never will be. I'm only good for one thing: destruction. I just need to make sure it's directed at the right people." She looked at me, her face rather serious. I tensed for the question. "So you're the real Nystrom assassin."

"Something like that," I answered, though it wasn't really a question.

"And they had you handling the terrorist attacks?"

I didn't have the energy to keep up the subterfuge. It had been a mentally draining time for me, trying to be the person she needed. I just hoped she wouldn't ask too many questions. "I didn't know it at the time, but that was part of the plan. They had the terrorists attack the city so I could be the big hero and stop them."

She shook her head. "They had terrorists murder random people as a small part of some other plan — like the attacks on Zaldia. These people have to be stopped. I can't tolerate their existence in the universe anymore."

"You know, even if we're completely successful in this, we're not going to end them with this one act."

"It will be a start." Diane glanced one last time at Rudle and headed for the door. "A nice, bloody start."

CHAPTER 35

It was called the Gray Beetle. Gray would not have been the word I would have used to describe its color, and it didn't in any way resemble the Earth animal known as a beetle. It was just a big, nearly black, hulking mass of a vehicle with a battering ram on front. It possessed extra-powerful thrust engines to allow it to break through walls while hovering. That would be fun to use ... especially in unintended ways.

And it wasn't that hard to steal, since we had Rudle's access card. There were a lot of feds hanging around the police station lately, so we wore suits and dark glasses. Diane made her hair black for the occasion, and I went with the fake facial hair again. We simply strolled in late at night as if we belonged and headed into the controlled garage when no one was around. In a couple minutes' time, we took off in the Gray Beetle. We landed in an empty lot far out of the way, disabled its locating device, and then took it back near Diane's hideout.

I noticed Diane had been very quiet. For a while I assumed she was just focused on the task at hand, but she also just seemed more distant to me. Something was going on with her, but I wasn't sure what. I started to realize that not knowing the other person's thoughts was one of the more infuriating aspects of interacting with other people. Usually there was nothing more irrelevant to me than the vapid thoughts of others. The only time I cared what others were thinking was when I was engaged in combat, but fear often brought my enemies' thoughts to the surface and made them quite evident. Starting to care about someone, though, made her thoughts surprisingly of interest to me, but they were also disappointingly impenetrable. I thought perhaps I should just leave her to work them out herself, but that conclusion was partially based on my not knowing what else to do.

"I have quite a bit of info," Dip told me. "Are you ready for it? I could send it to your local console."

I sat down at the small computer table in the hideout. Diane came and stood behind me. "Did Dip get what we needed?"

"I'm finding out. Dip, why don't you move to the computer's audio so Diane can hear you?"

"Because I might inadvertently reveal something you don't want me to, but I'll try it out." His cheery voice now came through speakers on the computer. "Can you hear me?"

"I can hear you," Diane said. "Nice to finally meet you ... and to know Rico's not just talking to an imaginary friend in his head." She seemed to perk up a bit; perhaps having another person to talk to — or a reasonable facsimile of a person — made her feel less isolated.

"Nice to finally talk personally to you, too ... What alias do you prefer?"

And then her mood deflated a bit. "Diane, I guess."

"Then I will use that instead of what I have recorded as your legal name."

"Just get to it, Dip," I said.

"Certainly." The screen changed to a number of images of Galactic Alliance officials. "These are Gredler's own files on the people who will be attending the conference, including which criminal syndicates they're linked to."

Diane studied the data. "This matches my own research. A number are Nystrom bought-and-paid-for, but not enough to influence the vote on the change in the Alliance — but they're probably the ones who will be propped up as leaders in Nystrom's power grab. Is this everyone who will be in attendance?"

"The list matches all the main officials who will be in the closed conference," Dip answered. "They'll each be accompanied by their own aides and security teams."

"And we can be sure with all the notice of Nystrom's intentions, those extra people will be syndicate thugs," I said.

"So many evil people ... in one room." I could see the passion come back to Diane's face. It was like a dog staring at a juicy steak.

"As for building security," Dip said, "Gredler tried to check up on that himself. And since he has full access, I now have full access and should be able to manipulate it until the codes are changed."

A number of different ideas ran through my head. "Good."

"Finally, when Gredler checked on his escape plan, that included the current access code for traffic over the city. That will only allow access, though, if sky control isn't being particularly observant."

I had plans for that. "Will you be able to get a craft into the conference if it's a one-way trip?"

"Um ... that is certainly possible."

"Um?" I asked.

"It's an optional syllable I can use when I'm busy processing information and trying to come up with a response. You told me to stop using it, but it's supposed to make me sound more human, so I thought I should use it again for the benefit of your guest, who may appreciate more human-ness."

Diane smiled. "Well, thanks."

"It did seem considerate, based on my considerate heuristics. Anyway, I have a few extra notes for you. As I am required by my programming to point out, your guest with the alias Diane is a wanted criminal, and what you're doing now is considered aiding and abetting by this planet's laws."

I sighed. "Thanks, Dip; that's really useful."

"Also, you seem to be planning a mass slaughter of Galactic Alliance officials. This is also illegal."

"Got it. Anything else?"

"Actually, I have something for Diane."

"Really? What?" she asked.

"To help with my data, I was wondering if I could ask you some questions about your impressions of Rico. We can skip over the ones that are sexual in nature if that makes you uncomfortable."

"That's enough, Dip. You can disconnect."

I saw that Diane was giggling. "Well, he's an interesting fellow." For some reason, it made me happy to see her happy. But the happiness didn't last long. "So," she said, becoming quickly more serious, "this is going to be pretty big, isn't it?"

"Well, that's the point. No one will be able to ignore this. Everyone will see how embedded the syndicates are within the government."

She nodded. "They're so powerful — so vile. What else can we do?" She had an odd smile. "No choice, really." And she was silent for a while — that frustrating unreadable silence where I knew something was going on in her head I wasn't privy to. And then suddenly she was all over me, kissing me and pulling off my clothes. It was a little weird. But I went with it.

* * *

She was much more aggressive this time, though strangely distant. I sensed she was trying really hard to get lost in the moment; I figured it wasn't so much that she felt passion for me as that she wanted an opportunity to escape her reality for a while.

Or maybe that was just in my own head. Maybe I had to admit that I didn't really know her motives. I was afraid that since she had a better idea who I really was, she would begin to reject me. Yet here she was, making love to me again, but I wasn't sure what that meant.

Afterward, she seemed to avoid eye contact. Maybe she was ashamed. I didn't know, and it was driving me crazy.

So I did what I always did when the world around me turned chaotic. I focused on the task at hand.

"We have a lot of work to do," I said as I got dressed. She nodded, doing the same. I spent some time looking over our weapons, preparing the explosives, and studying the layout of the capitol building we'd gotten from Gredler. I needed to have the plan well memorized, as well as the backup plan and the backup to the backup plan. That's always my advantage in these situations: no hesitation. I know exactly what I'm doing now and what I'm doing next. That simple sense of purpose in every situation is always such a comfort — to get lost in the moment and not worry about later. There is just the job at hand and nothing else.

But the truth is it was always so fleeting. I could live like that for moments, but my life as a whole would always be an aimless mess struggling for purpose. What was the solution to that? I didn't know. There probably wasn't one. I just kinda wanted to believe there was one.

I looked at Diane, who wasn't working but was instead sitting on the bed looking at a handheld. From the emotions showing on her face, what she was looking at wasn't mission-related. "What's the matter?" I asked.

"I'm sorry, but I had to check on my church." A tear glided down her cheek. "They've been my family for a decade, and I couldn't just mentally abandon them. I'm not that person anymore."

This wasn't helpful, but there was nothing to do about it now. "How are they?"

"On their message page, they announced that tomorrow is the funeral for Hana and her family. And then they left a message for me ..." She started to lose it. "They said ... that they love me and are praying for me."

"Do you think they believe you killed Hana and her family?"

"If they did, that's all the more reason I would need prayers." She looked up at me. "I wonder what they'll think of this massacre we're planning."

"No point in wondering," I said. "It's the only way to try and strike back at the syndicates. It's what we have to do."

"No choice," she whispered. She was quiet for a few seconds and then set down her handheld. "I can't do this anymore."

My reaction to this was unusual for me. A tingle down my spine. I think it was a physical manifestation of fear. "What do you mean?"

"Rudle was right: I'm such a hypocrite. Just look at this place." She set the handheld down and stood up. "I wanted a second chance, but I kept this place and stocked it with weapons 'just in case.' Just in case of what? I decided I wanted to be Melanie again? I set a trap for myself, and now I'm spiraling downward into it. I'm making all the same mistakes again. And I'm telling myself that this is my only choice — this is my only path — the same lies that kept me trapped for so long. I'm marching right into the abyss again, and ... I just need to stop. I can't go through with the plan."

I decided to try logic, though I suspected we were not operating in that realm. "All the syndicates will be there — this is our one big chance."

"I know. I kept telling myself that. This is for the greater good — but that's not what this is about to me. I'm angry; I want revenge. And it's all happening again. You saw how coldly I struck down Rudle. I'm tired of feeling so hollow inside. I'm done."

I took a deep breath and tried to think of the situation from her perspective. "Then what? We just let them all get away with it?"

That gave her a moment's pause, though I didn't really believe I had gotten anywhere with her. "We can give the information we have to others who can maybe act on it, but I'm not going to be part of a slaughter. I can't pretend it's righteous or that it must be done. There have been tyrants all throughout history, and they live, and they fall. This isn't worth my soul."

I decided one last try at an emotional appeal. "And the killers of your friend, her husband, and her children?"

She teared up. She was silent for a few moments and a couple times looked like she was about to speak but couldn't bring herself to say the words she had in mind. Finally the tears stopped, and her conviction seemed to firm up. "I know what I'm supposed to do, but I can't bring myself to say it. I'm too angry — I want to hurt the people who murdered my friends. I want to see them suffer. It's just like with my parents. And I know how empty that is, but I'm drawn to it. I'm just so filled with hate for them, but I know what I have to do to break free ... it's very hard. These people who destroyed my friends, my family ... and me ... they're just like us. They're broken people who need my sympathy, not my violence. I can't control their actions, but I can do the greatest thing that is in my power to do. I ..." She choked up but quickly got a hold of herself. "I can forgive them. I'm through seeking comfort in the suffering of others."

She cried some more — I didn't know if it was out of sadness or relief. "Should I just continue this alone, then? It's how I usually work anyway."

She snapped out of it a bit to grab my hand. "No, Rico. I still don't know everything about you, but I know you're in a dark place, too. And I'm not even trying to help; I'm just letting you take this doomed path with me."

I chuckled. "Sweetheart, you really don't know me, because you haven't dragged me down anywhere. This is by far the best I've ever been in my life."

"What I do know about you is that you can be so much more. That I can be so much more. But we have to leave this life behind. It sounds like with some help Dip could extract us from here. We can just leave this mess and not let it destroy us. I don't want to leave my family here, but it's the only choice I have to keep them safe."

"Then go. Leave me to what I do best."

"No, I'm not going to do this alone this time." She touched my cheek and pushed against me. "We'll go together. Start a new life together."

"You don't even know me."

"I know enough. I know ..." She hesitated, her lip trembling slightly. "... I love you."

As I looked into her eyes, sincere and longing, I knew she really meant it. I felt warmth on my cheek — something moving on it. A tear? Just that one statement broke me down. Simple words, yet it was like a spacecraft had plowed into me and left me paralyzed. I stood there, trying to comprehend what was happening to me, then realized there was nothing to comprehend. I loved her; she loved me. Was there anything more perfect? And I leaned in to kiss her.

And then the logical part of my brain finally broke up the party. Because where was this going? I could try settling down with her and living a quiet life — maybe have kids, which was just an abhorrent idea to me — but I would soon get bored. And then I would probably kill her, because it would be logical. I certainly would kill any children, because that was also logical, as they would mean nothing to me but might one day want vengeance. In the end, that's all I really am: a simple, logical being. I had some irrational emotions after all, which right now were telling me I didn't want to see Diane hurt, though they couldn't really provide reasons. But my logical side is the greater one. It's how I've survived. It's all I've really cared about. Being reasonable. And occasionally engaging my id with a little fun gun play.

So why was I here on this doomed path with some woman? Because I was in love with her. And these feelings for her kept me from wanting to think things through, because I knew where that would lead. I didn't want to face what I knew logic would tell me: that my relationship with her would only lead to tragedy. The happiest possible outcome was that she would die in this foolish assault against the syndicates while still believing the lie that I was someone who could ever love her back in the way she deserved.

But I didn't want her to die. Since I knew I couldn't be with her, whether she lived or died seemed logically irrelevant. Still, while I knew I had no hope of normality, Diane could live a normal life. And the thought of her happy was desirable to me for inexplicable reasons.

And thus I knew what I had to do.

I started laughing hysterically. I just lost it. The single tear from the heart was concealed by many more from laughter.

"What is it?" Diane tried to hide her hurt, but she failed. I usually didn't find pleasure in cruelty, but I usually didn't care either. This was an odd thing for me, though. It was as if by sensing her pain, I could feel it, too. I knew it was all in my head, but it was powerful.

I stopped laughing. "Sorry ... it's just that I saw how much you meant it, and ..." I chuckled some more. "I guess it's somewhat of an in-joke you're not privy to."

"This is funny?" She was still too hurt to be angry.

When something is no longer of use to you but can only get in the way, the logical thing is to kill it. "Jokes just compel you to share them — humor is a very social thing — so let me try and explain this one to you. I guess I can start by explaining me. When I was nine years old, my father shot and killed my mother in front of me."

She just stared at me, a little pity creeping into her face. "Oh ... Rico ..."

I chuckled. "Don't feel sympathy for me. If ever there was a nine-year-old boy who deserved to have his mother shot in front of him, it was me. But anyway, you're stepping on the punchline. Do you know what my reaction was to seeing my mother shot and killed? I turned to my father and asked him, 'Who is going to make dinner tonight?'"

Again, she said nothing and looked quite confused.

"Oh, come on! That's at least a little bit funny. You know the silly things kids say. I just saw her as someone who did household chores and could easily be replaced with a maid. I was only nine, so I hadn't quite learned I was supposed to pretend to have some sort of affinity for my mother so I didn't look freakish." I walked around the room, keeping a little distance from Diane. "You might ask why I didn't just naturally love my mother. It's because I lack that part of the brain that people associate with having humanity. I have no innate sense of right or wrong — everything is just a neutral action to me.

"Another childhood mistake was when I snapped the neck of the neighbors' puppy. It bit me, and I didn't want to get bitten again, so the logical thing seemed to be to kill it. I was so confused by the horrified expressions of the neighbors when what I did seemed so simple and logical. Of course, I didn't get the reason they'd keep the odd little creature around in the first place or what they meant by calling it 'cute.'"

Diane finally spoke. "You were born this way?"

"Not just that — I was designed this way. I'm not some child of God. I am a flawed creation of man. Nystrom scientists designed my DNA before I was born and used targeted surgeries to make me a highly intelligent, dispassionate warrior to use for their purposes. I was conceived as a killer, then raised by one of Nystrom's people and trained to be a hitman — which I've done quite prolifically."

She stared at me and then said, "I'm so sorry."

She pitied; it was greatly misplaced. "For what? I got to see the worlds from a different perspective from everyone else — unburdened by the irrational impulses people's own brains force on them. It's not like I feel bad about anything that's happened to me. I'm not even really sure what that means."

"But all you've done here ..."

"Was just me pretending to be what I thought people would expect to see from a hero. It was all for the job. But then I found out Nystrom was planning for this to be my last job for them — I'm too scary for even them to keep around — so I wasn't sure what to do, and now here I am following the whims of some emotionally loopy woman." I smiled — the one that usually made people shudder. "Anyway, that's where the heart of the humor is. You said you love me — and you meant it — but all you are in love with is just a hollow act. You're in love with someone who doesn't even exist."

She watched me silently for a while. I had delivered a lot of surprise blows quite quickly, and she didn't seem to know how to process it all. "Let me help you," she finally offered.

I laughed. "You? The mass-murderer trying to bury her guilt under some religion? I guess I should just feel lucky I've never known guilt and thus it's never motivated me to such high levels of idiocy. I'm bored with you now, Diane. I'm fed up with your silly little psychological drama. Here's a little tip for you: You're not special. There is no god looking out for you. You're just an emotional fool reading too much into her random circumstances."

She kept a firm gaze on me, but I could see she was breaking. "You can rage against me all you want, but you can't convince me away from what I know."

"Oh, I've spent enough time around you to know that deep down you don't even really believe your own nonsense." I then swung a quick punch, hitting her hard on the side of the head and almost knocking her down. She looked at me, now clutching blood on her cheek. I smirked. "Going to turn the other cheek?"

I could see by her clenching fists that she was ready to fight back, but she soon relaxed her hands. She then stood tall and faced me and stated slowly and steadily, "I love you, Rico."

This was not going exactly as I hoped. It was time to end it. "I can't believe all the time I've wasted listening to your prattle and subjecting myself to your idiotic, annoying friends — though at least with Hana and her family, that had a happy ending." I kicked her in the stomach and went to grab her while she was stunned. She tried to get a hand up, but I grasped her hair and then smashed her head into the wall. I then got behind her and put my arm around her neck and squeezed. "Now that I had my way with you," I said into her ear as she struggled against me, "you have nothing left to offer me."

I couldn't see her face as I kept the pressure on her neck, and I didn't really want to see the results of my effort. Eventually I knew by her limp form that she was unconscious, and I eased her to the floor and left her sprawled there to at least give the impression that I'd just tossed her to the ground when I was done with her. That coldly rational part of me said I should pick up a gun and end the charade for good, but that was exactly the part of me I was trying to protect her from. And that's what a sick and twisted person I am: The best way I could express my love was by hurting her so much she'd never want to be near me again. I loved her and she had loved me, but it wasn't enough. The only way she could possibly be happy would be for me to kill that love. Only her hatred of me would keep her safe. My path was doomed — it had been since my creation — but she still had the possibility of safety and happiness. The syndicates would still be after her, but I'd soon give them much bigger things to worry about.

I turned to leave but couldn't help taking one last look at her. I felt I had destroyed something of great value — of value I couldn't even comprehend. Certainly something I would never see again.

But what did it matter? What was one more person in the universe who hated me?

CHAPTER 36

It helps to know one's purpose in life. Mine is death. That's all I know I am good for. Killing. Spreading misery. If you believe in evil, then that's what I am: an evil. It's all I'm capable of being.

But there were still worse people out there. That's who I was going after.

I set the Gray Beetle to fly in a wide circle while I planned. I would be executing a modified version of the plan I'd been working on with Diane. We'd been putting together my magnum opus of death and destruction — it was too good to just let go. So I had a what. It just bothered me that I didn't quite understand why I was doing it. I was partly doing it because it had originally been Diane's idea. She may have changed her mind, but deep down she wanted to see all this evil crushed in righteous fury. Secondly, it would keep the syndicates occupied while Diane came to her senses and left the planet and everything on it for good. The final reason I was intent on this action was because I had nothing else to do. As I said, my purpose in life was to kill. And the syndicates were people in need of a killing. It just fit.

"I have done some analysis," Dip told me, "and this appears to be a suicide mission."

That caught me by surprise. "Your analysis can determine such a thing?"

"The odds of success seem low."

"You can never be certain about such things." He did have a point, though. Was he right that I was trying to get myself killed? I didn't think I wanted to die. I seemed more neutral on that issue. I didn't care if I died. Eternal oblivion didn't seem that far removed from my current state. "I need your help with something."

"Okay, but first I should inform you that your assaulting Melanie Fincher, who prefers to be known as Diane, was possibly illegal, though it may be looked at as self-defense considering the fact that she is a wanted murderer on this planet. You should contact the police to get an official decision on that."

"Not going to do that, but I need you to get me in touch with Gredler again."

"Will do."

Gredler soon answered. "Hello?"

"I just wanted to update you. I'm about to enter a risky situation to get more information. If you don't hear from me again soon ... well, good luck to you."

"If you help me here, I will follow through on my end of the bargain."

"Good. I thought of something, though. What type of guns does your personal security team use?"

"I ... don't know."

"Have them get Arco X5 blasters. In some daring public assassinations Nystrom carried out in the past, the assassins used personal energy shields that block a great deal of lighter gun fire. You need at least something of the Arco X5 level to contend. It might sound like overkill, but if Nystrom does try to assassinate you, it could save your life."

"Okay. Noted."

"Listen to me. I know. Anyway, I'm going dark for a while. Hopefully you'll hear from me soon." I ended the call. That was my final bit of preparation. I thought briefly about the very real possibility that I was going to die. By my own calculations, the odds were against me. In all likelihood, I would be killed, and the universe would move on — perhaps better for it. Did that mean anything to me? Did I care? I thought of Diane waking up, remembering what I did, and thinking dark thoughts of me as many have done before. Then hopefully she'd see my spectacular death in the news and move on, too.

Maybe I did want to die — to finally have an ending. I'd spent my whole life going nowhere in particular, but I still would have a conclusion. I hoped it would be a spectacular one, but I suspected it wouldn't be.

I stared up at the stars as if looking for God. For a moment I saw the beauty of the sky, but then my brain kicked in and I remembered that the pricks of light in the sky were only distant fusion infernos of no particular interest to me. The universe was large and purposeless. There was no meaning. Only finality.

I thought of my love for Diane. It — love — hinted of greater things in the universe. But it was just a lie. A sweet lie my brain had conjured up to get me to keep living despite the utter pointlessness of it.

I was done thinking. It was time to lose myself in something else.

"Dip, I need you to try to get me in contact with Morrigan now."

"Will do."

Eventually I heard an unsure voice on the line. "Hello?"

"Hey, Morrigan. It's Rico. We've had a bit of a bumpy relationship, haven't we?"

"Like when you shot Vance in the face? I liked Vance. I liked when she had a face. You shot a lot of people I liked — and others I didn't like but was responsible for — and now I have to answer the executives, 'Why are these people dead?' And somehow you only managed to stun Donner. I almost think you didn't kill her just to further annoy me —"

I heard some talking in the background, followed by, "Shut up, Donner! Just shut up!" Then Morrigan continued in a more subdued tone. "But I could just go on and on about me and my problems. So how are you and your girlfriend?"

"We had a bit of a falling out. It was sad."

"Well, you come here and tell me all about it."

"Are you at the bordello?"

"That I am. You see, I've had to lie low since *someone* told Gredler I'm with Nystrom — oh! That was you, wasn't it? It must have been hilarious."

"Okay, well I'm heading over to see you now."

"Great! We'll have a lovely talk."

"There will not be any talking."

There was some silence on her end, followed by laughter. "Awesome. Well, I have my dancing shoes on, so you'd better bring it, big boy. Bring the absolute best you have."

The end was coming. The thought made me feel empty inside. I was comfortable that way.

CHAPTER 37

"Can I help you, sir?"

The receptionist was a young human female who looked to be of no threat. There was a certain skepticism to her tone, though. Wearing some basic street clothes and a cheap-looking blue jacket, I was perhaps dressed a little too casually for such a fancy building. The lobby was opulent, decked out with sculptures of humans and Corridians, fountains, and a giant crystal- and gold-adorned chandelier dangling high above me. I hadn't had time to get a new suit since I'd been on the lam, though. "I am here to visit the thirty-first floor."

"Oh." More skepticism. That was supposed to be a very exclusive destination. "What's your name?"

"Rico Vargas."

She checked her computer screen, then looked at me and back at her screen. "Oh, I have you right here, Mr. Vargas. I'm afraid I don't have health records for you, though."

"Will that be a problem?"

"Federal law states that you must submit to some basic blood work before you can visit such an establishment. I can actually do it now. There will be a fee, though. Fifty."

"Fifty in what currency?"

"Standard Alliance dollars."

"Oh; duh. Of course." I fished out of my pocket a stick of my credit info and handed it to her. "Will this work?"

"Let me see." She scanned it. "Yes. That will work nicely." She handed it back to me. "I'll need to prick one of your fingers. Which hand would you prefer this on?"

Didn't really matter to me, but I held out my left, as I was slightly right-dominant. She pricked my ring finger with a small pin and then checked her computer screen. "You're good."

"Good to know."

"You'll need to see security now."

A security guard approached me — a Corridian male who also didn't look like much of a threat. He waved a clear, thin wand over me. It beeped at my pockets. "Could you please empty your pockets, sir?"

I complied and took out a small, folding knife I had with me. "I think this was it. Were you scanning for metal?"

"Among other things. Anyway, you can't take that up with you."

"Really?" It was just a little knife; that seemed a little extreme.

"I can hold it for you, Mr. Vargas," the receptionist offered.

"Oh. Okay. Thanks."

The security guard handed the knife to the receptionist and then waved his wand over me again. "Okay, you're good now."

"Just head down that hallway to the elevators and take the center one to floor thirty-one," the receptionist instructed me.

"Could you please let them know I'm on my way up?"

"Certainly."

"Thank you very much." I gave my friendliest smile. It never hurts to be polite.

I went down the hallway to the elevators, entered the center elevator, and hit the button for the thirty-first floor. Now Morrigan knew I was on my way and unarmed, and she probably suspected something was up. And these suspicions were confirmed when the elevator opened with no one inside. Then came the loud crash as the unmanned Gray Beetle smashed through the wall onto the brothel's floor, crashing around inside before coming to a stop near the elevators, where I assumed Morrigan's people were waiting with guns drawn. And that's when the explosives went off inside the Gray Beetle, sending fire, concussive force, and shrapnel in all directions.

Where was I? I had taken a second elevator to the thirty-second floor, a posh restaurant now filled with many alarmed patrons. I had made sure the Gray Beetle would pitch upward before it stopped, which had punched a minor hole in the restaurant's floor. The explosion had opened it up further, and while the patrons fled, I made for the smoky crevice and jumped down.

Smoke fought against emergency lighting. There was very little visibility, but I had an advantage over my enemies: I just had to kill anything that moved, while they most likely wanted to be more careful than that. My first order of business was getting a gun. There was a man trying to stand up near where I'd landed. I slammed his head into the floor and groped around for his gun. When I stood up, someone else stumbled by, and I grabbed a gun from her while elbowing her in the face. I then immediately fired on a couple of silhouettes I saw in the smoke. I had no idea how many combatants I was dealing with or how many were still alive, but all I was going to concentrate on was finding Morrigan. Maybe she'd been killed in the initial blast, but I doubted I would be that lucky.

I moved through the smoke, shooting anything I thought I saw moving. I spied someone out of the corner of my eye and turned and shot who I thought might be a female figure. I approached for confirmation, but then the smoke cleared enough that I saw a very determined set of eyes bearing down on me. She was quick but not quick enough, and I quickly had a lock right back on those eyes and pulled the trigger.

Nothing happened. An instant too late, I noticed it had gotten darker. The emergency lighting was gone, and the only light emanated from the many fires around the brothel. Morrigan had something in her hand — some sort of EMP device. That would only delay the guns for a second before they went onto backup circuitry, but a second was all she needed to close in on me. I barely got my hands up to block as her fist came toward me like a small wrecking ball trying to demolish my skull. She knocked me down, and I lost grip on my guns.

She could have just stood back and shot me, but she wanted to personally beat me to death to show her contempt for me. That was arrogance. That would be her downfall.

Just not now.

Before I could stand she pounced on me, but we were near the center of the blast and the weakened floor gave way. We fell and slammed hard into the floor below us, and the debris from above pelted us. I worked against my aching body to scramble to my feet. Morrigan was already standing two yards in front of me. There was no humor in her expression — she was ready to kill me.

She was much stronger than I was, but she was also much stronger than someone with her frame should have been. That meant she'd be easy to throw off balance if I could just get her to commit her full strength to a strike and miss. When she came at me, I ducked under her left hook while putting my full force into a body blow. The muscles were so strong in her abdomen it was like hitting a heavy bag. I assumed it hurt, but it didn't seem to faze her. She followed with a kick I couldn't dodge and had to block. I barely kept my balance.

I wanted to put distance between us, but that was just panic. I ignored it. Morrigan would be expecting a retreat and would be ready to use it. I had to figure out how to fight her in close, and that meant a lot of finesse and going for her vulnerable spots ... like her face. No creature ever likes getting hit in the face. And it would make her mad. She was the better fighter, so I needed her to make mistakes. She threw a straight punch that I dodged. She followed up with another left hook. I ducked under it and tapped her in the gut again, just wanting to make the connection and not worrying about the power behind it. Now came a roundhouse kick. I barely got out of the way, got behind it and pushed her off balance.

Now I had my small window of opportunity, and I slammed my fist into her face as hard as I could. She came right back at me with an elbow, but it missed, and I hit her hard in the head again. No fortified muscles there to soften the blow. She was hurting, possibly dizzy. This I had to keep building on.

She threw a panicked left and then a right, and I easily dodged both and came back once again as hard as I could to her face. Just as I connected I realized she wasn't trying to dodge the punch. As I hit her, it felt like a sledge hammer had smashed into my ribs. She had sacrificed another strike to the head just to make sure she got one clear blow on me, knowing that was probably enough to end the fight. And that's why brute force usually beats finesse.

It stunned me long enough for her to land a kick to my other side, shattering those ribs as well. I fell down and instinctively put my right arm up to protect myself, but she came with an iron grip on my wrist and then nailed my elbow, pulverizing it. I tried to get to my feet and pull free, but her foot shattered my knee. In a last-ditch effort, my left hand went for a hunk of concrete lying near me to throw at her, but she quickly grabbed my hand and squeezed until all the bones broke. Then her fist found my face, like a steel piston being jammed into my skull. I wasn't sure if the skull was broken — I was so rattled I was hardly sure of anything.

I don't remember what happened after that, probably due to the retrograde amnesia that tends to go along with violent blows to the head.

CHAPTER 38

I was in pain. And dizzy — probably suffering a nasty concussion. I couldn't see much — maybe my eyes were swollen. I thought I was sitting in a chair with my hands bound behind me. My arms were quite thoroughly broken, so I did not feel like moving them to test how bound I was. I tried to push off the ground to see whether the chair was bolted down, but my legs did not respond well, as they were apparently smashed to pieces as well. I was completely broken and helpless.

But I was alive.

"Dip, can you hear me?" I whispered.

No answer. That could mean lots of things. I tried not to worry about it for the moment.

"Is he awake?" a woman asked. Sounded like Morrigan.

I tried to focus my eyes. I recognized the red hair, but I was having trouble with the face. "Looks like someone really did a number on you." My jaw was still working, anyway.

"You should see the other guy." She knelt down in front of me. "Guess what, Rico? We're done with you."

"And yet I'm still here."

I could make out a nervous smile. "I know! Isn't that absolutely ridiculous?! It's not just me, right?"

"It's infuriating," said another woman in the room. "I just want to grab the first blunt object I see and go to town on him." My vision was pretty blurry, but she looked human, though there was something white — a bandage maybe — over her nose.

"I know you?"

She approached me angrily. "First you slammed my head into the ground, then you broke my finger and stunned me, then you broke my nose. Now it's payback time!"

Morrigan stood up and pushed her back. "Shut up, Donner! Just shut up! No one cares! And even if they did care … THEY'RE ALL DEAD! So shut up about your stupid nose and pinkie before I rip off your head and shove it up your ass!"

"Sounds like you may have some misdirected anger," I said.

She approached me again. "Oh, no. I have plenty of real anger for pretty much everyone at this point. You know, I'm starting to think this whole thing is some convoluted plot to get me killed, because it's about the only way I can make sense of it." She turned behind her. "Donner, get me a chair."

"Do you want a —"

"When does a simple command like 'Get me a chair' require further instruction, you useless twit? GET ME A CHAIR!"

"Sorry." Donner fetched Morrigan a chair. There didn't seem to be much to the room other than concrete walls and a couple of chairs. Morrigan positioned her chair in front of me and sat down.

"I don't plan to ever settle down and raise a family," Morrigan said.

"I don't really think you'd be a good mother."

She smiled. An angry smile. And she patted my sore, bruised face. "Thanks. I really needed that. Anyway, my point is that my people — the people I've trained and worked with and turned into real professionals — are the closest things I'll have to children. You see? And I don't know how much you know about mothers, since you're all weird in the head, but once you kill enough of a mother's children — and punch her repeatedly in the face — she starts to get kind of angry. I try to be professional, but right now all I want to do is rip off one of your limbs and beat you with it."

"I say we do it," Donner added.

"Or rip off one of Donner's limbs and beat you with it. I really want to kill you violently, but I can't. Do you know why?"

"It would be wrong."

Morrigan laughed an insane little cackle. "Still got that sense of humor. He's a funny guy, isn't he, Donner?"

"I don't think he's funny at all!" Donner yelled angrily.

Morrigan sighed. "She can't even banter. She is so utterly useless."

Donner looked confused. "What's banter?"

"SHUT UP, DONNER!" Morrigan screamed without turning around. She leaned toward me and whispered, "So who are you, Rico? Yes, you're a pathetic psychopath, but why are you so important? Are you like Donner here? Someone's nephew I got stuck with?"

I smiled slightly. "People just like me, I guess."

Morrigan stepped back. "Not well enough. Do you know what my orders were on this job?"

"You were supposed to make sure I died during it."

She stared at me a moment. "Yeah. Not sure how you know that, but it doesn't really matter now. And they were very specific about you dying making the hit on Gredler. But you can see the problem there — having to work with someone I'm also supposed to get killed. What if you figured out what was going on and struck back? Well, I guess that's not a hypothetical anymore."

"I figured it out because you were sloppy and tried to get me killed earlier in the game. You placed me at the café with no notice when the terrorists were attacking ... and I don't think those two ladies on the tram were just tailing me for intel."

She smiled again. "It would have made things easier if you had gotten killed, accidentally, early on. It would have allowed me to go on with my original plans. Didn't work out, though. And they actually threatened me — ME! Told me I'd be the target of the next hit if I or my people killed you. They threatened me not to kill you, some stupid hitman they don't need anymore and want to get rid of. Does that make any sense to you?"

"It's not my place to make sense of orders."

Morrigan frowned. "We're both just grunts, aren't we? Well, Anthony Burke was very specific in his instructions, and you don't cross him, do you?"

I felt an odd, sinking feeling. It was strange. I already knew he was okay with my death. I don't know why it would make a difference that he was the one who ordered it. Perhaps I was more sentimental than I would admit. I thought back to the meeting I had with him on Ryle and felt an odd feeling. Sadness, maybe. That feeling that something of value was gone forever. A much more common feeling for me lately. But it was silly. There was nothing about Burke to stir sentiment He was just who I took my orders from.

"Under different circumstances I'd pity you, Rico," Morrigan continued. "You're really a sad, inconsequential creature who's only good at one thing, and now no one has any use for you. Of course, since you're such a freak, this all probably means nothing to you, right?"

"Not really."

She leaned back in her chair. "And ya know the funny part? Well, I mean, so much of it has been absolutely hilarious — I've barely been able to catch my breath from all the laughing these past few days — but if I picked out the absolute funniest part, it'd have to be that the idea of you dying on this high-profile hit was so you could go out with some dignity." She stood up and smirked at me. "Well, Rico, do you feel like you have your dignity right now?"

"I'm a sociopath. Dignity has never been a concern for me."

She leaned down toward me. "Exactly! That's why this is all so stupid! You'd agree more than anyone that, now that we're done with you, we should just shoot you in the head! But, apparently for all your work, they wanted Rico — the boogeyman of the syndicates — to have a glorious death. And because of that desire, now here you are, tied to a chair, a bleeding, broken loser. Pretty ironic, right? I mean, that is a proper example of irony, I'm pretty sure." She turned to Donner. "That is a good example of irony, isn't it, Donner?"

"Huh?"

She looked back at me. "Completely worthless. By the way, we found and destroyed your ship. I know you had some AI on it and probably some sort of backup plan, but now it's debris floating in orbit. So let's just be clear on how completely hopeless things are for you."

There was no way of knowing if that were true — unless Dip got back to me — but it was not comforting. "Damn, my stuff was on that ship. Now you're just being mean."

"No, that's not mean." She smiled. "I have other plans for mean. Your detective/former hitwoman friend was captured by police."

My face twitched slightly at that news; I couldn't help it.

Morrigan's smile grew wider. "You *do* care for her! Wow. That's insane. I thought you were too mental to have human connections. And if we only had more time, I would fetch her from police custody, which would be simple enough, and then gut her slowly in front of you. It would be like a nice little psychological experiment to see if we could get a human reaction out of you. Still, I want you to know we will go get her after this is all over and ... I'm not sure exactly what we'll do to her, but it will involve lots of torture. It'll be fun. A job-well-done celebration involving her screaming very loudly. And she will beg for death a long, long, long time before she gets what she wants."

I thought of Morrigan's threat of cruelty against Diane versus the cruelty I'd already inflicted — pointlessly, since it evidently didn't keep her safe. Anger boiled up inside me, but it wasn't just directed at Morrigan. I pushed it down, as it was unhelpful. "You're taking this way too personally. That never ends well," I said.

"You're probably right. None of this is really your fault. You're like a child who doesn't understand the world and just lashes out in confusion. I know none of this was personal for you, but at the same time, you killed my people. I can't help but take that a bit personally."

"Your people were killers working for a criminal syndicate. We do nothing but spread misery in the universe. It will be better off without any of us."

Morrigan paused. "What the hell is that supposed to mean, you freakish psychopath?"

"I'm trying to look on the bright side here. There's no reason to get worked up when bad things happen to bad people."

She sprang at me, like a cobra to the kill, her fist smashing into my gut. "Then I guess this will make the universe happy!"

She knocked the wind out of me, and for a second it felt like my broken body wasn't going to be able to fill my lungs again and I was going to suffocate right there. But the air slowly came, and I lived another moment.

Donner walked over. "If we're supposed to keep him alive until we hear from the executives, you'd better not hit him again."

"Thanks, Donner!" she snapped. "Maybe I'll just have to hit someone else I don't have a standing order not to kill!" Morrigan looked at me. "Here's what happens now. I've sent word to Nystrom that you've turned against us and are now just a big bag of flesh and broken pieces of bone, so keeping you in this plan is rather useless now. When they finally tell me to do the sensible thing, I'm just going to walk into this room and shoot a big hole through your head. No need for further ceremony — I just want to get this done with, because we still have someone important to kill. You understand?"

I moved my head for a little nod. "Sounds reasonable."

"Glad you like it. So, Rico, you supposedly feel nothing about the deaths of others — any feelings on your own inevitable death?"

"Not really."

"You feel great fear just before the end, that I assure you." She patted me hard on my dislocated shoulder. It took a lot of restraint not to cry out.

"Morrigan."

"What?" She bent down to meet me face to face.

"I'd threaten you with a violent death, but you're smart enough to know that's pretty much an inevitability for you one day. My advice to you is to enjoy it, because whether or not the religious are right about the afterlife, you can be quite certain it will be your last chance to enjoy anything."

She backed away. "You're a funny guy, Rico." She wasn't smiling, though.

CHAPTER 39

Cold water splashed my face.

"He's still alive," I heard a woman say.

Apparently I had fallen asleep when they'd left me alone in the room. I had been dreaming, but I couldn't remember about what. It wasn't pleasant, whatever it was. Probably better than reality, though.

"Untie him," Morrigan said.

My hands were released, and it became obvious that my bindings had been the only things keeping me upright as I tumbled to the floor.

I felt a sharp kick to my ribs, which gave easily, as they were already broken. "Get up!"

I tried to comply, but all four of my limbs were broken and wouldn't support any weight. "I think I might need medical attention."

"No, you're good just as you are."

I looked up and saw Morrigan, dressed in black and looking quite combat-ready. Next to her was the other woman, Donner, dressed in a pantsuit and looking rather official — except for the bandage on her nose. Morrigan hadn't unceremoniously shot me in the head as she'd promised. That meant something.

I looked around the room for the first time since waking up but couldn't make out any details, as my vision was quite blurry. Perhaps an empty utility closet. I could faintly hear the hum of machinery nearby. "So where am I?"

"I don't think it really matters for you, Rico," Morrigan said.

"But I left my knife with the receptionist in the other building."

Morrigan stuffed a rag into my mouth. "And those were your very last words. According to the executives, we're not done with you yet, but the rest of this will require you to lie there quietly in a useless little meat pile. Think you can do that?" She lifted me up and threw me over her shoulder like a sack of potatoes. I let out a muffled cry of pain, but I was too broken to even squirm.

"We're clear," I heard Donner say as Morrigan carried me out into a dark, undecorated, deserted hallway. We soon came to another room, at which point I was dumped on the floor, causing me to scream into the rag.

"You give me enough time to make an exit, then come in here and shoot Rico until there's little left but ash," Morrigan said. "That clear?"

"Can't we just kill him now to be sure? It's not like anyone will know."

"Sure of what? Look at him. My orders are not to end him until after Gredler is dead. Let's just do this and then go out and get really drunk."

"Okay." Donner left the room.

I was able to position my head so I could see Morrigan. We were in a small room with no light except that from a tiny window near where Morrigan sat. She was putting together a sniper rifle. What a pathetic way to make the hit. Shooting from a distance implies fear, and I never liked to show anyone I was afraid.

Morrigan noticed I was looking at her and turned to me. "I might as well explain the plan, Rico: I snipe Gredler during his speech. I get out of here via my nice little escape route, and Donner 'finds' this room and is the heroic security guard who kills the infamous Rico. Oh, yeah! I forgot to tell you. You're infamous, because we leaked some of your exploits to the news agencies here. Anyway, Donner shoots you so many times that no one will be able to tell your bones were already broken. Yes, that's right! You're going to finally be done in by the complete and utter screwup Donner, since you're just not worth any more of my time. I hope you find your death abrupt and pointless."

It did seem a foolish death. That was sort of the point, I guess. A last, unwinnable fight against overwhelming odds — which was apparently how Nystrom now wanted my end to happen — only instead of doing that while serving them, I was weakly striking out against them. I fully expected to die while doing little more than making enough noise to disrupt Nystrom's original plans. My life was pointless, so I didn't see why I should have expected meaning from death.

Morrigan inspected her rifle and sighed. "I really wish I had more time to hurt you, Rico. I have some big anger issues to work out, but I guess Diane will just have to be the target of them. I'll work on her for days — weeks if I can manage. And I'll let her know it's because of you." She turned to look at me, a sick grin barely visible in the shadows of the room.

I could picture Diane in misery — her last agonized thoughts of her hatred for me. And it wasn't just images in my mind — I felt distress at the thought. Morrigan must have seen some reaction from me, because she looked satisfied at the psychological pain she'd caused and chuckled as she turned back to her rifle.

And that's what would have made this all even more pointless. I didn't even delay Nystrom's plans to kill Gredler. All I was changing was in what manner I died while the syndicate's plan went on without me. And in what way Diane suffered for it.

Or that would have been the truth if Morrigan had just shot me in the head as she had threatened. That's why I let myself react with distress to her threats against Diane, because the other involuntary action I was fighting was a smile.

I had a plan. A very foolish plan that I didn't actually expect to work. Yet it had already worked even better than I'd imagined. Because here I was in the conference hall, past security. And Nystrom's guard against me was completely down.

Of course, there was good reason for that. I had nothing left but the simplest of motor functions. But what better way was there to get the enemy to disregard you than to let them wreck and break you? I had fought Morrigan with all my might, but I'd expected her to win (and my plans had actually been much sketchier had I somehow succeeded in killing her). The variable I couldn't control was whether she'd just kill me outright, or if pressure from the syndicate would force her to keep me alive longer. The ploy was only to have the element of surprise against Nystrom's people here on planet, but I hadn't expected them to deliver me exactly where I needed to be.

For a moment I considered the possibility there was a higher power looking out for me. It would seem odd that He'd concern Himself with something as horrible as me, but people did speak of God using terrible things to his purposes before — like floods, plagues, and earthquakes ... And the angel of death.

I needed one more thing to fall into place if my plan were to work, and I soon heard a voice from above telling me everything was going to be all right.

"I'm in place, Rico," Dip said. "They did come after me, but I was able to misdirect them with a decoy ship. Are you ready?"

I could not respond, so I didn't.

"I can tell you are conscious, so I will go ahead. The event should occur on schedule."

The angel of death — sent by God to destroy the wicked. It was a fun thought, but if there was a God and He had a purpose for me, it existed beyond my reach. It would seem His concern would be better placed in protecting His faithful, like Diane. That was the one part of my plan that hadn't worked out at all, and she was now vulnerable to any one of the syndicates getting to her at any moment.

Except that they would soon have much bigger concerns. And certainly no one in this building would ever harm her.

"I will now implement the Fazium. I hope you're tied down, because your body is really not going to like this."

CHAPTER 40

Pain. My existence was nothing but constant pain. Claws ripped apart my insides. My skin was being boiled and torn. My head was engulfed in a raging migraine while simultaneously being cut apart with an axe. My toes were being pulled off with pliers. Any horrible thing you could imagine happening to your body, I could feel it going on all at the same time. It was pure physical agony — what some must imagine hell to be. Still, pain is just a signal to the brain. The brain then makes you want to panic, but a rational mind can overcome that animal instinct.

The Fazium was killing me — or at least with that kind of pain, I hoped death was coming soon. I'd had it put inside my body some time ago and given Dip the ability to remotely activate it. This was my last-ditch chance for recovery I'd thought of after Morrigan had removed my original hand years earlier. I now felt the Fazium spreading throughout my body and quite haphazardly forcing everything back into place based on how it had been programmed that a body should look like, mending flesh and bone in a rapid process. It was like surgery being performed on the entire body at once, which is why a coma is always induced before application of the drug. Overloaded with pain, my brain very much wanted to shut down, but unconsciousness was not an option for me right now.

Here was an advantage of my split brain: I let the lesser half process the pain. It was a bit like holding all of the pain at arm's length. I could feel all the agony, but the idea was to not let it envelop my whole consciousness and control my actions. Still, the pain was too much for that part of the brain to keep completely sequestered from the rest of me, and every bit of instinct told me to flail about and scream. But I fought it and remained motionless on the ground as I watched Morrigan in front of me, her attention focused on the scope of her rifle. I wasn't sure how much time I had, but I had to wait for the bones to be set in my limbs. Each second seemed like an eternity. Every nerve in my body was urging me to move. I tried to feel whether my arms were being forced back into place, but it was hard to separate one bit of pain from another when nearly every pain receptor in my body was firing.

Finally, I lifted my right arm. I couldn't feel it move through the screaming nerves, but I could see it. I didn't know if it was fully healed, but if it hurt for me to move it, it was just one drop in the ocean of agony. With a little coordination, which required much more effort than it usually would, I pulled the rag from my mouth.

I slowly worked to get to my feet. I couldn't feel the floor below me, as it felt like all my skin was being shredded apart, so I had no feeling in my limbs beyond that. Still, I relied on muscle memory to move my limbs in proper sequence. It was hard to concentrate — my body didn't want me to think about anything other than the pain — but soon I was on my feet, looking down on Morrigan.

I must have made a noise. She slowly turned around. It was quite dark in this room, so I guessed all she could see was the silhouette of a man — a standing man who should have been too broken to move. And she couldn't hide the fear in her eyes.

"Remember," I said, carefully working my tongue, which felt like it was being torn asunder like the rest of me, "when I told you about your violent death?"

I could sense her trying to bury the confusion, preparing to just kill me and figure out what had happened later, but it wasn't quite working. She was trembling. I was as she'd said: the boogeyman — a monster — and her natural response was to crush me quickly. She leapt at me and put her full strength into a punch to destroy the demon. But it was already over. She was no threat to me. I had fought her multiple times now, and I knew her movements. And in my present state, I had moved beyond the pain — beyond my own body. I floated past her fist with no effort, put my hand to her chin, and wrenched her head back as she threw every ounce of her momentum forward.

Through the window, I could see all the people gathered in an auditorium, looking toward a single stage which seemed to be protected with an energy shield. Apparently the vote was over, Gredler was now president of the Alliance, and the crowd was just waiting for him to come out and speak. Hundreds, perhaps thousands were inside. If things were as planned, they were mostly armed thugs guarding the politicians in the pockets of the syndicates.

I realized I had forgotten about Morrigan. I turned to see her lying in a heap on the ground. I had snapped her neck, but I didn't remember doing it. My mind was processing more stress than it had been designed to take, and as a result, I was having trouble concentrating on the here and now. But this was all simple enough for me — killing people — that perhaps it didn't need my intense concentration.

I took a pistol and what looked to be a remote off of Morrigan. "I'm guessing this was to turn off the energy shield for her kill shot."

"Hard for me to say," Dip answered. "Are you well enough for this?"

"I don't have time to take a sick day."

"The speech will be in five minutes — which is also when the package will be delivered."

I looked up at the vent above me. "I guess I'm going through the duct work."

"It's more of a maintenance area above the building. It has very high, automated security throughout."

On Morrigan's remote, I found a menu. One option was conveniently labeled "Disable Pathway Security." I selected it. "Is the security on now?"

"It has just been turned off."

"Direct me toward Gredler." I climbed onto a chair, opened the vent, and pulled myself up. I felt like I had full control of my body now and had adjusted to my new condition. I had gone from agonizing in pain to being so divorced from it that I felt nothing anymore. I was me.

I made my way though a small, darkened area past wires and pipes. Per Dip's instructions, I soon found a shaft that supported some cabling, and it was just wide enough for me to climb down. I descended until I landed in a maintenance closet. "Gredler should be just outside, waiting for his speech," Dip informed me.

I opened the door. Six security guards and Gredler were standing in front of me. And then the guards weren't. I never even felt slightly at risk, even as one guard got a shot off at me. I was untouchable now — that I was certain of. I bent down and grabbed two pistols from them — the Arco X5s. Gredler had listened to me, and now I was armed with my favorite weapons.

Gredler stared at me, too stunned to talk. I walked toward him. "It's your big moment now. You're going to change the galaxy."

"I thought we were working together!"

"Three minutes left," Dip informed me.

I pointed a gun at Gredler's head. "We are. Now we're going to go out there and talk to all those lovely people."

"You'll never make it out of there alive if you don't give yourself up!"

I pushed him toward the door to the stage. "Sounds like a challenge." Next to the door was a panel that controlled the energy shield. I made sure it was active and took Gredler onstage at gunpoint.

There were hundreds of people in front of me — a few political pawns of the syndicates backed by hundreds of syndicate killers, all posing as aides or security. And all the major syndicates I knew of were represented, including a few puppets of Nystrom. These were the criminals who thought they ran the universe, and all were now staring at me and the gun I had on Gredler. There were a few gasps when they first saw me, but only the uniformed security guards drew guns. Everyone else was smart enough not to escalate things with their rivals in close proximity.

Well, that would not do.

No one fled the area. If there were any innocents here, they were both foolish and unlucky to get trapped here with these people. And, anyway, even with Diane's influence, I still just could not make myself care. As has been well established, my purpose was to kill. Saving people was beyond me.

"You are on all the local television stations right now," Dip told me. "I assume this signal will travel quite far quite quickly."

I walked up to the podium, keeping a gun on Gredler. I hadn't planned to say anything, and with my body on fire I wasn't sure how coherent I could be. It seemed like there should be some introduction to the coming destruction for the viewers at home, though. Diane's intention had been to do as much harm to the syndicates as possible, and the best way to inflict harm on them was to expose them. But I wasn't here just for Diane, I realized. As I looked at all the smug criminals who held the power in the universe, a strange feeling bubbled up inside me, detectable despite the pain wracking my body: anger.

"Hello! What a great little show we're having! I'd like to congratulate Senator Gredler on becoming president of the new, more powerful Alliance — and I'd especially like to congratulate the Randatti criminal syndicate for helping their puppet to hold this powerful position. I know all you other syndicates wanted your own puppets in place here, but only one could do it, and it's nice to see that all you thugs and murderers can work together and compromise on occasion — especially when you see an opportunity to eliminate a powerful syndicate like Nystrom. You all plan to turn this joke of a democratic government against Nystrom. Of course, Nystrom has their own plans. They want to take out President Gredler in a spectacular fashion, something like this ..."

Without looking at him, I pulled the trigger on the gun I had pointed at Gredler. There were gasps, but no one could do anything while the shield was up. "Was that spectacular enough? It felt anti-climactic to me. But that is just the beginning of our fun day. With Gredler gone, I believe Nystrom plans to now show their strength and bully one of their own stooges into power. I don't follow politics very closely, but it's probably Senator Logston." Through the shield, I pointed my gun at a balding human now shrinking under my gaze. He was out of my reach. For the moment. "I don't think that plan is going to work, though. I don't think there will be any puppets left to dance."

The alarm system activated, and thanks to Dip's hacking, I could hear clicks and thuds throughout the room as the thick, secure doors locked, sealing all the entrances and exits of the auditorium, locking everyone inside. Now they started to panic. Now I could see the fear in them.

It wasn't enough to sate me.

"Listen to me!" I shouted over the yells of the trapped rats. "For too long you criminals have stolen and murdered with no fear of repercussions except from each other. You feel you are so powerful that you are above justice — you can do as you please, and nothing can rise against you. But I am here to tell you that your power is just an illusion. I am going to remind you all what small, weak, craven little things you are. No matter how many planets or how much fortune you hold, death still comes for you. That's who I am. I am death."

Though some of the thugs were working to open the doors, most were looking at me. I could hear a few of the experienced killers scoff, though. They knew that soon someone would get around the shield, and then I, a single man, would be dead.

"It's here," Dip said.

I smiled. "Prepare for the fires of hell."

And then it was as if the world ended. A tremendous crash caused the whole building to shake, and the ceiling above the auditorium caved in. A giant transport had crashed through the building, the front of it now inside and the rest sticking up out of the roof. As the dust settled, I could see the Calabrai terrorists spilling out of it, shouting and firing their weapons at everyone. And weren't they surprised when they found themselves in a large room full of criminal thugs quite prepared to fire back! Everyone had assumed the Calabrai were no longer an immediate threat, having been cowed enough for now. Still, when I'd sent them access codes (through Dip) so they could get a ship into the conference's air space, they'd obviously been able to throw together a bunch of guys with automatic rifles for an attack.

Within seconds, chaos erupted, with everyone shooting at everyone. All trapped inside, firing on each other in panic, and any alliances between syndicates ended in the chaos. I just hoped the cameras were still catching this so the universe could admire the symphony of violence I had made.

I crossed my pistols in front of me, waiting. And then there was a buzzing and popping as the energy shield gave out, no longer protecting them from me.

CHAPTER 41

What happened next was all a bit of a blur, like a half-remembered dream. With the combination of pain and euphoria, it was almost like I wasn't even there. I floated above it all, feeling no fear and no threat from syndicate thugs and terrorists fighting all around me. Logically, I knew that at any moment one stray shot could rip through me and end my life, but somehow I felt invincible. It wasn't just the drugs and pain messing with my brain, but something else. This room was filled with some of the universe's most powerful killers — people who thought themselves untouchable — and now they were spending their last few moments as weak and scared and panicked as any of their victims. All the misery they'd spread was now directed back at them. I was the instrument of this ... justice. What I felt, this feeling of power ... was righteousness.

With each trigger pull, someone evil and deserving of wrath fell dead. Most were too busy fighting each other to notice me, but the few who saw me coming for them had eyes filled with terror. Their last moments must have been spent realizing the truth of the matter: I *was* the angel of death, and there was nothing that could stop me.

It seemed to be over so soon, the auditorium just filled with the dead. I could hear the whimpers of a few survivors, but there were no more threats. I was the only man standing in the room. It was over. I had won. But how could it have ended any other way?

"Police are gathering outside and will breach the room soon," Dip warned me. "You should probably make your escape."

"What was that again?" I guess I hadn't paid much attention to the final part of the plan; I hadn't really thought I'd make it that far.

"Rear of the cruiser. Escape pod 287."

I noticed a TV camera pointed at me. I smiled into it and then headed into the crashed cruiser. Inside I found a few Calabrai cowering behind seats. I headed farther up the slanted floor of the destroyed craft. I can't remember if I shot the Calabrai I saw. I may have done so without even consciously thinking about it; my mind and body had almost been operating separately ever since the Fazium had taken effect. Eventually I was so far up into the craft that I knew I must be in the area sticking out of the roof. I found the escape pod Dip had indicated and entered it.

"Prepare yourself."

The escape pod launched, and out its viewport I could see the rest of the pods launch in different directions. With all the police force's resources currently in use trying to get into the conference hall, they wouldn't be able to spare the manpower to check all of the pods. After a few minutes, my pod was well outside the city and over the forest. The sky had darkened a bit with rain clouds, giving me further cover. The pod began to descend and eventually came to a sudden halt in a clearing.

"I'm on my way," Dip told me. "We'll need to be quick. We have some confusion to use as cover, but they're preparing further blocks on outgoing traffic that my authorization may not be able to circumvent. As you instructed, I passed all the information we had on syndicate connections within the Galactic Alliance to every media organization I could. I'll have to be radio silent for a few minutes, but I'll contact you again when I arrive."

I opened the pod. It had started to drizzle, and I could actually feel water drops on my skin instead of just pain. The Fazium was tapering off, and I was beginning to feel tired, both mentally and physically. But I smiled. I set my feet on the ground. My legs ached, but I could stand. And I felt good — better than I could ever remember. I was a new man; I had found purpose. The syndicates were vast, but I would continue to hunt them down and hit them where it hurt. I had just exposed to the public how entrenched the criminals were in their government. And not only that, I'd shown them as cockroaches to be crushed, not giants to be feared. Maybe it would rouse people to action as Diane had hoped. But whether it did or not, the criminals who thought they ran the universe would not rest easy. Not while I was after them.

I let myself enjoy the moment. The rain picked up, but the water felt good. It washed over me, cleaning off the old self, leaving the new. But the drug faded more, and as the pain throbbing throughout my body faded, for some reason I felt the aches more. The water was no longer pleasant but more like little rocks pelting bruised, raw skin. As the euphoria faded, a thought came to me: I wasn't some new being with purpose. I was just a pathetic, deluded, broken murderer alone in a dark forest getting soaked in the rain.

I tried to grab that feeling of purpose again — that faith — but it was gone, and reality was back. The Fazium and injuries must have messed up my mind to make me more susceptible to irrational thought, but my logical facilities had returned to remind me how pointless everything was. It didn't matter how much of the syndicates I hunted and murdered, I'd still be an empty, pointless being.

The only thing that didn't make any rational sense was that I was still alive, that I'd improbably survived it all. My real plan all along had been to die in that fight, and if that had succeeded I might have actually ended my life feeling I'd had a purpose in the universe. But I lived, and the torture of a useless existence continued on.

I looked up at the sky and the dark gray clouds dropping rain on me. "So do you exist?" I shouted to the darkness above. "And am I just some joke to you? I'm evil! Why don't you smite me? Why am I still here?" I knew I was probably talking to nothing. I looked down at the ground. "I just want to know what to do. Please, if you exist, I just need you to tell me what to do."

There was no answer from above. Only silence. Until Dip spoke in my ear. "I'm almost there."

Here came my escape, but what was I escaping to? Why was I trying to save my life at all? There was nothing left for me that was worth anything at all.

Diane. Caught up in my own drama and thinking I'd found purpose, I'd completely forgotten about her … natural for me, I guess. It's why I knew I could never be with her — I could never be about anything other than myself. But I saw my own life as worthless. The best I could do was use it to help someone more worthy of existence, who perhaps wouldn't have an empty and pointless life.

"Dip, do you have any updates on Diane?"

"I thought you intended to cease all involvement with her."

"Just tell me what's happening with her. Nystrom and the other syndicates are probably too preoccupied to go after her now, but I don't know how long that will last." I dreaded seeing her again after what I had done to her. And after she'd probably seen exactly what a monster I was in my huge, bloody spectacle before the cameras. But what she thought of me was unimportant. I just needed to make sure she was safe. And I had this silly little hope that if I accomplished this one thing of use, God would finally let me have my ending.

I could see my ship breaking through the clouds and descending to land in the clearing I was in. "I see that Diane is —"

The ship halted its descent, hovering a few yards above me.

"Why did you stop?" I asked after a moment's silence.

"I'm sorry, Rico."

"Sorry about wh —"

The ship exploded, and I quickly shielded my face from the fire and debris. Then there was another bang, a much smaller explosion. Like a gunpowder-based firearm being fired. And something hit me in the back.

My pain was gone again. And so was the feeling. I fell to the ground, and all I could feel was the rain on my face and the warmth of the burning pieces of my ship scattered next to me.

CHAPTER 42

It was no mystery who'd shot me. There was always one man who I'd assumed could take me down easily whenever he wanted to: my father. I just had begun to think he wasn't going to show up.

I didn't know what he'd shot me with, but I seemed to be paralyzed from the neck down. I could hear footsteps on dead leaves over the sound of the rain. I was rolling over, though I couldn't feel what pushed me. And then I was staring up at Anthony Burke, dressed in a dripping wet, long coat and hat, with an old fashioned-looking revolver in his hand, his dark, oddly sad eyes lit by the fires of my ship that weren't yet extinguished by the rain.

He knelt down next to me, returning the gun to a holster under his coat. He seemed quite certain I was disabled. "I knew in a fair fight, you'd outshoot me. I figured having your ship self-destruct in front of you would distract you enough to give me an edge."

My mouth still worked. "You made Dip destroy himself?"

"Soon after you installed that program, I took control of it. He's been reporting to me constantly since then. I didn't have sinister intentions; I just always liked knowing what you were up to."

"But then you knew my plans here."

He smiled. "Yes. Yes, I did. I even helped when I could. How do you think Dip got so good at hacking our communications? I was using him to feed you information. Since he was just a computer program, you never did think to suspect him."

True. I'd thought he was simple and logical like me — always with clear motives. Quite unlike Anthony. "So you ordered that I die on this job but then made sure I knew Nystrom was plotting to kill me?"

He nodded. "Yes ... it's complicated. Rico, do you know you were never meant to be a killer?"

I was startled by the notion, though my paralyzed body didn't outwardly show it, I assumed. "What do you mean?"

"You weren't originally intended to be a hitman — or to do any fighting at all. You were made to be highly intelligent and free from the emotional shackles that restrict most people's thinking. You were part of a long-term plan. The universe has been so chaotic, and it's long since been time that someone should seize control and bring order to it. But people have tried that forever, so we thought we'd make new people — better people — to lead a new order. You were meant to be a ruler, Rico. You were to be my son — made from my DNA — who would go on to inherit the universe. But it didn't work out."

Anthony's face was growing darker. I think my vision was fading just slightly. I couldn't tell if I was poisoned or bleeding out. "I never cared about being in charge."

He chuckled. "That was the miscalculation. We tried to take away your irrationality, and as a result you don't care about anything other than the present moment. You weren't the only one of you that we made, by the way. There were others made from the DNA of other Nystrom executives. But they were all menaces — constant dangers to anyone they were around and, despite their intelligence, there was no reasoning with them. They ended up being put down like dogs. Only you seemed to care about your own survival enough to adapt your behavior to get along with others. Nystrom still wanted to do away with you and forget the whole mess, but I fought for you. I saw potential in you. I figured in the least, with your intelligence and the modifications to increase your brain's speed, you could be a skilled killer, and you quickly took interest in that training. I hoped one day you would be something more, but no. You never seemed to care."

I was trying to process this revelation. I had assumed that I had been designed from the beginning to be good at killing — that while I wasn't quite the soldier intended by the program that made me, my identity and purpose were still to be an efficient killer. Instead, killing was just something Anthony had chosen for me when my initial purpose hadn't worked out. He could have chosen something else for me, and perhaps I would have devoted myself to it just as much. I thought a killer was all I was, but it was simply all that Anthony had imagined I could be.

"The executives never really trusted you — they remember too well the animals that the others like you turned out to be. So I don't think they ever fully trusted my judgment for keeping you around. Maybe they're right, maybe it wasn't good judgment. It's just ... you're my son. I was proud of what you were, and I didn't want to just discard you. But Nystrom has big plans. And I have my own big plans. It was time for me to let you go to show them my devotion to the cause."

I figured it was something like that. I wasn't too surprised that, in the end, I just wasn't more important than money and power to my "father."

"But you warned me," I said.

"Nystrom has their plans, but I have ... well ... bigger ones. I acted as though I wanted you to go out fighting like you deserve, but I had something else in mind for you. You see, Nystrom thinks they're big enough now that they don't need to hide in the shadows. They can rule outright. That might be true, but I see a problem. You see, we're criminals. People know that, and they'll never really accept us. We'll always have to use force to keep people in line. Like many other syndicates, we started as smugglers. Petty criminals. But as the governments expanded over too large a space and became weak and ineffectual, we found we were the only ones with the power and will to actually control things. Once you're powerful enough, I guess you're no longer really a criminal. You are the law. But can a bunch of thugs and murderers really be accepted as leaders?"

He smiled. This was his big idea he was telling me. This was his baby. His real child. "What we can be, though, are the villains who rouse people to action. Do you know why we're killing all those people on Zaldia?"

"Minerals?" It was my only guess.

"No. No one knows why we're there ... except me. I organized it for one purpose only. So we can ruthlessly kill innocent people and let all of civilization see it. You ever heard of the Nazis, Rico? A dictatorship that murdered millions of people back when humans were stuck on their home planet. They were so awful that everyone felt righteous in crushing them — that it was imperative to do anything to stop them. That's what I'm trying to make Nystrom — a powerful, evil organization that everyone wants to righteously rise up against and destroy. And destroy the other syndicates while they're at it. People will feel the need to do anything necessary to stop us and the others, and finally we'll have the effective nation the future needs. So yes. Nystrom needs to come out of the shadows. And then it needs to be destroyed. Under my guidance."

I started to understand. "You want the face of Nystrom and the other syndicates destroyed, and then you want to use the people's anti-syndicate fervor to build your own new government."

"Someone has to have the vision to guide things as they need to be."

I laughed. "Like when you made me."

"Mistakes will be made, son, but the universe is finally ready to move into the future. And your help was invaluable. The other leaders of Nystrom were hesitant to act on my idea. But now, with your spectacle exposing all the syndicates, people will rise up and demand an entirely new government. And I'll be there ... in the background, guiding things, as people wage war on the corruption in their government and the criminals behind it."

And that's what stung the most. I was trying to rebel. For a while, I was even trying to be righteous. But all I did was further Anthony's plans. He'd known exactly how I'd retaliate when I found out Nystrom had finally turned against me. Even when I thought I was doing something new and becoming someone different, all I was doing was acting my type and playing into his hands.

In Anthony's flame-lit face, I could see a twinge of remorse. It hurt him to kill me, but he'd decided other things were more important. That's just how people are. "You never did ask why I killed your mother," he said.

"I figured if I needed to know, you'd tell me."

"But you weren't curious?"

"People kill other people all the time."

He chuckled. "That's what I always liked about you. You were always simple, logical. You didn't get hung up on silly human conventions. I had such high hopes for you. I even had hopes for you after this job. I knew you'd lash out, and then I thought that with Nystrom in flux I'd be able to bring you back into the fold. But I can't now. Because you're broken. I thought my son could survive anything, but this broke you. Did I hear you shouting at God a few minutes ago? What was that about?"

A good question. "I'm just ... I'm lost, I guess."

"It's because of that woman. Diane, or whatever her real name is. Isn't it?" He looked angry. "Somehow she got in your head and you couldn't get her out. The things I would like to do to her ..."

"Please. Leave her alone." The words came out almost automatically.

He stared at me with a perplexed look on his face. "As you have probably realized, you're going to die very soon. What's it matter to you?"

"I ... don't know. Just please let her live. If you can do me one favor, get her to safety."

He slowly stood up. I could no longer see his face. "You were at times a difficult son to love. I was never much for affection, but I sometimes wondered whether you thought of me as anything more than someone who gave you orders."

"Not really. Maybe I had more respect for you than I had for other people. You seemed smart."

He chuckled softly. "*That* you respected."

"I did."

"But not now?"

I hadn't meant to phrase it in past tense, but it was true. "No. You have all these big plans, but in the end you're just another rat clawing at others for its share of garbage. Even if your plans work out and you have all the power you can imagine, you're still going to be no more than a silly, miserable fool."

"And this is a new opinion?"

No, not really. I had always seen the pursuit of power as pointless, but something was different now. I wanted so badly to leap up and grab Anthony and beat him until there was nothing recognizable left ... even though logically I knew how pointless that would be, and that it would bring me no happiness. Because it wasn't even really him I was angry with. "I just now realized how broken I am."

"We did make mistakes creating you, but —"

"Not that." I thought about my long, empty life. "You were a bad father, though. Perhaps I could have been something — done something better with my life with proper guidance. But you were too myopic to help me there — just focused on 'power,' as if that was a goal worth anything."

"I made you the best you could be in your circumstances!" he said angrily.

I took a deep breath, though it hurt some. "This is pointless. If I'm to die now, let me die in peace. You go rule the universe or whatever nonsense it is you're focused on."

Anthony stood still. "Do you hate me, son?"

"I don't think enough of you to hate you. I think it once mattered to me that I thought you cared for me, but I don't know why. Now I just want ... I sort of wish I never knew you. Then maybe I could have been someone else. Someone ..." I wasn't sure where I was going with that, but it soon became clear to me. I wanted to be someone Diane could love and who could properly love her back. And be content with that. But I wasn't going to share that with Anthony.

"I'm sorry, son," Anthony said. "This wasn't easy for me, but I can see from your rambling that it was probably the right choice. You're no longer your clear-cut, rational self, and that makes you dangerous. But it doesn't matter; I already killed you with the first shot. I don't hesitate on these sorts of things — I pick an action, and I follow through. That's how I survive. You'll be dead in a few more minutes. Goodbye." He turned and walked off.

So now I was alone, paralyzed, dying, and staring up at the rain that fell on my face. And I was angry for some reason ... but not with Anthony. I remembered Diane's talk of forgiveness, but forgiving my "father" was simple enough. He was just a fool — like every other sentient out there. But there was so much thoughtlessness in the universe that it seemed silly to obsess over a single instance of it.

But there was one person I couldn't forgive: myself. All this time, I'd known better than to be on the path I was on, but I'd pretended not to. I'd lied to myself constantly so I could keep going and never have to confront what I was. I'd said my problem with killing was simply aesthetics. I'd told myself that I was best alone and had nothing to gain from being around other people. And when I'd slaughtered the people at the conference, I'd told myself I was being righteous, when I was just indulging myself. My logic told me I had nothing to apologize for, but why did I always turn to it to justify myself? What was I fighting against? So what if I couldn't naturally feel that an action was right or wrong? I could still see the horrors of what I did. I could see the effect I had on people. And I chose to close myself to it. I chose it.

Even now, my logical side told me I was agonizing over nothing. The world was pointless, and it didn't matter what I did, because the end was always the same. But

I didn't care what that part of me had to say anymore. Look what it had gotten me: a miserable, meaningless death. Of course, it had never promised me any better than that. So why had I devoted myself to it? Why was I such a fool? Why didn't I even try to find something more in the universe? Was it all because I was scared to confront what I was? What I'd made of myself?

Of course, the realization didn't matter now. It was too late; this was my end. And there certainly was no father coming to embrace the prodigal son who decided to change his ways. He was the one who shot me.

A flash of lightning showed the silhouettes of trees far above me, the only witnesses to my imminent death. And the rain pelting my face was the only feeling I had left. I was going to die quite inanely, unmourned, and alone, my only comfort being that I didn't deserve any better. What was there in this life for me to hold on to, anyway? Everything in my life was so empty now. Except one thing. That brief feeling I'd had when Diane told me she loved me — when I saw that she meant it. I couldn't understand what it was, but I wanted to hold on to it.

Diane. The police had her, and she was an easy target for Nystrom. For Anthony. I had what I deserved, but I didn't want her to suffer anymore. It just didn't seem right.

I looked up as the lightning flashed again. "You have to protect her!" I called out. Did I believe in God now? I didn't feel like thinking it through — I just wanted Diane safe and had no other options left. "You can't let them hurt her anymore," I pleaded, my voice now more subdued. "Please."

Soon the rain lessened. I thought maybe it was a sign that He heard me. At least I simply chose to see it that way, as it provided some comfort. So I closed my eyes and waited for the end.

But I was so scared.

You're just slipping into oblivion, I told myself. *There's nothing to fear.* It was no use, though. I felt more alone than I ever had in my whole life. It was becoming an all-engulfing despair, a misery that felt never-ending. Was this the hell Diane had mentioned? Was that where I was going?

Frightened, I opened my eyes. I saw her face one last time. Heard her call my name. She looked scared. It pained me to see it, especially knowing that it was my fault. "I'm so sorry," I called out to her. "I'm sorry for what I did to you. Don't be sad, please."

And then she slapped me. "Rico!" she yelled again, this time louder.

I looked again and saw not just fear but also determination. "You're real?"

"Yes, Rico." I could feel her hand touch my face.

"How'd you find me?"

"I started tracking Dip's signal when he connected to the computer in my headquarters. And then we saw the explosion. What happened?"

I smiled. She was okay — she'd somehow gotten away from the police. "You need to get out of here. Others may come."

"We'll leave with you. Now what happened to you?"

"Shot. Also poisoned, I think. Can't move." My vision was fading still. I did my best to stay focused on her face.

"Verg, I'm going to need you to come help me move him. Can you land over here?" she called into a radio. "He's been poisoned — I'm not sure what. We need something for it." She looked at me. "Hang on, okay? Our ship is in a clearing nearby." She had kind eyes filled with concern for me. Despite it all, despite being the last person in the universe who deserved it, she still cared for me.

"I'm so sorry for what I said to you. For hitting you. I was trying to protect you. To keep you away from me. I'm nothing but death. I didn't want you coming back for me."

"Yeah, that was really stupid." I could see she was holding my hand though I couldn't feel it. "The least we mass-murderers can do is stick together and try to help each other climb out of the holes we dig, okay?"

"I should have listened to you. I ended up helping them with my big show. It was exactly what they wanted, what they knew I'd do. I should have listened to you about so many things." It hurt me to think she had seen what I'd done at the capitol, that she saw fully what a monster I am.

"Don't worry about that. You know the syndicates. You can help us figure out what to do next." So there was some utility in her coming for me, hoping I would be an asset in the fight against the syndicates. I couldn't have expected her to come out of mere concern for me. Not after what I'd done to her. This made more sense.

"I'm sorry I tricked you. I'm sorry I tricked you into saying you loved me. I'm sorry I made you look like a fool."

"Love doesn't make me a fool. You may think you don't deserve love — and I have been there, too — but it is stronger than any of our actions. I love you, okay? Not who you pretend to be, but who you really are. Do you believe me?"

I really wanted to believe. "You love everyone, though."

She smiled and stroked my hair. "But I'm here now with you."

It was hard not to think of her as a fool for coming for me, for not leaving me to die as I deserved. Especially after seeing what I was and after what I had done to her. But I wanted to believe her. I wanted to think I was someone worth her time and concern. I couldn't, but perhaps she saw something I was unable to. Her loving face did not reflect any scorn for what I was. I so wanted to reach up and touch her, but all I could do was stare at her as my life faded. "You're very beautiful. I don't know if I told you that. Women like to be told things like that. You're the most beautiful woman I've ever seen."

I hoped she would smile, but I saw tears streaming down her face. "Hold on, Rico. I didn't find you just to watch you die."

"No. Don't cry ... please. Please, Diane ..." I could feel my mind fading; it was painful to keep my thoughts together. "Be happy. Please smile. Please be happy. You deserve that. You're not like me. You've already given me more than I deserve."

I could tell my final moments were here. I'd had a lot of ideas of what my death would be like — sudden and violent, slow and pointless — but never in my wildest imagination had I thought I'd die with someone actually shedding tears over me. And even more preposterous would be that my last thoughts would be for the happiness of another. It was absolutely absurd ... but somehow it also made perfect sense. I couldn't quite understand it, but it's like everything I was looking for was right there. I'd wasted my life pursuing nothing, but there was something in life of real value, and it was here right now, hovering just out of my grasp. If only I had more time to understand. But it was too late now.

I felt myself being lifted. Diane went out of view, and I tried looking around for her, but I couldn't move my head. Then everything got brighter — maybe lights from inside a vehicle — but even the brighter light was fading along with my life. I saw what I thought was a man standing over me, and it looked like he injected me with something, but soon the all-encompassing darkness overtook me, and I lost view of him, too. Without thinking, I called out, "Diane!" I didn't know why. I was alone my whole life, but now I was terrified of being alone.

I couldn't see anything, but I heard her voice. "I'm here, Rico. Don't be afraid. I'm here."

I made my best attempt at a smile and relaxed, ready for the world to end. Yes, I realized now that I had wasted my life — had never even tried to make much of it, really — and given another chance, I would do things much differently. But death was mere moments away, and there was nothing I could do about that now. Instead, I decided to try and enjoy my last few seconds, feeling the presence of someone who actually cared for me standing by my side, strange miracle that it was. More than her presence, though, I thought I actually could begin to feel her hand squeezing mine. And then my final moments of consciousness turned to panic. Believing I needed to change my life and "better" myself were lovely idle thoughts before death, but what in the world was I going to do if I somehow lived?

ACKNOWLEDGEMENTS

First, I'd like to thank my wife, who has always supported my writing and who edited *Superego* and came up with one plot point that helped tie the whole story together. I'd also like to thank all my beta readers, including my sister, Sarah Fleming, Charlie Hodges, Steve Oglesby, Rick Woolard, Ed Killian-Keup, Michael Fisher, Dodsfall, Jeff Patterson, Jeff Ferrier, MD Persons, Rick Mount, Eric Krysinski, Nicola James Fiorvento, Randy McCarthy, Ray Pruett, Brian Goodman, and Robert Lowell. Thanks also to the readers of my blog, IMAO.us, who indulged me when I first posted the adventures of Rico as a short story there; that encouragement helped me decide to turn *Superego* into a full novel.

I would also like to thank Steve Russell and Gina Duvall and the rest of the writing group I was a part of way back when, who gave me the hard critiques I needed when I first started writing fiction. Also thanks to Michael Z. Williamson and Sarah A. Hoyt for all their help along the way. Thanks to Len Sherman for his comments on the manuscript. And a special thanks to Adam Bellow, David Bernstein, and the rest of Liberty Island for the opportunity to first get my novel out there.

In addition, I want to add a special thanks to Allison Barrows and Romas Kukalis (http://www.midsizemedia.com) for the great new cover for the second edition.

Thanks to my parents for always being supportive. Although my dad never liked "Sci-Fi," I know he would have humored me and read my book anyway. And thank you to God, Who always makes sure life is interesting.

ABOUT FRANK J. FLEMING

Frank J. Fleming is a novelist and senior writer for the satire site *The Babylon Bee*. He's also written satire books (*Punch Your Inner Hippie: Cut Your Hair, Get a Job, and Make America Awesome Again*) and columns for *The New York Post, USA Today,* and *The Washington Times.* Frank is a Carnegie Mellon University graduate and works as an electrical and software engineer when he's not writing. He lives in Austin with his wife and four kids and is a really cool dude.

Subscribe to his newsletter at FrankJFleming.com and receive a free story.

Made in the USA
Monee, IL
29 May 2020